Dacia Wolf

& the Fallen Prince

A dark and magical coming of age fantasy novel

Dacia Wolf

AND THE
FALLEN PRINCE

Book 3

Visit Mandi Oyster online at
www.MandiOyster.com

Facebook: https://www.facebook.com/MandiOysterAuthor
Instagram: https://www.instagram.com/MandiOyster/

*This book is dedicated to everyone
who dared to follow their dreams.
And to those who haven't yet,
there's no time like now.*

Chapter 1

Fireflies danced across the black velvet sky, lighting up, then disappearing like will-o'-wisps. Stars shone like diamonds, and a tiny moon smiled down at me. I lifted my face to the breeze and inhaled deeply, clearing the cobwebs from my head. The night air smelled fresh and clean.

Feeling more invigorated than I had for days, I strolled down the gravel road. Trees lined the sides, encroaching on the ditches. Rocks crunched under my feet, and the buzz of insects filled the air. For the first time in almost a year, I wasn't worried about demons, dragons, or mad sorcerers, but curfew was another story. I picked up my pace.

A twig cracked. I stopped and stared into the trees.

Not long ago, I would have been terrified that a dragon was about to jump out and attack me, but I had freed the dragons—and this was Bittersweet. Monsters had never followed me here before. I squeezed my eyes shut and sent up a silent prayer. *Not here. Please, not here ... not now.*

Another twig snapped. I sped up. Keeping my head still, my eyes darted from side to side. It was too dark to see more than a few feet, but I felt something watching me.

The breeze picked up, rustling leaves. I broke into a jog. Ten more minutes and I'd be home.

A burning smell filled the air. I slowed, turning toward the scent.

Fiery eyes blazed at me. A hollow space opened up inside my chest. A black hole that sucked all my happiness and hope into it. My hands trembled at my sides.

I took a step down the road, looking toward home. A soft growl halted my feet.

Slowly, I turned to face the trees. An enormous black panther stalked out of the shadows. Muscles rippled under ebony fur.

"No." The word escaped on a breath. I stumbled backward, slipping on the gravel. My ankle twisted, and I landed on my butt with my legs splayed out in front of me.

The panther lowered into a crouch. Its tail swished from side to side.

Power sizzled inside of me, heating my stomach, filling the abyss in my chest with warmth. I raised my hand. Blue sparks danced across my fingertips, igniting a fireball in my palm. The panther snarled, and blue flames shot through the air, striking the beast in the chest. They extinguished, absorbing into its body.

My stomach plummeted, dragging my spirits down with it. Shallow, quick breaths did little to ease my rising panic. A frantic beat pounded in my ears, drowning out all other sounds. I stared at the beast, my mind utterly blank.

The panther stood eerily still. Its eyes flared. Flames rippled within them, burning red, orange, and yellow.

I scooted back, and the beast pounced. Its claws dug into my skin, knocking me down. It glared into my eyes. A soft growl rumbled through its body, pulling its lips back and exposing its teeth.

Fear crept up my spine. My thoughts jumbled together.

Hot breath scraped over my face before fangs sank into my shoulder at the base of my neck.

I screamed, but the sound was muffled by the beast's body. Pain crashed over me with the force of a tsunami, then disappeared like the tide receding. My breath faltered, gurgling in my throat. Darkness surrounded me.

The sun was just beginning to spread its rays over the horizon. Pink and purple clouds filled the sky. I lay sprawled out on the side of the road. My shoulder throbbed. Pain stole my breath and muddled my thoughts.

I crossed my injured arm over my stomach and pressed my other hand to the ground, struggling to my feet, fighting dizziness.

Blood stuck my gray t-shirt to my body. I tugged on it, peeling the fabric from my flesh. Deep wounds punctured my skin. My shoulder throbbed.

Why? I let go of my shirt and hung my head. *Why haven't I healed?*

I took a couple of clumsy steps before realizing I couldn't go home like this. Instead, I teleported to Cody's house. Standing in the bushes, I rapped on his window, hoping not to wake anybody else.

He stumbled out of bed, wearing only black shorts. Rubbing his eyes, he staggered toward me. His blond hair poked up in all directions. He looked through the glass, and his shoulders slumped. He pushed the frame up. "Oh, Dacia, what happened?" Cody's hand trembled as he brushed the hair from his eyes.

I tugged the collar of my shirt back, revealing my shoulder to him. "I'm not—" my voice caught "—I'm not healing."

Cody pushed his screen out and reached down to pull me in. His fingers brushed against my arm, and I whimpered. He jerked his hands back. "Want me to try again? I'll be gentle."

"No, I'll get in." I floated off the ground and flew in through the window.

Carefully, he drew me against him. "What happened?"

I wrapped my good arm around his waist and lay my face against his chest. "A panther." I squeezed my eyes shut and sucked in a deep breath. "With fire in its eyes."

He stepped back, grabbing my hand and pulling me toward his bed. Sitting on the edge of it, he said, "Take my strength. Heal yourself."

"Are you sure?" I sat next to him. "If I heal myself completely, you'll be worthless all day."

He cupped my face and stared into my eyes. "Please." His thumb tenderly caressed my cheek.

"Lie back." I stretched out beside him, closing my eyes to fight against the nausea and agony, and prayed his parents wouldn't walk in.

Cool, healing energy spread through my body. My breathing evened out.

Cody's fingers traced my skin, slowing as he drifted off. I lay next to him until my pain was a dull throb.

I kissed his cheek, and his eyes slitted open. "Can I borrow a shirt?"

"Yeah." His voice was gravelly. "Tell me about the panther."

I crawled over him and grabbed a shirt out of his drawer. With my back to him, I pulled my bloodied one off, sucking in a breath as it rubbed against the wounds.

The bed groaned, and Cody's hands brushed over my arms. "Why aren't you healed?"

I looked over my shoulder at him, resting my fingers over his. "I didn't think I should take any more."

He sighed. "I'll get bandages."

I felt awkward standing there holding his shirt in front of me. His doorknob turned, and I closed my eyes, scared it would be one of Cody's parents.

"I'll be gentle." It was a relief to hear Cody's voice.

I nodded, lowering his shirt. I stood in front of Cody in nothing but my bra and shorts, covered in dried blood. Heat flooded my cheeks. I tucked a strand of red hair behind my ear.

"The panther." He wiped the blood off my shoulder with a wet cloth, careful not to cause any undue harm.

"It was tall." I held my hand several inches above my waist. "And ..."

"What?"

"I don't know how to say it." I turned toward him.

His gaze lowered for an instant before meeting mine.

I bit my bottom lip while I searched for the words. "It was a monster, not a cat. Its eyes were flames, and it absorbed my magic."

He spread some kind of cream on my wound before taping gauze pads over the punctures. Then he took his shirt out of my hands and tugged it over my head, lifting my hair out from under the collar while I pulled my arms through the sleeves. His fingers lingered on my neck. I raised my good arm, placed my hand on his shoulder, and touched my lips to his.

He held my head, crushing his mouth against mine. Warmth spread through my body, but I pulled away. "I have to go before your parents find me here. They wouldn't believe the truth."

"No." He laughed. "They wouldn't."

"Get some sleep." I squeezed his hand and started to pull away.

He held onto me, staring into my eyes. "Don't shut me out."

૪૭6৪৪

"I won't."

Leaning his forehead against mine, he whispered, "Be careful."

Stepping back, I teleported home, expecting my parents' full wrath or at the very least, their concern. Instead, they slept soundly in their bed.

Maybe they'd gotten used to me being at college, or maybe they just didn't care.

Chapter 2

I lay in bed with my back to the door, pretending to sleep until Mom and Dad left for work. Then I got up, cleaned my room, unloaded the dishwasher, and vacuumed.

Close to lunchtime, Cody called me. "You okay?"

"Yeah." I flipped through the channels, but there wasn't anything worth watching on TV. "Did you just get up?" I clicked the power button on the remote.

There was a long pause, and I knew he was thinking about lying to me. "Yes." The word was so soft I wouldn't have heard it if the TV was still on.

My stomach twisted. *I took too much.* "Are you okay?"

"I'm fine."

I scrubbed my hand down my face. "I thought I stopped in time. I shouldn't have taken so much."

"You healed?"

I glanced down at my shoulder. The throbbing had been persistent. The only other time I'd had a wound that wouldn't heal was when the demon, Nefarious, had attacked me. "No."

"Didn't take enough then."

I didn't answer. We'd had this argument before.

"If you need me, I'll ditch."

As much as I wanted to be with him, I wouldn't let him skip out on his siblings. "I'll be all right. I'm going to go to the park. I'll be on my best behavior."

The town park was a quiet and secluded wooded area. There were a few RVs and campers in the modern campground and some tents set up in the primitive campground, but since it was a Tuesday, the picnic areas were all but empty. I chose a table away from the road that was surrounded by trees on three sides. Taking a swig of my pop, I opened my book and began reading.

The main character had just been rescued when something caught my attention. I set my book down and stood to watch a black mist swirl through the air. It weaved and twirled, drifting toward me. Its dance was hypnotic.

Terror clenched my heart, but I couldn't move, couldn't look away. Evil emanated from the haze.

I knew I should run from it, but instead, I found myself stepping forward in a trance-like state, moving close enough to touch it. The mist undulated around me until I was surrounded. Terror rose inside me, but I was paralyzed.

The cloud merged together. As it did, it caressed the outline of my body with a tenderness that belied its appearance. It felt substantial, not at all like vapor. One tendril lingered against my face the way Cody's hand did before he leaned in to kiss me. I shivered in anticipation.

When the last wisp connected with the rest of the haze, a solid shape materialized in front of me. Once the transformation was complete, I looked into the face of the most beautiful man I'd ever seen. He was taller than Cody with hair as black as a raven's feathers and an olive complexion. His eyes were cold, and I sucked in a stunned breath as I stared into them. They were almost black, with an incredible depth to them. His face and body were chiseled perfection. My eyes widened, and my lips fell apart.

He lifted his hand, inching it toward my face, giving me a chance to pull away, but I stepped closer to him.

His fingers stroked my cheek, soft and smooth against my skin. I leaned into his touch, wanting him to pull me closer, to hold me against his body, to press his lips to mine.

I blinked, and Cody's face flashed before my eyes—golden blond hair and sapphire irises—and the desire that had come over me was gone. This man had no right to touch me. I didn't know him from Adam. Only Cody should caress my face; only Cody should hold me. I wanted to pull away from him, but I couldn't move.

"Dacia Wolf," the beautiful man said in a deep voice that was as smooth as silk. His other hand moved to the small of my back, drawing me against him. "It is a pleasure to finally make your acquaintance." His fingers slid from my face to my shoulder. I winced, but he didn't move his hand. He leaned down and brushed his lips against my cheek. My heart galloped. I wanted to get away from him, but I wanted him to pull me closer at the same time.

"I've waited a long time for this," he whispered in my ear. His hot breath on my neck sent shivers down my spine.

I didn't say anything in response; I couldn't. I stood there staring into his fathomless eyes, mesmerized.

"Cat got your tongue?" He chuckled, and a wicked grin spread over his lips.

"Who are you?" Color rose to my cheeks when I heard the husky timbre of my voice. I shouldn't sound like this with him. *What is wrong with me?*

"Mavros Malkin at your service." He took my hand in his and brought it to his lips—never looking away from my eyes.

"What do you want with me?" I hated myself for sounding so breathless.

"That depends."

I felt more like myself now. I knew what I wanted, and it wasn't him. Somehow, he was messing with my mind. I needed to concentrate to keep my feelings true. "On what?"

"On what you want me to be." He squeezed my shoulder, and the pain nearly dropped me to my knees. "I can be your worst enemy, or I can be your best friend and even more. The choice is yours. I will give you some time to decide. But, let me warn you; if you choose to be my enemy, I will destroy you." His voice was flat, emotionless, and I had no doubt he meant what he said.

"So, what does being your friend entail?" I didn't need another enemy, but I was positive I didn't want this man's idea of friendship either.

"Eternity."

"Wow"—my voice sounded more like my own, dry and sarcastic—"you take friendship seriously."

"Yes." His lips brushed against mine, and I lost myself again. "An eternity of this, Dacia," he whispered, drawing my body against his. Then his lips pressed against mine forcefully.

My defenses melted, and without my inhibitions holding me back, I returned his kiss, clinging to him. I felt alive and passionate. When Mavros pulled away, I was breathless and disappointed. I wanted more … I wanted forever.

I took a deep breath, inhaling the fresh air. It was cool and crisp. My head cleared, and I gasped. My hand covered my mouth, and I stepped backward, banging my hip against the picnic table.

"Don't bother pretending like you didn't enjoy that. You know you felt the earth move." He chuckled. "The choice is yours, Dacia. Eternity is a good option."

My eyes were still locked on his when he turned. I watched him dissipate, becoming vapor once again. As soon as he was gone, I was in control of myself—mind and body. I turned and ran to my truck as fast as I could. I sat behind the steering wheel trembling with fear and self-loathing. How could I have given in without restraint? What had I been thinking? The only thing I knew for certain was—whatever else this beautiful man was—he was nothing to be trifled with.

"Get a grip, Dacia," I said in a wavering voice.

Lifting my hand to put the key in the ignition, I realized my shoulder no longer bothered me. I pulled Cody's shirt back just to be sure I wasn't imagining things. Under the bandages, my skin was smooth and unblemished. "What in the world?"

Driving to Cody's house, I took the curves too fast. I couldn't wait to see him, but at the same time, I was terrified of what he would think of me.

When I got there, I couldn't muster the courage to go to his door. Instead, I sat in my truck in his driveway with my head on the steering wheel. Tears pooled in my eyes until they overflowed and cascaded down my cheeks. I wasn't ready for this. I didn't expect this to happen in my hometown, or for it to happen this soon. Aurelia told me it could be weeks, months, or years before I would be in danger again. I had hoped for years, but I should have known my luck wouldn't hold out for long.

Bang, bang, bang. The sound of Cody's knuckles rapping on my window caused my heart to jump into my throat. When it settled back in place, it was racing.

"You okay?" Even with my window up, I heard the alarm in Cody's voice. "Unlock the door."

When my heartbeat steadied, I opened my door and fell into his arms. With my head buried in his chest, I whispered, "It's happening again."

"Oh, Dacia." He held me against him and ran his fingers through my hair. "It'll be all right. I'm here."

But, will you be? I thought to myself. *When you know how he makes me feel, will you be here for me?* "I'm sorry, Cody. I know you were spending time with your family today. I shouldn't've come." I pulled away. Now that I was with him, I wasn't ready to tell him what had happened. I couldn't endure Cody's hatred for me.

"Needed to come. Glad you told me." He turned away, then back again. "Let me give them an excuse, and we'll talk. Be right back. Please … please don't go away."

Leaving was tempting, but where would I go? I couldn't hide from Cody. He'd find me, and when he did, what I had to say would sound so much worse.

When he came back out and saw me waiting, relief spread across his face. "Scoot over. I'll drive." He backed down the driveway and pulled onto the road. He lifted his arm, stopping before putting it over my shoulders.

"It's healed."

He held me close to his side. "Panther or dream?"

My head dropped forward. "Neither."

"Then what?"

"Cody, he was here." My voice sounded panicky even to my ears.

"He?"

"Mavros Malkin." I plowed my hand through my hair.

Cody's fingers tightened on the wheel. "Who?"

"First he was a mist. Then he turned into a person. I could tell he was evil, but …" My voice trailed off. I pulled away from Cody, sliding over to the passenger seat. My hands shook so bad it took three tries to buckle my seatbelt. "He …" I thought about his lips on mine, how I'd wanted more. The back of my throat ached.

Cody pulled onto the shoulder and turned the hazards on. "What is it, Dacia?" He reached toward me but dropped his hand when I pressed myself closer to the door. "What's wrong?"

My chin trembled. "I'm … sorry."

"For what?"

"I … I couldn't help myself."

He lifted my face so he could look into my eyes. "You're okay. You're safe."

I took a deep breath, then whispered, "Please don't hate me."

"Hate you?"

"You should. I wanted him to touch me. I wanted him to hold me." Pressure built up behind my eyes, and I fought to keep from crying. I didn't want him to feel sorry for me. He had every right to hate me, to be angry with me. It wouldn't be fair for me to play on his sympathy. "I … I even wanted him to kiss me. Cody, I'm so sorry."

"Whaddo you mean?" His face hardened, and anger flashed behind his blue eyes. "Did he?"

I'd known Cody most of my life, and I'd never seen him look like this before.

"Yes." My voice was little more than a breath, but he heard me. "I think he was controlling my thoughts. He made me want him. He was evil, and even though I knew that, I couldn't pull away from him." I was so ashamed of myself.

Cody backed up against the driver's side door, folding his arms over his chest to make himself inaccessible. He looked so hurt. I wanted to reach out and reassure him, but how could I? I'd wanted Mavros to hold me; I'd wanted him to kiss me. I wondered if it'd been so easy for him to control me because part of me wanted that. Even now, picturing his flawless face, I could see the allure. Was I so easily won over by beauty? I'd never thought of myself as being shallow before, but now I couldn't help but wonder.

"You love me?" Cody murmured.

I looked him in the eyes and answered, "More than any-thing … more than I ever dreamed was possible."

"Then we'll work this out." He dragged his hand down his face. "Tell me what happened."

My gut wrenched when I told Cody about the mist and about Mavros. I felt like I was going to be sick when I told him about Mavros' impossible beauty. As much as it pained me, I wasn't going to hide anything. I wanted Cody to feel like he could trust me.

"Cody … I'm scared."

He stared out the windshield. His face was stony. A mus-cle jumped in his jaw.

I looked down. Rocks and leaves covered the charcoal floor mat. "I couldn't move when he was near me … except closer to him. It was like he was a magnet drawing me in." I twisted my hands in my lap. *What would I do in Cody's place?* I remembered how torn up I'd been when we'd met Aurelia last year. Cody had stared at her, and I'd lost it.

"I couldn't control myself. I pictured your face and con-centrated on it." I reached toward him but let my hand fall onto the seat between us. "For a minute, I felt like myself again. I was able to resist him, but it didn't stop his allure complete-ly. He's going to come back, and when he does, I don't know what'll happen."

Cody didn't say anything, didn't move. He just stared straight ahead, not even blinking. When he finally did speak, he didn't hide the bitterness in his voice. "Make sure you think about me."

"I'm sorry." I reached out and traced his hand until he softened a little. He wove his fingers through mine, stroking my thumb with his.

"Not your fault," he said without looking at me. "Will try to keep that in mind, but won't be easy."

"I know, but he's not what I want. You are." I tried to smile at him, but it fell flat. "I'm not sure what Mavros is or what he wants, but he's not what he seems."

"Remember meeting Aurelia?"

I huffed out a laugh. "I was just thinking about that."

"Remember how jealous you were?"

"I hated her; I hated the way you looked at her." At the time, we'd known she wasn't human, but it wasn't until later that we found out she was a dragon. In her human form, she was beautiful, alluring, and sparkly. Cody'd done nothing but stare at her and stammer. I'd kissed Mavros like he was my long-lost lover returned from the dead. Cody should hate me.

"Forgive me?"

My eyebrows pulled together, and I tilted my head. "For what?"

"For being jealous and angry."

I unbuckled my seatbelt and slid over to his side, resting my hand on his thigh. "You did nothing wrong. But me? I suck. Forgive me?"

"Yes."

Lifting his arm over my shoulder, I snuggled against his side. As long as I was coming clean, there was still one secret I was keeping from him. One thing I hadn't told anybody. I needed Cody to know I had nothing to hide. "There is, uh, something I haven't told you yet."

His hand tightened on my shoulder. His entire body went rigid. "About Mavros?"

"No. It's nothing bad." I rubbed his leg, trying to get him to relax. "This happened at the end of school. For now, I'd like it to stay between the two of us."

"Okay."

"I'll never have to work." I tried to keep the grin off my face.

"Why?"

"Aurelia gave me some—" I tilted my head to the side while lifting my shoulder "—well, a lot of Draconian's treasure for saving the dragons. I don't need my parents to pay my college tuition anymore. I don't know how much I have, but I'm richer than I ever thought I'd be."

"Wow," he mumbled.

"I just wanted you to know." I held onto his hand and stared straight ahead. A field of lavender bloomed on one side of the road, and next to it, a field of sunflowers lifted their faces to the heavens. The contrast between the two was striking. On the other side of the road, trees stretched up, reaching for the skies. "I'm afraid things are going to be pretty rough, and if, uh … well, if something happens to me, I don't want you to think I was hiding anything from you."

Pain rippled across his features. "Like run off with Mavros?"

"I wouldn't do that, Cody."

"Not intentionally."

"I'm going to do everything I can to keep him out of my head, but it's not like it was with Draconian. Somehow, he gets through. Somehow, I lose all sense of myself." I hated myself for what I was doing to Cody, but he needed to know. "That's not what I was thinking, though. I was thinking more along the lines of if Mavros follows through on his threat."

"You'll stop him." He looked down at me and determination sparked in his sapphire eyes.

I wanted to share his confidence, but how could I stop somebody who had complete control over me? I rubbed my forehead. "Maybe I should run off. I doubt it would work, but I could try to hide from him."

"Not alone." He straightened, and his voice lowered. "We can leave tonight."

I'd already taken him from his brothers today. I couldn't let him leave without an explanation, and Mavros wouldn't just let me go.

"I can't let you do that; it would tear your family up. Besides, I don't know what I want. I just know I can't lose you. I'm afraid of what'll happen with Mavros." I turned away from him. I couldn't bear to see the pain in his eyes again. "I'm afraid of how he makes me feel, and I'm afraid he'll hurt you if you interfere."

"Don't worry about me, Dacia." His voice was soft. "I can take care of myself, and if not, you can." His fingers brushed against my face, asking me to look at him but not forcing me to. I tilted my head, and his blue eyes gazed into my green ones. The love I saw in them was infinite. "Want to run away, I will. Do anything for you."

The tightness in my chest threatened to keep me from responding. I rubbed at it for a moment before saying, "Hopefully, after this is all over, you'll still feel that way."

"I will." He kissed the tip of my nose. "Whaddo you wanna do today?"

"I should go back to the park to get my book. I left it on the picnic table when I ran away from Mavros, and I need to find out how Will gets back to Halt and the others."

"After that?"

I stared out the window. The lavender swayed in the breeze, bending toward the sunflowers. A year ago, clouds would have been rolling in, but I'd learned to control my powers enough to keep that from happening most days. I chewed on my lip, knowing he wanted me to stay with him, but I couldn't, not today. "I suppose I could drop you off at home, so you can spend some time with your brothers. You realize they're going to hate me for this, don't you?"

"They'll deal. They know you're important," he responded in typical Cody fashion. "You can hang with us."

"No." I shook my head. "I'll go home and read. I don't think Mavros will bother me again today. He said he'd give me some time … I imagine he meant more than a couple of hours."

"Sure you should be alone?"

I set my hand on top of his, gently rubbing my thumb along his pinky. "Yeah, I'll be okay. Maybe I'll cook supper for my parents."

While Cody drove to the park, he tried several more times to talk me into spending the rest of the day with him. As much as I wanted to, I couldn't. I wouldn't make good company, and his brothers deserved Cody's full attention. They only had a couple more weeks to spend with him before he had to go back to college.

After we retrieved my book, Cody drove to my house. He pulled into the driveway and stopped, staring straight ahead. "Couldn't let you drive home alone." He gripped the steering wheel so hard that his knuckles whitened. "Been attacked twice in two days."

I lowered my head, looking down at my lap. I knew where he was coming from, but I wasn't ready to deal with this again. "I know."

His head dropped forward a little, and he exhaled deeply. The tension released from his shoulders. He opened the door and got out, leaning against the hood of my truck while I gathered my nerve. We walked up the porch steps in silence, and he waited while I unlocked the door. "Please don't go anywhere. Me and Josh'll bring your truck back tomorrow." He held me tight, fear evident in his hug.

The front door opened, and my heart pounded against my ribs, fighting for freedom. The spoon I'd been using to stir the spaghetti sauce stilled.

"Dacia?" Mom sounded confused.

I exhaled a deep breath. "In here." I stood at the stove. The smell of garlic bread and spaghetti wafted through the air.

"Where's your truck?" Dad stepped into the kitchen. His bushy, brown eyebrows pulled together.

"Cody borrowed it. He's bringing it back tomorrow with Josh."

Mom followed behind Dad. Her green eyes lit up, and a smile touched her face, softening her features. "You didn't have to make supper. I would've done that."

"You always do." I shrugged, feeling for once like the daughter they deserved. "I was home, and it was easy enough to cook it while reading my book."

"You and your books." Dad laughed. "You always did have your nose stuck in one or another. Are you reading anything good?"

"Yeah." I held it up, showing him the cover. "I really like these books. It's one of my favorite series, and I don't get a lot of time to read between classes, studying, and my friends."

We ate at the table like a normal family. Mom and Dad asked how my day was, and even though I hated myself for it, I lied, then asked about theirs.

After supper, I did the dishes, then went to my room. I didn't have the energy to keep pretending life was a bed of roses. Lying on top of my comforter, I considered calling Cody to see if he'd come over. I knew he'd drop everything to be here, so I called Samantha instead.

"Are you and Dan still coming up this weekend?" I twirled a strand of my hair.

"Well … I was going to call you about that." Her voice was full of anguish. "Dan's parents want him to help out around the house. I guess they're painting or something. Anyway, I haven't seen him in a while, and I really miss him. But, if you want me to come without him, I will."

I knew how easy it would be to get her here. All I'd have to do was bring up Mavros and the panther. If I did, she'd find a way to stay here until we went back to college, but no matter how badly I wanted to see her, I couldn't be that selfish. "No, that's fine." I tried my best to sound sincere. "I see Cody almost every day, and it's not enough. I can't imagine being in your position."

"Thanks, Dacia." I could hear the relief in her voice. "So, uh, have your parents asked about your newfound control?"

"No." I laughed at the thought of them asking, at the idea that they could put their denial aside long enough to admit I was different. "They never will. My powers have always been taboo to them … don't ask, don't tell."

Samantha told me about her summer. Deana and Wayne had taken her to the ocean for ten days. The trip sounded like it had been wonderful, but my heart wasn't in the conversation. I'd been looking forward to seeing her and hearing her thoughts about Mavros but not over the phone.

Samantha never asked if I was having nightmares or if I'd met any new monsters, so I didn't bring it up. She'd find out when we were back on campus.

After hanging up, I tried to read, but I couldn't concentrate on my book. Dark skin and dark eyes kept flashing through my mind. I felt his hands on my face, felt desire spread through my body.

I set the book on my nightstand and knelt on the floor beside my bed. Folding my hands together, I prayed. "Lord, please don't let my dreams turn to nightmares. Please don't let Mom and Dad see me for what I am. Please don't let me wake up screaming or covered in blood. Please let me make it through the rest of summer without nightmares. Please keep me safe from Mavros. Amen." Then I climbed into bed and fought sleep until it finally overcame me.

Chapter 3

Mavros Malkin

The backyard looks magical. Mom and Dad have out-done themselves. Fairy lights glimmer in the trees. Every bed is perfectly groomed. Not a piece of mulch is out of place. Family and friends mingle, filling plates with food, dancing, and talking. The evening is warm. A million stars dot the night sky with only a few wispy clouds drifting over them.

As wonderful as it is, I can't enjoy it. Mavros stands beside me, with his arm touching mine. The warmth of his skin brands me even through his black, silk shirt.

"Dacia, who is your friend?" Mom asks. What she really wonders is why I'm with him and not Cody.

"This is Mavros. Mavros, this is my mom, Caitlin," I introduce them, trying to sound casual, but even to me, my voice sounds shaky.

"Mavros? What a unique name." Mom's red and silver hair is braided. The end dangles halfway to her waist. "I've never heard it before."

"It's Greek." His voice is silken, and I watch Mom's green eyes as she becomes mesmerized by him. "An old family name."

A blush creeps over her cheeks. "Well, it's nice to meet you. I hope you're enjoying the party."

"I enjoy any time I get to spend with your lovely daughter." He reaches for her hand, bringing it to his lips.

Mom is so transfixed by him that she can't see the anger or distress on my face. I want to warn her to stay away. I want to tell everybody to go home before he does something to them. As long as he's here, they are in danger, but all anybody else sees is a charming, beautiful man.

"And what a polite young man, too." My mother giggles like a silly, little schoolgirl.

"Thank you." He pulls his hand away. "May I have your daughter to myself for a few moments?" To my mom, I'm sure it sounds like an innocent request, but I know better.

"Of course," she answers. "Keep her as long as you'd like."

"I'm trying my best to do just that." He chuckles, then grabs my hand and tugs me away.

My fingertips tingle with the thrill of his touch. I hate my body for reacting to him this way. I don't want anything to do with him, but I don't want him to let go of me either. His touch makes me desire him just like I did the first day. I duck under his arm, pulling his hand over my shoulders, and wrap my arm around his waist. I want him to hold me tighter and never let go.

A voice in my head warns me to stay away from him. I pull back. "Let go of me."

"You don't want me to let go." He clasps my hand, brushing his thumb over mine. "You want me to hold you close and kiss you like I did last time we were together."

"I …" My voice falters. "I don't want to go anywhere with you … I don't …"

"Ah, the lady doth protest too much." He laughs and lifts his other hand to my face.

I look into his eyes and forget what I was going to say.

He leads me away from my party. When we stop, he turns to face me, never letting go of me. He holds my eyes with his gaze. I feel like he's staring into my soul—like he can see everything about me, every memory, every fear, every desire.

"Dacia, it's time for you to decide." His voice is gentle, loving. Without looking away from my eyes, he reaches up and brushes my cheek. Warmth lingers behind his touch, and goosebumps rise on my arms. He leans forward, his breath caressing my face. My traitorous body responds.

Tipping my head back, his lips press against mine, soft and warm. His fingers slide to my shoulders. As the kiss becomes more passionate, his hands move around my waist, tugging me against him. His body is all hard muscles.

This. This is what I want. Him forever.

"Dacia?" Cody whispers. There is so much pain in that one word.

For a moment, guilt flickers inside me.

Mavros' hand glides over my skin, and I no longer care that Cody is standing behind me. I tug Mavros' mouth down on mine again. My fingers tangle in his hair, holding on for dear life.

When he pulls away from me, I'm breathless and disappointed. I cling to him, but he retreats, not letting go of my hand. He glances at Cody, and when his eyes aren't locked on mine, I come to my senses.

Guilt claws its way up my throat, threatening to choke me. I clutch my stomach, hating myself, hating what my lack of self-control does to Cody. I start to turn around, but Mavros' eyes lock on mine, and I'm his once again.

"It looks like she chose me," Mavros says without turning away from me. He entwines his fingers with mine. I step forward. My other hand presses against his shirt over his heart.

"Dacia, I thought you loved me. I thought …" Cody's voice cracks.

"It looks like you were wrong." Mavros' malicious voice sends shivers down my spine.

Cody grabs Mavros by the arm and swings him around. As soon as I'm not looking into his dark eyes, I feel like myself.

I gasp. "Cody, I'm sorry." I sink to my knees and bury my face in my hands. My shoulders shake. I'm going to have to let Cody go to keep him safe.

"How dare you touch me." All the charm is gone from Mavros' voice. He sounds menacing and cruel. "You have no idea who you are messing with, boy!"

"Yeah, I do!" Cody clenches his fists. "The jerk who's stealing my girlfriend."

I press my hands into the ground and start to push up.

"Dacia, stay there." Mavros' words press down on me, holding me in place.

I try to stand, try to turn my head to look at them, but my body doesn't respond. Thinking of life, I try to break free from his hold, but I can't.

I don't know who throws the first punch, but I'm sure Mavros doesn't fight fair. And, I know who throws the last.

As soon as Mavros is gone, I'm able to move again. I crawl to Cody. He's in bad shape, worse than when Bryce, Alvin, Cassandra, and Vanessa attacked him. His face is bloody and unrecognizable. His ragged breath catches, then stops. I lift his head onto my lap and place my hands on his chest.

I think about life. Cody's superficial wounds heal, but it's not enough. His heartbeat never comes back. I lie my head on his chest and sob. It's my fault. If I was stronger, Cody would still be alive.

"Dacia … Dacia are you okay? Open your door!" My father's voice jolted me from sleep.

"I'm sorry, Dad." I wiped the tears from my face. "It was just a nightmare."

"Let me in." Panic choked his voice.

The last time I'd heard him sound like this, blue flames had danced along my walls. Dad had been standing in the hallway. Shadows and light had flickered over his face. His eyes had been wet with tears.

That was the night my parents learned to fear me, the night Jonathan died.

I stumbled to the door, unlocking it. Dad's eyes were wide. His hair stood every which way.

Touching his arm to calm him, I said, "It was just a bad dream, Dad. Go back to bed. I'm fine."

As soon as Dad left, I lay back down and clutched Glacier to my chest. I wished it was just a nightmare, but deep down I knew this was more. This nightmare was a premonition. Somehow, I needed to stop Cody from being killed.

Chapter 4

A Splash Of Drama

My eyes burned, but I couldn't allow myself to go back to sleep. I couldn't dream about Cody dying again. I wanted to call him, to hear his voice, to know he was okay.

Instead, I closed my eyes and concentrated on Aurelia. I hadn't tried to contact her since school ended. I had no idea where she was or even what she was. If she was in dragon form, would she respond to me?

Of course, I will respond to you, I heard her beautiful voice echo in my head. *Remember to only let thoughts out that you want to be heard.*

Yeah. I've got a lot on my mind, and I should've been more careful.

Obviously, there is trouble or you would not have contacted me. What is it? Leave it to Aurelia to get straight to the point.

I let her into my mind. She saw the visit from Mavros, the attack by the panther, and my nightmare about Cody. *I don't know if they're a team or separate threats, but Mavros terrifies me. He can get into my head, and I can't seem to keep him out. I can't let him hurt Cody.*

When is your birthday party? Her voice was tranquil.

Friday's my birthday. I rubbed my temples, trying to assuage the massive headache growing there. *I'm not sure when the party is. It's supposed to be a surprise. I just found out about it in my dream.*

I will be there. However, I may not be able to stay for more than a couple of days.

Thank you, Aurelia. My connection with her broke, but relief washed over me at once. There was nothing like having a dragon on your side to help make things seem better.

At 6:30, I called Cody. He answered on the fourth ring. "Dacia, what's wrong?" His voice was heavy with sleep.

I sank onto my bed. A sob escaped my throat. Hearing him steadied me. The panic that had resided in me since I woke up diminished.

"Dacia?"

"I needed to hear your voice."

"Why?" He sounded more awake now.

"A nightmare." I lay on my bed, cradling the phone against my ear. "If it's a premonition, it'll happen at my birthday party."

"Getting dressed; be there in ten." He hung up before I could argue.

Less than ten minutes later, Cody pulled into the driveway. I stood, looking at my doorknob for a minute before stepping out into the hall.

As soon as I walked into the kitchen, Mom set her coffee down. "Dacia dear, do you have nightmares very often?"

I hated not telling her the truth, but I looked her in the eye, shrugged like it was no big deal, and lied like a pro. "No, and when I do, I hardly ever remember what they were about anyway."

Dad walked into the room with Cody trailing behind him. "You were really upset when you woke up last night," Dad said. "Do you want to talk about it?"

Watching out the window so they couldn't see the truth in my eyes, I said, "I don't remember what it was even about—maybe it's because of my birthday. I'm getting older and will have to become more responsible soon. I don't know if I'm ready for that."

"Don't worry about that." Dad pulled me into a one-armed, sideways hug.

"No"—Mom spun her cup on the table—"you won't have much of a change. You've always been very mature."

"Good morning, Mrs. Wolf." Cody stepped up beside me, slipping his hand into mine.

"Call me Caitlin." Mom frowned at him. "Oh and good morning."

Cody squeezed my fingers. "Nightmare?"

"No big deal." I shrugged. "Are you ready to go?"

"If you are."

"You haven't even eaten yet." Mom stood and walked to the refrigerator. Opening the door, she stared inside. "Aren't you hungry? I can make you some eggs or pancakes."

"Cody's taking me to breakfast." I tugged on his hand, pulling him into the living room and toward the exit.

"Have a good day," Dad said as we walked out.

Cody's Camaro was in my driveway. I looked at it, then at him. I'd expected him to drive my truck over, but maybe he wasn't ready for me to have it back.

"Was in a hurry." He shrugged.

I sat in the passenger seat and strapped on my seatbelt. "So, I'm having a birthday party?"

Smiling, he put his fingers up to his lips and said, "Shh, it's a secret."

"Are Samantha and Dan coming up this weekend then?" My spirits lifted at the thought.

"Friday."

"My birthday is Friday … the thirteenth. Not that the date matters." I sighed. "But I think this one will live up to its reputation."

"Your parents'll wonder why we're sitting here." Cody nodded toward the house. "Where to?"

"Somewhere." I dragged my hand through my hair. "Anywhere."

He backed out of my driveway and headed toward Bittersweet, taking his time. He meandered down the gravel road, barely even kicking up any dust. Then he turned onto another one. In all the years I had lived here, I had never gone this way.

I knew he was waiting for me to tell him about my dream, but I wasn't sure how much of it he should know. Wasn't it hard enough for him to know how I felt when I was near Mavros? Did I really have to tell him that he might only have a couple of days left to live?

"Well?" he prodded once his patience ran out.

I stared out the window. The mountains played peek-a-boo through the trees. "I don't want to talk about it."

"So … either I die or you end up with Mavros." His voice was hard, matter-of-fact. "Or he killed me and ended up with you." He flipped his hand up. "Besta both worlds."

I listened to him talk so casually about the possibility of his imminent death, and I wondered why he stayed with me … why he would put himself through all of this. I knew he would say I was worth it, but no matter how hard I tried, I couldn't see it from his perspective.

"Yes, Cody, you died in my dream. Mavros pulled me away from the party and told me to choose. While he tried to, uh …" What was I supposed to say? *Well, Cody while I was locked in a passionate embrace with Mavros and kissing him like I should only kiss you, totally forgetting that you even existed, you caught us.* I couldn't tell him that; I couldn't keep hurting him. I closed my eyes and wiped my hand over my forehead. "While he tried to persuade me, you walked up behind us. He killed you, and I couldn't bring you back. I can't let it happen, but I don't know how to stop it."

"Didn't like seeing him persuade you. Huh?" Cody's expression didn't change, but his knuckles whitened as he clutched the steering wheel.

"No, you didn't."

As if he was talking to himself, I heard him whisper, "But did you?"

"He wasn't you." I hovered my hand above his knee, afraid he'd jerk away. When he didn't, I trailed my fingers over his leg, sliding my hand under the edge of his shorts.

His hands relaxed their hold on the wheel, but he never said anything. After another half hour, we reached an isolated mountain lake. He pulled over and stopped the car. There wasn't a soul in sight. I climbed out and breathed in the fresh air.

"This is beautiful, Cody," I said, breaking the silence that had lingered between us. I couldn't take it much longer. I felt like it was suffocating me.

"One of my favorite places." He sounded distant.

I was sure he was picturing the many ways Mavros could have tried to persuade me or picturing how he might die. He had every right to be angry, to be hurt. Who wouldn't be?

I walked over to him and put my hand on his arm. I wanted to comfort him without seeming pushy. "Cody, I'm not going to let it happen. I'll do everything in my power to keep you alive."

"I know."

"Then what's wrong?"

He tossed his head back and stared up at the sky. "Can't stop picturing it."

Tugging my hand down my face, I stepped away from him. I understood he needed time to deal with this. Jealousy was a beast, one that had to be vanquished alone.

While we walked to the water's edge, I told Cody about my conversation with Aurelia. "She'll be here Friday but probably not for long."

He skipped a rock across the still lake. Several more followed. "Can she help?"

I shrugged. "I hope so." I wanted to believe things would work out, but I had an ominous feeling. "I miss school."

Cody had been about to skip another rock. Instead, he lowered his hand, and his eyebrows pinched together. "Why?"

"Well, I miss having you all to myself. I miss the freedom. And," I felt my face flush when I told him, "I miss those days when I woke up in your arms."

Cody dropped the rocks and strode toward me. His hands slid onto my shoulders, then down my arms. Goosebumps trailed behind his touch. He kissed the top of my head. "Me too. Can't wait to wake up with you every morning. Maybe your nightmares'll end."

There was too much space between us. I closed the gap, pressing my body against his. "Wouldn't that be nice?"

He nudged my nose with his, tilting my head back. His lips pressed against mine, softer than velvet.

My stomach growled, and Cody backed away, chuckling. "Breakfast?"

"Can we walk by the lake first?"

"Yeah." Cody draped his arm over my shoulders, holding me against his side. The warmth of his body and the tenderness of his touch helped relieve some of my anxiety.

When we got to the lake's edge, I stuffed my socks into my shoes and waded into the water. It was cold—like mountain lakes always are—but invigorating.

"Come in with me." I wiggled my fingers at Cody, motioning for him to join me.

"That's okay. I'm fine here."

"If you're sure …" I laughed and scooped water into my hands, throwing it at him. A fountain erupted from the lake in front of me. The water surged forward, drenching Cody. He stood on the shore as wet as if he had dived headfirst into the lake. His arms were in front of him in a futile attempt to shield him from the deluge. His eyes were wide, and his mouth hung open.

"Sorry." I lowered my eyes, and my mouth curled into a wicked smile that I tried to cover with my hands. I felt bad about soaking him, but it was funny.

"How?" He shook his head like a wet dog.

"I don't know. I've never done anything like that before."

He mopped the water off his face. "Wonder if you'll ever max out."

"I don't know." I trailed my fingers over the water. "So far, I've been pretty lucky that stuff like this has only happened in front of you or Samantha. One of these days, it's bound to happen in front of my parents or classmates … or total strangers. Then I'll get taken away for experimentation or something. That'll be fun."

Walking into the water and taking my hand in his, he said, "Don't worry. Hasn't happened yet."

"You could've stopped to take your shoes off." I giggled.

"Why bother?" He clutched my hand tighter. "Wet as they were a minute ago."

"Sorry about that."

"You didn't mean it—" he smiled, and there was an evil edge to it "—but I'm gonna get even."

"For now, how about we get out of the water so you can dry off?"

He stalked closer, circling me. I turned, keeping him in my sights. Slowly, ever so slowly, he prowled around me. I held my hand out in front of me, waiting for him to strike.

He stared at something over my shoulder. I fought the urge to look, but he kept watching. His eyebrows pinched together. I glanced behind me. My gaze was off him for half of a second. He scooped me up in his arms and ran farther into the lake. I tried to wiggle free from his grasp to no avail. Still holding me, he dove underwater, dunking both of us. We emerged, giggling.

"You were too dry." Cody drew me into his arms.

I flipped my hair back. The water pulled the curls out of it, making it fall past my waist. "You didn't have to go under, too."

He shook his head. "If I'd've thrown you, you'd've flown off."

"Probably." The light breeze raised goosebumps on my arms. I shivered against Cody.

"Let's get out and warm up." He strode toward shore. With shoes on, his steps were sure.

The moss-covered rocks were slippery beneath my bare feet. I walked carefully, falling farther behind him. "Yeah." I pulled my shirt away from my body, but as soon as I let go, it clung to me again. "And we can dry off a little bit."

Cody poured the water out of his shoes. "Gonna take a month for them to dry."

"Maybe next time, you should just come in the water to begin with." I found a dry spot and stretched out on the rocks.

He sprawled out beside me. "Might be safer."

I snuggled next to him with my head on his shoulder. It was much warmer in the sun, so I called up a stronger wind, hoping it would dry us off before I died of starvation.

My mind wandered, and I found myself trying to figure out how Mavros could control me. Lying here with Cody felt so right. How could Mavros make me forget what Cody meant to me? How could he make all these feelings disappear only to be replaced by such a strong desire for him? And, most importantly, how could I make it stop?

I flipped over, and Cody followed suit. He slid his hand under the bottom edge of my shirt. His fingers were warm, comforting. I closed my eyes and fought the urge to sleep.

"Whatcha thinking?" Cody traced his finger along my cheek sometime later.

"How much I like being with you," I whispered, realizing I had nearly drifted off. "And, how to stop Mavros."

"Both at once?" He pulled his arm off of me and sat up. "Strange combination?"

"Not really." I knew I was about to upset Cody more, but he asked a direct question. Being me, I had no choice but to answer it. "I was thinking about how much I like snuggling with you. Then I wondered how Mavros can make me forget everything but him." Cody's mouth tightened, and I knew he was trying to control his jealousy. "I have to stop him, but I don't know how."

Through clenched teeth, he suggested, "Let me knock his head off."

"If he was just some other guy, I would." I wrung my hair out. "But, he's not. I don't know what he is. If I did, it might make things easier."

"Ask him?" He stared out at the lake.

"I don't know." I dropped my head into my hands. "He might tell me, but I really don't think he would. I get the impression he likes to be mysterious."

"Could try." He slipped his shoes on. "If not, maybe Aurelia can figure it out."

I stood up and started walking back to his car. "Maybe."

Cody was quiet throughout breakfast. He stabbed at his eggs and sausages like he needed to kill them before shoving them into his mouth. He didn't make eye contact with me.

As much as it hurt, it was less than I deserved. I had kissed another man. And, I had liked it.

By the time we left the restaurant, Cody seemed to have shaken off whatever thoughts had been eating at him. He leaned over the console in his Camaro and brushed my hair back, tucking a stray curl behind my ear. "Sorry."

"I know." I savored the warmth of his fingers against my skin and the love I saw in his eyes.

The rest of the day was like that. Anytime I got too quiet, Cody assumed I was thinking about Mavros. There were as many tense moments as there were good ones. I couldn't blame him for being jealous, but I couldn't convince him there was nothing to worry about either. I knew he felt insecure, and I didn't know how to console him. If he was this bothered by Mavros now, how would he react if he saw the two of us together? Was there any way to keep my dream from becoming reality?

Chapter 5

Fear of running into Mavros kept me locked up inside my house the next day. I lay propped against pillows reading. I did chores. I straightened my hair. I made chocolate chip cookies. I looked at the clock. It wasn't even noon yet.

Over her lunch break, Mom called. "Dacia, I need you to run to the store for me. I forgot to pick up some things. There's some cash in the cookie jar."

"Okay." My stomach plummeted, but I tried to hide my fear from her. "I guess I'll have to eat all the cookies then."

She gave me a short list of things to pick up. Cody and I had brought my truck back last night. Now I wished I'd left it at his house so I'd have an excuse not to go. I stood with my hand on the doorknob taking deep breaths. Finally, I got the courage to open it and step outside.

A cloudless sky greeted me, and a gentle breeze lifted my hair while I hustled to my truck. I locked the doors as soon as I sat in it. By the time I drove the five miles to the store, my shoulders ached.

Sitting in the parking lot, I scanned the area, searching for anything out of the ordinary. When I decided everything looked okay, I dashed in.

I glanced behind me while shoving items into the cart. After paying the cashier, I stood at the door, hoping nothing would happen on the short jaunt to my truck. I slid the groceries onto the passenger seat and floor, then hurried to the driver's side, leaving the empty cart in the stall next to me.

The drive home was much like the one to the store had been. I clung to the steering wheel. Fear turned every shadow into the panther, every person into Mavros. When I pulled into the driveway and didn't see anybody or anything, I relaxed somewhat. I walked around to the passenger side to get the groceries.

As soon as I opened the door, the hairs on the back of my neck lifted and cold chills crawled along my spine. Turning around, I saw the enormous panther. As soon as our eyes met, it lunged. Its teeth sank into my bicep.

Pain lanced through me. I punched the creature, knocking its head back. Its fangs tore through my skin, and it ran off into the trees.

Lava flowed through my veins, setting my insides on fire. The pain had no beginning and no end.

Tears poured from my eyes, burning a trail down my face. Blood bubbled up from the punctures. It dripped off my fingers, pooling near my feet.

Glancing at my house, I knew I wouldn't make it there before I passed out. I couldn't stay in the open and risk the beast coming back, and I couldn't focus enough to teleport.

I turned toward my truck and used it to steady myself. I took one step, and the ground lurched. Bile rose in my throat. My vision blurred with my next step. I lifted my hand to wipe it across my face and swayed. When I reached for the hood again, I staggered.

I tried to focus on life, but my thoughts just kept going back to the panther. What was it, and what had it done to me?

I lifted my foot, but it was sluggish and barely moved off of the ground. My toe caught on something, and I stumbled, falling to my knees.

Pressing my hand down, I tried to push myself back onto my feet, but everything spun, and I collapsed.

A black haze crept in at the edge of my vision. I blinked to clear my eyes. When I opened them again, Mavros stood above me. "Let me help you."

I nodded, and the world tilted. I pressed my eyes shut, hoping to stop the movement.

He lifted me into his arms. My pain eased as soon as he touched me. I sighed at the blessed relief and opened my eyes. I snuggled closer to him and breathed in his warm, summer nights scent. He carried me to the porch. "Unless you invite me in, I can take you no farther."

Glancing from him to the door, I said, "Set … me down … here." There had to be a reason he couldn't go in, and I wasn't ready to find out what it was.

He laid me down, careful not to jar my arm. "At least let me unlock the door for you." As soon as he let go of me, the pain ripped through my body again.

I dug my fingernails into the cedar planks beneath me and fought to hold back the scream that tore up my throat. Once I had control of myself, I whispered, "Yes. But don't go in." My voice was barely audible to me, but somehow, he heard it.

He went to my truck, grabbed my keys, jogged back to the porch, and held the door open for me. I crawled in and crumpled on the floor.

Pain pulsed through my arm, and I pinched my eyes shut to stop the room from spinning. I wanted Cody here with me. I needed his help, his strength.

Mavros stood outside the door, watching me. I pulled myself farther in and pushed the door shut with my foot. "Thanks," I mumbled before passing out.

"Dacia?" Cody's voice was panicked. "You here?"

"Yes." My voice came out in a whisper.

In a moment, he was at my side. "Heard your voice in my head and came as fast as I could." He knelt down next to me, gently turning my arm to examine the wound. "What happened?"

"The—" my eyebrows pinched together as I searched for a word for it "—not panther." My voice trembled. "It's enormous and way too strong … too fast to be a panther. I'm scared, Cody."

"I know." He lifted my head onto his lap and brushed my hair back from my face. "Me too."

"How am I supposed to stand against it, deal with Mavros, and keep you safe?"

"Dunno."

"I need you to bring the groceries in." He stood up to go, but I reached out and grabbed his hand. "Please be careful."

Cody made it in with the bags without any trouble. While I tried to regain some of my strength, he put them away. As soon as I could stand up, I stumbled into the kitchen and grabbed a bucket, filling it with soapy water. It sloshed over the edge when I carried it to the entryway, leaving more messes to be cleaned up.

I knelt down, careful not to use my injured arm, and cleaned the blood off the floor.

Cody came in as I was finishing. "I'd've done that."

"I know." I lifted my hand to him, and he pulled me to my feet. "I could use some help with my arm."

Cody led me into the bathroom and set me on the counter. While the sink filled, he grabbed a washcloth out of the closet. He dipped it in the water, then gently wiped the blood off.

I held my breath and bit my lip, trying not to cringe. My arm throbbed. Every slight movement sent agony flaring through the punctures.

Cody's mouth stayed in a firm, straight line. His eyebrows pinched together. He put antiseptic over the bite and cuts, then bandaged my arm. When he finished, he pressed his hands onto the cabinet beside me. "What happened?"

I crossed my wounded arm over my body, clasping the opposite shoulder. "When Mom and Dad ask, I fell down the stairs and cut my arm … no big deal." But, that wasn't what I was thinking. It was a big deal. My arm should have been healing. It shouldn't have been throbbing.

"I'm not your parents." There was no mirth in his eyes. They were hard and angry. "So, what happened?"

"I went to get the groceries out of the truck, and the panther thing attacked me. I punched it, and it ran off." I was still surprised by that. I couldn't have hurt it that bad. "I lay there until Mavros came. He carried me onto the porch and unlocked the door. He said he couldn't come in without me inviting him."

"Like a vampire?" Cody held his hand out to me. I took it and hopped down. "Must not be. He can be in the sun."

We walked into the kitchen, and Cody poured us each a glass of lemonade. I took a sip of mine, then said, "Unless Stephenie Meyer is right about that part, but I didn't notice him sparkling, and Edward did go into Bella's house without being invited." I shrugged and pain spiraled through my arm. "I crawled inside and shut the door." I shook my head. "I didn't know I called out to you. You could've been killed."

We sat in the living room and tried to watch a movie. I couldn't focus on it. My mind jumped between Mavros and the panther. I couldn't figure out what Mavros wanted with me and why the panther had disappeared.

I snuggled against Cody and gasped when my arm brushed his.

"First, your shoulder didn't heal. Now, this isn't." Cody cocked his head. "Why?"

"I don't know." I looked down, twisting my foot nervously.

"Take some of my strength."

"Are you staying?"

"Yes." I could almost hear his eyes rolling. "You should never be alone."

Chapter 6

*F*riday morning, I woke up to my arm throbbing. Touching the bandage, I felt heat through it. I unwrapped it and gasped. The wound was bright red and pulsating.

"Why?" The word escaped on a sob. *This doesn't make any sense at all. It was a big cat. Why can't I heal from this? Am I losing my powers?*

I sat on the edge of my bed and leaned forward with my head in my hands, trying to calm down. Cody would be here soon to keep me distracted while my parents got everything ready for my surprise party. Until I left with him, I had to pretend like I was okay.

Sometime during the day, Aurelia would arrive, and maybe she could help me figure out what was going on. I took several deep breaths. Once I calmed down, I headed to my closet to find something to wear. I didn't want Mom and Dad to know that their surprise party wasn't a surprise, but I also wanted to look halfway decent. So, I picked out an outfit that wasn't too nice but wasn't cut-off shorts either.

When I went downstairs, Cody was sitting at the table with my parents. "Morning, Dacia." He smiled at me. "Happy birthday."

"Thanks." I tried to look surprised to see him there. Mom and Dad had gone to a lot of trouble to keep this party a secret, and I didn't want to blow it for them. "What are you doing here so early?"

"Cody wanted to take you out for breakfast," Mom explained. "We were just waiting for you to wake up."

"You could've told me he was here."

"It's your birthday," Dad stated. "You deserve to sleep as long as you want on your birthday."

Mom stood up and walked toward me. She reached up and brushed a stray hair off my face. "By the way, how did you sleep last night? No nightmares?"

"Nope," I answered without looking at her. She didn't need to know the truth.

The panther had attacked so fast; there hadn't been time for me to scream. I was down another pair of pajamas, but there was no reason to be concerned about that anymore either. I had plenty of money to spend on new ones.

"Well, that's good news." Dad stood and gave me a hug. His body pressed against my arm. I squeezed my eyes shut, hoping to keep the pain from showing. "We're worried about you."

I stepped away. Cody looked from my face to my arm and then back again. I shook my head slightly. "It's nothing to worry about. Like I told you, I usually don't even remember what my dreams were about the next morning." The lie pressed down on me. I hated that I couldn't tell them the truth, but no matter how much I wanted them to accept me for who I was, I knew they couldn't. They needed me to be in control of my powers, confident, and strong. "It doesn't matter if they're good or bad." I remembered all of my horrifying nightmares and also the wonderful dreams I'd had while sleeping in Cody's arms.

Cody pushed his chair back from the table and stood. "Ready?"

"Yeah," I answered.

While Mom was hugging me goodbye, she pouted, "I can't believe my baby is nineteen today." She turned to Cody. "Can you believe she's nineteen?"

He shoved his hands in his pockets and nodded. "Since I am, yeah."

"I suppose that does make it easier," Mom admitted, but she still looked upset.

My eyebrows pinched together, and I tilted my head. "What's wrong, Mom?"

"Well, I can't believe my baby girl is a grown-up." She cradled her arms and looked down as if remembering holding me. "It seems like just yesterday I was bringing you home from the hospital."

It was so weird to listen to her talk like this. I thought I had been an embarrassment to them. I thought they were ashamed of me. I thought they thought I was a freak. Maybe I didn't understand my parents … maybe all this time I had been wrong about how they felt. Maybe my guilt over Jonathan had tainted me.

"I'm proud of how you turned out." Her pale green eyes glistened. "You've grown into such a smart, beautiful, wonderful young woman."

"Thanks, Mom," I said still hugging her.

"She's right, Dacia." Dad joined in the hug. "You make us both proud."

Cody cleared his throat. "Should go. Breakfast doesn't last all day."

"Oh, you're right." Mom stepped back, swiping at her eyes. "You two better get out of here."

"Thanks, Cody," I said when we were in his car. "That was a little overwhelming."

He nodded. "Saw you were gonna lose it."

"I've spent so long thinking they resented me." I stared across the yard into the trees, not sure what to think or how to feel. "It was nice to hear that they're proud of me." I swallowed a lump. "It was the perfect birthday present, but it made me feel a little awkward."

"Glad it made you happy." He took my hand in his. "Know it's been hard."

"So, what're we going to do today?" I asked in an obvious effort to change the subject.

"Your day. Whadda you want?" He turned the key in the ignition, and the engine rumbled to life.

"To spend it with you." I looked into his eyes. "I don't want to worry about the inevitable. I don't want to think about all the unpleasant things waiting for me."

"Start with breakfast." His stomach growled loud enough for me to hear it. He nodded at my arm. "How bad?" He backed down the driveway.

"It's not healing at all." I tried to keep the panic from my voice. "I don't know what's going on."

He put his hand over mine and squeezed it. "Maybe Aurelia can help."

"Yeah."

"Diamond?" he asked.

There was only one place to eat in Bittersweet, Diamond in the Rough. They had all kinds of food. For the most part, if you could think of it, you could order it.

"Sure." I chewed on my lip. "Do you know when Samantha and Dan are coming? It'd be nice to give them a heads-up before tonight."

"Late afternoon." He pulled onto the road, driving slowly to keep gravel from being thrown onto his car. "Told Dan to call when they get here."

"Okay, that'll make things easier."

Cody's lips pinched together, and he drummed his fingers on the steering wheel. "Samantha's staying at your house. Tell her about your nightmares."

I deserved that comment—I'd kept my dreams from them in the past—but my hackles rose in response. I wanted to snap at Cody, but instead, I bit my lip and promised, "I'll tell them everything."

He raised his eyebrows. I was sure he expected an argument from me. "Thank you. Know it's not easy."

"It isn't, but I'm trying to do better." I rolled my window down. The wind whipped my hair around my head. "I don't want you to worry that I'm keeping things from you. I want you to know you can trust me."

"Know I can." He ran his hand up my leg, sending tingles racing along my skin. "Doesn't mean I won't be jealous."

I rested my hand on his, squeezing his fingers tighter than I'd intended. "I'm afraid Mavros might come between us no matter what actually happens."

"Why?" He sounded confused and a little hurt.

"Well, I noticed that whenever I get quiet, you worry about what I'm thinking, and I can't blame you." I rushed through my answer.

"You're right." He nodded. "Trust you, though."

I looked at him, unsmiling, and said, "Yeah, uh-huh."

"I do. But it's tough. Hate—" he cleared his throat "—thinking about you two. Sometimes, can't help it."

"Don't give up on me." I pulled my bottom lip into my mouth. "I'm going to do everything I can to stop him."

"I know." He pulled into a parking spot and unbuckled his seatbelt. Then he waited outside the car for me.

I watched him, hoping this wouldn't be the last morning I'd spend with him. Opening my door, I got out and sashayed over to him. I hoped I looked sexy and not idiotic. Flattening my hands on his stomach, I pushed him back against his car and pressed my body close to his. I ran my fingers over his abs and up his chest.

He clutched my waist and smiled down at me. "What's this?"

I slid my hands up his neck, tilting his head forward until his mouth crashed down on mine.

He moaned and lifted me up. I wrapped my legs around his waist and clung to him. My pulse pounded. The pain in my arm flared. I leaned back gasping, and Cody lowered me to the ground, resting his forehead on mine.

His chest heaved, and his fingers trailed over my back.

I tucked my hands into his pockets. "I need you to do something for me." My voice was husky.

"Not staying home."

I closed my eyes and nodded slightly. "I didn't think you would." I huffed. "I had to try, though."

"Appreciate the attempt." He brushed my hair back. Then he wiggled his eyebrows while saying, "You can try again later."

Images from my nightmare popped into my head. If it had been a premonition, it would come true tonight. Even though I doubted he'd give in, I'd have to try again. Somehow, I needed to keep him safe. "Sounds like a plan to me."

Diamond in the Rough was filled with people I had lived by all my life but never really known. I felt self-conscious walking in there. I shouldn't have; nobody paid any attention to me. A few people waved to Cody, but I might as well have been invisible.

While we waited for our waitress to bring our food, Cody said, "Your parents told everybody not to bring gifts, but wanted to give you something."

He handed me a small box wrapped in dark purple and tied with a silver bow. Careful not to rip the paper, I opened it. The jewelry box was small. I figured it was earrings, but when I opened the lid, a ring sparkled up at me.

Cody drummed his fingers on the table. "It's a promise ring."

"It's beautiful, Cody. Thank you." I whispered over the lump forming in my throat. Tears welled up in the corners of my eyes. I didn't deserve his affection. I couldn't believe that after I kissed Mavros he still wanted to give me this.

"Not as beautiful as you—" he took the ring out of the box and slid it on my finger "—but you're welcome."

I held my hand out in front of me, admiring it. The gold band was thin. A small oval diamond was offset by rubies and smaller diamonds. It was delicate looking and perfect. Smiling at him, I asked, "What does it promise?"

His eyes sparkled. "That I'll love you forever. That I'll be there through the ups and downs and everything in between. That one day I'll make you my wife." He reached across the table, brushing his fingers along my cheek. "And anything else you want it to promise."

"Anything?"

He nodded.

"That you'll stay away tonight?" I held my hand over his.

He pulled away. "Anything but that."

Throughout breakfast, I kept glancing at the ring on my finger. It was a beautiful, unexpected gift.

Cody and I spent the whole day together, enjoying each other's company. We did our best to keep conversation light and avoid the subject of Mavros until Samantha and Dan arrived. As luck would have it, we met them in the park where I'd first encountered Mavros.

When we drove through the park gates, my stomach lurched, and my heart raced. The air in the car thickened, becoming impossible to breathe. I gasped, but the only response was a tightening in my chest.

Cody rubbed my neck. "Breathe, Dacia."

"Can't," I said around the catch in my throat.

"It's okay."

"It's not." This was the place I'd met Mavros. I was afraid he'd be here, afraid of what he'd do to Cody.

Cody drove slowly, whispering to me, trying to soothe me while he looked for Samantha and Dan. We found them sitting at a picnic table, holding hands. The sight of them helped ease my anxiety.

They made such a cute couple. Samantha was petite with friendly, soft brown eyes and long, brown hair. Dan was about an inch shorter than Cody with broad shoulders, auburn hair, and an angel's smile.

When I stepped out of the car, I saw the surprise on their faces. It seemed they weren't aware that it was no longer a surprise party. "So, you're painting this weekend, huh?" I said, giving Samantha a hug. "It's good to see you."

"Yeah, I had to come up with something." She sounded a little embarrassed. "Your mom said it was a surprise party."

"It was—" Cody shook Dan's hand "—'til Dacia had a nightmare."

The picnic table sat over a graveled area, keeping the grass from growing underneath it. I kicked at the rocks, not wanting to look at anybody. "I met my next adversary, and in my dream, he tried to kill Cody at my birthday party. It … uh … gave the secret away, but my parents don't know it isn't a surprise."

"So, did you meet him in real life or just in your dream?" Dan asked.

I tugged a shaking hand through my hair. "No, I met him here of all places."

"What is it this time?" Samantha asked.

I looked at Cody. I knew it would hurt him when I told them about Mavros, and I felt horrible for it.

"Go ahead." He waved his hand at me. "I'll be okay."

Dan and Samantha shot us curious looks but didn't say anything.

The picnic table was in a clearing, surrounded on three sides by trees. I scanned the area, looking for anything out of place. Small animals, insects, and birds filled the forest with the usual sounds. A bunny munched on clover. It seemed safe.

I sat down on the bench and folded my arms over the table. Cody stood at the end of the table between Samantha and me, staring into the trees.

I focused on my hands, not daring to meet anybody's gaze. "Mavros Malkin is gorgeous, and when he looks into my eyes,

I can't think about anything but him. All I want is for him to touch me."

"Oh," Samantha said at the same time Dan said, "That's not good." Their expressions were identical masks of sorrow as they looked from me to Cody.

"When he first appeared, he was a mist that slowly transformed into a tall, dark, handsome man." I pinched my eyes shut and dragged both hands down my face. "He wants me to be his friend."

"Friendship's good." Samantha shrugged, lifting her palms like she didn't see the problem.

"For eternity." Those two words gave me the heebie-jeebies. I rubbed my arms and cringed when my fingertips came too close to my wound. "But I don't think I need friends like him. I'm not sure what he is, but when the mist was near me, I could sense it was evil."

Samantha placed her hand on Cody's arm. She looked up at him, then lowered her gaze to the ground. "So, how do you fight someone or something like that?"

"I don't know how to fight him." I stared at the table. Initials were carved over its scarred surface. "I don't even know how to resist him. All I know is that if my dream was a premonition, he'll show up at my party tonight, and all Hell will break loose."

"What she means is: I'll find them … together. He'll kill me. She'll try to revive me. Won't work." Cody's face remained an emotionless mask, but his eyes grew cold and hard.

"I'm sorry, Cody." I reached for his hand, but he sat beside me and wrapped his arm around my shoulder careful not to touch my wound.

"You've got your own demons." He rested his head on top of mine. "Don't worry about mine."

"Just drop me off, then leave."

"When I said try again, didn't mean like this." His voice sounded light, but pain flickered in his eyes.

"Aurelia is supposed to be here sometime today." I siphoned off some of Cody's strength without meaning to. As soon as I realized I was doing it, I tightened the leash on my powers. "I'm hoping she has some answers. Maybe she can tell me what Mavros is and give me some idea of how to stop him."

Dan shot me a mirthless smile. "Well, we'll do whatever we can to help you."

"I'm not sure if we can do anything except be here for you." Samantha reached across the table and squeezed my fingers.

"That's good enough." A heartfelt smile curved my lips. "Friends make everything easier."

"What does Mavros want anyway?" Samantha asked.

"Me," I said like that was obvious.

"Yeah … but why?" Dan flipped his hands up.

The wind picked up, and I wondered for a minute if it was my doing. "Oh, uh, I really don't know."

"I'm sure we'll find out," Samantha said, "but, now for more important things. Was that a ring I saw on your finger when you reached for Cody's hand?"

"Yeah, a promise ring." I lifted my hand, and a smile spread across my face. "Cody gave it to me this morning."

"Wow … that's beautiful." She looked at Dan. It was a look that said your turn.

"It was quite a surprise." I dropped my hand below the table and rubbed Cody's leg. "There's more to tell you since you're staying with me. I've been attacked by a monstrous black-panther thing a couple of times, and I've been having nightmares."

"Not good." Dan rubbed his chin. "Is the panther a dream?"

"Yes, but I've also survived its attacks twice already."

The blood drained from Samantha's face. "Do you think you're going to have to deal with them both at the same time? Is there some connection?"

"I'm not sure what's going on." I tried to sound nonchalant, but my voice wavered. I pointed at my arm. "The panther attacked me yesterday. It isn't healed. Mavros showed up right after that and helped get me in my house. He tried to get me to let him in, but I wouldn't. He said he couldn't enter."

Cody squeezed my shoulder but didn't say anything.

"So, he's a vampire?" Samantha shook her head like she couldn't believe she was even saying it.

The bunny darted into the trees. My grip on Cody's leg tightened in response. Fear curled in my stomach. The others watched me. I shook my head. "Something tells me no."

"Then what?" She rubbed her chin.

"I don't know." I shrugged, and my arm pulsed in response. "I'm hoping Aurelia can answer that for me."

"It sounds like you're having an eventful summer." Dan shot me a smile that didn't reach his eyes. "I'm sorry we haven't been here to help you."

"It's okay." As much as I wanted them nearby, my life was a mess. "You're safer when you're not around me."

We hung out at the park as long as we could without Mom worrying whether or not Samantha and Dan would make it to my party on time. After the initial conversation, we moved on to more pleasant topics, like how the last two weeks had been for them and what they'd been up to. It was good to see the two of them, and I felt a little weight lift off my shoulders when I explained to them what had been going on with me.

"Don't forget to be surprised when you see us." Samantha leaned out the window to remind me.

"I've been working on my acting for the last week. It's hard to hide all of this"—I waved my hand through the air—"from my parents. Anyway, as far as Mom and Dad are concerned, I seem to be a fairly good actress."

After Samantha and Dan left, my anxiousness returned. Would Aurelia arrive in time? Would she be able to help me stop Mavros, or was I on my own?

"Just contact her," Cody instructed.

"Hey, I thought I was the mind reader," I said, acting indignant.

Cody shrugged. "Know you."

"Yeah, probably better than anyone else." I wrapped my hand around his arm and laid my head on his shoulder. "I'll wait. I'll see her tonight."

"So, uh …"

"What?" I sat up and looked at him.

His mouth opened and closed. He dragged a hand down his face before looking at the ground. When his voice managed to come out, it was quiet and broken. "Shouldn't ask, but need to." He looked up at me, his eyes begging me to understand. "How does he persuade you? If I'm gonna see it, I'd like to know."

"You don't have to see it." I ran my hand down his arm, but he just stared at me, waiting. "Are you sure, Cody?"

"Not knowing is worse than what you'll tell me." His hand trembled as he ran it through his hair. It fell down flawlessly feathered. "I've imagined you with this perfect man in a hundred different scenarios. Just tell me … please."

"First, I have to tell you, he is not a perfect man. He is beautiful but far from perfect."

"Okay."

"Second, if you're going to picture me with the perfect man, it shouldn't be too difficult." I tried to smile at him, but his anguish made it hard. "I'm with him right now."

"Thanks." He entwined his fingers with mine.

"Well, uh … are you sure, Cody?"

He nodded in response.

In his eyes, I saw the pain he tried to hide, and I wished there was some way I could console him. "A very passionate kiss"—shame burned my face—"that I initiate."

"Least I know."

"I hope not." I looked away, unable to hold his gaze. "I'm hoping it wasn't a premonition."

"Yeah, there's always that," he said, but he didn't sound convinced.

When we arrived at my house, everything looked normal including Cody's expression. Somehow, he managed to conceal his true emotions. Jealousy, fear, apprehension, and misery were no longer visible on his face. He looked like the same old, good-natured Cody.

I stared at my house, the yellow two-story I'd lived in since I was six. The wrap-around porch made it look warm and inviting. I wondered where all the guests had parked. There was no evidence that party-goers waited inside.

Cody took my hand in his. "Ready?"

"Not really." I shook my head. "How about you?"

"No." He squeezed my fingers and opened his door. "No choice."

As we walked through the doorway, a chorus of "surprise" rang out. The living room was full of relatives that had never seemed to like me, neighbors I didn't know, and the few people in my life that I called my friends.

I didn't have to act like I was surprised. Sarah, the Dean of Phlox University, and Aurelia stood next to Samantha and Dan. I hadn't expected Sarah to be here. She was a middle-aged woman with graying hair and soft hazel eyes. On campus, she was my mentor and surrogate mother.

My eyes were drawn to Aurelia like a moth to a flame. Her skin sparkled under the overhead light. Her long hair fell to her waist. Every strand was perfectly in place. Her gold, cat-like eyes met mine, and there was something in them I didn't want to see.

Fear.

Even with that, my heart lightened when I saw the two of them, and for the first time, I felt like I might be able to handle the upcoming night.

"Wow." I looked around the room taking everybody in.

Mom and Dad moved over to hug me. "Happy birthday," they said in unison.

"Thank you," I said with a smile. "So, is this why Cody kept me out all day?"

"Yeah, we had a lot to do," Dad said. "We've never had a surprise party before."

"It takes a lot of work and coordination," Mom added.

"This is great." I held onto Cody's hand, hoping his touch would center me.

"The party is actually out back." Mom turned and led the way through the room to the sliding glass door. "Why don't we head on out?"

As I walked across the room, I hugged or shook hands with all the well-wishers I passed. When I made it to Aurelia, she pulled me close and whispered in my ear, "Dan and Samantha caught Sarah and me up to speed."

"Thanks," I told her trying to be inconspicuous. "We'll talk outside."

She sniffed as she pulled away. "You are injured."

I nodded. All of the hugging I'd done since getting home made my arm throb. I tried to put it out of my mind, but the pain pulsated with every beat of my heart, and the wound burned with fever.

Stepping onto the deck, I was amazed by the transformation of the backyard. The landscaping was always beautiful, but with the decorations my parents put up, tonight it was magical. Paper lanterns hung over the make-shift dance floor. Many of the trees were covered in twinkle lights. The koi pond reflected them, making the water sparkle.

A DJ played soft background music. Tables were set up on the outskirts of the dance floor. One table off to the side was covered in fruit trays, sandwich trimmings, chips, and dips. In the center of it was a spectacular tiered cake.

It was all too much for me. I wasn't used to this kind of attention, and if Mavros showed up, tonight wasn't the best night to have so many witnesses.

While I took everything in, Cody's family came up to me. Susan pulled me into a hug. "Happy birthday!" She patted my back. "Brent and I are so happy you and Cody finally started dating."

"Thank you." A genuine smile spread over my face. "Did you see what he gave me?" I stepped back and held out my hand.

Brent and Susan looked from my ring to Cody. "Promise ring." He grinned at them.

"Very nice," Susan said.

Brent patted my back. "He's a lucky guy."

"Thanks, but I'm the lucky one." I grabbed Cody's hand, not wanting him to get away from me.

Cody's siblings all wished me a happy birthday before darting off.

While Brent and Susan talked to me, I kept thinking how much they'd hate me if they saw me with Mavros and how torn apart they'd be if Cody died.

It took longer than I would've liked, but we finally made our way to Samantha, Dan, Sarah, and Aurelia. They sat at a table away from everyone else. "I'm so glad you're all here." I had said that a lot tonight, but this time I meant it.

"Aurelia told me it's beginning anew." Sarah patted my hand. "I'm so sorry you're going through this again, but I thought maybe I could help you out. I need a few students to come back to campus early to help me get ready for the new semester." She winked. "I thought maybe the four of you would be interested."

The tension in my shoulders instantly eased. Leave it to Sarah to help me out of a bad situation. I didn't want Mavros or the panther anywhere near my parents, and I didn't want them to keep worrying about my nightmares. "That would be perfect."

"I'll have to talk to my parents." Samantha grinned at Dan, and I knew she was excited about the possibility of spending more time with him. "I don't know how willing they'll be to have me go back early, but hopefully, I can talk them into it."

"I'm not sure either," Dan said. "If I can, I will, though."

"What about you, Cody?" Sarah asked.

"If Dacia goes, I go." Determination set his jaw. "She can't be alone."

I didn't think Mom and Dad would keep me from going, but I worried the peace we'd found would disappear. "When can we go back? The sooner the better."

Sarah looked at my parents and Cody's standing together talking. "Discuss it with your parents and let me know. You can come as soon as tomorrow."

Aurelia put her hand on my shoulder and sent her strength flowing through me. The pain in my arm lessened but didn't disappear.

I raised my eyebrow at her in question.

"You need to get back to your full health." She lowered her hand. "I am afraid I cannot heal this completely, though." She looked at Sarah. "If you are done, I have information to share with everyone."

Sarah nodded at Aurelia. "I'm finished."

I scooted my chair in and straightened my back in attention. "This is the conversation I've been waiting for."

"I believe the panther and Mavros are one and the same."

"Really?" My mind went into immediate denial. Why would Mavros have saved me if he was the panther? It didn't make sense.

I was pulled out of my thoughts as Aurelia continued, "Mavros means black and Malkin is another word for cat. If he is who I think he is, Mavros Malkin is, in reality, a very dangerous demon. He is able to shapeshift, and the mist, the panther, and the human are not the only forms he can take." Her pupils slitted, and for a moment, I saw the dragon within. "Hopefully, I am wrong. Conversely, if I am not, he is a very dangerous enemy. I will know for sure when I see him. I realize now is not the best time to tell you this. However, if he does show up tonight, I want you to be aware of what you are dealing with."

I tugged my hand through my curls. "Great. A shape-shifting demon who's after my heart."

Cody wrapped his arm around my shoulders and pulled me closer to him. "You'll get through this," he whispered in my ear.

"I hope you're right." Then to myself, I added, *I hope we all make it through this.* "It explains why I can't heal from this wound, though." I held up my arm. "The panther attacked me yesterday, and it's not getting any better."

"Give me your hand, Dacia." While Aurelia held my hand, a cool sensation worked its way up from my fingers to my wound. The pain diminished until only a dull throb remained. My arm no longer felt feverish.

"Thank you." I wanted to pull the bandage off to see how the bite looked, but it could wait until I was alone. "So why did Mavros act like he was saving me after the panther attacked me?"

"I imagine he was trying to gain entry to your house." Aurelia sat completely motionless. A gentle breeze lifted her hair off her shoulders. When it quit blowing, not a strand was out of place.

"Well, I guess I'm glad he hadn't gained control of me." I drummed my fingers on the table. "The other day I probably would have invited him in."

"Be careful around him," she warned me, "and do not under any circumstances allow him entry to your house."

"I'll do my best," I promised. "If he shows up tonight, I'll have to make sure nobody else invites him in." I looked at Cody. "I'll have to stay with him until he leaves."

He closed his eyes and sucked in a deep breath, slowly releasing it through his mouth, nodding his head so slightly that I almost missed the movement.

I wasn't hungry, but I figured my parents would be upset if they didn't see me eat. All of us grabbed a plate of food and sat back down at our table. We weren't alone for too long. Cody's three brothers and sister joined us.

Britny sat on Cody's lap. Her long blonde hair was pulled back in an intricate braid that would take me days to recreate. Josh, Dawson, and Brandon looked like younger versions of Cody, but their personalities were all different. Josh was all about hunting and fishing. Unless he was playing sports, Dawson could rarely be seen without a book. Brandon was always telling stories or jokes.

Britny stared at Aurelia, tilting her head and smiling shyly at the dragon in human form. Finally, she whispered, "Are you a fairy?"

"No." Aurelia smiled, a magnificent smile that lit up her whole face.

Looking from side to side, Britny leaned in closer. "Then why do you sparkle?"

Aurelia's gold eyes twinkled. "It is how God made me."

"I wish He woulda made me sparkle." Britny plopped her chin down on her hand. She had a dreamy look in her eyes. "Someday, I'm gonna find a fairy." She stared at all of us as if daring us to tell her she wouldn't.

Samantha's eyes glossed over, and I imagined she was remembering the first time she saw one. "If you look really hard, you might."

Britny beamed.

I shook my glass at Cody, so he'd know where I was going, and got up to refill my punch. Mom had made my favorite kind, raspberry sherbet and clear pop. I filled my cup, took a big gulp, and topped it off again.

Weaving my way through people, I wandered back to my table. It was a beautiful night. Stars dotted the sky. The crescent moon hung low over the western horizon.

I sidestepped one person and ran into another. Punch splashed against my skin. "Sorry," I said without looking up.

"Just who I was hoping to run into." The silken voice sent a wave of fear rushing through me.

I jerked my head up.

Mavros' eyes gleamed, and a wicked smile played on his lips. "I hope you're having a happy nineteenth birthday."

Trying to keep my voice from trembling, I said, "I was. Are you enjoying my party?"

He leaned in close. His breath warmed my skin. "Very much."

"Dacia, who's your friend?" Mom fidgeted with the end of her red and silver braid.

I hadn't even realized she was in the area, but when I heard her question, I thought I would be sick. It took everything I had to keep my composure.

"This is Mavros. Mavros, this is my mom." My mind raced as I tried to figure out a way to get out of what was coming next.

"Mavros? What a unique name," Mom commented. "I've never heard it before."

"It's Greek," he responded. "An old family name."

"Well, it's very nice to meet you. I hope you're enjoying the party."

"I enjoy any time I get to spend with your lovely daughter." Just like he had in my dream, he charmed her when he kissed her hand.

"And what a polite young man, too." She giggled like a love-struck schoolgirl.

"Thank you." He bowed slightly. "May I have your daughter to myself for a few moments?"

"Of course." Mom's fingers trailed down Mavros' arm, and I wondered if he was somehow controlling her. "Keep her as long as you'd like."

"I'm trying my best to do just that." He chuckled, then grabbed my hand and started to walk away.

My pulse thrummed, and heat flared through me. "Let go of me." My voice shook, and I didn't know if it was from fear or desire. How could his touch do this to me? Would I become immune to it?

"You know you really don't want me to let go." He turned toward me and brushed his fingers along my cheek. "What you want is for me to hold you, to kiss you like I did last time we were together."

I kept my gaze focused on the tip of his nose, afraid that if I looked into his eyes, I'd be lost. "I don't want to go anywhere with you ... I don't want to do anything with you. I need to get back to my party before anyone realizes I'm gone."

He leaned down so his breath caressed my ear. A pang of desire shot through my body. "If you don't come with me willingly, I'll force you. Neither one of us wants that."

He led me to the edge of the timber, clutching my arm. Pain thrummed through my wound, keeping beat with my heart. In my dream, we had stopped a few feet from here, but he went deeper into the trees. He didn't stop until we were out of sight from prying eyes.

A war waged inside me. My desire to be with Mavros struggled with my fear for Cody and my guilt over betraying him.

Mavros' thumb brushed over mine, and my heart fluttered. I didn't want him to let me go. I wanted him to embrace me. I longed to feel his warm lips pressed against mine. Somewhere in the back of my mind, I knew I shouldn't be thinking these things, but I couldn't remember why.

"Dacia, it's time for you to decide." Mavros traced the line of my cheek. His fingers were tender and loving, gentle against my skin. He leaned forward, and my heart raced in anticipation. I felt the warmth of his breath on my mouth. A faint smile played on his lips. He looked even better than I remembered.

"Your heart sounds like it's about to take flight." He laughed. "Are you excited about something?"

I couldn't wait any longer. I pulled him closer to me and pressed my lips against his. He moaned in contentment and kissed me with more desire than I knew was possible.

Dacia, I heard Aurelia's voice in my head, *where are you? Cody is searching for you. We tried to stop him.*

That brought me back to my senses, but I couldn't let Mavros know. I pulled away from him, and anger sparked in his eyes. *Mavros took me into the woods,* I thought to Aurelia. "What am I supposed to decide?" I sounded breathless, but after a kiss like that, who wouldn't be?

"If you will be mine." His hands dropped to his sides, and he took half a step away from me.

"But … why do you want me?"

"You captured a balor demon. You defeated a dark wizard with fifteen dragons under his control. You are young and powerful." He reached for me but let his hand drop. "I want you by my side … for eternity."

I heard someone walking toward us and felt Cody's presence. I couldn't let him see Mavros and me together. I couldn't let my dream become reality. My chest tightened, and the temperature seemed to drop. "Cody, please go away." My voice trembled.

Mavros' eyes flashed, dark and terrifying. "When you're mine, you won't care about him."

Cody stepped out of the trees, not heeding my warning. I looked from his eyes to Mavros', and I felt myself being drawn in. Mavros lifted his hands to my face, gently caressing my cheeks with his thumbs.

"Dacia, no," Cody cried out as his heart broke in two.

"She doesn't want you," Mavros said, never taking his eyes off mine. Then he leaned into me, brushing my lips with his. My arms wrapped around his neck, pulling him closer.

His mouth crashed down on mine. My fingers wove through his silken hair. I stood on my tiptoes, pressing my body as close to him as possible.

He lifted me just as Cody's body slammed into him. I was thrown to the ground. The air fled from my lungs.

Chapter 7

Friday The Thirteenth

"**H**ow. Dare. You. Touch. Me!" Mavros said through clenched teeth.

"Leave Dacia alone." Cody's voice was deep and ominous. I heard his fury and despair and hated myself.

"You have no idea who you are messing with, boy!"

"The jerk who's stealing my girlfriend. That's all I need to know."

All of this happened before I could even scramble to my feet. I pressed my hands to the ground, and Mavros said, "Dacia, stay there."

Mavros' power pinned me. I couldn't move, couldn't even turn to look at them. My dream replayed in my head. Cody would die if I didn't stop Mavros. It took all my strength, but I climbed to my feet.

Somehow, I managed to keep my voice firm when I said, "Mavros, if you harm Cody, if you even touch him, I will choose to be your enemy."

Confusion flickered through his obsidian eyes. "So be it." He turned his back on Cody. "He is insignificant." He took a step toward me. "You are what matters. After all, you'll forget about him soon enough."

His eyes locked on mine, and I felt my resolve weaken. Desire ignited in my body, and I longed for Mavros to wrap his arms around me and pull me into his embrace. His lips had been soft, and fire coursed through my veins with the remembered passion of our kiss. And, as Mavros had predicted, Cody was all but forgotten.

"Dacia." Cody's pain-filled voice pierced my heart. "Dacia, choose me … not him."

I felt myself returning to my senses, and so did Mavros. He turned around in a flash and sprung at Cody.

Rage filled my body. I leaped at Mavros. All my hatred, all my uncertainty was taken out on him. My fists were on fire as I threw punch after punch at him. Sparks flew into the night sky but didn't seem to do any damage to Mavros.

"Dacia!" Aurelia grabbed my shoulders, pulling me off of him. "Take Cody back to the party."

As I turned my back on them, Mavros said, "Well, well, well, if it isn't the magnificent dragon. It's been a long time, Aurea."

"Not long enough," Aurelia countered.

I didn't stick around to find out how the conversation would end. I wanted Cody as far away from Mavros as possible, and I needed to get away, too. I couldn't trust myself with Mavros. I couldn't believe Cody had seen me react to Mavros like that. *What will he think of me now?* I wondered.

You cannot afford to think about that. You have to get Cody to safety. You can beat yourself up later, Aurelia said.

My mind reeled. *How had Aurelia heard my thoughts?*

I wanted to make sure you were in control, Aurelia's voice rang through my head again. *I see now that you are.*

"Cody, let's go." I reached for his hand, but he jerked away from me, shoving his fists into his pockets. "We've got to get back to the house."

His jaw clenched. His eyes were hard and angry.

I looked down, not wanting to see his love turn to hatred. "Please, Cody."

He trudged forward. His pace faltered, and he stared beyond me. "Do you love him?" His voice was hard and distant.

Mavros was close enough to hear my answer. I didn't love him and didn't think I'd ever be able to, but if I said that where Mavros could hear it, I was afraid of what the repercussions would be. If I didn't say it, would Cody understand I was trying to protect him? I rubbed my hand down my face. "Can we talk about this when you're safe?"

"No." His teeth ground together. "I need to know now."

"He's everything you're not, and you're the one I love." I took a step closer to Cody, and he took a step farther away.

"How'm I supposed to believe that when you looked at him like that?" His voice cracked, and it broke my heart in two. "When you kissed him like that?"

Mavros laughed. "She won't resist me for long."

"Get Cody out of here now, Dacia." Aurelia's voice was a growl.

"Please, Cody." All I wanted was to get out of here. I didn't want Mavros to hear Cody's doubt. I didn't want him to know how torn up I was. I didn't want him to know how much this was hurting Cody.

Cody shook his head and planted his feet. "Tell me."

"I don't know, Cody. I don't know why I can't turn away from him … why I can't tear my eyes away … why I can't be true to myself or to you." I projected my next thoughts to Cody to keep Mavros from overhearing them. *I need to figure out what he is and what he wants. I need to destroy him before he destroys me. I need to stop him before he destroys us. I don't love him. I love you.*

"She can't get enough of me," Mavros' voice filled the silence. "When I'm near her, I'm all she wants. You can't compete with that, *mortal*." He spat the last word.

"I'm sorry, Dacia." Cody's rigid stance crumbled, and he looked broken. Pain filled his voice and shone in his eyes. "I thought I could handle this, but I can't."

"Cody, no matter what you think about me … no matter how you feel about me … we've got to get back to the house." Stretching my hand out, I stepped closer to him. "Mavros will kill you if he gets the chance."

෮෮80෨෨

"He already did." He raked his fingers through his hair and looked at me. His eyes held none of their usual love. They were hurt and betrayed.

Cody spun around to walk away from me. I didn't know what he was planning on doing, but I didn't want to find out. I jogged the few remaining steps between us, grabbed his arm, and before he could yank it out of my grasp, I teleported to my room. I didn't think anybody would be there, but I was wrong. Samantha, Dan, and Sarah were waiting for us.

Cody pulled his arm from my grasp and stalked to the door, keeping his back to me.

Sarah looked between the two of us. "What's wrong?"

I turned away from them, unable to hide my shame. I imagined myself in Mavros' embrace, pulling his face to mine, seeing it from Cody's perspective. He'd never forgive me. He shouldn't. I didn't deserve his forgiveness or love. I was weak. I should've fought Mavros, not swapped spit with him. I buried my face in my hands. "Cody found me with Mavros."

"He's here?" Samantha asked.

"Yes, Aurelia is with him now." My voice sounded thick. "I'm not sure what's going to happen."

"You'll save everyone." Cody's voice was soft, but it did nothing to hide the cruel tone. "That's what you do. Isn't it?"

I sank to the floor, and tears flowed from my eyes. "I do my best." I sobbed. "I didn't … I didn't want to hurt you. I don't know why I can't help myself. I wish I could."

Cody lowered himself to the ground next to me. He pulled my head to his chest and wrapped his arm around my shoulder.

"Sorry," he whispered in my ear. "I shouldn't act like this. It's not your fault. Please don't cry."

"You don't have anything to apologize for." I didn't deserve his comfort or support. I tried to pull away from him, but he held me tighter. "I do. I am a terrible person, and I don't deserve you."

"You are also the guest of honor, Dacia." Sarah's voice was stern and authoritative. She stood with her hands on her hips, daring us to argue. "I know it's not what you want to hear, but you need to get back out there to your party. You need to stay close to Samantha and Dan—and Cody, if he's ready to go out. If you want to keep this from everybody, you need to get back out there and act like everything is fine."

"Okay." I wiped the tears from my eyes and stood up.

"Why don't you splash some cold water on your face?" Sarah clasped my shoulder. "Then we'll all go out together with the pretense that you were giving us a tour of your house."

Somehow Cody slid into a happy, carefree personality that probably fooled all but those closest to him. I saw the pain in his eyes. Samantha, Dan, and Sarah talked, managing to keep the conversation light.

As soon as we stepped outside, Mom said, "Where've you been?" Before I could answer, she grabbed my hand and pulled me over to the cake. "You need to blow out your candles."

Mom and Dad stood on either side of me. Dad said, "Can I have your attention?" When people turned to look at him, he continued, "Thank you all for coming. We're grateful to have all of you here to celebrate Dacia's nineteenth birthday." He squeezed my shoulder. "She's always made us proud, and we can't wait to see what's next for her."

Mom lit the candles and started singing, "Happy birthday to you ..." Everybody else joined in.

I closed my eyes and made my wish. *Please help me stop Mavros without anyone getting hurt.* I blew out the candles, and after people quit clapping, I thanked them all for coming and making my day so special.

It seemed like an eternity had passed before Aurelia returned. I looked at her with raised eyebrows, but she shook her head and said, "Later."

"So, are you joining our slumber party?" Samantha asked her.

"I am."

"What about you, Sarah?" I asked. "Where are you staying?"

"There's a bed and breakfast in town, an old Victorian house." She pointed toward Bittersweet. "I dropped my stuff off there this afternoon. It looked pretty nice." Sarah looked at Cody and me. "I got your parents together while you were gone. It's okay with them if the two of you come back to campus early."

"That was easy." Cody's arm was across the back of my chair, but he hadn't touched me once since we left my room.

I stared at my hands folded on the table. The knots in my stomach tightened, causing my breath to catch. "Are you sure you want that now?"

"Thought I made it clear." The muscles in his neck and jaw tightened, and another wave of guilt washed over me.

I lifted my hand, but stopped before touching his face, afraid he'd cringe. "That was before I broke your heart and permanently etched that sadness into your beautiful blue eyes."

"I knew—you told me what I'd see—looked anyway." Regret took the hard edge from his voice. "You saved my life. I should've thanked you."

Watching people dance and talk and eat, I worried about what would happen if Mavros decided to return and wondered if while I was here, any of them had invited him inside. "Does it feel like Friday the thirteenth to anybody else?"

"Things are going to work out; you'll see." Sarah rubbed my hand. "It'll look better in the morning."

A humorless laugh fell from my mouth. "Unless I'm covered in blood with worried parents banging on my door."

"Mavros didn't kill Cody." Samantha leaned against Dan, holding her glass up to her mouth.

"That's got to be worth something." Dan took Samantha's glass and set it on the table. The two of them sauntered toward the pond. Samantha's white skirt swished with each step she took.

Mom appeared from nowhere. I closed my eyes and shook my head, hoping she hadn't heard any of that conversation. I didn't want her to know about the world of demons and dragons and all of the things that go bump in the night. She looked like she was enjoying herself, so I assumed our discussion had gone unnoticed.

She put her hand on my shoulder and asked, "Are you enjoying your party?"

"Yes, Mom." I plastered a smile on my face. "It's great."

"Why don't you and Cody get out there and dance? I haven't seen you out there at all tonight."

"I'm not sure Cody feels up to dancing." I didn't want him to feel obligated to look at me, let alone touch me.

He stood up and offered me his hand. "May I?"

I was a little surprised, but when I placed my hand in his, a genuine smile turned up my lips. "Of course."

He pulled me close, wrapping his arms around me as we swayed to the music. "Give me time." His voice was soft and his eyes sincere. "I'll be okay once I get the images out of my head."

"I'm sorry." I slumped, watching our feet.

Cody lifted my face and stopped moving. "Please … please don't say that again, Dacia."

"I have to apologize." I couldn't look him in the eyes. I hated myself and could never apologize enough for what I'd done. "Those images will never be gone. You'll always remember."

"You couldn't help it. You'd've stopped him if you could." He brushed my hair back. "Every time you apologize, it sends stabbing pains through my chest. Know you're sorry. I forgive you. You've just got to give me time to deal with it."

I started dancing again. If we stood still for too long, people would wonder what was going on. "I love you, Cody." I squeezed his arm. "I love your patience. I love your faith in me, and I love that you can forgive me for this. It's good to know that at least one of us can." My stomach churned. "I'll never forgive myself whether it was my fault or not."

He bent down and nudged my nose with his, tipping my head back. His lips touched mine. "You need to. If you don't, Mavros'll win."

"Even so, I don't know if I can."

We danced for a couple more songs before Dad cut in. "Are you enjoying your party, or is it a little too much for you?"

"Well … uh, it is a lot of attention, but it's nice," I answered him.

He sounded more than a little concerned when he said, "I hope you don't mind that we told people not to bring gifts."

"No, I don't mind at all."

"So, uh, I guess you're going to be leaving pretty soon." His shoulders hunched. He seemed smaller. Crow's feet perched beside his eyes. His salt and pepper hair was shorter than I'd ever seen it. Whether it was to cover its thinning or just for something different, I wasn't sure. As if he knew what I was thinking, he straightened and smiled at me.

"Yeah, Sarah mentioned having us go back Sunday or Monday. I didn't know she was going to talk to you and Mom before I had a chance."

"We'll miss you, but we can't keep you here forever. You're growing up so fast," he said. "And it seems like college has been good for you."

"It has." I looked at my friends sitting together, laughing and talking. "It's helping me come out of my shell."

"Just don't stay away so long this time." Dad had always seemed so strong and aloof. I wasn't sure where this vulnerability was coming from. Had my parents changed, or was I just now seeing them for who they were? "Come home more often this year. Don't wait for the holidays."

"I'll try, but with all the homework, I don't always have a free weekend." I needed an excuse in case things didn't go well with Mavros. I couldn't come home again until this was over.

"Do your best. Mom and I get lonely here without you." We danced in a comfortable silence for a while. "I'm glad to see you have such good friends there, too. They seem like good kids."

"They are." I looked around for my friends. Samantha and Dan danced not far from us. Cody spun Britny around, making her laugh out loud. Then he lifted her up and swayed to the music. Her feet dangled near his knees. Sarah and Aurelia were still sitting at the table. Their heads were bowed together. "I'm lucky Samantha and I got stuck as roommates, and it was good to see them again. I've missed them. After seeing them every day, it was hard to go the last few weeks without them."

When the rest of the guests were gone, Mom and Dad found me. They took turns hugging me and telling me goodnight. "Don't worry about the mess," Mom said. "Your dad and I have all day tomorrow to get it cleaned up."

"Goodnight, darling." Dad gave me another quick hug before turning to everyone else. "It was nice to meet you all."

As soon as they were out of earshot, Aurelia decided it was time to talk to us about Mavros. We sat at the table farthest from the house to keep my parents from overhearing.

"Time does not mean the same thing to dragons as it does to humans. Hundreds of years ago—maybe even millennia—

Mavros crossed my path. I had trained a girl a little younger than you, Dacia, and Mavros wanted her."

"What happened?" I blurted out.

Aurelia's eyes had a faraway look to them. The normally vibrant gold looked tarnished. "Patience, young one."

"Sorry."

"Her name was Elizabeth, and she was a lovely person." She focused on me, bringing some of the luster back to her irises. "You remind me of her. I think it is your spirit. Like you, Elizabeth wanted nothing to do with him. She did not give in when he asked her to join him. She was a good person and very talented. However, she did not have your strength or courage, and her true love did not stand by her side. Unfortunately, she died before her time. When Mavros realized he could not win her over, he killed her."

She turned to face Cody and continued, "Cody, you are stronger than Richard could ever have dreamed to be. If you turn away from Dacia, she will fail as Elizabeth did. Stand by her. Give her your love and support no matter how much it hurts. Try to remember that Dacia's heart belongs to you, even if it does not seem that way."

He placed his hand on top of mine. "I'll do my best."

"Mavros cannot force Dacia's decision. He can make her feel like he is the only man in the world. He can ask her to join him while her defenses are down. He can even make her believe that he loves her, but he cannot compel her to choose him."

"I saw them." Cody's face darkened, and he folded his arms over his chest. "Won't take much."

"You're right." Once again, I wanted to reach out to Cody, to comfort him, to let him know he was the one I loved, but what if he rejected me? What if he didn't want me anymore? "Aurelia contacted me just in time to bring me to my senses. That's probably what saved you, Cody. I was aware when you showed up, but then I made the mistake of looking into Mavros' eyes. Once I did, I was under his spell again."

"Then don't look in his eyes," Cody said through clenched teeth.

"The same thing happens if he touches me." I looked at my hands folded together on the table. Cody's promise ring sparkled at me. "And, when he approaches me with people around, I can't stop him from touching me."

"What does he want with Dacia?" Samantha asked. "And, what did he want with Elizabeth?"

"My best guess is that he wants Dacia on his side so that he can go through with whatever diabolical plan he has." She cocked her head as if listening. I'd seen her do it so many times last semester, and I finally understood.

"Arion's here. Isn't he?" I reached for his aura, but he must've been blocking me.

"Yes." She smiled.

Samantha bounced in her seat and clapped her hands together. "Can we see him?"

Aurelia shook her head. "Most people would see him as a horse, but Britny would have seen him as a pegasus."

"Okay." Samantha's expression did a one-eighty.

"I am certain you will see him again." Aurelia's gaze never lingered on any of us for too long. She was constantly monitoring the trees.

"So … Mavros." I drummed my fingers on the table. "Why would it matter? If Mavros was doing something evil, I would try to stop him no matter what."

"No, Dacia, once you make a promise to a demon, you are bound to it. There is no turning back."

"Oh, well that's good to know."

Dan huffed out a startled laugh. "Definitely need-to-know info there."

Avoiding looking at Cody, I said, "When I was with Mavros, I asked what he wanted with me. He said he wants me because of my power, so Aurelia's guess is probably right."

"So, how does she stop him?" Sarah tapped her finger against her chin. "And what happened after Elizabeth was destroyed? Wouldn't Mavros have been able to do whatever it was he wanted if she was out of the way?"

"I am not sure." Aurelia's eyes glistened. "I will see if I can find out what happened to Mavros after he killed Elizabeth. Maybe some of the elder dragons know. I lost track of him while I mourned her passing."

I stood up and paced beside the table. My thoughts were jumbled together, threatening to bury me beneath them. I needed to move to keep that from happening. "How long are you going to be around?"

"I will see if I can get registered at Phlox University for the fall semester." She looked at Sarah, then turned her gaze on me. "You are going to need help."

Sarah nodded. "I can pull some strings and make it happen."

"Didn't think you could." Cody watched every step I took.

Aurelia nodded. "I had other commitments. However, this is more important. Dacia is going to need our help and support if she is going to get through this, and we need to make sure she gets through this." She looked at me, and her face was filled with warmth and pride. "Dacia, you are destined for greatness. You have proven that with Nefarious and again with Draconian. You are also a friend to the dragons. There are not many humans throughout history who have been able to say that."

"All of us will help her in any way we can." Samantha drummed her fingers on the table. "Dan and I will talk to our parents about going back to school early."

"It would be best if you were not alone." Aurelia focused her attention on Cody. "Mavros stands a better chance if he can get her by herself."

"I'll sleep on the couch 'til Samantha shows." Cody shot me a sideways glance.

Sarah looked from me to Cody and shook her head. "I don't know if I should allow you to sleep in her room unchaperoned."

Anger ignited in Cody's voice. "I'm not trying to take advantage of her!" He slammed his hand down on the table, and I wondered how much more he could take before he exploded.

Aurelia settled her hand over Cody's. Then looking at Sarah, she said, "Mavros would not want Dacia if she was impure."

Heat crept up my neck and onto my face. I looked at my feet and twirled a curl around my finger. "Well, that was embarrassing."

Dan lifted his hands, palms up. "Sounds like you have your answer."

"What?" Samantha glared at him.

"Oh, come on … you all know you were thinking it." Dan rubbed his hand along his jaw. "You could make Mavros give up."

I folded my arms over my chest. "I am not losing my virginity to keep Mavros away!"

"Dacia, calm down." Sarah stood up and looked at all of us. "We're still at your parents' house."

"You're right." I took a couple of deep breaths then said, "Cody and I agreed to wait, and after Mavros—" I pulled my hand through my hair "—I don't …"

"What?" Cody's eyes blazed. "Know if you want me?"

"No. God, no." My heart plummeted to my feet so quickly that I couldn't keep standing. I sat next to him. "I'm afraid you won't want me anymore."

He stretched his hand out but let it drop between us.

Everyone else looked away. Samantha pulled her locket around its chain. Dan was suddenly very interested in the grass, and Aurelia and Sarah quietly talked to each other.

I grabbed Cody's hand, praying he wouldn't yank it away. His fingers tightened on mine. Relief surged through me. I stood, and he followed me to the koi pond. When we stopped, I wrapped my arms around his waist, and he pulled me against his body.

"Cody, I love you. I will only ever want you, no matter what it might look like." I ran my hands along his back, wishing this night had never happened.

His hands trailed over my arms. "We could get married."

"Do you really want to?" I pulled back and looked up at him.

"Eventually."

"Me too." I pressed my hand to his cheek. "Eventually."

"If it'll keep *him*"—his voice was full of venom and hatred—"away, I'll marry you now."

Rubbing my thumb along his cheek, I said, "I think it's too late. I think he'd kill one or both of us."

"Yeah." He held his hand over mine.

Even though Cody had just offered to marry me, I felt like our relationship was more fragile than ever. Cracks had marred the surface the moment Cody saw me with Mavros, and when I'd kissed him without abandon, those cracks had shifted until deep fissures covered the terrain.

I looked at the others sitting at the table. "We can see what Aurelia thinks."

Cody held my hand as we walked back. He stared into Aurelia's eyes with a challenge in his, and I was glad she had her dragon under control. "Will he go away if we get married?"

Samantha gasped in surprise. "It seems to me like that would make him really mad, and he'd just decide to kill you."

"I am afraid Samantha is probably right." Aurelia nodded. "If the two of you would have been married before Mavros entered the picture, that would have been different, but since you were not, I doubt he will give up his claim on Dacia so easily."

"Maybe that was why I was having those dreams," I said as the realization struck me. "They were telling me to marry you. If we would've, none of this would be happening."

Cody pulled me close, wrapping both of his arms around me. "It'll work out," he whispered in my ear.

Sarah shook her head and grimaced. "Well, I guess after hearing all of this, maybe the best option is for Cody to sleep on the couch. That way we can make sure Dacia is safe." She looked from me to Cody. "It's not my place to make these decisions, but since we can't let your parents know what's going on with you, I think it's the only choice."

Aurelia stood up. "I need to know what their room numbers will be."

"I can get that information to you tomorrow." Sarah's perfectly trimmed eyebrows pinched together. "Why, though?"

"Their rooms need to be blessed before they arrive."

Chapter 8

Stranger Danger

The shadows are long. Birds fly back to their nests to settle in for the night. Insects serenade each other.

I walk through the park, searching for Cody. My pulse thrums in my ears. The staccato beat pushes me faster. Aurelia told me not to be alone. She warned me I'm more susceptible to Mavros if I am.

"Cody!" I shout his name, but there is no answer.

Picking up my pace, I round a corner. A little boy sits alone at a picnic table. I turn, searching the area but don't see anyone else. "Where are your parents?" I meander toward him.

"I don't know." His lip wobbles. "We were hiking, but now I can't find them."

The roaring in my ears diminishes. My heart goes out to him. "Why don't you walk with me? I'm looking for somebody, too."

He looks up at me with sad brown eyes. "I … I'm not supposed to talk to strangers."

"My name's Dacia." I stop moving toward him, not wanting to scare him.

He chews on his lower lip, then finally says, "I'm Felix."

"Well, let's go see if we can find your parents."

We continue down the road in the direction I'd been heading. The shadows in the trees darken as night closes in. Unintentionally, I drift toward the middle of the road. "Do you live around here?"

"No, I live far away." Felix tilts his head and points. "I think I heard something over there. Will you come with me?"

I swallow the lump in my throat. "Yes"—the word shakes—"of course."

He leads me to a trail in the woods. An owl hoots, and Felix turns to me with wide eyes. "I'm scared. Will you hold my hand?"

I stretch my hand out to him. When his fingers fold against mine, a tingling sensation rises from my fingertips and up through my arm. I close my eyes, realizing I've made a huge mistake.

"Why?" My voice sounds hollow.

Mavros' fingers caress my cheek, then my neck. "You can trust me and want to help me when I'm a small child. Why can't you now?"

I stare at the ground, thinking about Cody, trying to resist Mavros. His touch is gentle. I feel alive. "Because you're not trustworthy. You're trying to manipulate me."

"Look at me, Dacia." His soft voice is laced with pain. "Look me in the eyes and tell me that you don't see sincerity there. Tell me that you can't see how much you mean to me, and I will leave you alone."

I look into Mavros' eyes and feel myself being drawn to him once again.

"What do you see, Dacia?"

"Desire." I pull my hand from his and wrap my arms around his waist.

"Can you see how much you mean to me?"

I trace my tongue over my lips and step closer. "Yes."

His finger skims along my face, trailing down my neck, and over my shoulder.

Heat flares in my stomach. I slip my hands into his back pockets and pull his body against mine.

He leans down. His breath caresses my face. "Stay with me then. Be mine forever. Let me show you what love means." His nose brushes against mine. He teases me with his lips, bringing them almost to mine, then drawing back. He cups my face and grazes his mouth over mine. "Will you be mine?"

"Ye—"

"Dacia?" Cody's voice halts my answer. "Where are you?"

I suck in a breath and stagger back.

Mavros clenches his fists at his sides, making his veins bulge along his muscles. His soft, seductive voice turns acidic. "This is the last time that *boy* will disturb us."

His chiseled body softens, blurring at the edges. A black mist flows from his chest. The vapor coalesces into a cloud in front of me.

"Cody, get out of here!" I shout before flying off in search of him.

Cody stands at the edge of the timber watching the black smoke solidify into Mavros. I dart between them, lifting my hands to block Mavros.

"Don't touch him." I narrow my eyes and plant my feet. "If you do, I'll never be yours. Never."

Mavros' form blurs as he steps toward me. Tendrils of mist weave with the breeze, lifting behind him like ethereal wings. "If you do not choose me, you choose death."

I lower my hands slightly, ready to beg for Cody's life if I have to. "But, if you kill Cody, that's the choice I'll make. I won't live in a world without him."

Mavros prowls closer until only a thin strip of air separates his body from mine.

I reach back, clasping Cody's hand, keeping him behind me, keeping me grounded.

The warmth emanating from Mavros' skin is almost enough to put me under his spell.

I gaze at Mavros' forehead, careful not to look into his eyes.

"The window of opportunity is closing." He lifts his hand toward my face but doesn't touch me. "You have until mid-September to decide." His thumb reverently brushes against my cheek.

Flames of desire leap through my body. My heart races. I clutch Cody's hand tighter, pulling his strength into me.

"Make the right choice." Mavros' breath caresses my ear.

I bite my bottom lip pulling it into my mouth, stifling a moan. My fingers loosen as I pull away from Cody.

Mavros disappears, and I realize he's going to win. If given enough opportunities, I will vow to be his forever.

Chapter 9

Saturday morning, I woke up and stretched like a cat. Aurelia stood at the window, staring out at the trees. "Morning." My mouth was fuzzy from sleep.

"Good morning, Dacia." She turned toward me, and her slitted pupils rounded as they dilated. "How did you sleep?"

I sat on the edge of my bed and pulled underclothes out of my nightstand. "A little boy needed my help. He turned out to be Mavros." Heat crept up my neck and over my cheeks. "He's very … persuasive." I fanned my face. "I don't know how I'll resist him."

Samantha rolled over on the air mattress she'd shared with Aurelia and propped her head on her hand. "Isn't there a way to keep him from mesmerizing her?"

Aurelia shook her head. "Not that I am aware of. I will speak with my elders as soon as they are willing to meet with me." She looked out the window again and let out a long sigh.

I wondered what she was thinking. Was she preparing herself for loss, like with Elizabeth? Was she trying to gather herself for another semester of college? Or was she longing for freedom?

"I'd appreciate any advice they can offer." I pulled a t-shirt and shorts out of my dresser. "We're supposed to meet Cody and Dan in less than an hour. If we're late, they'll worry."

Driving to Diamond in the Rough, I clenched the steering wheel, butterflies swarmed in my stomach. Their wings beat against my insides. With every breath, they multiplied.

What if Cody didn't want to see me? What if Mavros intercepted us? What if Mavros did something to Cody and Dan?

By the time I parked my truck, my hands ached. As we walked inside, Aurelia's voice in my head startled me. *This is where I leave you. Be careful.*

You, too, I thought to her.

The guys stood by the door. Cody watched everyone coming and going. His eyes were tight, but when they met mine, he visibly relaxed. A genuine smile lifted his lips.

As soon as I was close enough, he pulled me into a tight hug, clutching me against his body. "How'd ya sleep?"

"Good." I wrapped my arms around his waist. "No painful nightmares."

He let go of me, jerking back as if I had burned him. "Didn't hurt you. Did I?"

"No." I shook my head and held my arm out. "It's healed."

We sat in a booth. Bittersweet was a small town where almost everyone knew each other. At times, I loved that, but it also meant people were anxious to pick up any gossip and start spreading it before anyone else got ahold of the news.

My aunt, Cindy, was our waitress. "Well, hello again." She handed us our menus, then pointed her glittery pen at me. "That was quite the soiree your parents threw last night."

"Yeah." I smiled at her. "It was totally unexpected."

She tapped her chin with a long, red fingernail. "Since Bill and I weren't supposed to bring a gift, why don't I get your breakfast?"

"Oh, you don't have to do that."

"I insist." She pulled out her order pad. "So, what'll you have?"

We placed our orders and talked while we waited for our food to show up. Cindy brought our breakfast over and shoved the ticket in her pocket. "Happy birthday, Dacia."

"Thank you." I smiled at her, realizing this fight was one I could back down from.

She kissed me on the cheek and hugged me before walking away.

"When are you going to Phlox?" Dan shoveled a forkful of hash browns into his mouth.

Looking at Cody, I shrugged. We hadn't discussed it, but the sooner I could get away, the happier I'd be. It was bad enough that Mom met Mavros at my party last night. I didn't want my parents any more involved in this facet of my life.

"Tomorrow morning?" Cody asked.

My shoulders relaxed. "That'd be great."

Samantha looked at Dan. "I don't know what Mom and Dad'll say."

"We'll be there by next Saturday no matter what." Dan took a drink of his orange juice.

Dan and Samantha left early in the afternoon. They both wanted to talk to their parents in person about going back a week early. I would've liked to spend more time with them, but I understood.

After we said our goodbyes, Cody sat on the edge of my bed. "You'll be okay if I go?"

I shoved the clothes I was holding into my duffle bag. "You don't have to stay. Spend some time with your family."

He stood up and took my hands in his. "What about him?"

"I promise to stay here." I grabbed the belt loops on his shorts and pulled him closer. "I have to finish packing and spend time with Mom and Dad. Then Aurelia will be back before I go to sleep."

He put his hands on my shoulders, holding me back. "Promise."

"Promise." When Cody pulled his hands back, I leaned my forehead against his chest. "I don't want to see him either."

He tilted my face up and looked into my eyes. "You leave … a lot."

"Unless Mom and Dad make me, I'll be here. I swear."

"Call me if they do." He bent down and pressed his lips to mine.

Cody follows me. His blue Camaro is never far behind as I drive down the highway. It's reassuring seeing him there, but I wish we could've ridden together. I'd feel more comfortable with him beside me.

The three-hour drive feels never-ending. My favorite songs blare through the speakers, but my mind keeps wandering.

I turn onto the road that'll take me to Althea when I see movement at the edge of my vision. I look at the passenger seat. Black smoke pours in through my vents.

My first thought is that my engine is on fire, but the smoke smells like warm, summer nights.

Mavros solidifies in the seat next to me. "You were going to leave without saying goodbye?"

"I go to college." I stare at the road, refusing to look at him. "I have a life."

He reaches for my hand, but I jerk it away, swerving into the other lane. My heart races. I flip on my signal and pull onto the shoulder.

"Are you trying to kill me?" I shout at him. In my frustration, I make the mistake of looking into his eyes.

"Quite the opposite." He lifts his hand to my face. "I'm trying to save your life."

I nuzzle my cheek against his palm, loving the feel of his skin against mine.

"You're about to make a bad decision."

There's a knock on the window, but I can't pull my attention away from Mavros. "I'm going to show you what will happen if you don't choose me."

Red and blue lights flash in the darkness. Sirens blare, racing to my parents' house. Flames lick the night sky. This smoke smells of ash and death.

Mom and Dad are nowhere to be seen. My heart catches in my throat.

"Is anybody in there?" a fireman shouts.

My hands cover my mouth, holding in a scream. I nod. "My … my parents."

Another car pulls up. Cody jumps out and runs to me, throwing his arms around me. "Thank God you're okay, Dacia. I was so scared." He looks around. "Where are Caitlin and John?"

I point, unable to find my voice.

"Oh, no."

As if a whirlwind picks me up and moves me, I'm now standing with Cody at the cemetery. Wayne and Deana sit in front of the flower-covered casket. Wayne's arm is wrapped around Deana's heaving shoulders.

When the minister starts talking, I fall into Cody. Somehow he manages to keep us both standing. "Samantha Waters was a beautiful, intelligent young woman with a long life ahead of her. She and her beloved, Dan Tamarin, were taken from us all too soon. The hole in our lives will eventually heal, but a piece of us will forever be missing. Those of us who knew and loved Samantha will never forget her."

The world spins, and I'm watching the scene play out from high above. Cody strolls across campus, his backpack thrown over his shoulder. The panther stalks him, then pounces. Claws and fangs tear through his flesh.

Mavros sits next to me in my truck. His hand is still on my face, wiping away my tears. "The lives of the people you love the most were taken because you would not join me. As much as you have suffered, your pain does not begin to compare to mine. I'm offering you my heart and soul for all eternity. Don't spit in my face."

The scene shifts again. Mavros and I stand outside my dorm room. He stares into my eyes. "Be mine, Dacia. Free me from my curse, from this eternal Hell."

I shake my head. "I can't."

His fingers morph into a massive paw. Before I can register what's happening, he slashes it across my throat. The force knocks me to the floor.

I grab my neck and think about life. My wounds don't heal.

Mavros transforms into the panther. He mauls me. Then he prowls down the hallway, leaving a trail of bloody pawprints.

Darkness closes in, and I welcome death.

"Dacia!" Dad pounded on my door.

I woke up, gasping for breath but unable to fill my lungs. My neck and body were ravaged. Blood clogged my throat. I tried to suck in air. My lungs burned. I thrashed against my bed, tangling myself in my sheets.

"Everything is fine, Mr. Wolf." Aurelia's words were thick with magic. "Go back to sleep."

Dad stopped pounding on the door. Aurelia placed her hands on my neck, and soothing energy flowed through me.

Air flooded into my lungs. I sucked it in greedily.

Aurelia stared down at me, holding my hand, continuing to heal me. Her tawny eyes were filled with immense sadness. She stayed by my side until all my dream wounds healed. While I changed clothes, she cleaned up my bedding. She held the bloody sheets in her hands and burned them.

When I lay down, she used her magic to force me to sleep.

Chapter 10

Cold Shoulder

By the time Cody knocked on the door, my stomach churned, and anxiety tightened my chest.

I had to keep Mavros from hurting my family and friends, but I had no idea how to protect them without giving in to his demands.

While Dad greeted Cody, Mom pulled me into her arms. "I thought we'd have you for another week." She stepped back and wiped her eyes. "I'm not quite ready to say goodbye yet."

A lump formed in my throat, trapping any words I might have said.

Then it was Dad's turn. "Don't be a stranger."

"I won't." I patted his back, hoping this wouldn't be the last time I hugged him. Then I clutched Cody's hand and walked out onto the porch.

"Drive careful," Dad said at the same time Mom said, "Be safe."

Cody opened my truck door. "Where's Aurelia?"

"She left this morning." I looked up at Mom and Dad, hoping they couldn't tell how scared I was for them. "She's trying to find out whatever she can."

Squeezing my hand, he said, "I'll follow." He brushed his lips over mine, then walked to his car.

My hand shook when I reached for my seatbelt. It took several tries before I finally heard it click into place. *Three hours.* A glance at Cody let me know he was as worried about the trip as I was. I took a deep breath, smiled at my parents, and backed out of the driveway, cranking the radio to drown out my thoughts.

Every movement, every cloud that passed over the sun, temporarily darkening the sky, made me clench the wheel tighter and glance at the passenger seat.

My fingers were stiff. My shoulders ached. My pulse pounded.

When we pulled into the dorm's parking lot, Sarah was waiting for us. "Right on time," she said as I stepped out. "I gather your trip was uneventful."

"Nothing bad happened." I flexed my fingers and stared at the mountains.

The power and beauty of nature rejuvenated me. The tension in my shoulders lessened. The snow-covered mountains rose to the clear blue sky. Fluffy white clouds drifted above them, casting their shadows over the flower-covered ground. Marmots sunned themselves from the safety of boulders. The air smelled fresh and clean, and there was a crispness to it that could not be found at lower elevations.

"It's good to have you here." Sarah patted my back. "It'll be better for you to be away from your parents until your nightmares stop. It's also probably best if they don't get in Mavros' way."

Cody slid his arm over my shoulders. "That had me worried."

"Me too." I closed my eyes and tried to pull myself together. "The panther attacked me twice, and Mavros approached me three times. Sooner or later, he would've threatened my parents."

"Hopefully, he'll stay away from Bittersweet now that you're here." Sarah walked toward the dorm, jiggling her keys as she searched for the right one.

We followed behind her. I was glad to be back on campus. I'd faced two monsters here and walked away. I could do it again.

Sarah stuck the key in the lock. "I want the two of you to stay together, and don't go out after dark unless Aurelia is with you."

"I'll do my best to keep Dacia safe." Cody held the door open for us.

I strode in. "I'll do my best to keep everyone safe without endangering myself in the process."

"Let me know if you need anything." Sarah stayed outside, looking over her shoulder toward her office. "I have a lot to catch up on before classes resume next week, so I'll be spending most of my time in my office."

"Thanks, Sarah. I appreciate you talking my parents into letting me come back." I stepped outside and gave her a hug.

"Just stay safe. That will be thanks enough." She smiled and hurried off.

Cody and I made several trips to our vehicles, carrying everything in. I unpacked a few things before deciding it didn't all have to be done today.

"So whatcha wanna do?" Cody plopped down on the couch, throwing his arm over the back of it.

Sitting beside him, I said, "It's getting late." I rubbed his leg. The feel of his skin against mine helped soothe me. "The room is blessed, so if Aurelia's right, Mavros can't get in here."

"So we stay." Cody ran his fingers along my jaw, and I leaned into his touch. He stood, turning his back to me. "Movie?"

My eyebrows pinched together, and I stared at his back. His muscles were tense, his posture rigid. "Sure."

Cody walked over to a box and pulled out the first movie he saw. He stuck it in the DVD player and sat in Cookie Monster.

What'd I do? I tilted my head and looked at him.

He ran his hand down his face. "Made a promise." He folded his hands together and looked at the ground. "Can't get carried away."

"We won't." I rubbed my arms. "I'm not ready … not yet."

He sat beside me, pulling me against him. "I am." He brushed my hair back. "Won't push you, though."

Halfway through the movie, there was a knock on the door. "C—"

Cody clamped his hand over my mouth. "No invitations." He walked to the door and looked through the peephole. Opening it, he said, "Hey, Aurelia."

"Any luck?" I stood, facing them.

She stepped into the room and pulled the door closed. "No, the elders were in meetings and would not see me. I looked through the archives but found nothing. I will keep searching until they grant an audience with me." She walked to the window and stared outside. "Arion would like to see you tonight. He will meet you here at dusk if that is okay with you."

I lifted my shoulders. It would be dark soon, but Arion would keep me safe. "Yeah, I'd like to see him."

Cody frowned at me. "You forgetting?" He turned to Aurelia. "Sarah doesn't want us out late without you."

"That seems reasonable." Aurelia brushed imaginary lint off her navy blouse. "However, Dacia will be safe with Arion."

Arion—a pegasus who owed his life to Aurelia—and I walked along the beach at Falcon Lake. Aurelia had already explained to him what was going on with Mavros, but he wanted to hear it from me. I didn't mind retelling my story to him. He had a comforting presence that made me feel safe.

Stars filled the evening sky, and the moon reminded me of the Cheshire Cat's smile, reflecting on the cascading waves. A cool breeze blew over Falcon Lake, and a shiver ran down my spine. Along with it came an ominous feeling.

I stopped walking and stared into the trees. "Arion, we need to leave now."

"What is it?" His ears perked up, and I knew he was listening for some previously unheard sign of danger.

"Just a feeling," I told him. "I think something bad is going to happen."

"Climb on. I will get you out of here."

I turned to hoist myself onto his back, and the giant panther sprang. It grabbed Arion by the throat. My first impulse was to scream in terror and run, but I held my ground. Lightning bolts shot from my fingertips, hitting the beast in rapid succession. It turned its back on Arion and stalked toward me. Blood dripped from its fangs, and a fierce snarl tore through the night air.

The beast leaped forward. Its front paws landed on my shoulders, knocking me to the ground where I was pinned by the enormous cat. Its teeth grazed my throat.

As I awaited my death, the panther transformed. Human hands pressed down on my shoulders. Slowly, the beast became Mavros. His lips brushed my neck, and my body relaxed. My fear gave way to desire. I lifted my hand to brush it against his face.

Arion whimpered, and I focused on him. Blood stained his shimmering fur.

Mavros' mouth moved against my ear, his breath sent shivers through my body. "We don't have to be enemies, Dacia. Things could be different between us."

My body urged me to succumb to him, but I fought the impulse. "You tried to kill my friend. How does that make us anything but enemies?"

"That wasn't my fault." His voice was flat, matter-of-fact. "How can I be blamed for my instincts? Panthers eat horses."

"You're not a panther," I snarled through clenched teeth, "and Arion is *not* a horse!"

"Pegasus—" he skimmed the tip of his nose along my jaw, and my body shivered "—horse … they both taste the same."

Frost coated the ground next to me. My breath fogged the night air. Then my body literally turned to ice.

Mavros threw himself off me and yelled, "Damn it, Dacia!" His handsome features turned hard and angry. At that moment, I was sure that if he could touch me, he'd kill me.

It took all I had to hold my fear at bay. I knew if I gave in to it, I wouldn't be able to stay frozen. I walked to Arion, keeping Mavros in sight.

"Don't. Touch. The. Horse. Dacia." His voice was a harsh growl, causing me to tremble with fear.

"He is not a *horse*!" I threw my arms around Arion's neck and teleported to Aurelia's lair. Treasure filled the cavern, but the only thing I cared about was Arion. His breaths were shallow. Blood still pulsed from his neck.

I held my hand over his shredded flesh and thought about life. When the flow of blood lessened, I called for Aurelia. *I need your help. Arion is dying.* Within seconds, Aurelia was at my side. We both concentrated our healing powers on Arion. When we finished, his breathing was harsh but steady.

Sitting back, I knocked down a stack of gold coins. They tinkled over each other as they tumbled to the ground. "I'm sorry I didn't keep him safe."

"This is not your fault." Aurelia squeezed my shoulder. "It is mine. I should have gone with you."

I didn't agree with her, but now wasn't the time to get into it. "I hope it's okay I brought him here." I didn't know what she'd think of me coming to her lair uninvited. "I needed someplace we wouldn't be seen."

Her lips pulled back, and her pupils slitted. Then she shook her head. She must've been fighting some internal battle. "It was good thinking. What happened to him, though?"

"Mavros is the panther." I held my head in my hands. "He snuck up on us and went straight for Arion's jugular."

"I wonder why he went after him, not you."

"He said it was instinct." I stared at the gold and jewels until they blurred. "But, I think he was getting him out of the way so I'd be alone with him. He called Arion a horse, and that infuriated me." I ground my teeth together, feeling the ire build in me again. "I froze."

"Dacia, fear—"

"No, Aurelia." I shook my head. "I wasn't scared. I turned into a giant ice cube." I remembered Mavros' body pressing against mine, his hard muscles, and gentle caresses.

Aurelia's eyes widened. "You found one of his weaknesses. Ice. I should have guessed."

My lungs filled to near bursting, and a smile spread across my face. "Yeah, I did." With a way to fight him, maybe I could keep my friends safe. "Mavros was touching me when I did it. It burned him or hurt him somehow. He couldn't come near me. I rushed over to Arion and teleported him here."

"Thank you for saving his life." Aurelia held her hand over her heart. "It means as much to me as if you had saved my own."

"You're welcome, Aurelia." I stood up. "I should get back to Cody. He's alone, and I don't like it."

She looked from me to Arion. "I am going to stay here tonight. He needs me more than you do."

"Keep him safe." I teleported back to my room and found Cody pacing the floor.

He rushed toward me. "So much blood." He held me at arm's length, scanning every inch of me.

I looked down and noticed for the first time that my shirt and arms were coated in Arion's blood. "It's not mine."

His gaze settled on mine. "Whose? You okay?"

"I'm fine."

His fingers brushed my neck. "This yours?"

"Arion's." I remembered the panther's fangs brushing my throat, then Mavros' lips. My face flared with heat. "Let me wash this off, and I'll tell you everything."

I sat in Big Bird, not sure if Cody would want to be beside me. Staring at the lilac carpet, I replayed the evening's events, trying not to leave out anything. "If Mavros is willing to hurt Arion, I'm afraid to leave you alone for even a minute."

He knelt in front of me, lowering his head to look into my eyes. "Don't worry 'bout me. I'll be all right."

"I'll worry. I can't live without you." I kissed his cheek.

He pulled me onto his lap and pressed his lips to mine. Our kiss deepened, becoming more passionate.

When he drew back, I couldn't help but compare it to Mavros' kisses. With Cody, I felt eternal love and passion. With Mavros, it was all about desire and control. As long as I could keep my head when I was around him, it was possible Mavros would never touch me again, let alone kiss me.

Cody and I curled up on the couch together and drifted off to sleep. My last coherent thought was whether or not Cody could keep my nightmares away again tonight.

Chapter 11

Cody and I walk hand-in-hand along Falcon Lake. The waves wash over my bare feet. Sunset turns the clouds a soft pink. Within minutes the entire sky is ablaze with reds, oranges, pinks, and yellows. The sunset reflects on the surface of the lake. A crescent moon rises in the East. I stop walking to take it all in.

"This is beautiful," I say in a soft whisper. "Sunset is my favorite time of day."

"Sunrises are good."

"Yeah, they just come a little too early for my liking."

"Used to." He stands behind me, wrapping his arms around my waist. "Don't sleep like you did. Saturdays in high school I'd call at noon, and you were sleeping."

"I miss those days." I fold my arms over his. "Sleeping 'til noon was nice."

He chuckles softly. "You're up before me now."

"Only because I'm too scared to sleep." I gaze at the magnificent display Mother Nature is putting on, wishing I could get lost in it.

He rests his head on mine. "Why are you scared to sleep?" His voice turns silky.

My heart slams to a stop. The breath catches in my throat. *No. How?* Trapped in his embrace, I turn slowly, knowing I'm not going to like what I see.

Mavros' dark eyes stare into mine. The heat of his body and the scorching intensity in his eyes burn all thoughts of Cody from my mind.

"Nightmares," I answer.

"Dacia," he says, not relinquishing his gaze on me, "I want you to promise me something."

"Anything," I answer in a husky voice. I'll do anything to keep this beautiful man next to me.

"Promise you'll *never* freeze yourself again when I'm around."

The anger in his voice makes me recoil. I don't want him to be angry with me. "I promise, Mavros."

"Promise what?"

I cock my head to the side. *Why's he acting so weird?*

He clutches my arms. "Tell me what you promise."

"I promise, Mavros ..."

His grip tightens and excitement lights his eyes.

"… I will never freeze myself when you are around again."

"Do you realize you cannot break a promise that you make to me?" He radiates smugness.

My eyebrows pinch together. "No, but why would I?"

He brushes the hair off my face. His fingers are tender now. "You'll try, but you won't be able to. Since this is a dream, if you wouldn't have said my name, you might've found a way around it, but now you're bound."

"What do you mean this is a dream? Sometimes you don't make any sense. Besides, I don't want to break any promises that I make to you." I snuggle against him. "I just want you to hold me and watch the sunset with me. It's almost as beautiful as you are."

Leaning forward, he kisses me on the forehead. "Dacia, my love, you amuse me sometimes."

"I'm glad I make you happy." I rest my head against his shoulder. His skin is so warm I can feel it burning through his black silk shirt. "Do you always wear black?"

"Yes." He smiles. "It suits me."

"Dark and mysterious," I murmur, "or tall, dark, and handsome. They both suit you."

"I need you to do something else for me."

"Anything."

His lips pull up in a smirk. "Forget what we were talking about. Forget the promise you made me."

Chapter 12

Trapped By Fear

Morning was not my favorite time of the day, but waking up in Cody's arms made it more enjoyable. I opened my eyes and found him watching me. "How'd ya sleep?"

"Pretty good, I had a weird dream, but it wasn't a nightmare." My eyebrows pinched together. Parts of the dream flitted away, and the harder I fought to remember, the more I lost. "I was standing on the beach with you. Then you turned into Mavros, but he didn't try to hurt me or anything."

Cody's expression grew pained for an instant, but he quickly covered it up. I knew he didn't like me dreaming about Mavros, and I understood that. "How'd you sleep?"

"Really well." A soft smile spread across his face, making him look boyish. "Could get used to this. Sarah'll let me stay 'til this blows over."

"Yeah, and afterward there'll be another monster trying to kill me or something. You'll always be watching over me, making sure I don't sneak out or get hurt."

He blew out a breath. "There's always that." Wrapping his arms around me, he drew me against him.

My arm throbbed under his grip. "Ouch."

"What?" He jerked his hand back.

I tugged my sleeve up. A bruise in the shape of a hand wrapped around the top of my arm. I pulled my other sleeve up and found a matching bruise there. Closing my eyes, I tried to focus on the details of my dream, but it became foggier. "I don't know where they're from." I lay down next to him, resting my head on his chest. The beat of his heart steadied me.

"You always remember." He shook his head. "Even when they kill you."

"But I don't." I tugged my hand through tangled curls, trying to remember, but nothing came to mind. I shook my head. "I need to find out how Arion is." I needed to do something other than lie there thinking about what waited in the shadows for me.

"He'll be okay."

I closed my eyes, and the image of Arion popped into my head. Blood soaked his pristine fur. *Aurelia, how's Arion? Is he okay?*

He is getting stronger, she answered. *Demon wounds can be very tricky and tend to take a while to heal. You did well, Dacia. He would not be alive without you.*

He would've done the same for me.

I will be here with him for a couple of days at the very least. If you need me, I will come, she promised. *I owe you for this.*

No, you don't.

Please stay close to the dormitory, she said. *I do not want Mavros to hurt you or Cody while I am indisposed.*

We will. Guilt pressed down on my stomach. *Tell Arion I'm sorry I didn't keep him safe.*

He does not blame you. He told me you knew something was about to happen and tried to get him away.

I was relieved Arion was in good enough shape to talk, but guilt still twisted my gut. *I should've been faster.*

I pressed my hand against Cody's chest and sat up. "Aurelia doesn't want us to leave."

"Me either." He sat next to me, combing his fingers through his hair. It fell into place, and I envied him. My hair would look like a red afro if I combed it without wetting it first, and right now, it was probably sticking out in a hundred directions.

Cody tilted my chin up. "Whatcha thinking?"

"That I probably look awful."

His thumb skimmed along my chin. "Never."

My skin tingled behind his touch. I ran my hands along his bare chest, contemplating knocking him back down and spending the day lying on the couch with him. Instead, I got up and called Sarah.

"Sarah can't meet with me until 4:30, so what are we gonna do all day?"

We spent most of the morning playing games: Boggle, Othello, and Scrabble. After lunch, we decided we didn't want to spend the whole day in my room. We walked to Lupine Fieldhouse to shoot hoops, but the doors were locked.

"We can go to the other court." I grabbed Cody's hand and started pulling him across the green space.

"No." He tugged back, stopping me. "Don't want you in the open."

As if fighting monsters wasn't bad enough, when they were in my life, I felt like a caged animal. The walls closed in, and I needed my space. I dragged my fingers through my hair. It was too soon to start this again.

Cody and I went back to my room, and I paced in front of the couch like the tigers at the zoo.

"Dacia, please." Cody patted the cushion next to him.

I stopped, looking down at him. "I hate being trapped. Why couldn't they bless the whole building? The whole campus?"

He grabbed my hand, pulling me onto his lap. "I'm trapped, too." He wrapped his arms around me. "Least we're together."

I rested my forehead against his. "I'm sorry. I shouldn't complain, but I hate being cooped up. I get caught up in my thoughts and see all the bad things that might happen."

He kissed my chin, then the tip of my nose. "How can I help?"

"I don't know." My head dropped forward.

We watched movies until time to leave for Sarah's office. I tried to keep my mind from wandering, but I felt like Sisyphus, eternally doomed.

Trees lined the sidewalks between Wisteria and Cacomistle Halls. The fresh air recharged me. Birds sang and insects hummed. Squirrels jumped from branch to branch, and chipmunks darted to and fro.

I sensed no danger. My steps slowed. Cody stopped, waiting for me to catch up. When I did, he pressed his hand against the middle of my back, quickening my pace. His body was rigid, his eyes alert.

We walked past both of the men's dormitories, choosing the route with the most visibility. As soon as Cacomistle Hall came into view, Cody sped up even more.

The three-story stone and timber building looked like it had always been here. Centuries-old pine trees surrounded it. Enormous boulders were strewn about where glaciers had deposited them.

As soon as we stepped inside, Cody noticeably relaxed.

The office was dark, no flames danced in the stone fireplace. I looked toward the seating area, remembering how nervous I'd been the first time I came here. I'd fully expected to be expelled for setting Cassandra Nightshade's books on fire. Instead, Sarah had been excited to meet someone with powers. She'd told me about the prophecy, and I'd thought she was certifiably nuts.

Timber columns formed a cathedral ceiling, and the massive windows framed a spectacular view of the Snowfire Mountains. Looking at them centered me.

We climbed the rustic-looking stairs to the second floor. Sarah's door was open, so we stepped inside. I knocked on the oak moulding. "Hello."

"Have a seat." Sarah's voice came from her office in the back. "I'll be out in just a moment."

Two couches faced each other separated by an oak coffee table. Cody and I sat on the one with the best view of the mountains. Normally, he'd be right next to me with his arm over my shoulders or his hand on mine, but he sat at the opposite end of the couch. Instead of focusing on him, I studied the room. Not much had changed since the last time I'd been here. All the ash had been cleaned out of the fireplace, and fresh logs waited for their turn to provide warmth and ambiance to the room. Bookcases still lined the walls. Some new titles had taken up residence on their shelves. Among them were two of my favorite books: *Prince of the Fallen* by M.H. Woodscourt and *Assassin's Odyssey* by C.T. Ortega.

We only had to wait a few minutes for Sarah to come out. She sat across from us and smoothed out her tan slacks. "So—" she tilted her head, looking at the distance between Cody and me "—what did you need to talk to me about?"

I leaned forward with my elbows on my knees and told her about Mavros attacking Arion.

Her hand flew in front of her mouth, covering her gasp. "Will he be all right?"

"Aurelia thinks so." I twisted my hands together.

"But you don't?"

Cody scooted closer, placing his hands over mine, as if that could stifle my guilt. "Dacia blames herself."

"The fault doesn't lie with you." Sarah's couch shifted when she stood and walked over. "Mavros is to blame." She rested her hand on my shoulder. "It sounds like you saved Arion."

"I should've been faster." I choked back a sob. "I'm supposed to keep everyone safe."

"The only one who expects that is you." Sarah squeezed my shoulder and stepped away. "You need to keep yourself safe. If Mavros comes after you, teleport to your room as quickly as possible, but please, don't go anywhere else alone."

"We won't," Cody said.

Sarah paced behind the couch she'd been sitting on. "You need to be extra vigilant … I need you to stay safe."

"We'd planned to go to Althea." Cody sat back, pulling his hand off mine. "But without Aurelia, didn't."

Sarah nodded. "That's good. There's enough on campus to keep you busy."

"Everything's locked," Cody said.

"I'll have that fixed immediately." Sarah sat across from us again and looked directly at me. "I'll have the ball cages unlocked, too. I don't want you to get bored."

"I won't go looking for trouble." I tried not to sound angry. I knew she was right, but I hated being reminded of my faults. "Sometimes, though, it's better to face life head-on than to wait—cowering in the corner—for it to pass you by."

"Courage is a commendable trait." Sarah nodded. "Just wait until you're ready. If you act too soon, you'll fail."

I raised my hand in the Girl Scout's salute. "I'll do my best not to do anything stupid and not to jeopardize anybody … including myself. I don't want anybody to get hurt. I just want to get through this somehow … to figure out how to stop him and to move on with my life."

"That sounds like a good plan to me, Dacia." Sarah looked at the clock, then stood. "I've got one more meeting. I'll have the fieldhouse and library unlocked right away." As we walked to the door, she said, "Why don't you two join me for supper? I'll meet you in the cafeteria at six."

Phlox University's swimming pool was Olympic-sized, and Cody and I had it all to ourselves. We changed into our suits and met at the shallow end.

Cody waved his arm at the pool. "Show me what you can do."

"Other than soaking you—" I smiled and threw water over him like I had at the lake "—I don't know what I can do with water."

Cody grabbed me around the waist and plummeted underwater. When he brought us up, his eyes sparkled with mischief. He wiped the water off his face, then mine. His thumb brushed over my lips a moment before his mouth crashed down on mine.

I wrapped my arms around his waist and pulled his body against me, backing against the pool wall.

His hands trailed over my shoulder blades and down my spine, exploring every inch of exposed skin. It had been too long since he'd touched me like this. Heat flared beneath my skin, and I felt alive for the first time since Mavros had come into my life.

I ran my fingers over his back, along his ribs, and up his chest, memorizing the feel of him. My tongue brushed against his, and a moan slipped from my lips.

His hand slid down my leg, lifting it. I wrapped them around him, and any space that had been between us disappeared.

He was who I wanted. Mavros was an inconvenience that I would have to deal with. Cody was my forever. My happily ever after.

I wove my fingers through his hair, then trailed them down his shoulders. My lips slid off of his, trailing kisses along his jawline to his ear.

"Dacia." Cody pulled back. Alarm flickered across his face. "Water's warm enough."

I pushed him away and thought about snow and ice. "Better?"

"Yeah." He swam across the pool.

I fell onto my back and floated. Guilt pooled inside of me. I could have hurt him. I needed to get a handle on myself. I couldn't let my powers get out of control ever again. I couldn't allow anybody to be hurt again.

Once I was calm, I swam up to Cody, reaching for his hand, but I let mine drop before making contact. "Did I hurt you?"

"No." He shook his head. "Startled me."

"You sure?"

He dove underwater and surfaced several feet away from me. "Yeah."

"Then why are you clear over there?" I pulled my bottom lip into my mouth and hoped I didn't sound as desperate as I felt.

He lifted one side of his mouth in a half-smile. "You're not ready, but I am."

"Oh." My jaw hung open for a second. "Sorry." I back floated, staring at the ceiling high above me. Thinking it would be nice to have a pool float, I shaped the water around me and used it to hold me up. When I tired of that, I swam to the deep end, using the water to propel me forward. I summoned waves and whirlpools.

Cody stayed near me, watching me test out my powers, but he didn't touch me again.

Finally, he pointed at the clock and said, "Time to go."

I watched him pull himself out of the water. The muscles in his back flexed, and I wanted to wrap my arms around him again, but I knew it wasn't right to push him.

By bedtime, I was exhausted. I crawled onto the couch with Cody. He wrapped his arms around me, running his fingers through my hair. I snuggled into him with a sigh. He was warm and comfortable. He was my happy place.

Chapter 13

A Life For A Life

*E*verything is black, the walls, the floor, the ceiling. I'm stuck in an obsidian void, staring into Mavros' rage-filled eyes. Every muscle in his body is taut, and I can sense his hatred and envy for Cody.

"Dacia, this is not the way things are supposed to be. You belong with me. This *boy*"—he spits the word out—"is nothing more than worm food."

"No." I hold my own for once. Maybe I can look into his eyes without being enchanted because of the hatred in them, or maybe, hopefully, I'm getting stronger. "I belong with Cody. He is my soulmate … the only one for me."

"If you choose him over me, you will watch him suffer an agonizing death." Mavros grabs my arm. His fingers burn my skin. "If you choose me, I will let him live his pathetic, little human life, and he will eventually die on his own. But, I will not stand by and watch the two of you together! That is not an option."

"So, don't watch," I say through clenched teeth. "I love him, and nothing you can say or do will stop that."

"You are destined to be mine!" Anger distorts his features. His eyes narrow, and his irises blacken with hatred. Cords bulge in his neck as his jaw clenches.

"No! My destiny was to defeat Nefarious," I yell, unable to control my anger. "I did that. The rest of my life was supposed to be my own!"

"No, Dacia." Mavros laughs, a dry humorless laugh. "That is where you are wrong. There is so much more to that prophecy that you don't know."

My breath catches in my throat. I tremble with rage and fear. His words ring true, and even though I don't want to hear it from him, I ask, "What are you talking about?"

"Join me ... be mine, and I will divulge the rest of it to you." He stretches his fingers out, begging me with his eyes to entwine mine with his. "Otherwise, you will have to find out for yourself."

I shake my head, and his hand falls to his side. "Tell me." I hate the pleading tone of my voice. "Help me find a reason to trust you."

"Nice try." He grins at me, and the look nearly disarms me.

I narrow my eyes at him and fold my arms over my chest. I can't let him distract me. "You expect me to give up everything, and you will give me nothing in exchange."

"No, if you give up your human, I'll spare his life … for you, Dacia." He prowls around me, and I turn to keep my eyes on him. "If you don't give him up, he'll die, but not before he suffers as no mortal has ever suffered. The choice is yours, and the clock is ticking."

I woke with a start. My heart pounded loud enough to wake the dead, but somehow Cody slept through it. I was grateful for that. I didn't want to have to tell him that I was dreaming about Mavros again.

I settled back down and thought about my dream. I knew part of this conversation would happen, and I wondered what I would choose when the time came. I couldn't let Cody die, but I couldn't choose Mavros over him either.

Chapter 14

I woke up in Cody's arms feeling rested and loved. *I could get used to this*, I thought to myself.

I wanted to stay there curled up with him, but it was time to start a new day, like it or not. "Cody." I trailed my finger along his arm, hoping not to startle him awake.

"Mmm." His eyes slowly opened, then drifted shut again.

"I'm going to take a shower and brush my teeth. I won't be too long."

"Kay." He opened one eye and said, "Stay in the building."

I kissed the tip of his nose before getting up. "I will."

I stepped out into the hall and found it empty. Cody and I were the only two staying in the dorm right now, but I wasn't used to the silence. It seemed so out of place here. Even though I always walked softly, my footsteps echoed throughout the hallway like a herd of elephants tromping through it.

Just as I pushed on the bathroom door, I felt somebody watching me. I closed my eyes and slowly turned around.

Mavros leaned against the wall dressed all in black. Except for the rage in his eyes, he looked quite relaxed. His right foot was crossed over his left. When he spoke, his tone was anything but casual. "I don't like seeing you sleep in his arms."

"Then don't watch me sleep." I flipped my hands up. *He watches me sleep? Do I ever have any privacy?*

He pushed off the wall. "Yesterday, at the pool was a little much."

I clenched my fists, my fingernails digging into my palms.

A smile played on his lips as he stepped toward me.

What right did he have to watch me? Was there a way to stop him from doing it?

He took another step closer, his gaze roving over my body.

"What?" I snarled the word.

"Has anybody ever told you that you are just … so damned cute when you're angry?" An impish grin tugged at his lips.

"Why would you even say that? Are you just trying to piss me off?"

"No, actually, I am trying to make you mine." The anger had fled his eyes, leaving them soft. I looked down, hoping not to fall under his control. "I thought you knew that."

A humorless laugh escaped me. "I'm not sure your intentions are honorable."

"Tell me what to do to win your affection." He strode closer but didn't touch me … didn't try to control me. "Help me, Dacia."

"I love Cody," I answered without looking into his eyes.

"I know, but I want to be a better person." The sincerity in his voice was overwhelming. "I can't do that without you."

I felt myself being drawn in again—this time without him touching me and without looking into his eyes—and I knew I had to keep it from happening. I couldn't let him gain control of me. "But you're not even a person. Are you?"

"Well, not technically, no, but you think of Aurea as one. Don't you?" His words begged me to believe him, and I found myself wanting to.

I couldn't trust my voice, so I nodded in response.

"With you in my life … with you to keep me on the straight and narrow … I could be good enough. You could think of me as a person, too. Can't you find it in your heart to help me?"

He was baring his soul to me, and I felt my heart going out to him. He sounded so innocent. He sounded like he could be good. I wanted to believe him, but even if I did, it wouldn't change things. My heart belonged to Cody.

I made the mistake of looking into Mavros' eyes. My pulse quickened. I closed the gap between us and reached out to him. Without thinking twice, he pulled me into his arms and pressed his lips to mine. If he would've asked again at the moment, I would've given myself to him for all eternity.

While Mavros held me, I wasn't conflicted or tormented. I felt alive. My body tingled with excitement.

"This is how it could always be, Dacia," he said in his silken voice. "With me, you'd never age. You'd always be young and beautiful."

"But, what would I have to give up?" I leaned my head back and looked into his eyes. "Everything has a price."

"Nothing you would miss." The softly spoken words caressed my ear.

There was something I was forgetting, but all I could think about was Mavros' touch … his promise. Was there anything I could want more than this? How could I?

"In time you would see that Cody was nothing … that he meant nothing to you."

Cody … how could I have forgotten him? Even with all of Mavros' impossible splendor, I shouldn't have been able to forget Cody.

"No, you're wrong! Cody's my life."

"Oh, is he?"

"Yes!"

"How easily you can forget your life. If I wouldn't have mentioned his name, would you have remembered he existed?" His voice was condescending, and I knew he was right.

I stepped back, focusing on his black boots, not daring to look into his eyes. "If you wanted me to forget him, why did you even bring him up?"

"I wanted you to realize that he isn't that important to you. If he truly mattered … if you loved him like you say you do … would you forget him every time you see me?" Once again, his voice was velvety smooth. He sounded so sincere that I almost fell for it, but I knew deep down that he was playing me. He wanted something from me, and it was time for me to realize that he was no less of a monster than Nefarious or Draconian had been. He just came in a nicer-looking package.

"Cody is my life!" I jabbed my finger at him. "The fact that you can control my thoughts and feelings doesn't make them any less."

"Are you so sure about your feelings, Dacia?" His hand brushed against my face, tilting it up until he stared into my eyes. I tingled from his touch and was his again. "Don't you want this? We could be a great team."

For a moment, I considered his offer. However, something held me back. Just as I was about to make the biggest mistake of my life, I pictured the most beautiful blue eyes I'd ever seen and returned to my senses. "No, it's a great offer, but I think I'll have to pass."

Mavros' retribution was swift. He reached up and slashed me across the chest with a panther's paw.

I stumbled back. Pain blossomed across my shredded chest. Blood ran out of my mouth. I lost my balance, falling to my hands and knees. The lights faded, and I slipped into oblivion.

"Dacia."

The voice sounded a thousand miles away. I tried to peel open my eyelids, but they felt like they'd been sealed with superglue.

"Dacia."

I recognized it this time. Cody. He came for me. *Oh, God. What if Mavros is still here?*

Cody pulled me into his arms and rushed down the hallway. "What happened?" His voice was muddled and far away.

"Mav—" The word scratched against my throat but came out as barely more than a breath. "Mavros."

Cody laid me on the couch. "I'll call Sarah."

"Demon," I whispered. I still couldn't open my eyes, but I could feel his fear.

"C—" His voice cracked. "Can you get Aurelia?"

Aurelia, help.

I don't know when Cody came back to me. I don't know who was with him. I don't know how long I slept before waking up to find Aurelia standing over me. The couch crinkled with my movements. Plastic covered the cushions. I lay between sheets dressed in only the bandages that wrapped around my chest and pajama shorts.

"Water," I croaked.

"Cody, get Dacia some water please," Aurelia said to him.

He brought me a bottle of water, placed one hand behind my head for support, and helped me drink some of it. "Not too fast," he cautioned me.

"Now, can you let Sarah and Nancy know she is awake?" Aurelia turned to me. "How are you feeling?"

"Better than when Cody carried me here." My voice sounded better, but it was still scratchy.

"I would hope so." She held my hand, and her energy flowed into me. "That was three days ago. I have been trying to keep you alive since Tuesday morning."

"Three days?" I gasped. I couldn't believe it had been that long.

"Three and a half," Cody said, sounding exhausted. "It's Friday afternoon."

I turned to look at him and gasped in pain. He rushed back over to me. "You all right?"

"I just need to remember not to move." I tried to smile, but pain turned it into a grimace. "Are you okay?"

Black bags circled Cody's eyes, making them appear sunk in. His skin was pale, his hair stood up like he'd pulled his fingers through it too many times, and dried blood crusted his clothes.

He didn't say anything. He knelt beside me with his hand on my leg. It looked like he was fighting to keep his eyes open.

"He has not slept," Aurelia answered when it became obvious Cody wasn't going to.

"I must've been in bad shape."

"You barely breathed." Cody stared at the floor. "Barely held on."

"It has been a long time since I had to treat wounds this bad." Aurelia squeezed my hand before standing up.

"I can't believe I was out for three days." I tried to push myself up so I wasn't flat on my back. Pain sucked the air from my lungs and pinched my eyes shut.

"Stay still." Cody's voice shook.

"I need a drink."

This time Aurelia lifted my head and held the water bottle to my lips. "Last time you were mauled by a demon, it took a while for you to heal. That was just a wound to your leg.

This was your chest. Your heart and lungs were damaged. Your ribs were broken. No normal human would have survived. You scarcely pulled through."

Cody rubbed his hands over his face. "Didn't think you'd make it." Tears lined his eyes. "None of us did."

"I'm glad to prove you wrong then." I was still trying to get my head wrapped around the idea that I'd been out for three days. "Have Samantha and Dan been here?"

"No, they will be here tomorrow." Aurelia twisted the lid back on the bottle and set it on the ground.

"It's probably best they weren't." I yawned, and my eyes slid shut. "Nobody else needed to see this."

"Why'd he attack?" Even though Cody was trying to hide it, I could hear the rage in his voice.

"Because in the last possible second, I saw your beautiful blue eyes and told him no." I reached for his hand. "If he'd've asked a minute sooner, things might've ended differently."

Cody twined his fingers through mine. "Think he knows you survived?"

"He knows." I remembered the anger in Mavros' eyes. "He told me he didn't like seeing me sleep in your arms. He was watching us then. So ... I can only imagine he's been watching since."

"We need to be careful what we say and do," Aurelia said.

"Oh, Aurelia." I covered my mouth with my hand. "Is Arion okay?" *How could I have forgotten him?*

"Yes." She tilted her head to the side, and I wondered if she was listening to him. "Like us, he has been very concerned about you."

"I'm sorry you had to leave him."

"You needed me more than he did," she said. "You would have died if I had not stayed by your side. Whether you would have come back or not is another question. One I am not ready to find out the answer to right now."

"Thank you." I yawned again.

"Both of you need to rest." Aurelia's words were laced with magic.

When I woke up a few hours later, I could make small movements without severe pain. Cody slept soundly on the floor next to me. Aurelia sat by my feet. Her revitalizing energy flowed into me. Even though my strength was returning, I had a long road ahead of me.

When Cody woke up, Aurelia took him to the men's dorm so he could take a shower and change clothes. While they were gone, the doorknob rattled. Something scratched against the wood.

Fear clutched my heart. My breathing accelerated. Sweat beaded on my forehead.

I tried to pull myself to a sitting position. My ribs ached, and something tore in my chest. Blood seeped through the bandages. I fell back against the couch, panting.

My heart pounded in my ears, blocking any noises coming from the hall. I closed my eyes and tried to calm my breathing.

"Dacia, let me in." Mavros' voice slid over me like Aurelia's had when she'd told me to rest.

I pressed my hand against the couch, trying to push myself up.

"I can help you if you let me in." His voice was smooth. "I can take your pain, take your suffering. I can end this."

My arm shook, but I pushed myself up to a sitting position. I swung my legs around. Sweat dripped into my eyes.

"Dacia, let me heal you."

I fell off the couch and dragged myself across the floor.

"I can take away your pain forever."

My muscles trembled. Each movement sent shockwaves of pain rippling through my body. Tears dripped off my chin, splashing against the top of my hand.

"You're almost there, Dacia. I can hear your heartbeat. It calls to me."

I stretched my hand up, reaching for the handle.

"Dacia, no!" Cody's voice snapped me out of Mavros' hold.

Mavros roared, shaking the walls. "I'll kill you for this, *boy*!"

Cody lifted me, gently carrying me to the couch. "Looks like we came back just in time."

As soon as he laid me down, Aurelia pressed her hand over my reopened wound. "She cannot be left alone again."

Before I passed out, I felt my chest mending.

Chapter 15

The breeze blows across the water, sending ripples dancing toward the shore. I spin in a circle, taking in the scenery. Lodgepole pines surround the lake on three sides. The fourth side is taken up by a mountain I don't recognize. The sun is high in the sky. A few clouds flit by.

I fold my arms across my body to block the chill. Tape scrapes against my fingers. I look down to find I'm at this lake wearing only my bandages and pajama shorts.

Mavros stands a few feet from me, staring across the water. "Dacia." He steps toward me.

"What do you want?" I scramble back.

"Your forgiveness." He lifts his hand, palm up, reaching toward me.

I look at it, shaking my head. "You almost killed me."

He slips his hand into his pocket and kicks at the ground. "I was angry. I was wrong." He looks at me through his eyelashes. "I never wanted to hurt you. All I want is for you to love me."

Repeatedly shaking my head, I take another step back. My foot hits a rock, twisting my ankle. Mavros starts toward me, but I hold my hand up. "You want more than that. I just don't know what it is." I shuffle back. "And, if you want love, you're going about it the wrong way."

"Why do you think I want more?" His shoulders slump forward, making him appear smaller, broken. "I want you to say you'll be mine." Rubbing the back of his neck, he whispers, "And, I want your forgiveness." He holds his hand out, trudging toward me. "Please."

His voice is so broken that I look into his eyes.

"Please forgive me?"

"Of course." I close the gap between us. "I know you didn't mean to hurt me. You only want what's best for me."

He opens his arms, and I step into his embrace. "Can't you see I'm what's best for you?" His voice is soft and seductive.

"I can see you believe that."

He leans his face down to mine and brushes his lips in a line from my ear to my mouth. My body quivers in anticipation and my breathing accelerates. "Are you sure that's all you can see?"

"I can see that I want you to kiss me." I grab his shirt with both hands, curling my fingers in it, pulling him closer. "Please?"

He doesn't answer. He just brings his lips down to mine and kisses me. It's a hard, fierce kiss. I feel all of his anger in it, but even so, it leaves me wanting more.

"Dacia, will you be mine?" He breathes into my ear.

I press my body against his, craving his warmth, his touch. "I …"

He puts his hands on my shoulders and pushes me back. His fingers dig into my skin.

"I don't know why, but I can't answer right now." Tears tumble down my cheeks. "I want to say yes, but something's holding me back."

Anger flashes in his eyes for an instant before he covers it up. "Then when?" He steps away, turning his back on me.

The wind blows across the lake, raising goosebumps on my exposed skin.

He glances over his shoulder. His eyes have softened, and I wonder if I'd mistaken his anger. "When will you answer me?"

"Do you have any idea how expressive your eyes are?" I rub my arms, trying to warm them. "Every emotion shows in them."

"Then surely you can see my love for you."

"I've seen desire and passion, and anger flits across them from time to time. I've seen jealousy and even sincerity, but I can't remember seeing love in them." I rub my arms, trying to warm them.

He crosses to me, pulling me into his embrace. I slide my arms between him and his jacket, savoring his warmth. "Then before you make your decision, I will make sure you find it there. You will see how much you mean to me."

Chapter 16

*L*ight flickered through my eyelids, brightening, then darkening. I forced my eyes open. Cody paced in front of the couch.

"Hey." My throat was scratchy, and the word slid out like a bad come-on.

Cody stopped instantly, turning to look at me. "How you feeling?"

I pressed my elbows into the couch and scooted back. Pain tore across my chest. "Like a demon tried to rip my heart and lungs from my chest." I tugged on my lower lip with my teeth. "I thought I'd feel better this morning."

He sat by my feet, massaging them while he watched me. "Wish I could help."

I pulled my hand through tangled curls. "I hate to ask, but … what day is it?"

"Saturday." He slouched down, stretching his legs out.

"Where've you been sleeping?"

He pointed. "The floor."

"Why?" I looked around. "You could've slept in my bed or one of the chairs … or your bed."

He shook his head. "You can't be alone, and I wanted to be close."

I looked down and noticed my bandages had been changed. I didn't want to think about what led to them needing to be changed, so I said, "Maybe you can join me here tonight."

"How're you sleeping without me?"

"You mean, how'm I dreaming."

"Well, yeah." He looked away, not meeting my eyes.

Cody didn't want to hear about me holding and kissing Mavros. He didn't want to know how good Mavros could make me feel, or how I longed for his touch. "Mavros apologized to me in my dream last night. I'm just glad he didn't hurt me. I'm not sure my body could handle another injury, even from a dream."

With Cody's help, I got up and walked around several times throughout the day. My strength was returning slower than I'd have liked but faster than most people's would have. Anytime I left the room, Cody or Aurelia went with me. I wasn't sure I'd ever be left alone again. The attack was enough for them to think I needed to be guarded, but crawling to Mavros last night was a downright embarrassing reason for them to keep me under constant observation.

Students filled the halls, moving into their rooms, chatting with friends. Aurelia helped me put a sweatshirt on to cover the bandages.

I still hadn't seen the wound. I wasn't ready to face it.

Samantha and Dan showed up late in the afternoon. They came in laughing and excited, but their moods changed when they saw me lying on the couch. "What happened?" Samantha asked.

"Mavros attacked me Tuesday morning." I sat up. The scabs pulled, and pain lanced through my ribs, pinching my expression. "I didn't wake up until yesterday afternoon."

"She was in bad shape." Aurelia knelt in front of me, holding her hand out, wanting me to take more of her strength before she left.

"If you need me, you know what to do." She turned to Samantha and Dan. "Do not go anywhere alone. Dacia was just going down the hall for a shower when Mavros attacked her."

"More people here now." Cody sat beside me, leaving a gap between us.

I wondered if he thought he'd break me if he got too close. "It'll be easier for Mavros to blend in." I placed my hand over Cody's, needing his touch to center me. "I don't know if he'll attack any of us in the open, but he might lead one of us away."

"Be careful." Aurelia turned toward the door.

Samantha and Dan followed her out of the room to unpack their cars.

While they were out, Cody and I paced from one end of the room to the other. He stayed close by, ready to help me if I stumbled.

Samantha and Dan came back in carrying her things. Dan set down a couple of boxes and said, "Cody, can you give me a hand while Sammi unpacks."

"Sure." He led me to the couch and helped me get situated. "Don't leave."

I grabbed Cody's hand. "Please be careful. He promised to kill you."

"You stay. I'll help him." Samantha's eyes were wide. "This isn't going to be as much fun as I was hoping." She and Dan started for the door. "I'm sorry we weren't around when you got hurt."

"I'm not." I pulled my hand through my hair. "Cody looked pretty bad when I woke up. I'd hate to put too many people through that."

"Remember when Nefarious attacked?" Cody clutched my hand. His eyes looked haunted. "That was her leg. Mavros ripped open her chest … her heart and lungs. For three days, we … we thought she'd—" his voice broke, and tears glistened in his eyes. "Aurelia said she might come back, but it was scary."

I looked around the room, then out the windows, wondering if we were being watched. "Mavros has been keeping an eye on us. So we need to be careful about what we say and do in here."

"Can do," Dan said. "So anybody up for a movie?" He plopped down in Cookie Monster.

"What about your stuff?" I asked.

"Tomorrow," Dan said.

"Might as well watch a movie." I rested my head on Cody's shoulder. "I can't do a whole lot anyway."

Samantha curled up on Dan's lap. "So, I'd like to know what happened first."

I should've expected Samantha and Dan to want to hear all the details, but for some reason, I hadn't. My hand trembled as I pulled it through my hair, trying to steady myself enough to delve into it.

Before I could say anything, Cody began. His voice shook, and his eyes were hollow, but he made his way through it. "So, Aurelia is trying to figure out what Dacia needs to do."

"Sunday night, Arion wanted to see me." A weight settled in my stomach. I stared at the lilac carpet. "Mavros attacked him."

Samantha gasped. Her fingers dug into Dan's arms. "Oh, no." She shook her head. "Is he okay?"

Cody rubbed his hand along my leg. "Dacia held Mavros off and saved Arion."

Samantha lifted her eyes to the ceiling. "Thank God."

"How'd you stop Mavros?" Dan wiped the tears from Samantha's cheeks.

I pulled my hand down my face. "I turned into an ice cube, and he couldn't touch me."

"What made you do that?" Samantha asked.

"He … uh …" I pulled on my bottom lip with my teeth, and Cody's grip on my thigh tightened. "He always feels so warm. He was lying on top of me, and it was instinct."

Cody extracted himself, careful not to hurt me. He walked to the window, keeping his back to me.

Samantha watched him, then turned to me and mouthed, "Sorry."

Dan glanced between us, frowning. He shifted as much as he could with Samantha on his lap. "At least you know something you can use against him."

I felt like there was something I should know about turning to ice around Mavros, but whatever it was skittered away like cockroaches when the light flicks on.

Chapter 17

Cody slept on a blanket on the floor beside the couch. I rolled onto my side and gazed at him. His lips were parted slightly. The lines of his face softened in sleep.

I reached down, grimacing as the scabs on my chest stretched, and traced my finger along his jaw.

"What?" His eyes shot open, and all of his tension returned. "You okay?"

I yanked my hand back. "I didn't mean to startle you."

"Need something?" He jerked to a sitting position.

"Well"—I patted the couch—"my pillow could use a break."

His lips curved up in a crooked grin. "Oh, could it?"

"Yes." I squished it. "See how flat it's getting."

"You sure?" He tilted his head, looking from my hand to my face. "Don't wanna hurt you."

"Please." Laying with him on the couch felt right, the way things should be. His first class of the semester started in a couple of hours, and it terrified me. My mind ran through a constant loop of all the things that could happen to him. "I'm worried about you."

"I'll be fine." He traced his fingers along my arm, careful not to hurt me. "Don't leave while I'm gone. Please."

"I won't, Cody." I squeezed his hand. "I'm still not over the last injuries. I don't need any more for a while."

"Need some strength?"

His offer tempted me. My body ached, and fatigue tugged at my eyelids. "No. You need to stay alert."

I closed my eyes, savoring Cody's warmth and strength. When I opened them again, Cody and Dan were dressed and ready for class.

Somebody knocked on the door. I lifted onto my elbows. While Dan opened the door, Cody stood beside me like a loyal Doberman.

"Hello." Aurelia stepped into the room. "How are you feeling?"

"Sore." I lay back down. "Tired."

She perched on the edge of the couch and clasped my hand. Her energy rushed through my veins. "I will walk Cody and Dan to class. Then I will come back here to keep an eye on you."

"No." Cody crossed his arms over his chest. His stance widened. "She needs you here."

"The room is blessed." Aurelia let go of my hand. "Mavros cannot enter."

"Last time we left her"—Cody said through clenched teeth—"she crawled to him."

I pinched my eyes shut. That was not one of my proudest moments, and I feared I'd never live it down.

"Yes." Aurelia stood. Her golden hair fell to her waist, sleek and smooth, never a strand out of place. "Dacia's injuries had left her groggy. All of her energy was being used to heal her wounds. She did not have the concentration to fight Mavros. She does now. Plus, Samantha will be here to stop her if that happens again."

"Please, Cody." I folded my arm over my stomach, trying to get comfortable.

He knelt next to my head, brushing my hair back. "It's what you want?"

"Please. I won't go anywhere."

He kissed my forehead, then stood. "Let's go then." Looking into Samantha's loft, he said, "Keep an eye on her."

Samantha peered over the edge and saluted him. "Aye, aye, captain."

I paced until Aurelia came back. My legs were weak and shook with every slow, shuffling step I took. Stumbling, I grabbed the back of the couch for support.

"Dacia—" Samantha descended her ladder "—they'll be okay. Sit before you hurt yourself."

I let go of the couch and resumed pacing. "I can't. I should be with them, protecting them. Instead, I'm stuck here going out of my mind."

She stepped in front of me, reaching for my hand. "You need to get better before you can help anyone."

I sat, resting my head against the back of the couch. My pulse pounded against my wounds. "So, never?"

Sitting beside me, she said, "You're getting better."

"But I need to be better now." I pressed my hand against my chest, willing my body to heal.

A knock on the door sent my heart racing. "Is … is it him?" My voice was barely a whisper.

"Let me in," Aurelia said.

I slumped down. Relief drowned the fear, but the rush of adrenaline left me trembling.

Aurelia sat next to me, holding both of my hands in hers. "You need to get your strength back. You should have sensed my presence."

Releasing a deep sigh, I closed my eyes. "I haven't sensed anyone lately. I'm not healing fast enough." I tugged my hand through my hair. "I'm useless."

"No, you're not." Samantha's voice was harsh.

Aurelia squeezed my fingers. "Using your power takes energy."

"Right." I rolled my eyes. *Why's she telling me this? I already know it.*

"Your powers are being exerted as you heal. You are unintentionally using them, which leads to exhaustion."

Samantha sat down in Big Bird, propping her elbows on her knees. "That actually makes a lot of sense."

Aurelia pumped her energy into me until she had to leave to get Cody and Dan. While her strength coursed through me, my exhaustion faded. My arms and legs regained some of their strength. Before my energy could dwindle, I got ready for class. I threw on a t-shirt, but my bandages could be seen through it. I pulled a charcoal gray Phlox University hoodie on over the top. It was too warm for a sweatshirt, but I didn't want people gawking at me.

By the time Aurelia brought Cody and Dan back, I was lying on the couch again, fighting sleep. Cody lifted my head and sat down. "Sure you wanna go?"

"I should."

Aurelia knelt in front of me, once again taking my hand in hers. This time when she pushed her strength into me, my eyes jolted open. A tsunami of vitality surged through me. "Why so much?" I asked.

"I need to research while you are in class." She kept a firm grip on my hand. "Before you run into him again, I need to get this figured out."

"Will she be strong enough?" Dan's hazel eyes narrowed in concern.

Aurelia nodded. "I will be back in time to walk to Shakespeare with Dacia."

"Glad you're here." Cody's fingers entwined with mine. "And, not just because I'd hate that class."

Leaning my head back, I looked into Cody's eyes. "I figured you'd like Shakespeare. He's history. Isn't that your thing?"

"He doesn't make sense."

Dan shook his head. "Not to me either."

"Well, in all honesty—" Aurelia let go of my hand and stood, straightening her cream-colored slacks "—I really liked the guy."

"You knew Shakespeare?" I sat up slowly to avoid causing more pain.

"I have known a lot of people in my lifetime. He was a quiet, reserved, inquisitive man. Life and its sorrows fascinated him." She started for the door, looking over her shoulder. "If I am to get back in time to go with Dacia, I need to leave now."

With those words, my skin felt cold and clammy, my insides churned, and I was lightheaded. A sense of unease filled me at the thought of Aurelia leaving campus. From past experience, bad things tended to happen when she did. *Hopefully, not this time,* I thought to myself.

Kalmia Hall was one of the closest buildings to the dorms, but I felt like we were crossing the entire state. Cody carried my backpack for me, claiming I needed to save my strength. None of us talked.

As we walked past a group of students, I heard a couple of guys talking. "Yeah, I heard about that. I think she must be crazy."

"Probably, I mean who's ever heard of a black panther in this part of the country, let alone one that big."

"If there was one, you'd think it'd be out there"—he pointed to the trees—"not hanging out around the dorms."

"Well, that was interesting," I said to no one in particular.

"What, Dacia?" Dan asked.

"A large black panther has been spotted hanging around the dorms."

"Mavros." Samantha covered her mouth with her hand. "He'll leave everyone else alone; won't he?"

"I don't know." I closed my eyes and shook my head. "I don't know what he wants. He wants me to join him, but for what?"

"Hopefully, Aurelia'll find out," Cody said, taking the words out of my mouth.

I sat through Scientific Computing without hearing a word Professor Granite said. He was a middle-aged man with a salt and pepper mullet, matching mustache, and gray eyes who had taught a few of my other classes.

By the time we left, my strength was waning. I tried to hide it from the others. I didn't want them to worry.

Cody held my hand on the way to Sedum. Without meaning to, I siphoned off some of his strength. "Sorry."

"Take what you need." He wrapped his arm around my waist and pulled me closer.

I wanted to relax into him, but I expected Mavros to appear at any moment. With my energy sapped, there was no way I'd be able to protect myself, let alone my friends. When Dan pulled the door to the cafeteria open, I slumped with relief.

"You okay?" he asked as I walked past him.

I shook my head in disgust. "I'm stupid."

Samantha's face scrunched in a look of bewilderment. "What?"

I swung my arm in front of me in an all-encompassing gesture. "Just because we're inside, I shouldn't feel safe. Last time he attacked, I was inside."

Dan grabbed Samantha's hand and pulled her into the lunch line. "Every minute without him is one to be grateful for."

True to her word, Aurelia returned to the dorm in time to walk with me to class. When she showed up, I was slumped against Cody, taking his strength.

"Take more." He mumbled. "Done with class. You need it."

I pulled away. "I've taken too much."

"Me and Sam would be happy to help." Dan flipped his thumb between the two of them.

"I will lend her my strength on the way to class," Aurelia said.

I kissed Cody on the cheek. His eyelids fluttered but didn't open. Grabbing my backpack, I asked Aurelia, "Did you have any luck?"

"Yes." She lifted my bag off my shoulder. "After class, I will discuss it with you all."

I let out an exasperated sigh. "Fine. You walking with us, Samantha?"

"Yeah." She kissed Dan. "Stay here with Cody."

"No problem." He held her waist. "I've got homework to do."

My mind was wandering when Dr. John Rowan walked into class. I had seen him around campus, but I never knew who he was before. He was a tall, thin man in his mid-forties. He had brown hair with some gray starting to show in it. He appeared stern, but when he smiled, he looked affable enough.

During class, I found myself more concerned about what Aurelia would say than what Dr. Rowan was talking about.

"Dacia, are you okay?" Aurelia asked when we left the building. "You seem distracted."

I tugged my hand through my curls. Loose hairs clung to my fingers. I let them fall, blowing away in the wind. Students strode across campus. Some sat in the grass, enjoying the warm fall day. They laughed, biked, rode skateboards, napped in hammocks, and I was trapped, caged by my fear. "I am. I'm terrified of what you're going to say." We walked to Primrose Hall to get Samantha. "After Draconian, I thought I'd have more time." I watched my feet. "I'm not ready for this."

She squeezed my shoulder. A burst of energy lifted my head and quickened my pace. "Thanks."

"I hoped you would have more time, too." She lowered her hand. "However, it seems like evil is drawn to you."

Samantha strode toward us. As soon as she joined us, we turned around to go back to the dorm. "Is everything okay?" she asked.

I nodded, then focused on Aurelia. "Is this how it is for everyone like me?"

"Everyone must walk their own path," she answered without looking at me.

What aren't you telling me?

Now is not the time, Dacia.

"It's never the time," I mumbled.

When we got back to my room, I fell onto the couch next to Cody. His eyes drifted open. The irises rolled back, and then closed again.

"Is he okay?" I held my hand against his chest, feeling the steady rhythm of his heartbeat. "I must've taken too much."

She held onto his hand. "Try to wake him now."

"Can you keep doling out your strength like that?" Dan's nose wrinkled, and he leaned forward. "You've been helping Dacia and now Cody."

"I have plenty to give."

I ran my finger along Cody's jaw.

"Back already?" Cody's eyes opened, and he sat up straight. "Everything okay?"

"Class is over." Dan closed his book. "You slept the whole time they were gone."

I dropped my head. "I took too much."

"You needed it." He rubbed his eyes, then focused on Aurelia. "What'd you find out?"

Samantha put Dan's books on the floor and sat on his lap.

Aurelia stood at the window, staring outside. "Mavros is a greater demon, one of the strongest to have ever stepped foot on this planet."

"Lovely." The word slipped from my mouth unintentionally.

Aurelia turned and shot me a grief-stricken imitation of a smile. "He cannot stay on Earth without binding himself to a mortal woman."

Dan pulled Samantha against him, probably grateful she wasn't Mavros' target. "At least you know your role now."

"Yeah." Samantha's eyes shone with sorrow. "No wonder why he's trying so hard to win you over."

"But why me?" I asked.

"To make my life a living Hell." Cody's voice hardened a little more with each word.

Dan's hand never stopped moving along Samantha's arm. "Because you are one of the few people who could stop him."

Aurelia nodded at him. "Quite possibly." She sat down next to me, feeding me her strength.

"I'm okay." I tried to pull my hand away, but she held it tighter.

"You must heal soon." She patted my leg. "Mavros, like all demons, can only return to Earth once every 999 years unless summoned. The last time he was here, he killed Elizabeth. After her death, he was banished to the Abyss. If he cannot win you over in the allotted amount of time, he will once again be cast out."

Cody perked up. "Allotted amount of time?"

"Forty-five days."

I felt my eyebrows raise and my mouth twist into a humorless grin. "So, all I have to do is stay strong until he gets sent back, and this will be over." I pulled away from Aurelia and paced in front of the couch. "That sounds too easy. There has to be more to it."

"I doubt he plans to leave you or your friends alive if you turn your back on him, Dacia." Her pupils slitted, and for a moment, I glimpsed the dragon beneath the surface. Anger and hurt rippled her features. "His vengeance will be swift and deadly."

"Not good," Samantha said.

Dan tightened his grip on Samantha. He pinched his lips together, and the dimple on the right side of his face sunk in. "So, how does she beat him?"

"I do not know." Her form settled. Her eyes almost appeared human again. "He has only been defeated once, and it was not by a human."

I had been pacing away from her. I turned too quickly and lost my balance. My chest tightened, and pain lanced through my body.

Cody jumped up, steadying me. "Who?" he asked.

Aurelia bared her teeth. It was an odd expression on her, but I'd seen her dragon do it before. I knew how terrifying it was in her natural form. "I have been forbidden to say, lest I break a pact made several millennia ago."

I sat next to Cody, no longer sure of my strength. "What can you tell us?"

"Until Mavros is able to lure a mortal into his trap, he can only return to Earth for forty-five days once every 999 years. His time on Earth is fleeting, and as it grows shorter, he will become increasingly desperate."

"If you were there, why didn't you know this?" I felt like I was accusing her of lying, of keeping things from me, but I didn't understand.

She took my hand. Power rushed through my veins. "I was young. Elizabeth was one of the first beings I was asked to protect." She pinched her eyes closed, and pain rippled across her features. "When I failed, the elders sent me into isolation. I mourned Elizabeth's death in solitude."

Her sorrow seeped into me, and I squeezed her hand.

Samantha bit her lip. "So you didn't know anything about Mavros when you were sent to protect her?"

"No." She stood and walked to the window. "We have to tread carefully where he is concerned. We are not allowed to interfere."

"You said that before." Dan leaned forward. "Why? What do you mean?"

"I cannot elaborate." She opened the window, and the breeze lifted her hair. "It is imperative that I do not give too much information away."

"Okay." Slumping against Cody, I asked, "Is he stronger than Nefarious?"

"Not necessarily stronger but more cunning." She tapped her finger against her chin. It seemed like the more time she spent with us, the more body language she picked up on. When we'd first met her, she was eerily still. "Nefarious was evil. All of his intentions were evil. He was here for only one purpose, and he thought he was strong enough to win. Mavros, too, is evil. However, he knows he needs you. He will do everything in his power to captivate you. If he does—if you agree to be his—he will destroy everything you know and love while you stand by his side watching. You will have immortality but at a heavy cost."

I pulled Cody's arm over my shoulder, needing him to steady me. "Since I don't want immortality at any cost, I'll have to do my best to keep putting him off until I can figure out a way to stop him."

"Why wouldn't she try to stop him?" Samantha stilled Dan's hand by placing hers over it. "Dacia isn't like that. She has morals."

"It has nothing to do with morals. Once you make a promise to a demon, you cannot go back on your word."

Realization slammed into my chest. The air was sucked from my lungs, and a wave of dizziness swept over me. "Oh, my God." Every head in the room turned to look at me.

"What have you done, Dacia?" Aurelia asked. "What did you promise him?"

"In a dream, after Mavros attacked Arion, he made me promise something." I concentrated on the dream, but the details were muddled. "He told me I'd want to go back on my word but I wouldn't be able to. He said that since I said his name in my promise, I wouldn't be able to get out of it."

Cody lifted his arm from my shoulders and stood up. "What, Dacia?" He sat in Cookie Monster, clutching his head. "What did you promise?"

Tears pooled in my eyes. "I swear I don't remember. It was a dream. How can dreams affect reality?"

"You must be diligent even in sleep." Aurelia rubbed my arm. "Mavros is probably right. Whatever you promised will most likely be binding, and I fear you will discover your oath at the worst possible moment."

I swiped at my eyes. "You warned me any promise would be binding. I should've known better."

Samantha shook her head. "It was a dream. Nobody blames you."

I looked at Cody. "Nobody?"

"Nobody." He gazed at me, hurt and fear dwelled in the depths of his blue eyes. "But, what if … what if you already bound yourself to him?"

"I do not believe that was the promise she made," Aurelia said.

"I know I'm newer to this than the rest of you—" Dan cleared his throat "—but, I was thinking about everything you told me about Nefarious. Didn't you have a necklace or something that let you know when he was near? Does that work for all demons or just him?"

Cody, Samantha, and I looked at each other and shrugged. Then I said, "I don't know. Maybe I should get that back from Sarah and try it. If I know Mavros is around, it might help me focus on something other than him or teleport to safety or something."

"That was a really good idea, Dan." Samantha beamed at him. "We were there. We should've thought of it."

"If that works, you might be able to avoid him completely." Aurelia nodded, tapping her finger against her lip. The action reminded me of Sarah. "As long as your friends are with you, you could keep them safe, too. When did you first see Mavros?"

"The Tuesday before my birthday," I answered.

"We will assume that was his first day on Earth," she said. "That would mean you have thirty-two more days before he returns to the Abyss."

I walked over to the calendar and marked a big "X" on September 23rd. "If your assumption is correct, this will all be over by September 23rd, one way or the other." I flipped the calendar back and forth between August and September, trying to convince myself it wasn't that long and that I could do it. "At least, I know it's not going to last forever. Maybe I'll even be able to go home for Christmas."

Cody stood behind me, wrapping his arms around my waist. "You can do it." He rested his chin on the top of my head.

I folded my arms over his. "Thirty-two more days. Piece of cake," I said with false enthusiasm.

"Keep thinking positively." Aurelia's voice was full of confidence and encouragement. "I know you can get through this."

"I'm about a third of the way there." I was trying to sound optimistic, but on the inside, I was panicking. I wanted to silence my inner voice, but it kept repeating, *Oh, my God, I still have thirty-two days to go. I'm never going to make it!*

"On the way to class this morning, Dacia overheard a couple guys talking about a panther being spotted around the dorm." Samantha sounded uneasy. "Do other students need to worry about Mavros?"

"For now, I believe there is no need for anybody outside this room to worry," Aurelia answered.

"Okay." Samantha sounded a little more relaxed.

Aurelia stood, looking at me. "If it is okay with you, I need to check on Arion."

"Go ahead." I blinked, and she was gone.

I tugged my hand through my hair. "Before I collapse, I need to see Sarah."

"I'll go, too," Cody said.

After calling her, I grabbed Cody's hand. The world blackened. Our bodies squeezed in and stretched out. Light seeped in through my eyelids. I stumbled forward. Cody lifted me, carrying me to the couch.

"Take my strength, Dacia." He held me against him, and his energy seeped into me. I slowed the flow to a mere trickle, not wanting to take too much. He'd spent enough of the day sleeping.

Sarah came out of her office and stood in front of us. "Are you all right?"

"She's weak," Cody answered for me.

My mouth opened, but the words wouldn't come out. Taking a deep breath, I tried again. "Aurelia said I'm using so much energy healing that I'm exhausting myself."

"How are your injuries?"

Once again, Cody saved me from talking. "Better, but not good."

I clung to Cody, allowing his strength to burn off my exhaustion. "I need the amulet."

"Why?" She sat across from us, running her hands along her pewter slacks, smoothing them out.

"Mavros is a demon," Cody answered. "The amulet worked on Nefarious."

"So, maybe it works for all demons," Sarah finished for him.

"It was Dan's idea," I said.

She rubbed her jaw, shaking her head. "We should've thought of it. We were all there and saw what it could do."

Cody lifted me slightly, resituating me in his arms. "Maybe we were too close to the problem."

Sarah raised her finger and walked to her office. I thought she was getting the amulet, but she came back with a planner. She flipped a page back and forth. "I can't get it for a day or two. Do you think you can get by until then?"

My stomach plummeted to my knees. "I'll be careful." In all honesty, I was disappointed. I'd hoped I'd be able to walk out of here wearing the amulet. A lot could happen in two days. The entire universe could come crashing down in that amount of time. I could swear my loyalty to Mavros by then.

Chapter 18

Angels And Demons

Tuesday followed the same pattern as Monday. I was on edge, expecting Mavros to show up and cause a ruckus. I sat in my classrooms staring at the doors, looking over each student, wondering when he'd show up. When Cody, Samantha, and Dan were away from me, I worried about their safety.

As often as she could, Aurelia grabbed my hand or my arm and sent a stream of power flowing through my body. With each burst of energy, my wound healed a little more.

I felt strong enough to eat dinner in the cafeteria. I sat with my back against the wall and watched the door anxiously.

"Relax," Aurelia said.

I shook my head. "I can't. I have a bad feeling. Mavros has all but disappeared since he attacked me." My hand fluttered to my chest at the thought of his claws ripping into my flesh. Even though I was better, I was far from healed. My torso was wrapped in bandages, and at times, breathing was difficult.

Cody looked from my hand to my face. "You okay?"

"Fine, reaching up was just an instinct."

He took my hand in his, gently rubbing his thumb over it. "Don't overdo. If we miss class, we miss."

Samantha smiled at me. "He's right."

Dan, Cody, and I all turned to look at her. "Who are you, and what did you do with my Sammi?" Dan asked.

When we got back from dinner, Marcy stood in the hallway. As soon as she saw us, she said, "I'm not going to have to kick Cody out of here nightly, am I?"

"No," I told her. "He's turned over a new leaf. He no longer stays in girl's dorms longer than he should."

"Good." She tossed her hair over her shoulder. "It got a little old last year."

I shrugged. "Well, you know, things could be worse. You could have demons or crazed magicians trying to kill you."

"Uh-huh." She looked at me like I had three heads. "That could happen."

"I'm just saying … life could be worse." I raised my eyebrows and tilted my head. The hint of a smile played on my lips.

"Good to see you, too," Cody told her as we walked by.

When we were in our room, Samantha looked at me like I'd lost my mind and said, "What was that about?"

"I don't know." I laughed. "She just irritates me some-times. We should've seen about renting a house."

"That would've been cool," Dan agreed.

"I don't think my parents would've gone for it." Saman-tha's lips pinched together. "Besides, where would we get the money?"

My mind flashed to the treasure Aurelia had given me. We didn't need to rent a house. I could buy one for us. Maybe if I made it through this, we'd have to consider getting out of the dorms next semester.

"I know, but it was a good thought." We stepped into our room, and I said, "Cody's going to have to stay here, and I don't want to put up with Marcy banging on the door every night."

"It'll be okay." Cody went to the fridge and grabbed a bot-tle of water, holding it out. We all nodded, and he tossed one to each of us. "We got good at hiding last year."

Samantha snuggled against Dan on the couch, chewing on her lip. "Do you think Dan should stay, too? I don't know if it's a good idea for him to leave on his own every night."

"I think it would be best for him to stay." Aurelia stood by the door. "We have no way of knowing if Mavros will try to kidnap anyone to use as leverage. We need to do whatever we can to avoid that." She tilted her head, and her eyes had a faraway look in them.

"You can go to Arion. We'll be fine." I turned to Samantha and Dan. "If you're going to stay, you can sleep in my bed."

Samantha's eyebrows scrunched together and her eyes narrowed. For a second, I thought her claws might come out.

I patted the back of the couch. "I'm going to curl up on the couch with Cody. It keeps my nightmares at bay, and apparently, it really annoys Mavros."

"I'm not sure annoying Mavros is the best idea," Dan said, "but, I think keeping your nightmares away is a good thing. If you can get some sleep, you'll be able to think better."

My head rested on Cody's chest. I was comfortable and content, but sleep wouldn't find me. I rolled off the couch and grabbed a bottle of water. After downing half of it, I paced, growing more restless by the second.

I'll just go out for a minute, I thought to myself. *I'll be fine. Some fresh air will be good for me.*

Knowing I was making a mistake, I snuck into the hall and pulled the door shut without making a noise. Most of the time, I would've had to worry about Aurelia, but she was with Arion.

Standing outside the door gazing up at the beautiful night sky, a gentle breeze blew, lifting the hair off my neck. I searched for familiar constellations and took pleasure in breathing in the fresh air. I felt revitalized even though I knew I should feel guilty. If Cody woke up, he would be a nervous wreck, but I belonged out here. I wanted to go for a walk but knew that would be carrying it too far.

With a huff, I turned to walk back into the building and stepped right into Mavros' arms. He held me for a brief moment, sighing with contentment.

He stepped away, releasing me. "You heard me calling, and you came." His words were practically purred. "I was afraid you'd resist me."

Staggering back, I pressed my hand to my chest. "You called me?"

"Yes." He lifted his hand but let it fall to his side. "I've missed you, Dacia." Standing between me and the door, his stance was relaxed.

I could've teleported to my room, but I didn't feel threatened. "What do you want with me?"

"Eternity."

"But, why me?"

"You're perfect."

"Perfect." The word came out on a laugh. "No, I'm not."

"Ah, and she's humble, too."

My cheeks warmed at his comment. "Nobody's perfect." I kicked at the ground with my toe. "So … why?"

"You are beautiful, intelligent, and powerful, but more importantly, when I am near you, I feel alive. My heart beats faster." He strode closer. His dark eyes softened. "The palms of my hands sweat. Butterflies flutter obnoxiously in my stomach. Of all the women in the world, you are the only one who makes me feel this way. You, Dacia, are the only one for me. When you're near, I realize why I never stayed on Earth before. Without you here, it wouldn't have been possible for me to be happy. Now that we've met, I know you are the reason for my existence." He reached out and took my hand in his. "Don't you feel the same way about me?"

With him touching me, it was hard to concentrate on anything else, but somehow, I managed to tell him the truth. "Not the same. I feel passion and desire when I am with you. Right now, I want you to pull me closer to you. I want you to kiss me and hold me and never let me go, but I don't love you."

"If you want me like that, then say yes." His fingers grazed my cheek, and I leaned into his touch. "If you would say yes, I could hold you forever and never let you go. You would learn to love me as I love you."

I shook his hand off my face. "I will *always* love Cody."

He dropped my hand. His eyes flashed before he turned his back on me. Hatred radiated off him. "If Cody was no longer in the picture, would you change your mind about me?"

He didn't try to touch me or make me look into his eyes. He stood with his hands in his pockets, his back to me. Was he asking me without having me under his control because he wanted me to like him or was this just another trick of his?

"If Cody was out of the picture, it would be the end of my world. It would take me a long time to get over him … if I ever did." I watched him for the slightest movement. If he gave any indication that he was about to attack, I'd teleport to the safety of my room. "I think it would be months, if not years, before I even considered dating again."

"But, by then it would be too late for me." His shoulders slumped. "What will it take to make you mine?"

"I'm sorry, Mavros, but it'll never happen. I gave my heart to Cody. It's no longer mine to give away."

He turned to face me, staring me straight in the eyes. His eyes looked dark and tormented. Instead of feeling tingly all over, I felt terrified.

In the span of a breath, I was surrounded by darkness. Wherever I was, it was pitch black, and I was positive this place had never seen the sun. I stuck my arms out in front of me and walked forward, feeling my way. There was only nothingness. I tried to teleport out, but I couldn't visualize anywhere.

The darkness overwhelmed me. My breathing grew rapid, then forced. I felt like an incredible weight pushed down on me. I tried to calm myself, to focus on my lake, but irrational fear dug its claws into me. A small whimper escaped my lips.

"Dacia." Mavros' voice sounded menacing here. "This is what it's like in the Abyss. Will you send me back there for another thousand years? Have I done anything to you that would make you think I deserve this kind of punishment?"

I didn't answer his question. I didn't want to make him any angrier. I needed him to get me out of here before the weight of the nothingness crushed me.

"Don't send me back there." His words were a plea.

My heartbeat drummed in my ears. I closed my eyes and tried to master the terror. "What would you do if you stayed here?"

"No one's ever asked me that." He chuckled. "Well, I would make it a better place to live."

"Better for who?"

"Are you asking me all these questions to avoid answering me?" His voice sounded closer.

I reached out, needing contact to help center me. My fingers slid through the air. I spun, feeling for something, anything. "I'm sorry. I don't know what to say." I wrapped my arms around my body, trying to hold back the horror. "You're a demon. You're evil. Why wouldn't I expect you to do terrible things? Don't demons thrive on fear and pain?" I had never been so scared in my life, and knowing that at any moment Mavros might turn on me, made it all the worse.

"Just because I am a demon, you think I'm evil?" He laughed, but it was humorless. "The world is not so black and white. I suppose you think all angels are noble?"

"Aren't they?" My trembling legs gave out, and I fell to the ground.

"No!" The panther's growl followed the word.

I clutched my chest. The memory of pain flared through my wounds. A sob escaped my lips.

"Isn't your devil a fallen angel? How did Lucifer fall if he was righteous and honorable? Did your god cast him out for being too noble?"

"I don't know." My voice quivered. "So … you're not evil?"

"You should give me the benefit of the doubt."

"You attacked Arion. Then the next day you attacked me." I stared into the Abyss, hoping to see something. "Neither of those incidents was justifiable."

"It was instinct when I attacked the horse. And, you will never know"—his voice softened—"how truly sorry I am for what I did to you. If I could go back in time and change it, I would. I am sorry I hurt you, Dacia."

"Sorry?" I yelled at him. "You almost killed me. I missed three days of my life, and I'm still not healed."

"Please forgive me. I'm trying to be a better person for you." He sounded closer.

Something grabbed my hand. I screamed in surprise and jerked away.

"I didn't mean to startle you." Mavros' arms wrapped around me. He lifted me to my feet. Still holding me, he asked with his voice silky smooth, "Do I seem evil to you?" His hand brushed against my cheek.

"I don't know." His touch centered me, drawing out the dread from the place. I stepped closer to him, needing his warmth to burn away the chill that had settled deep inside me. "I don't know what to think. Somehow, you control me, and from past experience, I'd say that's not a benign quality."

"Trust your instincts." His breath tingled against my neck.

"Take me out of this place?" I pressed my body closer to his. "It's closing in on me."

"Not until you answer me."

"If you won't take me out of here"—I stepped back—"even though you know what it's doing to me, then I'd say you're not good. You may not be evil, but you're not good."

He growled into the darkness. A gust of air blew across my face, and then I was standing outside the dormitory again. "I want you to see me for what I am, Dacia. I want you to realize that I'm not evil, no matter what your dragon friend told you." His eyes implored me to believe him, and for once, even though I was looking into them, I wasn't under his control.

"So, prove it to me." I lifted my shoulders in a shrug, raising my hands in the air. "Give me some time to come to that conclusion on my own."

He stepped toward me. His steps were slow, measured, as if he didn't want to startle me. He took my hand in his and stared into my eyes.

My wound pulsed, throbbing like it hadn't for days. My fingers fluttered over my chest, and I sucked in a deep breath.

Before dissipating into smoke, he caressed my cheek and brushed his lips across mine. "If that is what you want."

He was gone, and I was left standing there wondering what had happened. Was he not what he seemed? Was he the exception to the rule … a good demon? Was he to the devil what the devil was to God? I kept picturing his eyes before he vanished. They looked so vulnerable.

I tried to sneak back into the room, but Cody was waiting for me. "Where've you been?"

I considered telling him that I went to the bathroom, but I told him the truth. "I went outside for some fresh air and found out that Mavros had been summoning me."

"Why, Dacia?" He ran a trembling hand through his hair. His sapphire eyes were wide with fear. "What were you thinking? You could've been killed."

"Can we talk about this in the morning?" I asked. "We're going to wake up Samantha and Dan."

"Too late," Samantha said, shaking off the dregs of slumber. "You might as well spill."

I walked over to the couch and sat down. "I suppose it doesn't matter what I was thinking. Does it? I was being summoned by a demon. I don't know if I could have kept from going out there." I looked up into Cody's face and saw that all his anger over Mavros had been replaced with fear and concern.

"Not good." He took my hand in his.

"No, but he let me go." I leaned forward with my elbows on my knees and stared at the carpet while I told them what had happened. "I honestly don't know what to think about this."

"What do you mean?" Cody sounded incredulous. "You're not considering his offer; are you?"

"No, that's not what I mean." I raked my fingers through my hair. "But, is Mavros really evil? Why would he bring me back here instead of keeping me there until I gave in and told him I'd be his? I don't know how long I'd've lasted. I've never been so scared in my life."

"Really?" Dan's voice rose in astonishment. "You've had more to be afraid of than anybody I've ever known."

"Yeah." I finally looked up. "That's kind of my point. I was that scared, and it's not like I'm afraid of the dark or afraid to be alone. Even when I thought Nefarious was going to kill me, I wasn't that scared. But tonight, I was horrified. Mavros could've used that terror if he'd wanted to. If he's evil, wouldn't he have?"

"So … uh, can't demons bring on irrational fear?" Samantha peered over her loft railing. "Was it something he was doing to you so he could make himself look better when he safely returned you?"

"I don't know." I shook my head. "I suppose he could've. I really don't know what to think. I don't like that he can make me leave my room against my better judgment. I don't like that he can control my thoughts and feelings. I don't like that I have no idea how to stop him. I'm scared."

"Hopefully, the amulet works." Cody wrapped his arm around me and pulled me closer. "Maybe it'll keep him from summoning you."

"Maybe." I laid my head on his shoulder. "Maybe it won't do anything at all except look gaudy and out of place around my neck."

"Have a little faith, Dacia." Samantha grabbed her pillow and burrowed under her covers.

"I'll do my best." I turned off the light. "Let's get some sleep? Maybe Mavros will leave me alone for the rest of the night."

"Let's hope." Cody lay down, and I snuggled against him afraid to close my eyes.

Chapter 19

Demon Marked

As Aurelia walked me to our Shakespeare class, she lectured me about listening to Mavros. "He is playing you for a fool, Dacia. Deceit and manipulation are the areas in which demons excel."

"But he seems so … I don't know," I furrowed my eyebrows and thought for a moment before saying, "sincere … convincing."

She looked at me out of the corner of her eye. "If you knew you were going to be banished for 999 years, you would do your best to sound convincing, too."

"Ugh! It's not like I want to tell him I'll join him." I took a deep breath and said in a calmer voice, "I … I don't know. I guess I feel bad for him. If the Abyss is what he showed me, nobody should have to go through that torment."

"I know." Her voice was calm and soothing. "You are a trusting person, and you have a hard time dealing with those who are not honest. If … no, when he is sent back to the Abyss, he will not stay there for long. Demons are not tied to one world as humans are. They can travel between all of them. He may have a similar curse on him in each realm, but he will not be stuck in the Abyss."

I watched my feet as we walked. "Why would he try to manipulate me? Why not keep me imprisoned? He knew how scared I was. Why not force my hand?"

"Maybe he thought he would stand a better chance if he could convince you he was good." She rested her hand on my shoulder, sending her energy into me.

"You don't need to do that." I shrugged. "It healed over-night." I ran my hand down my face. "There's not even a mark."

Her eyebrows pulled together as she looked from my face to my chest and back again. "Good," she said as she pulled her hand away, but the tone of her voice and the look on her face made me think it really wasn't good. I wondered what she suspected but doubted she'd tell me.

"It is possible Mavros will employ other methods as the deadline nears, but for now, I think he wants you to like him. I imagine he feels it is a better way to win your loyalty, and in your case, he is probably right."

My backpack slid down my arm. I hefted it back up, holding onto the strap. "Yeah, you catch more flies with honey than vinegar. As far as I'm concerned, though, honesty's always the best policy."

I spent all of Shakespeare class thinking about what Aurelia told me. Was I that gullible … that easily manipulated? I never thought of myself that way before, but Aurelia had a good point. Demons thrived on fear and chaos, and right now, my world was feeling pretty chaotic. Everyone was disappointed in me for trusting Mavros. Not for the first time, I wondered if he looked more like a monster, would it be easier for me to believe he was one. I wanted to think I wouldn't feel any different, but I couldn't quite convince myself of it.

On the way to Sarah's office, I asked Aurelia, "So, am I just taken in by his looks? Is that why I can't see that he's evil?"

"I believe there is more to it than that." She paused. "His appearance is an obstacle, but he is trying to convince you he is good. Nefarious and Draconian did not show you a decent side. For the most part, since Mavros is trying to seduce you, he has concealed that part of himself from you, and when he was unable to hide his dark side, he came up with convincing excuses for his actions. He is trying to make you sympathize with him."

"And, it's working." I dragged my hands down my face. "God, I'm so dumb."

"Is it working?" The wind whipped Aurelia's hair around her head. Gray clouds darkened the sky. "It is not supposed to rain today, Dacia."

"Sorry." I stopped and sucked in a deep breath, concentrating on my mountain lake, feeling serenity wash over me. The gusts settled into a gentle breeze.

"That is better." Aurelia resumed walking. "It seems you are suspicious of him."

"Yeah, I suppose I am." I twisted my earring around. The slight action helped me think. "But, I also find myself wondering … doubting. I thought I was a good judge of character. Now, it seems like I'm a pushover."

Aurelia opened the door to Sarah's office and ushered me in.

"Hello, ladies." Sarah set her papers on the coffee table and focused on me. "Is everything all right, Dacia? You look distressed."

"Mavros summoned me to join him last night—" I sighed "—and I did."

"Oh, dear." She gasped.

"It's not as bad as you think." I put my backpack on the floor and sat down. "He was nice—for the most part. Anyway, I'm not sure which side is up anymore."

Aurelia stood behind the couch and explained in more detail, but I didn't listen. I thought about Mavros. He looked so vulnerable last night when he left me. Could he have been faking his anguish?

No, I said to myself, *he was sincere.*

The pain had been so clear in his eyes. Every emotion showed there. He couldn't hide it when he was angry, just as he couldn't hide his true feelings. It had to have been genuine.

Sarah walked over and rested her hand on my shoulder. "Trust your instincts, Dacia. They've been pretty good to you over the past year."

She left the room, and when she came back in, she held a box with the amulet in it. I was nervous to see it. It was from a part of my life that I thought was over. I was afraid seeing the amulet would bring Nefarious back to the forefront of my mind.

She carried it over and handed it to me. I opened the box and looked down at the amulet that had protected me from Nefarious. It was a diamond-shaped pendant on a heavy gold chain. In the center of the pendant was a sapphire set to look like an almond-shaped cat's eye with an onyx pupil. The gold around the outside edge of the pendant was smooth with diamonds inlaid on each of the four corners. The inside was rough with inscriptions that said in some ancient language, "Find courage within yourself."

I took the amulet out of the box. "Here goes nothing." I gingerly placed it around my neck. Like it had the first time I put it on, a warm sensation rushed through my body. My skin tingled and the hair on the back of my neck stood on end.

Unlike last time, the amulet glowed as if Nefarious himself was in the room with us. "It's not working." I pulled it forward and stared down at it.

Aurelia stood in front of me and looked at the amulet like it was a puzzle. "Sarah, will you try it on?"

I rubbed the back of my neck before lifting the chain over my head and handing it to Sarah. I had no idea why Aurelia wanted her to wear it. Obviously, it wasn't working anymore.

As soon as it was in Sarah's hand, the glowing stopped. She put it around her neck and shivered. "It feels weird; doesn't it?"

"Why isn't it glowing on you?" Pressing my hand against my chest, I wondered if my wound had something to do with it.

Aurelia nodded at me. "Dacia, touch it now."

As soon as I touched the amulet, it glowed a brilliant blue. "Why?" A lump formed in my throat, threatening to cut my voice off.

Aurelia led me to the couch and sat beside me. "Mavros has marked you."

"What? How?" I slumped down and dragged my hand through my hair.

"It may have happened when he kissed you or when he attacked you." Aurelia patted my leg, but I found no reassurance in the action. The idea of being marked by a demon was repulsive and frightening. What did it mean? Could the mark be removed?

"The how and why do not matter. What matters is that you cannot wear the amulet, but maybe one of your friends can."

Sarah slipped the necklace back into the box. "I'm not sure that'll help."

Aurelia nodded. "Mavros will most likely still be able to summon her, but hopefully, they will be able to let Dacia know if he is nearby."

"Well, I guess that's better than nothing," I said with a long, drawn-out sigh. I stared out the windows at the mountains, but for once, I found no comfort in them. "What does it mean?"

Aurelia and Sarah both looked at me. Their confusion was obvious.

"That he marked me." I flipped my hands up and frustration laced my voice. "What does it mean?"

Aurelia cocked her head and tapped her lip. "It means his essence is inside of you. It could be from his venom, or he may have intentionally tainted you somehow." She patted my knee. "I am unsure of the repercussions of being demon marked. It may be how he can infiltrate your dreams or how he called you to him last night."

"Great." I leaned forward with my head in my hands. "So, does Cody wear the amulet because he's with me more, or does Samantha wear it because she has classes on her own?"

Sarah leaned forward like she wanted to comfort me, but she wasn't close enough. "Why don't you let them decide that, Dacia?"

"Sure," I agreed.

The three of us walked to the door. Sarah pulled me aside, wrapping her arm around my shoulders. "Keep your chin up. Things are going to work out. You can do this."

"I hope you're right." I pulled my hand across my forehead, trying to rub the stress away. "But, I'm not too sure about that. What if he lures me out again tonight but doesn't let me come back?" My words were rushed. I covered my mouth with my hand and took a deep breath. Tears pooled in my eyes, blurring my vision. "I'm really scared, Sarah. I have no idea how to stop him, and Aurelia hasn't come up with anything either. If something doesn't give, I'll probably end up being responsible for destroying the world."

She gave me a quick hug. "I know things seem dismal, but I have faith in you."

Aurelia and I walked back to my room without saying anything to each other. I was stuck in my head, wondering what other side effects being marked by a demon might have on me.

As soon as I closed the door, Cody asked, "She have the amulet?"

"Yep." The p popped out of my mouth.

Samantha spun around in the desk chair. "So, it didn't work?"

"Nope." Once again the p made a popping sound.

"As soon as Dacia touches it, it starts glowing." Aurelia put her hand on my back and nudged me across the room. I plopped down in Cookie Monster, unconsciously rubbing my hand back and forth over the arm. "Sarah was able to wear it, so we thought maybe one of you could."

Dan sat down in Big Bird, looking from me to Aurelia. "Why does it glow when Dacia wears it?"

"Aurelia says I've been marked by a demon." I bit my lip.

The blood drained from Samantha's face. "What does that mean?"

"It means that his essence is in her." Aurelia stood behind me with her hand on my shoulder. "I imagine it will be until he returns to the Abyss. If I am right, nothing she does will change that."

"Lovely." I dropped my head into my hands.

"How did she get demon essence on her?" Dan asked.

Aurelia hesitated. "It could be …"

Cody interrupted her, running a shaking hand through his hair. "Please … I don't wanna know."

"Okay." I started pacing. "Cody's with me more, but Samantha has classes on her own. So, the two of you need to decide who will wear it, or if either of you will. Or, Dan if you want to, you can." I stopped in front of the window, hoping the peacefulness of the mountains would settle over me.

I wanted to go off on my own somewhere to sulk, but I knew that wouldn't go over very well. I heard them discussing the amulet, but tuned it out. I was trying to figure out how to avoid Mavros and how to beat him in the end. However, no matter how much I thought about it, I couldn't come up with a viable solution.

Cody grabbed my hand and pulled me onto the couch beside him. "You okay?"

"I'll live … hopefully." I tried to smile. "How about you?"

"I'll live. You'll make sure."

"Pizza or cafeteria tonight?" Samantha asked.

I knew she was trying to get our minds off Mavros, but it would take more than food for me.

"We could head down to The Avalanche." Dan stretched his legs out in front of him and slid down in the chair, looking quite relaxed. "Do you feel like getting off campus?"

I shook my head. "You guys can. I'm gonna stay here."

"We'll stay with you." Samantha picked up the phone. "I'll call it in."

I looked at each of them. "So, who's the lucky one?"

"Me." Cody lifted the chain. I could almost hear his eyes rolling. "Was weird when I put it on."

I cocked my head at him. "How'd I miss that?"

"You were staring out the window." Dan pointed to the one looking out at the mountains.

Cody threw his arm over my shoulder, and we sat in silence for a moment. I was glad he was there. He knew me well enough to back off when I needed him to, but he also knew that I needed him. Right then, it felt pretty good to be able to curl up next to him.

"Ow." Cody's hand flew up to his neck, and he yanked the amulet out from under his shirt. The sapphire's glow lit up the room.

"Dan or Samantha will have to wear it," Aurelia said. "Apparently, Cody cannot touch you if he is."

Samantha reached her hand out. "I'll wear it."

"Didn't think it'd get so warm." Cody dropped it on top of his shirt.

I couldn't quit staring at the amulet. "If you don't want to wear it, you don't have to, Sam."

"No, somebody should." She took it from Cody. "We don't know if it'll work anyway. If he's like Nefarious, it should glow anytime he's around, but if he's like you, it'll only glow if he touches one of us. It'd be nice to find out."

I dragged my hands down my face. "It'd be even nicer if we didn't find out."

"Yeah, but realistically, we're going to." Dan patted the arm of the chair, and Samantha sat beside him.

"I know. I'm sorry. I just feel … lost." I twisted my hoodie strings around each other. "I'm afraid Mavros'll get me to leave one of these nights and not bring me back. Or, if he can lure me out, what's to stop him from luring you guys out? And, if he can make me go outside by myself, why can't he just make me agree to be bound to him?"

Aurelia cocked her head as if listening. She nodded. "You have to make that decision freely. He can dazzle you and leave you breathless before he asks, but the decision must be made of your own free will."

I rubbed my arm. "Mavros can be quite charismatic."

Samantha rolled her eyes, and Cody jerked his arm off my shoulders, pulling away from me.

"What?" I flipped my hands up. "He is. If it weren't for Cody, I may have fallen for his act. But, like I told Mavros, I already gave my heart away."

Cody leaned forward, folding his hands together. "Don't forget that."

"When he holds me—" I cleared my throat, hoping nobody heard how husky my voice sounded "—or looks into my eyes, I do forget. I'm afraid I'm going to lose you because of him."

"Yeah." Cody rubbed my leg.

I focused on the way his hand felt against my skin and let my memories of Mavros slip away.

"Tears me up, but he's controlling you"—he stared at the floor—"making you feel that way. It'll take more than that for me to walk away."

"I hope so."

Aurelia looked at me with more emotion in her eyes than I remembered ever seeing in them before. Fear and concern mingled together. She blinked, and they were masked again. "I will stay close by as often as I can. If I sense that you are leaving the building, I will stop you."

"Don't neglect Arion." A sad smile touched my lips. "He needs you, too."

She walked to the door, stopping before opening it. "He is getting better. I will leave now, check on him, and be back before nightfall. Be careful."

Chapter 20

Whisked Away

The urge to go outside was overwhelming. I covered my head with a pillow and pulled Cody's arms around me, but I couldn't fight the impulse any longer. I snuck into the hallway.

Aurelia leaned against the wall, waiting for me.

"I'm sorry." I combed my fingers through my hair, trying to tame my curls. "I couldn't resist any longer."

"Do not be ashamed." She pushed off the wall and walked toward the stairs. "The best of us cannot ignore the call of a demon. Shall we?"

It took me a few seconds to comprehend her words and actions. For a moment, I wondered if Mavros could control her.

She seemed more likely to lock me in my room and throw away the key. "Really?"

"If you do not go to him, he will keep summoning you." She glanced over her shoulder. "At least if I am with you, you will be safe."

The two of us stepped outside together. One moment, the black panther strolled toward us. The next, a god among men sauntered over. I sucked in a deep breath as I took in Mavros. I tried to picture him differently, but I couldn't—he was chiseled perfection.

"This is not between us, *dragon*." Mavros spat out the word with all the venom he could muster. "You know that you cannot interfere."

"I am not," she responded. "I am here as Dacia's friend. That is within my power."

"Make sure that you don't overstep your boundaries." His eyes softened as he gazed at me, and he held his hand out. "Dacia, my love, will you walk with me?"

I reached out, unable to stop myself, and placed my hand in his. A jolt of electricity shot through my fingers, leaving my body tingling. He enfolded me in his arms. His supple lips pressed against mine. Somewhere in the background, I heard Aurelia growl, but she didn't move toward us.

When he pulled away, black bat-like wings sprouted from his back, blotting out the stars. He held me around the waist and flew off toward the Snowfire Mountains. I remembered thinking, *Aurelia is not going to like this,* but I didn't care. Flying through the night sky with him was exhilarating. The warmth of his body kept the chill away.

He landed near a mountain lake and set me down. "I'm sorry, but I didn't think we needed a babysitter."

"It's fine." I rubbed my arms, trying to warm them. "It's beautiful up here but cold." I wasn't dressed for a trip to the mountains. I was wearing my pajamas, shorts and a t-shirt. I didn't even have shoes on.

"I should've thought of that." He took his leather jacket off and wrapped it around my shoulders. "I just wanted to get you away. Without time with you, how am I supposed to prove my love?"

I slipped my arms into the coat's sleeves and lifted the collar to my nose, breathing in deeply. It smelled like warm summer nights and something I couldn't place. "Help me find some firewood?"

Mavros held my hand while we collected sticks. We piled the branches in a rock ring at the edge of the lake. Then I concentrated until a ball of fire ignited in the palm of my hand. I threw it, and the wood burst into flames. Mavros sat down on the beach, and I snuggled up against him, resting my head on his shoulder.

"I have something for you." He slid his hand into his jacket pocket, pressing his body against mine, and pulled out a black velvet box. When he handed it to me, his eyes were filled with something different … hope, maybe?

"Oh." I'm not sure if the gift or the look in his eyes surprised me more. I lifted the lid to find a panther intricately carved from a black star sapphire hanging on a silver chain. "Thank you. It's beautiful."

"Anything for you." He smiled at me, an angelic smile that didn't belong on the face of a demon. He took the necklace out of the box and fastened it around my neck. His hands brushed against my skin, and goosebumps rose all over my body.

"This is nice," I said. "It's very peaceful here."

He rubbed my arm. "I'm glad you like it. The time I get to spend with you means a lot to me. If you do send me back to the Abyss, I'll carry this time with me to help me get through it."

"Why would I send you back to the Abyss?" I felt like he was speaking Greek. He didn't make any sense at all. "I want you to stay right here with me." I pressed my fingers against my chest, emphasizing my words. "I want you to be with me forever."

Mavros stood up and walked to the other side of the campfire. "Do you really want me to stay?"

"Yes." I watched him, trying to figure out why he'd left my side, taking his warmth with him when he walked away. "I want you to stay."

He looked away from me. "Will you be mine so I can?"

"I …" My voice faltered. The words caught in my throat. I looked down and saw the ring on my finger. "I'm sorry." I looked back up in time to see his shoulders hunch forward. "I'm sorry, but I can't do that. I can't be with you. I'm with Cody."

He walked back over, stopping in front of me, and looked down. "Haven't I shown you my feelings for you are true?"

"You've shown me passion and desire." I fiddled with the necklace he gave me. "You've shown me you can be kind and gentle, but I haven't seen love."

"Then I'll have to keep trying." He sat next to me but didn't touch me this time. "I imagine the dragon is getting anxious. Would you like me to take you back?"

"That's probably a good idea," I said. His eyes met mine, and I snuggled against him. "But, this is the most relaxed I've been in a long time."

"We could stay … for a few more minutes … if you'd like." He pulled me closer. His warmth seeped into me.

I sighed in contentment. "Just a few." I felt his breath against my cheek and tilted my head back.

"Somehow, I will find a way to convince you," he whispered in my ear.

We sat on the beach a while longer. The gentle lapping of the waves and the crackling of the fire were hypnotic. I stared into the dancing flames. The tension in my shoulders eased. I closed my eyes and imagined how life could be with Mavros.

"We should go."

I opened my eyes to find a contented smile on Mavros' lips. "You look happy." I reached up, tracing my fingers over his mouth.

"How could I not be here with you?" He stood and helped me to my feet.

I faced the lake and acted like I was scooping water in a bucket. I threw the water on the fire to douse the flames. When it was out, Mavros sprouted his wings and flew off into the night with me in his arms.

He set me down in the shelter of the trees near Wisteria Hall. "Thank you for a wonderful evening, Dacia." He brushed his lips over mine and disappeared.

When I walked back into my room, four relieved faces looked up at me.

I pulled the door shut quietly. "I'm sorry."

"It is not your fault, Dacia." Aurelia walked over, evaluating me. "I told them what happened. I explained that I took you outside. I had no idea he would take you away. I am the one who should be sorry. He would have kept calling you. I thought it was the best decision. I was wrong."

"He took me into the mountains." I didn't look at any of them. I didn't want to see the disgust on their faces. "He tried to get me to choose him, but I didn't."

"Were you cold?" Cody's hands curled into fists. His body was rigid.

"Oh." I tugged Mavros' jacket off and threw it on the floor. The warmth leached out of my body. I stared at his coat, wondering how I could've forgotten I'd been wearing it. "I was. I wasn't planning a trip to the mountains. I'm still in my pajamas. I don't even have shoes on."

I stepped toward Cody, but he backed away. "I … I didn't mean to go. I thought Aurelia would stop me." I sank to the floor and put my head in my hands. The panther dangled from my neck. My hands trembled, making it impossible to unclasp it. "I can't …" A sob caught in my throat, stopping my words. "I can't get this off!"

"A necklace." Cody groaned. "He's giving you jewelry?"

I hated myself for what this was doing to Cody, but how could I stop it? I couldn't avoid Mavros. I couldn't ignore his summons.

Samantha knelt beside me, lifting my hair to take the necklace off. "Ouch!" she yelled when she touched the chain. She jerked her hand up and stuck her fingers in her mouth. After a moment, she pulled them out. "I can't take it off you, Dacia. It burned me."

Cody ran his hand down his face. His lips turned up in an angry smile. His eyes narrowed.

I stood and reached out to him. "I'm sorry," I whispered.

Without saying a word, he stormed out of the room, slamming the door behind him. A few seconds later, we heard Marcy yell, "Cody Hawks, what are you doing here this time of night?!"

"Leaving!" he yelled back at her.

"I'm reporting this tomorrow morning!"

My heart plummeted, leaving me hollow and broken. I doubled over, gasping. When the room started spinning, I fell to the floor. The soft ticking of the clock crescendoed until the silence was as loud as Cody slamming the door had been.

"I am singlehandedly ruining everything. I should have just put up with it. I should have put headphones on and ignored him."

"You know that would not have stopped it. They"—Aurelia pointed at Samantha and Dan—"might think that would work, but we both know better. You do not hear him calling. You are just drawn out to him. There is nothing you can do to stop it."

"Is that true, Dacia?" Samantha sat on the floor beside me.

"Yes, if I'd heard him, I would've known what I was walking into last night." I took a deep breath and turned to Aurelia. "Can you keep an eye on Cody for me?"

"Yes." She headed out the door.

"He'll be back." Dan's hair was tousled. He was shirtless, and his hands were stuffed into the pockets of his pajama pants.

I shook my head. "Why? Why would he come back?" I swiped at my eyes. "Would you? If your girlfriend was cheating on you, sneaking out in the middle of the night to see another guy, would you forgive her?"

"It's not like that, and you know it, Dacia." Samantha's voice rose in anger.

"Why isn't it?" Without Cody, I'd never get through this. I would've promised my heart to Mavros if I hadn't thought of Cody. "The guy I'm sneaking off to see is a demon, but it has to hurt Cody the same as if I was sneaking off to be with any other guy on campus. It has to break his heart to wake up and find me gone, to have me come back wearing a necklace given to me by another guy … wearing his jacket. I couldn't be that forgiving. Could either of you?" I looked each of them in the eyes, daring them to deny the truth.

"But …" Samantha looked away from me. "He loves you."

"I do." Cody reappeared in the middle of the floor with Aurelia at his side. "But, don't know if I can do this." He looked calmer, but fine lines of anger etched his face.

"You have to," Aurelia said. "If you do not stand by her, she will suffer the same fate as Elizabeth. Thoughts of you make it possible for her to say no to him. Without you, she will fail."

A muscle in Cody's jaw ticked. "So, I'm supposed to deal with her running to Mavros, and what? Be happy about it?"

What Cody said was a repeat of what I'd just told Samantha and Dan, but hearing it from his mouth, ripped my heart out. All the torture I'd been through in the last year had nothing on the pain I felt now. I folded myself into the fetal position, closed my eyes, and let my tears flow.

Cody blew out a weighty sigh. "I'm sorry, Dacia." He knelt beside me, his thumbs wiping the tears from my face.

I heard the door close and realized Samantha, Dan, and Aurelia had left. I sat up and faced Cody. "I-it's fine. I understand." He looked like he was going to start talking, so I held my hand up to stop him. "I couldn't handle it. I hate myself for doing this to you. I hate that I'm too weak to stop him from controlling me."

"Don't … don't hate yourself, Dacia."

The pain in his eyes about undid me. "Why shouldn't I? All I do is hurt you." I stared down at my hands, twirling my promise ring on my finger. I hadn't had it very long, but in that time, I'd gotten used to it being there. A fist clenched my heart, squeezing an extra beat out of it, when I realized I was going to have to give it back to him. "It's better if I hate myself than if you hate me."

"Don't hate you." His voice was a little less than a whisper.

"Not yet."

Cody had always been the rock in our relationship, but he looked vulnerable hunched over with his hands on his lap. He ran his fingers through his hair and let out a ragged breath.

"Can't hate you for this. Not your fault. Can't help that he controls you. Can't help that he set his sights on you."

"Maybe not, but … I can't keep doing this to you." I took my ring off before I could change my mind and held it out to him.

"Don't want that back. Please, don't make me, Dacia." He pushed my hand away. "Give me time."

The ring sat in the palm of my hand. The ruby sparkled. "It'll keep happening. I can't stop it."

Cody curled my fingers over and pushed my hand down. Then he pulled away like he couldn't bear touching me. "Didn't like seeing you in his jacket." His voice was soft, but anger and betrayal simmered in it, threatening to erupt. "Don't like him giving you gifts." He dragged his hands down his face. "Didn't mean to hurt you."

I lifted my hand, wanting to comfort him but afraid he'd pull away again.

He looked at my hand, then my face. "Don't know how to handle it. I'm jealous 'n' angry."

"Do you think I don't know that?" I clutched my promise ring, unsure if I dared to put it back on. If I did, I wasn't sure if I could take it off again without losing a piece of myself. "Do you think I don't see how this is destroying you? I hate it! I wish there was something I could do, but I can't. All I can do is sneak out of here like a rat being called by the Pied Piper. I'm breaking your heart, and I hate myself for it!"

"Stop saying that." His voice was harsh, and his irises were icy.

I held the ring out again. "Please … please take your ring back. Find somebody else. Somebody who'll be good for you."

Tears dampened his eyes. "No, Dacia, please don't." He wrapped his arms around me and pulled me onto his lap. His hand ran through my hair as he rocked back and forth. "Please don't. Don't hate yourself. We'll find a way through."

"How?"

"We will." He pressed his cheek against mine. "We love each other. We'll get it." He peeled my fingers back, revealing the ring. "Put it on. We have what? Twenty-eight or twenty-nine days? We can make it, right?"

I couldn't say anything. I wrapped my arms around his neck and buried my face in his chest.

Chapter 21

*M*y eyes were swollen and sore when I woke up. I wasn't ready to face another day. My dreams had been filled with visions of Cody leaving me, and even though I woke up in his arms, I knew there was a chance they would come true. If he'd seen me in Mavros' arms last night, he'd hate me as much as I hated myself. He'd know there was a reason for his anger.

"Hey." Cody's voice was husky. "You okay? Nightmare?"

"Why do you care?" It came out harsher than I'd intended. "How can you?"

He pressed up onto his elbow and looked at me. "Whaddo you mean?"

"With everything I put you through, why do you want to be with me?"

"I love you. It's not your fault. Once Mavros is in the Abyss, things'll go back to normal."

"Normal?" I laughed humorlessly. "What's normal? Nefarious … Draconian … dragons … Mavros. There is no normal."

"So, you don't wanna try?"

"I don't understand why you do." Once again, I was hurting him, and this time I could do something about it. So, why wasn't I stopping?

"Dacia, you're my world … my life." He brushed my hair back from my face. "You're going through a lot. Sorry for the way I acted."

"For the way you acted?" I jerked away from him, not understanding how he could take the blame. "What about the way I acted? How can you blame yourself? This is all on me, Cody. I'm the bad guy, not you. I'm the one who snuck off to be with a demon. I'm the one who flew off into the mountains with him. I'm the one who came back still wearing his coat. Not you. You did nothing."

"Please, Dacia, please … don't do this." He squeezed his leg between mine, pulling our bodies closer together.

"You left me in my dream." I pressed my hands against his chest, holding him back far enough for me to look into his eyes. "I can understand that. I can't understand why you're holding me now."

"Because I love you … because I promised to take care of you." He held my hand up and twirled my promise ring. "Promised to love you forever, and I will."

"Are you sure this is what you want?"

"You're mine, Dacia. When you accepted that ring, you made a promise to me." Anger colored his voice. "Just because Mavros made a play for you, don't expect me to back down. I'm gonna fight like hell to keep you."

"But, he doesn't fight fair." I remembered the dream I had before my birthday. Cody's broken body filled my vision.

"That's okay." A slight smile pulled up his lips. "I have the advantage." He put his hand over my heart. "This belongs to me."

"Hear, hear." Samantha cheered him on.

"Good speech, Cody." Dan peered over my loft at me.

I looked at the three of them and couldn't help but smile. "Well, I'm glad you're ready because you're in for one hell of a fight." I traced my fingers along his face. "Are you sure the prize is worth it?"

"Only prize I want."

Even though I didn't want to, I got up and went to class. I needed to pretend my life was normal. So far this week, going to classes had been a waste of time. I hadn't paid attention in any of them. My grades were going to suffer this semester if I didn't start concentrating during lectures and doing my homework.

My first class was Creative Writing. Of all the classes I'd taken this semester, there was a better chance this one would hold my attention. Aurelia walked me to the door before telling me she was skipping. "I want to spend some time with Arion. He needs to get out and exercise. I will be waiting for you when class lets out."

"Be careful." I walked into the room feeling like there was a lead weight in my stomach.

I sat at my desk, doodling on a piece of paper. With every stroke of my pencil, I saw the look of disgust on Cody's face when he realized I had Mavros' coat on. I saw his revulsion when he saw the pendant dangling from my neck. I kept hearing the door slam, the sound of him walking away. How could I keep from hurting him? If I managed to send Mavros back to the Abyss, would I win, or would I end up losing everything that mattered?

"May I sit here?" somebody asked.

"Yeah, sure," I said without looking up.

The chair scraped across the ground, and the owner of the voice plopped down so close to me that I felt the warmth radiating off of his body.

I slid my chair away from him and started shading the mountain scene.

A hand shot between my paper and my face. "My name is Damon."

How rude, I thought to myself. I shook his hand just to get him to move it. "I'm Dacia. Are you new here?"

"Yeah, I actually just got here yesterday."

With that comment, I looked at him for the first time. He wore a tight black t-shirt that failed to hide his muscular body. His hair was dark and tousled. Glancing into his eyes, I sucked in a startled breath. They looked just like Mavros'.

"What's wrong?" He edged his chair closer to mine than was necessary. "Is everything okay?"

"Yeah, I'm fine." I moved my backpack and scooted away from him. "You remind me of somebody."

A playful smile tugged at his lips, drawing my attention to his mouth. "Somebody you like, I hope."

"Yeah, somebody I like even though I shouldn't." My voice trailed off. *Why can't you just keep your mouth shut?* I thought to myself.

He raised one eyebrow. "Why not? Did he do something to you?"

"It's complicated." This wasn't something I wanted to discuss with a total stranger. I went back to doodling, hoping he'd drop it.

"Well, if you need to talk or need a shoulder or whatever, let me know." He edged closer. "Like tomorrow night, we could go to dinner."

"Oh." My pen slipped, rolling off the desk. "I can't, but thanks for the offer."

Damon bent over and grabbed it. Then he seized my hand, gently wrapping my fingers around the pen.

I was too shocked to move, to pull away, to tell him to get out of my space.

His fingers brushed mine as he pulled away. "Maybe some other time then."

"I'm, uh …" I lifted my hand, pointing at my ring. "I'm flattered, but my boyfriend wouldn't like that."

He leaned closer to me. "You don't have to tell him." His eyes sparkled with mischief.

"Do you know anybody named Mavros?" The question popped into my head and out of my mouth at the same time. Mentally, I slapped my forehead.

"No, why?" His face didn't give anything away. He didn't look surprised by my question or on guard or anything.

"That's just who you remind me of. It's your eyes. They look just like his." *But they don't have the same effect on me,* I thought to myself. *Thank God!*

A cocky grin drew my focus to his mouth. He licked his lips, and his smile widened. "Is he as charming and attractive as me?"

"Uh, well, he's the best looking guy I've ever seen, and he can be very charming."

"So, what's the deal?" His fingers brushed my shoulder. "If you like him so much, why are you with this other guy?"

"It's complicated." I pointed my pen at him. "Remember?"

"Oh, so we're back to that again?"

"Unless the two of you want to share your words of wisdom with the rest of the class, could you please quiet down?" Professor Fisher asked. "They actually pay me to talk, and since I need the money, I would like to do my job now."

"Sorry." Heat crept up my neck and onto my face.

When class was over, I shoved everything into my backpack and darted for the door. I was hoping to avoid another conversation with Damon. His persistence was overwhelming.

Unfortunately, he fell into step beside me, closer than comfortable. "So … what other classes do you have?"

We walked through the hallway surrounded by students. Voices bounced off the ceiling, and footsteps pounded against the tile floor.

"I have Mythology this afternoon and Scientific Computing and Shakespeare on Mondays, Wednesdays, and Fridays. What about you?" I asked more to be polite than anything else.

He smiled a cute lopsided smile. "Oddly enough, I have the same schedule."

"Oh, well that's quite a coincidence."

"Or … maybe it's fate." He shrugged and held the door open for me.

As soon as we stepped outside, the fresh, clean air whisked away the stale scent from the hallway.

I lifted onto my toes, searching for Aurelia. As soon as I saw her, tension fled from my muscles. I veered toward her, and Damon shadowed me. As we strode closer, I noticed her watching Damon and looking between the two of us. She fell into step beside us, and Damon didn't even seem to notice her. Of all the things I'd seen since starting college, this was the strangest. Everyone stared at Aurelia the first time they met her. Some people never quit staring.

He grabbed my elbow, stopping me. "Can I join you for lunch?"

"Look, Damon"—my voice was harsher than I meant it to be—"you seem like a nice guy, but my dance card is full. I already have a guy trying to pull me away from Cody, and I don't think I can deal with another one right now."

He nodded and dropped my arm. "So that's the complication with Mavros. Okay, I'll back off. I'll listen if you want to talk. I'll be here if you want me to be, but other than that, I'll lay off."

"Thank you." I smiled at him. I hadn't expected that to go so well.

"See you in Mythology." He turned around, heading back the way we came from.

"What did you tell him about Mavros?" Aurelia asked in a fierce whisper.

"His eyes look like Mavros'." I dug through my backpack, searching for my sunglasses. "He was being relentless, so I asked him if he knew Mavros. I wanted to see if his expression gave anything away, but it didn't. Anyway, I told him that Mavros was a complicated subject, and that was the end of it." I hefted my bag onto my shoulders, and we started walking again.

Aurelia glanced over her shoulder a few times. I wondered if she sensed Mavros, but she didn't try to hurry me along.

"What?" I asked after she looked again.

"There is something about Damon that rubs me the wrong way. Something feels off about him."

I stepped closer to her and lowered my voice. "I think he's Mavros." I kicked a rock. It bounced along the sidewalk before rolling into the grass.

Aurelia's pupils slitted, and a nearly invisible stream of smoke blew out of her nostrils. "I will not skip classes if that is the case. You seem to be a magnet for trouble." Her dragon hovered just beneath the surface.

I looked away from her, afraid of challenging her and making things worse. "I wish I wasn't. I'd change it if I could."

"I know you would." She rested her hand on my shoulder.

I glanced at her. Her pupils were round again. "Why is evil drawn to me?" With her already riled up, it probably wasn't the best time to ask, but I needed to know.

"They feel your strength." She lowered her hand. "I have never seen another like you, and unfortunately, evil is drawn to power. All the demons, all the villains will want you to stand with them. Each of them will want you for their own. They do not understand that you are a phenomenon ... a genuinely good person."

I stopped walking and lowered my head. I didn't want to hear what she had to say. I longed for peace. I didn't want me or my friends to keep going through this. How long could I keep them safe? "I'm never going to get a break. Am I?"

"I hope you do, Dacia." Sympathy and sadness filled her golden eyes. "However, I do not see it happening, not for a long time. I thought you might have a chance, but then Mavros showed up. It was too soon. Nothing should have happened to you ... not for months or maybe even years. There was a possibility it was just a coincidence that Draconian found you so soon after you defeated Nefarious, but Mavros has proven it is more than an unfortunate twist of fate."

I swallowed the lump in my throat and turned my eyes away from hers. "That's not what I wanted to hear, but thank you for telling me the truth." I turned back to her, feeling tears roll down my cheeks. "I can't keep dragging my friends through this. I can't keep endangering their lives."

"If Arion has taught me anything, it is that you need friends, and they need you." She gave me a sideways hug. "You cannot leave them out of this. I know that is not what you wanted to hear, but whether you like it or not, they are part of your life."

My pulse ratcheted up as fear twisted my gut. "How can I keep putting them through this? How can I continue allowing them to be tortured and kidnapped and traumatized … and maybe even killed?" I felt like I was stuck in quicksand, slowly being pulled under.

Students veered around us. Several looked at me with concern, others indifference, and some disgust. I wiped my eyes and focused on each step.

Aurelia's voice was soothing. "They love you and want to help. If they could, they would move mountains for you." She held the door to Wisteria Hall open. "If standing by your side is the most they can do, they will take the hardships that come with that decision. You have to let them make their own choices. If it becomes too much for them to handle, they will walk away on their own."

Before starting up the stairs, I turned and looked her directly in the eyes. "I know that I need them, but are you sure they need me?"

"Yes."

I trudged up the stairs, trailing my hand along the railing. "Cody is not going to like Damon." He'd already put up with enough thanks to Mavros. He didn't need to see Damon vying for my affection too.

She nodded. "It promises to be an interesting afternoon."

Cody, Dan, and Samantha beat Aurelia and me back to the room. Samantha sat at the computer doing her homework. Cody and Dan leaned forward with controllers clutched in their hands. Their cars raced across the television screen. Dan's crossed the finish line first. He pumped his fist in the air.

As soon as Cody finished, he looked over his shoulder at me. "Hey. How'd it go?"

I tugged my hand through my hair. "I need to talk to you."

Cody's face fell, and he patted the seat next to him.

"There's a new guy on campus." He looked at me funny but let me continue without interrupting. "He's in all of my classes, and he seems to be interested in me."

"And?" His voice was distant.

I grabbed his hand. "I love you. I don't want anything to do with anybody else. And, I don't trust Damon. His eyes remind me of Mavros."

"That doesn't sound good," Samantha interjected.

Glancing over my shoulder at her, I said, "No, I'm more than a little concerned."

"If he is Mavros and the amulet works, we should find out in Mythology," Aurelia said.

Cody pulled his hand out of mine and slumped down, leaning his head on the back of the couch. "Do I hope it's more competition or that Mavros is in all your classes?" He covered his face. "The fun never ends."

Walking to class, Cody held my hand, but he seemed aloof. I shouldn't have done it, but I wanted to know what he was thinking. After a slight hesitation, I eavesdropped on his thoughts.

More competition? I'm nothing special, nothing like her. If he's Mavros, there's nothing I can do about it, but if he isn't, he better be ready for a fight.

Samantha, Dan, and Aurelia walked in front of us, talking amongst themselves. I pulled back on Cody's hand, slowing him down. "I know you don't want to meet Damon." I kept my voice low, hoping to keep the conversation between us. "I know you're trying really hard not to let this bother you, but I want you to know he means nothing to me. He never will."

"Thanks, Dacia." He squeezed my hand. "Means a lot."

The classroom was empty when we walked in. I sat in the back with Aurelia and Cody on each side. Dan and Samantha took the seats in front of me.

I drummed my pen against my desk, watching the door, wondering how Damon would act. I only had to wait a few minutes to find out. Even though I didn't want anything to do with him, I couldn't help but admire the way he walked into the room with an air of confidence nobody deserved to have.

His eyes met mine, and a smile lit up his face. "Hello, Dacia." He sat down in front of Cody and angled his desk toward mine.

"Hi, Damon. These are my friends: Cody, Dan, and Samantha." I pointed at each of them as I said their name.

He kept his eyes focused on me. "Nice to meet you."

Samantha reached around Dan, sticking her hand out for Damon to shake. "Welcome to Phlox University. I hope you like it here."

"Thank you." He took her hand, never taking his eyes off me.

All through class, every time I looked up, Damon was staring at me. A cocky grin pulled his lips up.

Cody's fists were clenched. He ground his teeth together.

I ran my hand along his leg, trying to get him to relax, and prayed Damon wouldn't do anything during class.

As soon as Dr. Cedar dismissed us, Damon said, "Are you sure you don't want to go out with me this weekend?"

I stared at him with my mouth hanging open. "Uh, seriously?"

"Yeah." He stepped closer to me. "I know you think Cody's the love of your life, but you might find out differently if you give me a chance."

Cody stepped forward. I grabbed his belt loop and thought to him, *Please don't. It's what he wants.*

I took Cody's hand, leading him out of the room. Damon fell into step beside me. "I'm with Cody, and I'm not going out with you. So, please give it a rest!"

He tucked a strand of hair behind my ear. "Okay, for now. You'll think about me. You'll wonder what it'd be like to be with a real man." His fingers brushed my cheek as he lowered his hand. "In the end, you'll choose me." A smile covered his face. It was a smile that promised trouble.

"What an ass," Cody said through clenched teeth as Damon walked off in the other direction.

Cassandra stomped past us with her friends. She spun around, her face red with anger. "So, one guy's not good enough? You have to have them fighting over you?" She threw her arms up. "I don't get what they see in you."

In my first semester at Phlox University, I'd had enough of Cassandra to last my entire lifetime. I didn't need her holier-than-thou-attitude. "I imagine they see that I'm not you, and that's more than enough to satisfy most guys."

"One of these days, you're going to realize that you're not all that." She waved her hand up and down, emphasizing her point.

I shrugged off her insult. "I've known that all my life. I think you're the one who's finally figuring it out."

She stepped closer. Bryce's hand shot out, clutching her arm. "It's not worth it, Cassi. Let's go." She shot me a look that could kill and stormed off.

I watched her stomp away, wondering if she would ever be civil to me. "It's a good thing Mavros wasn't interested in her. She'd have joined him without a second thought."

"Yes." Aurelia looked at me, then at Cassandra and her friends. "Either Mavros enjoys a challenge or he wants to ensure that he will not be threatened once he is able to stay on Earth."

Cassandra was far enough ahead of us that I started walking again. "Wouldn't others like me stand against him?"

"They would." Aurelia strode beside me, keeping an eye out for any signs of trouble. "However, you are the most powerful human on Earth right now."

"I don't want to be." I kicked a rock into the trees. "I just want a normal life."

"Well, if Mavros wouldn't have chosen you, he might've won already." Samantha walked backward in front of me. "I know you don't want this responsibility, but I'm glad you're here protecting us. You're good at it." She turned back around without missing a step.

"She's right." Dan looked over his shoulder at me. "If somebody else had the power that you have, they might not use it for good. Luckily, besides being powerful, you've got morals."

Would you think that if you knew I'd read Cody's mind or if you knew how Mavros made me feel? I wondered to myself.

"My turn." Samantha glanced around to make sure nobody was paying attention to us. "When I shook Damon's hand, the amulet lit up like the Fourth of July. He's definitely Mavros."

"Good to know." Cody blew out a relieved sigh. "Only one guy to deal with."

"The bad part is I had to shake his hand before anything happened." Samantha fiddled with her bracelet. "We won't know when he's near like Dacia did with Nefarious. The amulet won't be very helpful."

"I hoped it would work, but it looks like Samantha is right," Aurelia said.

I pulled my hand through my hair, wishing that something could work in my favor. "Well, there's not really any sense in wearing it if that's the case. If you want to give it back to Sarah, we can."

Samantha shook her head. "I'll keep it on for a while. You never know what'll happen."

"In the meantime—" I looked at Cody, knowing he wouldn't like what I was about to ask "—what am I supposed to do about Damon?"

"Easy." Dan shrugged. "Tell him you know who he is."

I rubbed the back of my neck afraid of what Cody would think of what I was about to say. "Maybe I can use this to my advantage."

Aurelia tapped her finger against her lips. "Maybe if you string Damon along, you can keep Mavros from summoning you at night."

"Ugh." Cody groaned, clenching and unclenching his fists. "Why can't Dacia just be with me? Why does this have to be so difficult?"

"If it keeps me from going out to him at night, is it worth it?" I knew this was tearing him up, but I also knew he wanted what was best for me. "It's not like I want to be with him, but I think he's safer as Damon than as Mavros."

"Mavros is willing to do whatever it takes to get Dacia alone with him." Aurelia's voice was gentle, her eyes sympathetic. "When he is Damon, he does not have the same effect on her. For some reason, he has not tried to control her yet."

"It's not like I have to go out with him." I fidgeted with the panther pendant, unintentionally drawing Cody's attention to it. "I need to be nice to him in class and let him think I might go out with him."

"It should keep him satisfied for a while," Aurelia said, "maybe even long enough that we can figure out what to do."

Cody's shoulders slumped. "Don't like it, but I'll do what I can." He sounded defeated.

Marcy turned onto the sidewalk in front of us. Her ponytail bounced against her shoulders. Seeing her made me realize Cody and I needed to be elsewhere. Grabbing Cody's hand, I stopped him. "We need to see Sarah."

The others watched us.

"Why?" he asked.

I closed my eyes and pinched the bridge of my nose. "Last night."

"Doesn't need to know I was a jerk." Anger or maybe regret colored his voice.

"Marcy caught you in the hall. We need to let her know it won't happen again."

"Yeah." He let go of my hand and turned around. "Suppose."

Cody and I walked to Sarah's office in silence. His head drooped, and his face was stony. I hadn't even made it through one day without hurting him. Could we make it through four more weeks, or would our relationship crumble all around us?

Cody stood in front of Cacomistle Hall. He took a deep, steadying breath and reached for the door.

"Wait," I said.

He lowered his hand and watched me in the reflection.

I reached for his arm, and he tensed. Dropping my hand, I said, "I'm sorry, Cody. I don't know what else to do."

"Yeah."

The wind picked up, whipping my hair around my head. "I don't want this. I don't want him."

He slowly turned. His eyes were red. "Will we make it through this?"

"Oh, Cody." I wrapped my arms around his waist and pressed my forehead against his chest. "I love you, and nothing's going to change that."

His hands brushed over my shoulders and down my back. "I'm scared."

"Me, too."

Hand in hand, we walked inside. Alicia sat behind the desk. Her blonde hair stuck up like a porcupine's quills.

"Hi." I went up to the desk. "Can you let S— Dean Aspen know we're here?"

She nodded, waving toward the seating area with her manicured fingers.

We'd barely sat down when she said, "Go on up."

Sarah stood at the door, waiting for us. "Well, you saved me a trip." Her expression was stern, her voice grave. She ushered us in and paced in front of us. "Marcy was here this morning ranting about you, Cody. Why were you causing a commotion?"

"We were fighting." He stood with his hands shoved in his pockets, staring at the floor.

"At three in the morning?"

His shoulders tightened, and his jaw twitched.

"That's when I got back." I waved at the couch. "Why don't you sit down?" I told her everything, not leaving anything out.

"Cody." Sarah's expression had softened.

He looked at her. His face was a blank mask.

"I understand this is difficult for you."

A strangled smile fell from his face. "That's an understatement."

"If you are going to stay there, to keep Dacia safe, you are going to have to follow the rules." She folded her arms over her chest. "You cannot be seen there again."

"I'm sorry, Sarah. I won't."

I was impressed with Cody for not making excuses.

"You've put me in a difficult position." Sarah stood and paced behind the couch. "If you get caught there again, I'll have to expel you for the rest of the semester. That won't do anybody any good."

"She was wearing his coat and a necklace." He stared down at his hands. A muscle ticked in his jaw. "Jealousy got the best of me."

"Make sure Marcy sees you leave tonight and every other night." She patted Cody on the shoulder before sitting down and focusing on me. "The amulet isn't helping?"

Rubbing my hand along my forehead, I looked at Cody. I didn't know how much more he could handle. "Cody can't wear it. If he touches me, it burns him."

She tilted her head, and her eyebrows pressed together. "Why?"

Cody squeezed my knee, then stood and walked into the hall.

"I suppose for the same reason it glows when I touch it." While Cody wasn't in earshot, I told Sarah about Damon and our plan for me to lead him on for as long as I could.

That night when Mavros summoned me to join him, I woke Cody. "I need your help. Mavros is calling me to him. I don't want to go, but I can't help myself."

"Whaddo you need? Tell me, and I'll do it."

"Hold me tight, and don't let go."

He wrapped his arms around me, and I nuzzled into his chest. His head rested on mine, but I still felt Mavros' pull. I kissed Cody's neck, making my way up to his mouth. His lips were soft and warm against mine. The heat between us ignited, and he returned my kiss with unbridled passion. I wrapped my arms around his neck and twined my fingers through his hair, tugging him closer to me. His hands traced down my back. One hand traveled down my leg, pulling it up over his.

Mavros continued summoning me, but the draw lessened.

"It's working," I whispered.

A smile played across his lips. "Can do this every night."

"You'd probably do this every night even if it didn't help." I ran my hands over his chest, memorizing the feel of his body.

"Yeah." His voice was husky. "I would."

"He won't forgive me for this." I kissed his chin. "I'll pay for it."

"Sorry." He pulled me closer, tilting my face up. The tips of his fingers glided over my cheeks, and his lips brushed across mine, drowning out Mavros' call.

Eventually, Cody and I drifted off to sleep.

Chapter 22

What Choice Do I Have?

Mavros and I are at the lake in the mountains. Cool wind raises goosebumps over my exposed flesh. The moon hangs low in the sky. A pink glow spreads over the Eastern horizon.

He stands with his back to me. I stare into a campfire, watching the embers. They flicker from red to orange to gray and back again.

"Dacia, why do you insist on doing this to yourself?" His voice is low with a hard edge. "Why won't you accept you were meant to be with me so we can move on?"

"Because I wasn't meant to be with you." I rub my arms, trying to warm them. "I was meant to be with Cody."

He pivots to face me. "I don't want to kill you, Dacia. I want you to be with me … forever, but if you continue along this course, I will have no choice."

I look up at the stars, knowing that if I meet his eyes, he'll control me. "You always have a choice. You can always change your path."

His steps crunch over the rocks. "But, why would I want to?"

"You said you wanted to be good." I close my eyes, lowering my head. "You said not all demons are evil. Prove it. Let me have the life I want. You'll return. Maybe next time, she'll want you. Maybe she won't have given her heart away already."

"And, maybe she'll return me to the Abyss." He stops in front of me. The tips of his boots nearly touch my bare feet.

I take a step back. "That's the chance you'd have to take. So, are you good or are you evil?"

"I'm a demon." He leans in, whispering in my ear. "What do you think I am?"

"You can be anything you want."

"Look at me, Dacia." His voice compels me.

I fight the urge to lift my head, to look into his face, but the pull is too strong. My eyes are drawn to his. Long, dark lashes frame obsidian irises. Desire washes over me.

"Do you really want me to go away?" His voice is silky smooth.

"No." I reach my hand out, cupping his cheek. His skin is soft and warm. "I want you to stay with me forever."

"Why do you keep trying to send me away?"

I drop my hand to my side and whisper, "Cody." His name breaks Mavros' hold over me.

"Ugh, I'm so sick of that name." He turns away from me. "If you send me back to the Abyss, you sentence Cody to death, and it will not be a quick one at that, my love. I will make him suffer … just as you are making me suffer."

I stumble back. "So you're leaving me no choice?"

"Well, as you so kindly told me earlier, you always have a choice." He spits my words back at me, then turns to face me again, looking into my eyes. "I know it's in you to make the right choice. When the time comes, Dacia, you will choose me."

Chapter 23

The sun peaked in through a crack in the curtains. My legs were tangled with Cody's, and his arm was thrown over me. He looked peaceful and relaxed, but I felt like a thousand spiders crawled through my stomach.

Fear of what the day would bring pressed down on me. I didn't want to flirt with Damon. I didn't want to lead him on. I knew who he was, and I wanted nothing to do with him, but that wasn't the plan. The plan was for Aurelia to skip classes again and for me to pretend to fall for Damon's act.

I disentangled myself from Cody, grabbed my clothes, and went down to the bathroom to shower. By the time I got back, the others were awake.

Cody's mask was back in place. I sat beside him, taking his hand. He rubbed his thumb along mine.

As soon as Samantha was dressed and ready for class, I teleported all of us to Cody and Dan's room. While they showered, I paced.

Samantha walked to the window and stared outside. "He'll be all right, you know."

"Will he?" I thought about how he'd looked after I'd returned the other night and what seeing me in Mavros' coat had done to him. I thought about how I'd feel if our places were reversed. "I wouldn't be."

On the way to class, more students milled about, discussing the black panther. Panic spread through me, tightening my chest, clenching my stomach, and weakening my legs. What if Mavros started attacking students to force me into making a decision? I only knew a handful of them, but everyone here had families and friends. Whether I knew them or not, all of their lives mattered.

"I saw it, too," a girl said. "It just sits outside the dorm staring up at somebody's room. It's kinda creepy."

"Yeah, Dave said he saw it, but when he turned for a double-take, there was nothing there but black smoke."

"I wonder what he's smoking." Drew Crocus, Cody's first roommate here, laughed. "I think it's time someone takes that cat out."

"Not a good idea." Cody stopped. He rubbed the back of his neck. "Let Dean Aspen know. She can call the DNR or something."

Drew smiled at him, one of those looks that promised trouble. "Where's the fun in that?"

"Staying alive." Cody shrugged.

When we were far enough away, I said, "I hope they don't do anything stupid."

"We all do." Samantha looked over her shoulder at me.

Aurelia joined us in class since everyone else was in there with me. When Damon entered, I felt the eyes of my friends on me.

"Hi, Dacia." He passed by my desk.

"Damon." I nodded at him. I watched him walk away, wondering what he was up to.

He turned, saw me looking at him, winked, and smiled. He sat a few seats down from me. Throughout class, I glanced at him a few times. He faced forward, listening to Professor Granite. On the way out, he was a perfect gentleman, holding the door open for me and my friends.

"Was that for my benefit?" Cody asked when Damon was out of sight.

"I don't know." The relief was evident in my voice.

"I would be more inclined to believe it was for Dacia's," Aurelia said.

You are going to be on your own this afternoon, Dacia, Aurelia projected her thoughts to me. *Neither Arion nor I will be watching over you. We need to find out what Mavros wants, and I fear the only way is to let you be on your own. If something happens, teleport back to your room.*

Are you sure? I asked her. *Can't you turn invisible and make sure I'm okay?*

I do not know if he can sense me. We will find out later, but I do not want your first meeting with him to be jeopardized by my presence.

Walking to Shakespeare, part of me was thrilled to be on my own, but part of me was terrified. I knew what Mavros was capable of. Without supervision, it could be like when he attacked me in the hallway. I took a deep breath and walked through the door. Damon wasn't in the classroom yet. I sat at a table near the back of the room and pulled out my paper and a pen. I drew a lion's head while I waited for him to show up.

He sat at the table beside me, hooked his foot around my chair, and pulled me closer to him. His leg pressed against mine. It took everything I had not to jerk away from him, but I needed him to think he had a chance.

"So, have you been thinking about me?" he asked with the confidence of someone who already knew the answer, and once again, I was thankful he didn't try to control me in this form.

"Well"—I twirled a curl around my finger—"a little more than I'd like to admit."

"I knew you would." A cocky grin brightened his face.

"Class is starting." I brought my finger to my lips. "I don't want to get in trouble again."

Damon rested his arm on the back of my chair throughout class. Every so often he'd play with my curls, brush my shoulder, or rub my neck. Every instinct told me to pull away from him, but instead, I leaned into his advances, allowing them to continue.

When class was over, Damon picked up my books and walked out with me. "Would you like to go to dinner with me?"

"You're persistent." I looked up at him through my eyelashes. "I'm not ready to do that yet. I can't stop thinking about you, but I … I'm with Cody."

"Won't you give me a chance?" He looked at me like a sad puppy.

"Let me get to know you." I brushed my fingers over his arm. "Give me some time."

"That's more than I dared hope for." He brought my hand to his lips and kissed it. "Maybe I'll see you around this weekend."

"Maybe." I tried to sound hopeful.

He continued walking with me. The wind blew my hair across my face, and Damon brushed it back. His hand lingered on my cheek. "Will you sit with me?" He pointed at one of the school's many benches.

This was what I was supposed to be doing, so even though I wanted to run off in the other direction, I nodded. "For a little bit."

As soon as we sat down, he threw his arm over my shoulders and pulled me closer to him than I was comfortable with.

However, like with Mavros, it felt good to be with him. He didn't control my mind like he did as Mavros, but I wondered if he had some control over my emotions.

"I'm glad you're reconsidering." He brushed his fingers along my neck, and I leaned into his caress. "There's just something about you that makes me feel like the two of us belong together."

Does he really think he's fooling me? Doesn't he realize I know who he is? "I'm drawn to you, too."

"But," he said. I shot him a curious look. "You forgot to say but. You know. But, Cody's in the way."

"If I hadn't known Cody all of my life, maybe I would feel differently." I bit my lip, pulling it into my mouth. "But, I can't break his heart unless I know for sure I'm doing it for the right reasons."

"Sit here with me for a while." He stretched his legs out in front of him and leaned back, closing his eyes. "We don't have to rush into anything. I just like being with you."

While he wasn't looking at me, I studied his features. I'm sure most girls and a lot of guys would have been flattered by his attention. He didn't look perfect like Mavros did, but he looked real … handsome. And, even though I knew he was a demon, he was likable. I was pretty sure his true colors weren't shining through, but … what if they were? What if he was good?

"What are you thinking?" He peeked at me through a slitted eyelid, catching me staring at him.

"Just that it's nice to sit here with you … comfortable." I chewed on my lip for a second. "It's kind of like I've known you forever."

"It does feel right." He scooted closer to me. "I know you think Cody is what you want, but are you sure? Or, are you just going with the flow because you're afraid of change?"

"No." I laughed. "Change doesn't scare me. I'm with Cody because he's comfortable, but he's also more than that. When I look at Cody, I see our past, our present, and I also see a future with him. I know that he loves me even though I am flawed, and I love him."

"Well, if I'm going to win you over, it sounds like I've got a lot of work to do." He sighed.

Stretching my legs out in front of me, I rested my head on his shoulder. "The best way to lose me is to push too hard."

"Thanks for the advice." His fingers trailed along my arm. His touch was soothing. "I'll keep that in mind."

I was hoping that would be his response. He had no chance to win me over, but if I could make him slow down in his pursuit, things would be easier.

As I lay down with Cody that night, I hoped Aurelia was right and Mavros wouldn't try to summon me. Hopefully, befriending Damon had been the right thing to do. I rested my head on Cody's bare chest and snuggled up against him. As I did, a soft sigh escaped my lips.

"What's wrong?" Cody ran his fingers through my hair.

"Nothing. That was a good sigh … a this-feels-right sigh." I rubbed my hand along his arm.

"It does." He kissed my forehead. "My favorite parta the day."

"Mine too." The lights were off, but the glow of the streetlights shone on his face.

"Except for being afraid to go to sleep."

"My dreams haven't been too bad lately." I closed my eyes. "It's been a while since I've been hurt in one of them."

"Let's not jinx that."

Chapter 24

Learn From Your Mistakes

The panther is bigger than I remembered. It steps from the trees, prowling toward me, growling.

"Mavros, stop! If you hurt me, you will regret it."

Flames dance in his eyes. He steps forward, closing the distance. I lift my hands, backing away.

The cat springs forward, knocking me to the ground. He stands on top of me, and his fangs press against my throat. "Please, Mavros, don't hurt me," I beg, careful not to move for fear of his teeth clamping down on me.

A black haze surrounds me, and the panther disappears, replaced by Mavros. His body pins me to the ground. "Some people never learn from their mistakes." His voice is so low it sends shivers marching along my spine. "I didn't expect you to be one of them."

"What mistake?" I force my voice not to waver.

He whispers in my ear, "For starters, coming outside alone. Not realizing that panthers have instincts and thinking I wouldn't hurt you in that form." His words are quiet, but I hear the annoyance in his voice. "Those are all mistakes. Ones that you've made before, and now I'm thinking they're ones you'll make again."

I slowly, carefully edge my hand up and touch his face. "You didn't hurt me even though you could've."

He leans into my touch. "You're lucky."

"Maybe … or maybe you wouldn't hurt me." I wrap my other hand around his waist. "You did once, but I don't think you will again."

"So, you trust me?" He trails kisses from my ear down my neck.

I close my eyes, hating what his touch does to me. "Yes … no … I don't know, but you need me. It's against your best interests to harm me."

His eyes harden, and his lips pull back in a snarl. "So not only am I untrustworthy but also selfish?"

"No." My heart races. My breath comes out in shallow gasps. He's turning my words around, and I'm terrified he's looking for a reason to hurt me.

"You're still snuggling up on the couch with Cody at night." He presses his teeth against my throat. "That's another mistake … one I fear will get you both killed."

I slide my hand under his shirt, hoping to distract him. "It doesn't have to be this way."

Clouds darken the sky. Lightning flashes, followed instantly by a loud clap of thunder. Fat raindrops plop against the ground, hitting my face. I turn my head.

He wipes the water off my cheeks. "Yes, Dacia, it does. I have two choices—to win you over or return to the Abyss. Would you return?"

"No." Rain pelts the ground, making pine needles and mud splash onto my face.

"What would you do to keep from returning?"

"Not what you're doing." I let go of Mavros and shield my eyes. "I wouldn't threaten someone I claim to love. I wouldn't threaten that person's friends."

He grabs my shoulders and transports me to the Abyss. "To escape from this, Dacia, are you sure? Is there anything you wouldn't do to keep from returning here?"

A heavy weight presses down on my chest. Sweat beads on my forehead. I gasp for air, wanting to scream. I know Mavros feels me panicking, but he does nothing.

After what seems like hours but was probably only minutes, he asks again, "Are you sure you wouldn't kill to keep from returning here?"

"I'd rather die." My voice shakes.

"I. Don't. Have. That. Choice."

"Then yes … yes, I would kill to stay out of here." My words are scarcely a whisper, but he hears me. Tears spill from the corners of my eyes. I hate myself for giving in, but there's no way I would be able to endure the Abyss.

He presses down on me. "Are you evil?"

"Y—" my voice catches "—yes."

"No, Dacia, you're not." He returns me to the real world and straddles me, not touching me. "You're one of the most decent and moral people I've ever met."

He brushes my eyes and cheeks. A tingling sensation follows his fingertips. I lean into his touch, savoring it, wanting more.

His voice softens. "Would it be so bad to spend eternity with me?"

I grab his shirt, resisting the urge to give in. "No, not if that was all you wanted." *But, something tells me there's more.*

Chapter 25

Because Nice Matters

I woke up feeling awful. I'd admitted to Mavros that I'd be willing to kill to stay out of the Abyss. Did I give him a green light to kill my friends? Would he hold my admission over me? Guilt welled up inside of me. I shouldn't have to be held accountable for my actions in my dreams, but I knew there was always the chance I would be.

"Hey, Dacia." Cody yawned. "How'd you sleep?"

I tried to keep my voice down. I didn't want to wake up Samantha and Dan. I didn't want them to know what I'd done. They'd never look at me the same. How could they? "I told Mavros I'd kill to keep from returning to the Abyss. I'm not sure how he'll use that little piece of information or if he's even aware of it."

"You wouldn't. You'd've spared Draconian if you could've." Cody brushed the hair back from my face.

My head fell forward, and my shoulders hunched. I squeezed my eyes shut. "But if my choice was to end somebody's life or return to the Abyss, my opinion might change."

"Really?" He lifted one eyebrow.

I rubbed my finger over it. "You don't have to pretend to understand. I know I'm just as evil, just as hideous as the monsters I've faced."

"No, you're not." His voice rose in anger.

So much for keeping things quiet, I thought.

I heard stirrings and knew Samantha and Dan were awake now. Cody held my face in his hands and stared into my eyes. "Think you would, but you couldn't. You'd never pull the trigger."

"I'd like to think so. I don't want to be a monster, but he took me there again in my dream. It's a terrifying, horrible place." I pulled my hand through my hair and looked away from him. "I think I'd do everything in my power to keep from going back there, and if that meant killing someone …" I let my voice trail off without finishing.

Cody changed the subject. "Let's go to Althea. Catch a movie. Get dinner. Maybe it'll help."

"If Aurelia'll go." I pulled the covers off and sat up. Mud dotted my pajama shirt. *What in the world?* "You probably don't want me going anywhere without her."

"I'm sure she'll go," Samantha said, sounding sleepy. "And … for the record, I agree with Cody. You'd never pull the trigger."

Dan climbed out of my loft. "Even I know you better than that."

We spent most of the day in Althea. Time away from campus seemed to lift my friends' spirits, but I was drained.

I lay down on the couch with Cody. I'd only been asleep for a little while when I woke up. I looked around, trying to discover what jolted me from my dreams about Cody, but everyone else was asleep. I heard somebody calling my name and realized avoiding Mavros all day hadn't been a good idea.

I plugged my ears. I covered my head with my pillow. He continued to call, and I felt myself being pulled toward him. I got off the couch and headed toward the door. Knowing that if I stepped out into the hall Aurelia would be waiting for me, I teleported outside.

Mavros leaned against a tree with his hands tucked in his pockets. When I appeared in front of him, he looked stunned for a split second before changing his expression to one of smugness.

I spun around. Wisteria Hall was behind me. Most of the windows were dark, but a few night owls remained. A handful of people were still out and about. Hopefully, nobody saw me appear suddenly.

Folding my arms over my chest, I glared at him. "How did you make me do that?"

"Do what?"

"Teleport to you."

"My secrets are my own." He strolled toward me. "I wasn't about to let you ignore me like you did the other night." He reached up and caressed my cheek. Heat coursed through my body, and flames ignited under his touch. "By the way, if I were you, I wouldn't do that again." His hand moved down to my neck, and his grip tightened. His eyes sliced into mine before he released me, and I was free to think on my own.

Staggering back, I rubbed my throat. "I need to sleep at night. Sometimes, I'm going to ignore you."

"It's not the fact that you ignored me." His eyes narrowed. "It's the method you employed."

The campus lights shone down on us, stretching our shadows across the ground. "I told you from the beginning what Cody means to me. It's not like you didn't know."

"No." He paced like a big cat at the zoo, reminding me he was a top predator. "You've never hidden the fact that you would choose him over me, but that doesn't mean I enjoy seeing you and him together."

Trying to stay warm, I rubbed my arms. If Mavros was going to keep drawing me out, I needed to start sleeping in a sweatshirt. "I also believe I told you that I don't want you watching me in my room."

"Yes, you did." He reached out and took my hand in his. As soon as he touched me, I forgot our argument. I forgot everything except how beautiful he was. "What would you like to do tonight?"

"As long as we're together, I don't care." I snuggled against him, and he draped his arm over my shoulder.

He held me against his body, and mine reacted to him. My pulse quickened; my breathing increased. I longed for him to kiss me. Instead, wings sprouted from his back, and we flew off to Falcon Lake. We lay on the beach, my head resting on his chest, and stared up at the night sky. The sound of the waves crashing against the shore relaxed me even more.

"How do I prove my love for you?" Mavros ran his fingers through my hair then down, along my arm. "What will it take?"

"This is a good start." Goosebumps trailed his hand. "Just lying here with me, holding me, not trying to manipulate me … that all helps."

"What else?"

"I don't know. I've only been in love once." I lifted onto my elbow, looking down at him. His expression was peaceful and calm. "Cody and I were friends forever. Our relationship grew from there and became what it is now. I don't know how it happened; it just did. One day, we realized how much we were giving up by ignoring our feelings. Suddenly, it was worth risking our friendship because what we were losing by not trying meant so much more. When I'm with Cody … You don't want to hear this. I'm sorry."

"If it helps me win your heart, please continue," Mavros said. I was surprised by the tenderness in his voice … surprised there could be so much compassion there.

"Okay, well, when I'm with Cody, I feel safe and comfortable." I thought about all the little things he did for me on a daily basis. Carrying my backpack, holding the door open, just sitting quietly with me when he knew I was too overwhelmed to do anything else. "I know he'll do whatever it takes to keep me safe. When I look at him, I see our future together."

He ran his hand through my hair. "What do you see when you look at me?"

"A bad boy … someone dangerous." I bit my lip, not sure how he'd take my answer. "I see somebody who would steal my heart only to turn around and break it."

"That's not what I want." He sounded distressed. "I want forever … not just a human's version of forever. I want an eternity with you by my side."

"And, you wouldn't break my heart?" I trailed my hand over his body, feeling hard muscles through his silk shirt.

His eyes fluttered shut. "I'd do my best not to. I can't see the future. I can only promise my heart and hope you take it. I won't push you, but I'd like to spend more time with you. I'd like to see if you could learn to love me as I love you."

"Thank you for not pushing." I kissed his cheek. Then I wondered why I'd done that. Somewhere in the back of my mind, I knew he must be controlling me, but I didn't care.

"I should get you back before I cause too much trouble."

Mavros held me against his body and flew me back to campus. He set me on the ground in front of the dormitory and tilted my chin up. "May I?" His voice was soft.

I cupped his face in my hands and nodded. His mouth crashed down on mine, and his arms wrapped around me. I moaned against his lips, tangling my fingers in his hair. He chuckled and pulled away.

Looking up at the building, he said, "Your friends are waiting for you."

A shadow passed in front of my window, and my stomach dropped. "I should go." I turned and ran inside.

Nobody was around, so I teleported into my room. Cody pulled his hands through his hair, then punched the wall.

"Cody, I'm sorry." I crossed the room to him.

He jumped in the air and spun around. Surprise registered on his face. "You're okay." Tension eased from his body, relaxing his shoulders. He opened his arms, and I ran into them.

"I'm so sorry." I pulled him against me. "He didn't want me to ignore him, so he …" I looked up at him. "He made me … I teleported to him, Cody. How'd he make me do that?"

"It's okay, Dacia." He pulled me against him, clinging to me. "Thought he'd hurt you. Thought we'd find you too late … if at all." He stepped back and swiped at his eyes. "Let Aurelia know you're safe."

Holding onto Cody's hand, I let Aurelia know I was back.

Samantha and Dan sat together in Big Bird, watching Cody and me. I led Cody to the couch. As soon as we were situated, Samantha asked, "So, what did he want?"

"He said he wanted to see me." I hoped Cody could handle hearing about Mavros and knew that if roles were reversed I wouldn't be able to. "He didn't try anything. He flew me to Falcon Lake, and we watched the stars."

"You should be doing that with me." Cody sounded hurt, and he had every right to be.

"I'm sorry, Cody. I would've rather been with you. Please know that." I clutched his hands and willed him to know the truth.

"I do, but couldn't've been me."

"What do you mean?" I jerked back.

"Can't go on our own." Cody stood and walked away. When he turned back, his lip was pulled up in a snarl. "Who knows if we'll ever be able to be alone."

I reached out, hesitating to touch him. He stepped closer, taking my hand in his. "We could, Cody. If it was just the two of us, I could keep you safe. I can't protect everyone all the time, but I could protect any one of you."

Samantha cleared her throat, drawing my attention. "Are you sure about that?"

"If you don't think I can, why do you keep telling me I'll get through this?" I snapped.

"Keep your voices down or Marcy will come knocking," Dan said.

"You're right." Leaning back, I closed my eyes and rubbed my forehead. I needed to calm down. "But, how can you say you have faith in me and not believe I can keep one of you safe? I don't understand."

Dan's voice was soft and filled with concern. "Maybe because Mavros attacked you in the hallway."

Cody and Samantha nodded.

"He surprised me. That experience taught me that nowhere is safe from him." I dragged my hand through my hair. "I won't make that mistake again."

Chapter 26

Shortly after Cody and I woke up Sunday morning, Aurelia came over. She sat in the chair and leaned forward, whispering, "Dacia needs to spend time with Damon today. Otherwise, Mavros will come calling again tonight."

"No." Cody shook his head. "Needs to stay away."

"Cody"—I fought to keep my voice steady—"she's right. If I stay away, he'll do whatever it is he did last night."

"You're killing me." He groaned and turned his back on me.

I put my hand on his arm and felt him tense at my touch. "I don't want this. I'd rather be with you, not him, but you're more likely to lose me if he calls me away at night."

"Hate this." He looked over his shoulder. His face twisted in pain.

I knew he wasn't mad at me, but I felt so guilty. It wasn't fair for him to have to deal with this all the time. He deserved a normal life with normal problems just as much as I did.

"Why don't we get Drew and some of the other guys together and go shoot hoops?" Dan suggested. "You can take your frustration out on the court."

Looking up at the lofts, I rubbed my eyes. "I'm sorry we woke you up again."

"It's okay." Samantha yawned. "But, what am I supposed to do all day?"

"You can be on my team." Dan shot her one of his amazing smiles.

She laughed. "I suck at basketball."

"Cheer me on then."

"That is a good idea." Aurelia nodded at Dan. "I will keep an eye on Dacia and bring her back safely." She turned to me. "When you are with him, I want you to keep a connection open with me. That way if things start to get complicated, I can help you."

"Do you think he'll be able to sense you?" I asked.

She shrugged her slender shoulders. "We will find out."

"When?" Cody's voice was emotionless, his face a blank mask.

When it became obvious that I wasn't going to answer, Aurelia said, "The sooner she sees him, the sooner she can get back here."

I pulled my hand through my hair. I hated what I was doing to Cody, but I couldn't see a way out of this. "I'll be ready in about a half-hour."

Dan and Samantha left to round up people to play basketball, and Aurelia went back to her room to give Cody and me some privacy. I sat down with him and pulled his arm over my shoulders, snuggling up against him. I traced my fingers along his jaw and down his neck. He put his hand on top of mine and held my eyes with his. "Promise you'll be careful." He lifted his hand to my cheek and caressed my face with his thumb. "Promise you won't take any risks or play hero. Promise to come back."

"I promise."

August mornings in the mountains tended to be chilly. I threw a hoodie on over my t-shirt and went outside.

I stood just outside the door, trying to decide where to go to find Damon. Shoving my hands into my pouch, I walked toward the green space.

Damon sat on a bench with his arms spread across the back of it. He was wearing a charcoal sweatshirt and blue jeans. When he saw me, he smiled a warm, welcoming smile I couldn't help but return.

He looked all around. "Alone? Where's your entourage?"

"Playing basketball." Slowing my pace, I walked toward him. "Normally, I'd be with them, but I wanted some space."

"Admit it; you were thinking about me." He winked.

"A bit cocky, aren't we?" I raised my eyebrow at him and laughed. Then remembering what I was supposed to be doing, I lowered my head and looked through my lashes. "It's hard not to." I thought about Mavros and Damon all the time, but I gave him a different reason for it. "Have you looked in a mirror lately? You're gorgeous."

"Thanks. So does this"—he pointed to the two of us—"mean you're considering changing your mind?"

"I'm keeping my options open," I replied without making any promises. I had to be careful what I said to him because even in this form, a promise to him was a binding pact.

"I'm glad to hear it." He stood. "I'd hate it if I didn't stand a chance with the prettiest girl on campus."

I felt myself blushing. *What is wrong with me? He's a demon.*

Nothing is wrong with you, Dacia. Aurelia's voice startled me.

If nothing is wrong, why am I blushing? Why am I flattered by a demon's comments?

You are human, and he is charming. You are doing fine.

Damon tilted his head like Aurelia does when she's listening to Arion, I wondered if he could somehow hear Aurelia's thoughts, too.

He brushed his hand up against mine. "So, what do you want to do?"

"We could go for a walk. It's a beautiful day, and I love to look at the mountains."

"You should've come out earlier. There was a herd of elk grazing over there." He pointed to the valley they frequented.

"I could watch them all day, and I love it when moose come down." Excitement rushed my words. "It's amazing how they adjust from having no antlers to having those huge racks. You'd think they'd get headaches or stiff necks from holding their heads up."

Damon walked next to me but not uncomfortably close. "You have a deep appreciation for nature."

"Yeah." I tucked a strand of hair behind my ear and wondered how he could be so easy to talk to. "I respect all life—plants, animals, even insects. I am astounded how some of them can survive up here in the mountains. I love the krummholz."

His eyebrows pinched together, and he cocked his head.

"Oh." I laughed. "Sorry. The stubby, gnarled trees that live up at the higher elevations. If they had grown down here, they would be some of the tallest trees around. Instead, they fight for survival every day. It makes my life feel a little insignificant."

"Nothing about you is insignificant." He shot me a sideways glance. "I've only known you a few days, and I know that much."

Trying to hide the stupid grin his words brought on, I looked away from him. "You have to stop complimenting me. You're embarrassing me. I'm not all that."

"You can say that again." I recognized the voice before I turned to see Cassandra behind us. "Where's Cody?" She fluffed her hair. "Maybe I can go console him."

"Cody's not available." Damon's voice hardened. "Dacia and I are walking together. Nothing more."

"Then why don't you walk with me?" She offered her arm to him.

"No, thank you. I'm enjoying Dacia's company."

Cassandra spun on her heel, but I reached out and grabbed her arm. She stiffened, and I realized that no matter how she treated me, she hadn't forgotten what I was capable of.

"Cassandra, I don't know if you realize this or not, but the perfect guy for you is Bryce. He'd do anything for you."

"Bryce?" She chewed on her lip and twisted her earring. "We've been friends forever."

"So were Cody and I. Maybe you should give it a try. How many other people call you Cassi?"

"Whatever." She stomped off.

Damon watched her walk away, then turned toward me. "She hates you. Why would you try to help her?"

"Because I don't believe in hate." I lifted one shoulder toward my ear.

"You really are amazing."

"No." I shook my head. "I just try to be the best Dacia Wolf I can be. Nobody else is going to do it for me."

He jogged a couple of steps to catch up to me. "You do a good job."

"Some days I don't, but I try." I bumped my elbow into his arm. "Anyway, enough about me. What brought you here?"

"Fate … I'm hoping." He stuffed his hands into his pockets. "I love the mountains, and this is a good school."

We walked through the green space. Then followed a path along Rose River where the forest surrounded us. Without being under his control, I would've been terrified to be alone with

Mavros like this, but Damon didn't make me feel that way at all.

We hiked in a comfortable silence. I couldn't believe how at ease I could be with him since he didn't seem to be influencing me in any way. He never tried to touch me. He wasn't staring into my eyes. If he would've come to me like this to begin with, he'd have had a better chance of stealing me away from Cody. Damon was likable, and he didn't scare me like Mavros did.

Be grateful he was not aware you would feel this way, Aurelia said.

Believe me, I am, I thought back. *I just feel really guilty about feeling anything but hatred toward him.*

You do not believe in hate, she reminded me. *You did not just say that for his benefit. You are a good person who believes there is good in everyone else. You would not be who you are if you believed differently.*

"What are you thinking?" Damon's eyes seemed accusing, but maybe it was a result of my guilt.

"Well …" I stopped to look at a mushroom growing near the base of a tree. "Just that I'm enjoying myself."

A smile brightened his face, crinkling the corners of his eyes and stealing my breath.

The sun beat down on us. I took my hoodie off and tied it around my waist. The morning had slipped by in a blur. "I should go back. I've got homework to do."

He put his hand on the small of my back, turning me around. The panther pendant bounced against my chest as we walked.

Damon glanced at it. "Cool necklace."

"Thanks." My fingers went to it unintentionally.

"From Cody?"

"No." I tucked it under my shirt, feeling it warm my skin. "Mavros gave it to me."

Rubbing his neck, he said, "And … it's complicated."

"Right."

When the dorm was in sight, he said, "I'm glad I got to spend time with you today. I didn't expect to see you until class tomorrow."

"Yeah, it was nice," I said and actually meant it.

Damon and Cody were alike on one point. Neither of them believed in leaving me without walking me to my room. He held the door open for me and headed off down the hallway.

This is where I leave you. Aurelia sounded irritated.

Thanks. I grabbed a book off my shelf and plopped down in Cookie Monster, fully intending to read. Instead, I thought about Damon and Mavros. *How can someone with a smile like that be a demon?* I knew it was shallow, but a great smile should mean a great person. Evil shouldn't be able to be housed behind a friendly mask.

I got up, pulled a bottle of water out of the fridge, and walked back to my chair. *Is it really all an act? Or is he a good demon?* I heard the key in the lock and realized the time for this line of thinking was over for now.

When Cody, Dan, and Samantha walked in, I asked, "How was your game?"

"We creamed 'em." Dan shot an imaginary basketball, then grabbed Cody's shoulder. "I love it when Cody's on my team."

Cody didn't seem to share Dan's enthusiasm. Lines of tension spider-webbed from his eyes, and I knew what was on his mind.

Not knowing how he felt about me, I stayed sitting in Cookie Monster. I screwed the cap onto my water and set it on the floor. "I'm okay." I looked into his eyes, hoping to see relief, but his expression didn't change. "Nothing happened. Damon was a perfect gentleman. Cassandra saw us together and wanted to know if she could console you. He told her there was nothing going on because I was with you."

"That's surprising." Samantha stood by the fridge and tossed waters to Dan and Cody.

"Yeah, it wasn't what I expected." I lifted my hair off my neck, pulling it into a ponytail. "He never touched me, never tried to make a move. When I told him I had homework, he walked me back. No harm done." I knew that wasn't the case in Cody's eyes, and if roles were reversed, I wouldn't have been thrilled about letting him go off with another girl.

Cody stood behind the couch and chugged his water. As soon as he finished, he walked to the door. "I'm gonna shower."

Dan kissed Samantha, jumped up, and left with Cody.

I dropped my head into my hands. "Maybe I should've told him Damon was a total jerk."

"Was he?" Samantha's voice was soft.

"Not at all."

"You shouldn't have said that then." She leaned toward me. "But, maybe you should try to sound like you didn't enjoy being with him."

I looked into her brown eyes, knowing she was right. "But I did." I pulled the band out of my hair. "I didn't think I should lie."

When they came back, Cody was aloof. He sat in Big Bird and looked anywhere but at me.

Pretending my heart wasn't splintering more with each beat, I worked on my homework. Samantha and Dan left with Aurelia keeping an eye on them.

I set my books on the floor and knelt in front of Cody. "Let's get out of here … go for a walk."

"Aurelia's not here." Cody shook his head and rolled his eyes.

"No." I ran my hand along his leg, hoping he wouldn't pull away from my touch. "Just us. I can keep us safe."

His smile was hopeful.

We walked out of the building hand in hand. The sun was starting its descent behind the mountains. The air, though still warm, was beginning to cool.

We followed the path to Falcon Lake. By the time we got there, stars dotted the sky. Yellow streaks shot across the horizon.

Cody slipped his hand from mine and draped his arm over my shoulder. I tucked my hand into his back pocket. We meandered to the playground and sat on the swings.

Insects serenaded us. An occasional owl joined in the song. The last of the sun's light disappeared behind the mountains. Millions of stars brightened the night sky. Their reflections danced across the inky blackness of Falcon Lake only to be interrupted as ripples crossed the surface. I felt like we were the only two people in the world.

"This is nice," Cody said softly.

I twisted in my swing so I faced him. "From now on, no matter what monster is after me, we need to try to spend some time like this."

He smiled at me, and it was a fantastic smile—genuine, caring, and excited. My lips curve up in response.

We lay down on the beach and looked up at the stars. I couldn't help but compare this to my experiences with Mavros. With Mavros, I felt like my mind wasn't my own. I was always fighting to remember what was important to me. With Cody, I felt right. I wished life could be this way all the time. I loved having Cody's arms around me. Even though I knew he couldn't protect me from the monsters in my life, I felt safe and loved.

A sense of peace washed over me, and my eyes drifted shut. I don't know how long we stayed like that before Cody's grip tightened on my waist.

My eyes sprung open, and I stared into the panther's fiery irises. A menacing growl rumbled from its throat.

"Don't hurt him, Mavros—" I sat up, blocking Cody with my body "—instincts or not."

The beast's lips curled back revealing a mouthful of sharp teeth. My body cooled, but nothing else happened. Fear clenched my heart when Mavros didn't back away. I concentrated on ice and tried again to freeze my body.

The panther seemed to sneer before edging around me.

I circled with him, keeping between him and Cody. He stepped closer, and I realized that if he attacked, I'd survive, but Cody wouldn't.

I lifted my hand. Ice shot from my fingertips. The cat jumped back. I grabbed hold of Cody and teleported back to my room.

Cody lay on the floor with me sprawled over his body. Both of us were breathing hard. The room was dark.

"That was close." Cody's voice shook.

Chapter 27

My New Mantra

*M*avros leans against a tree, all long, slender muscles clad in black. He blends in with the night, a god among men.

No. I shake my head. *He's a demon in a beautiful package, not a god.* Tucking my hands into my pockets, I saunter away from him.

"Dacia." His voice is a low growl. "Don't. Walk. Away. From. Me."

I glance at him over my shoulder. His body is rigid, and he seems to be restraining himself with great difficulty.

Not wanting my back to him, I spin around. "What?" I toss my hands up.

"Why were you with him?" He stalks toward me.

"Because I love him." I take a step away.

Still prowling toward me, he asks, "Why did you attack me?"

Widening my stance into a defensive posture, I say, "Really?"

He nods.

"You wouldn't back off."

He narrows his eyes. "I told you I wouldn't hurt you again."

Flames ignite in my palms. "To get to Cody, you would've."

"If I'd've wanted him dead, he'd be dead." A menacing grin spreads across his face. He smacks his hands together, and my flames shoot toward him, absorbing into his body.

I drop my hands to my sides, not sure what he just did. "How?" I shake my head, knowing he won't answer anyway. "I thought you couldn't help what you did when you were a panther. I thought it was instincts."

"When I see you, I try to override my instincts … your safety is my top concern." He stands with his hands behind his back.

I take another step away from him. A twig snaps under my foot. "Promise you won't hurt Cody." I start to look over my shoulder, but I don't want to take my eyes off of Mavros. Unsure of what's behind me, I stop moving.

"I can't make that promise." He strides forward until he stands toe to toe with me. "If you choose to let me return to the Abyss, I will hurt him. I've already promised you that." The menace radiating off him is palpable.

I want to get as far from him as I can, but I need him to trust me. "Promise not to hurt any of them until I decide." I run my fingers along his arm.

He looks from my hand to my face. Surprise shines in his eyes. "No." He shakes his head. "I don't make those kinds of promises."

Reaching down, he takes my hands in his. *This is a dream. It's a dream. It's my dream, and I'm in control.*

"Dacia, I want you to make me a promise." His voice is intense, and I fight to stay in control.

I focus on the bridge of his nose, not looking into his eyes, not wanting to fall to his charms. "What?"

"Promise not to use ice against me." He trails the tips of his fingers along my jaw.

"I …" I bite the inside of my cheek. "I can't." *This is a dream.* I repeat my mantra over and over again in my head.

He presses his thumb into the palm of my hand, blood pulses to the surface, and fire surges through my veins. I drop to my knees. "Promise," he growls through clenched teeth.

"No." I force the word out.

The pain retreats, and he pulls me to my feet. He traces a line from my ear to my neck. I want to give into him, but I continue chanting, *This is a dream, this is a dream, this is a dream …*

He brushes his lips across mine. "Promise." His voice is soft, but there's a dark undercurrent to it.

"No."

He holds me against his body, running his hands down my back. Then he swipes his hand. Blood pours from four deep gouges across my stomach. My legs weaken, and I slump to the ground, gasping for air.

"Oh, Dacia." Cody's voice was a combination of grief and horror.

I forced my eyes open. I was curled up against him on the couch, and both of us were covered in my blood. Pain rippled through my body as I rolled onto my back.

"Towel." I gasped.

Cody sprung from the couch, retrieved a towel, and hurried back to me. He eased me up and wrapped it around me. I pressed it against my stomach, hoping to staunch the blood flow.

"Need anything else?"

I shook my head, and he went to the sink to wash off. Closing my eyes, I concentrated on healing and life.

"What are you doing?" Samantha's voice was heavy with sleep.

"Washing," Cody answered.

She flicked her light on. "Oh, my God! Cody, are you okay?"

"Fine." He waved at me. "Dacia's blood. Looks like a panther attack."

Dan jumped down from my loft and came over to me. "Are you okay?"

"Sure." I tried to make myself smile to reassure him, but I cringed. My voice wavered. "Mavros wanted me to promise not to use ice, but I wouldn't." *Aurelia, I need your help.*

I am on my way.

"Cody, Dan, you might want to hide. Aurelia is …" She stood in front of me. "Never mind."

"How bad is it?" She knelt beside me.

I lifted the towel away, and she placed her hands on my wounds. A cool sensation spread relief to my body.

"I didn't promise." I clutched the towel, trying to hold the pain at bay. "I kept telling myself it was a dream and that he had no control over me."

"You did well." Her voice changed, becoming thick. Magic emanated from her words.

Even though it went against my nature, I let my defenses down. I didn't fight her spell. I knew she wouldn't harm me.

"Sleep well, Dacia."

My eyelids grew heavy, and I fell into a deep dreamless sleep.

Chapter 28

Decisions, Decisions

For the next couple of weeks, the days followed the same pattern. Cody played basketball with Dan while I spent time with Damon—always with my link to Aurelia open. We went for walks and talked. Sometimes he held my hand or threw his arm over my shoulder, but most of the time, he gave me space. As the days passed, I began counting him as one of my friends. I knew I shouldn't. I knew he was a demon, but I couldn't help myself. He was charming and fun to be around.

Through my link with Aurelia, I felt her discomfort with Damon, but she didn't stop me from seeing him. She never talked to me about him after he walked me to my room. She never told me I was getting too close to him. She always closed off her connection to me as soon as he left. Mavros stayed away as long as I spent time with Damon, and that was her main concern.

Damon pulled me to one of Phlox University's benches. I sat down, but he stood in front of me, pacing two steps in one direction and then back again and again. "Dacia, you've been spending time with me every day after classes."

"Yes." I had a feeling I knew where this was going. I'd begun to hope he wouldn't ask. "I like spending time with you."

"It's been two and a half weeks." He looked at me. His eyes held a deep sadness in them. I wanted to reach up, caress his face, and tell him things would be okay, but I kept my hands firmly at my sides. "I've been patient. I've seen our friendship grow, but it's never been a secret that I want more. Will you go out with me this weekend? It doesn't have to be anything fancy, just dinner at The Avalanche."

If you do not go with him, I am afraid Damon will disappear, and you will be left to deal with Mavros. In Aurelia's words, I felt her sadness and fear.

"Can I think about it tonight and let you know tomorrow?" I grasped my arm above the elbow.

His shoulders slumped forward. "Sure." He scrubbed his hand down his face. "I guess that's better than no." He reached his hand down to help me up, then walked me back to my room.

"Are you ever going to invite me in?" He stood in the hall, looking in.

"Not until I decide what to do about Cody. He'd never understand if he saw you in my room."

"Please don't say no." He took my hand and lifted it to his lips before heading toward the staircase.

When Cody, Dan, and Samantha came back to the room, I was sitting with my head in my hands, trying to figure out what to do. Cody sat as far from me on the couch as he could. "Not gonna like this, am I?"

I looked up at him and saw that the expressionless mask he had donned for the last couple of weeks was firmly in place. "Damon asked me on a date. Aurelia thinks that if I turn him down, Damon will disappear and Mavros will start calling me out at night. I'm not sure which is the lesser of two evils. If I tell Damon yes, he'll want more—more dates, more than walks, more than kissing my hand when he says goodbye. I don't know if I can deal with more."

Cody didn't change expressions, didn't move, didn't say a word. He'd been this way since I started spending more time with Damon, and even though I couldn't blame him, I wished he would show some emotion, show me he cared. I wished he would let me in.

"Did you give him an answer?" Samantha asked.

I looked around the room, meeting all of their gazes. "I told him I'd let him know tomorrow. I wanted to know what you guys thought."

"Difference does it make?" Cody's voice was hard and cruel. "Been dating him for two weeks."

"Not because I want to." My voice was low and steady, but inside I felt anything but in control.

"You like him. You enjoy spending time with him. Don't pretend you don't." He got up and headed toward the door. "I'm gonna shower. Do whatever."

Cody's words shattered my heart, breaking it into a million jagged pieces that cut my insides to shreds. A chill shuddered through my body, and a sob escaped through clenched teeth.

Samantha sat down beside me. "You know he doesn't mean it. He loves you, and he's trying to deal with this."

The dam holding my tears back was about to break. I knew that if I looked at her, it would burst. I held my head and focused on breathing. "I know it's hard on him, and I know it's eating him up. But, it's not what I want either. I want to spend time with Cody. Damon is my friend, but Cody's my life."

Dan's face scrunched up in disgust. "How can you be friends with Damon? He's a demon. He's Mavros."

They'd never understand. They hadn't spent time with him and didn't see him the way I did. "I know, but sometimes it's hard to remember that. He's nice, polite, and funny."

"He's. A. Demon." Dan stood by the sink, splashing cold water on his face.

I walked to the window and looked outside. The aspen trees stood out against the pines and spruces. Their leaves were bright yellow. Too soon, they would litter the ground, and winter would be upon us. "I know"—I raked my fingers through my hair—"but are all demons evil? Obviously, all angels aren't good, or the devil wouldn't exist."

"I know you don't see it." Samantha's hands were folded in her lap, and she looked at them, not me. "Mavros isn't a good guy. He's manipulating you, trying to get you to join him."

"How can you be so sure?" Folding my arms over my chest, I turned and stared at her. "I've seen his eyes, seen the emotions there." I shook my head. I wasn't going to change her mind. "That's not what this is about. Do I go out with Damon in two days, or do I risk the wrath of Mavros if I say no? It's not much of a choice; is it?"

"I think Aurelia is probably right." Dan walked over and stood behind Samantha. His hair poked out every which way. "We've agreed from the beginning that Damon's safer than Mavros."

"If I go out with him, it could be the end of me and Cody." I slid my promise ring up and down my finger. *How could things have gone so wrong so quickly?* "I don't know if he can handle this."

"Hopefully in two weeks, this will all be over." Samantha rubbed my arm.

"Yeah, there's that."

"I'm gonna hit the shower." Dan leaned down and kissed the top of Samantha's head.

I pinched the bridge of my nose, hoping to hold it together. "Make sure Cody's okay."

"I will."

"I'll walk with you as far as the bathroom." Samantha jumped up and grabbed her bag. "I need a shower, too."

Left in the room alone, I decided to call home. "Hi, Mom," I said into the receiver.

"Hello, dear. How are you doing?"

"I'm a little lost right now." Tears trickled out of my eyes. "Cody and I are having some problems, and I don't know what to do."

"Well, tell me about it." I imagined her sitting down on the couch, folding her legs under her.

I let out a long sigh. I wanted to tell her everything, but I couldn't. "There's this other guy."

"Oh." The surprise in her voice was obvious. "Cody's been there for you forever, but he's your first boyfriend. It doesn't hurt to keep your options open."

"That's not it, Mom." I blew out a long breath and cleared my throat. "This other guy likes me, and he's nice. But, he's just a friend. He asked me on a date, and …" *Now, what do I say? I can't tell her why I should go out with him. This was stupid.*

"Oh, I see. You don't want to ruin your friendship."

I leaned my head against the back of the couch and stared up at the ceiling without really seeing anything. "I'm afraid that if I say no, it's going to ruin things. If I say yes, it'll definitely ruin things."

"Then you just need to decide which is more important"— her voice was matter-of-fact—"dating Cody or being friends with this other guy. I imagine you already know the answer."

"Yeah, I do. Thanks, Mom."

"When are you coming home?"

"Hopefully, in a couple weeks, I'll be able to."

I paced the room waiting for Cody to come back. When the knob turned, I tensed and watched the door. My body slumped forward when I realized it was Samantha. She looked at me, then over her shoulder. "What?"

"I thought you might be Cody."

"Oh, I'm sorry." She closed the door and sat her bag down. "Can't you tell?" She tapped her head.

I pulled my hand through my hair. "Too stressed." I resumed pacing. "He'll be back … Won't he?"

"He will." She grabbed books out of her bag and sat in front of the computer. "Just give him some time to calm down."

Aurelia?

Yes, Dacia.

Cody …

I saw what happened. He is fine. He will make his way back to you. Until then, Arion and I will keep an eye on him.

Thank you. Can you keep an eye on Dan, too?

They are together.

By the time Cody and Dan came back, I expected to see a groove worn into the floor. Cody stood by the door while Dan pulled Samantha into an embrace. "Let's give them a few minutes," he said.

Cody stayed where he was. He wouldn't look at me. Pain tore through my chest. I tried to take in a deep breath, but it lodged in my throat. "Why … why can't you look at me, Cody?"

A muscle ticked in his jaw. He looked up but not at me. "Do you wanna date him?"

"No. I decided not to. I wanted to tell you, but …" I let my sentence hang in the air.

He shuddered as he took in a breath. His eyes met mine, and for the first time in weeks, there was emotion in them. "I'm sorry." He crossed the room to me. "Thought you wanted him. You've been getting closer. Thought I was losing you." He stopped in front of me, reached toward my face, then hesitated, dropping his hand to his side.

"I don't want anyone but you." I closed the gap between us. "I thought you knew that." I raised onto my toes and wrapped my arms around his neck. He put his hands on my waist, and I felt them trembling. Pulling me against him, he buried his head in my neck.

"Tell him yes." Cody lifted his head and brushed my hair back. "Not what I want but for the best."

"I'd rather deal with Mavros than lose you."

"Tell him yes." Cody swallowed and lowered his head. When he started talking again, I had to strain to hear him. "Tell him yes. That way Mavros will leave you alone at night."

"Let me know tomorrow if that's still what you want. I won't tell him yes unless you're sure." I leaned my head against Cody's chest and listened to the steady rhythm of his heart. Samantha and Dan found us that way when they came back.

Chapter 29

What Choice?

I wipe my sweaty palms on my shorts for the umpteenth time. As soon as Dr. Rowan dismisses class, I have to tell Damon my decision. Bile rises into my mouth at the thought.

Damon looks over at me and mouths, "Are you okay?"

I shrug and go back to pretending to take notes. When class ends, Damon picks up my backpack and tosses it over his shoulder. We walk out together, finding a bench to sit on, like we've been doing for the last couple of weeks. He throws his arm around me, in a casual way, not an embrace. We watch students hurry to and from classes, and I begin to relax. The silence is comfortable, not tense at all.

"Have you decided?" Damon looks at me. His dark eyes are filled with hope.

I suck in a deep breath and release it slowly. "Yeah, uh, I'm sorry, but I can't go on a date with you. I'm not ready yet. Can you give me more time?"

"More time?" Anger fills his voice. "Don't you think three weeks is enough?"

"It's a big step. I'm … I'm not ready."

"So you've been leading me on?" His arm tightens on my shoulders, holding me in place. "I see the way you look at me. You enjoy spending time with me. You don't throw my arm off your shoulders or pull your hand away when I hold it."

"I'm sorry, Damon." Tears dampen my eyes. "I thought I was ready, but I'm not, not yet."

His expression is cold and hard. His teeth lengthen into fangs. My pulse quickens, but fear paralyzes me. Damon leans in. His lips brush my neck before his teeth tear through my jugular vein.

"I'm done being your friend." He swipes the back of his hand across his mouth, wiping my blood away before he disappears.

I slump forward, falling to the ground. I feel my heartbeat slow, feel blood flowing from my neck, feel my life slip away.

I woke up in Cody's embrace. The dim glow of the streetlights through the curtains shone on him. Blood soaked into his shirt and ran down his arms. My hand fluttered to my neck. Dried blood. No gash. "Cody," I whispered in his ear.

"I don't wanna go to school, Mom," he mumbled.

"Cody, you're talking in your sleep." I gave his arm a gentle shake. "Wake up."

"What?" His eyes popped open. "You okay?"

"I had a nightmare, and it looks like we took a bath in blood." I got off the couch. "I'll teleport you to your room so you can take a shower."

Cody stood and looked down at himself. "That'd be good. Can't clean this in the sink."

"Sam, Dan, wake up," I said.

"Uhn," Sam mumbled.

Dan sat up in bed and looked down at us. His eyes widened, and his voice was louder than it should've been. "Are you okay?"

"Bad dream," I answered. "I'm taking Cody to his room so he can get cleaned up."

"Good idea." Samantha tried to hold back a yawn.

Aurelia, keep an eye on Dan and Samantha, please.

Your room was blessed. They are safe there.

I grabbed Cody's hand. "Ready?"

"Sure."

While Cody rounded up his shower essentials, he asked, "What happened?"

"I said no." I lifted my shoulders and tried to sound nonchalant.

"Guess that settles it." His hand shook as he reached for his bottle of shampoo. "You gotta say yes." Cody's voice didn't show the discouragement I was sure he felt.

I walked over to him and put my hand on his arm. "I won't do anything that'll make me lose you."

He looked me in the eyes, his face was stern, unflinching. "Tell him no and this happens, you'll be out several days. By the time you wake up, Mavros won't play games. Then you might lose us all. Go on that date."

My chin dropped to my chest. I couldn't see any other way out of this either. "Hopefully, that'll hold him off for a while, but what if it doesn't?"

"Least you tried." Cody pulled his shirt up over his head. His abs were flexed. A fist of desire clenched in my stomach. I turned away from him, fanning my face with a notebook I found on his desk. "I'm gonna jump in the shower."

I gave him a little finger wave and watched him walk out the door. When he came back, my heart flipped. He stood in front of me with nothing on but shorts. His skin was damp. I stepped up to him, placing my palms on his chest.

Cody laughed. "Love that look, but you're covered in blood."

"Oh." I pulled away from him and heat rushed to my face.

"Hold that thought 'til you get cleaned up." He brushed my lips with his thumb before kissing me softly.

We teleported back to my dorm, and I headed to the showers. By the time I got back, Cody was asleep on the couch. With a sigh, I snuggled against his bare chest and fell asleep.

Chapter 30

Completely Broken

I walked out of Shakespeare with Damon. His shoulders were hunched, lacking his usual confidence. He reached for my hand but pulled back. I saw him look at me through the corner of his eyes, but I wasn't about to make this any easier for him.

We sat on our normal bench. Like in my dream, I stared off into the distance. I knew what I needed to do, but my heart told me not to.

Damon turned toward me and grabbed my hands. "Have you decided?"

"Yes."

"Yes, you've decided? Or, yes, you'll go out with me?" Hope widened his eyes and brought a slight smile to his lips.

I opened my mouth, but the words fought to stay inside. *You can do this, Dacia,* I thought. I opened my mouth again, and this time, they came out. "Yes, to both."

His smile broadened, lighting up his entire face and making my heart do a somersault. "You've made me the happiest man on campus." He leaned forward and brushed his lips along my neck.

My body tensed in response. I clutched the bench, waiting for his teeth to sink in, but that didn't happen.

Instead, his hand caressed my cheek. "Thank you." His husky voice murmured in my ear.

My heart raced, and my body softened. A nervous laugh escaped my lips. "I'm glad you're happy," I whispered and was ashamed to admit I meant it.

Dan and Samantha were curled up on the couch. Cody stood at the window, staring outside. His shoulders hunched forward. "How'd it go?"

"He didn't kill me—" I set my backpack down and leaned against the wall "—but ..."

"But what?" Samantha knelt on the couch, peering over the back at me.

I tugged my hand through my windblown curls. "But nothing." I remembered Damon's hand brushing my face and wondered what was to come. "I just wish there was another way."

"There isn't." Cody turned. His body was tense, and his blue eyes were icy. "This is the only way."

I walked toward him, slowly stretching my hand out like I would with a frightened animal. "Let's go out tonight. Just the two of us."

Cody smiled a sad smile and shook his head. "I'd like that. More than anything, but … no."

"No?"

"Mavros can't see us out. He can't know it's a farce." He stepped around me, refusing to look at me. "See if Arion can watch me? I'll sleep in my room."

"Oh." My legs wobbled. I sank down against the wall and lowered my head to my hands. "Oh."

"He watches." His voice was ragged. "You understand that; don't you?"

"I …"

The door clicked. I looked up. Cody and I were alone. He sat in Cookie Monster. His elbows rested on his knees. He studied his feet. "He'll know if we're together. It can't be both ways."

I covered my face. "Then I want you."

"Know that can't happen." A tear rolled down his cheek and dripped off his chin.

Holding back a sob, I knelt in front of him and put my hands over his. "I'm sorry, Cody. I'm sorry I'm always hurting you."

"Coupla weeks." He attempted to smile, but it looked more like a grimace.

I looked down, shaking my head. "That's the thing."

He tucked a lock of hair behind my ear. "You'll defeat him."

"Maybe, but … I should've told you earlier. Aurelia doesn't think it'll change. She thinks I'll fight one monster after another." I took a deep breath and tried to keep my voice steady. "It's never going to end. Ever."

Cody's thumb brushed my cheek. "Didn't think it'd be easy," he whispered, "but, never thought it'd be this hard."

I leaned into his touch. "I'm sorry. I don't want this. I don't want Damon or Mavros. I don't want to see you hurt."

"I know. Only way, though." He pulled his hand away. "Maybe next time, they won't want your love."

"Let's hope."

He leaned down and whispered in my ear, "I'm not letting go. Just stepping back. I love you." He kissed the top of my head, got up, and walked out.

I curled up on the couch and clutched Cody's pillow to my chest. His scent lingered on it—a cold winter's day before a snowstorm, fresh, brisk, and clean—causing tears to pool in my eyes. I didn't move when the door opened.

Samantha walked over and sat on the floor in front of me. She brushed the hair off my face. "Aurelia told us about Cody. Arion's guarding him."

I nodded, unsure if my voice would even come out.

"You can sleep in your bed if you'd like." Dan sat in Big Bird, rubbing the back of his neck.

I shook my head.

"You sure?"

"I …" My voice was gravelly. I cleared my throat and started again. "The couch smells like him."

"Are you okay?" Samantha's soft brown eyes were filled with remorse.

I shook my head. "I really don't want to …" A sob escaped. I took a deep breath. "I can't talk right now. I'm going to sleep."

I pulled Cody's pillow closer to me and breathed him in.

Chapter 31

Cody stayed away all day. I didn't see or hear from him. I thought about going to his room, checking the basketball court, or calling him to make sure he was okay. But, why would he be? His girlfriend was going on a date with another man. No, not a man, a demon. I couldn't understand why he'd ever want to see me again.

Samantha offered to hang out with me, but I knew I wouldn't be good company. "Go with Dan." I rubbed my hand over my mouth. "Make sure Cody's all right."

Instead of pestering Cody, I spent the day pretending to read. I couldn't pay attention to the book. My insides trembled. I liked Damon, but I didn't want to date him. I didn't want to face the consequences of a date gone wrong. If the date lived up to his expectations, we would all be in trouble. If it didn't, there was a possibility I wouldn't make it home.

Damon knocked on my door a few minutes before six o'clock. When I opened it, he said, "You look beautiful."

"Thanks. Samantha picked this out." I was wearing black pants and a green silk shirt that brought out my eyes. "You look pretty nice yourself." He was dressed all in black. His eyes were bright with excitement.

"Aren't you going to invite me in?" His smile lit up his entire face, tearing down my defenses.

I started to swing my arm back in a welcoming gesture but caught myself. "Not tonight. You wanted to get off campus, remember?"

"Yes, shall we then?" He held his arm out for me to take. We walked out to a black Mustang with dark tinted windows. He held the door open but stopped me before I could get in. The back of his hand brushed against my cheek. He leaned forward, closing the distance between us. "Thank you," he breathed.

I felt my pulse quicken. "F-f-for what?"

"Saying yes." He wrapped his arms around me and pulled me against his body, an embrace I couldn't have escaped from if I'd wanted to. His lips brushed across mine, curving them into a smile when I didn't recoil. He lowered his mouth, and

I was lost in a passionate, all-consuming kiss. When he pulled away from me, I stumbled forward.

"Sorry," I mumbled as he caught me.

"Don't be sorry." He ran his thumb along my cheek. "I like this Dacia … vulnerable and passionate."

My eyes widened and I swallowed. No matter how much I liked Damon, I didn't want to be vulnerable around him.

He helped me into his car and shut the door behind me. When he walked around to get in, I felt myself come to my senses. *Aurelia,* I thought, *I'm going to need you tonight. He's controlling me, and I don't know if I can fight it on my own.*

I will be nearby, she responded.

As soon as we started down the road, Damon took my hand in his. The warmth of his skin made a tingling sensation spread throughout my body. Pleasure intermixed with fear. Fear that I might make a promise to this demon, a promise I would regret for eternity.

I closed my eyes and tried to picture Cody's face, the blue of his irises, the curve of his lips, but his eyes kept darkening until they were as black as night. His face transformed into Damon's, and it became harder to remember exactly what Cody looked like.

When I opened my eyes, Damon was watching me instead of the road. Smiling at him, I asked, "So, where are we going?"

"I packed a picnic dinner, and we're going to Pine Ridge Park to watch the Althea Artists perform *Faust.*"

Hearing *Faust* snapped me back to reality. "Isn't that the play about the guy who sells his soul?" I knew it was, but I wanted to see what kind of reaction I would get.

"Yes." He showed no emotion, no familiarity with our situation.

"I don't understand that. One lifetime." I stuck my index finger up in front of me. "One. That's all we have to get through to spend eternity in Heaven. Why blow it to spend eternity in Hell?"

"Selling your soul is a bit ridiculous." My mouth dropped open at his words. "But, if you choose to live forever, you never have to leave this world behind."

"Losing everyone you love is a steep price to pay for immortality. Isn't it?"

"I suppose that depends on whether or not you're alone." His thumb caressed my hand. "If you're with someone you love, death seems like the more costly choice."

I shrugged. "I don't know. I'm not afraid of death."

His laugh was humorless. "That's what everyone says until they're standing face to face with Death himself."

"I've stood on the shore, waiting for the boat." I remembered climbing aboard, the feeling of peace that had settled over me.

His eyebrows rose as he turned to look at me. "You have?"

"Yep."

"When?"

"A few times over the past year, but I really don't want to talk about it. This is our first date." I tried to sound excited. "Let's not ruin it with morbid conversation."

I'd never been to Pine Ridge Park before. It sat on a hill overlooking Althea. The peaks of the Snowfire Mountains rose behind the town. I breathed in a sigh of contentment. I could've sat at the park all evening just looking at the mountains. Instead, Damon spread a blanket down on the ground and pulled fried chicken and potato salad out of a picnic basket. We ate in relative silence.

When I finished, Damon stood and reached for my hand. Helping me to my feet, he bowed and asked, "May I have this dance?"

I chuckled. "There's no music."

"Sure there is." He pointed to one of the Althea Artists just as he turned on a radio. Soft music drifted over to us. Damon put one hand on my waist and held my hand in his. My other hand rested on his arm. He pulled me closer to him, leaving just a sliver of air between us. Heat radiated off his body, and somehow, I resisted the urge to move closer, to press my body against his.

Damon danced like a pro, and it was easy to follow his lead. *This is so different from dancing with Cody.* I pictured his face for an instant before it was replaced by Damon's dark eyes and hair, Damon's seductive smile. I leaned my head on his shoulder and let myself get carried away by the music.

Dacia. I heard the warning in Aurelia's voice but chose to ignore her. I was enjoying myself. Why did she have to interfere? *Dacia, think about Cody. Think about your love for him. You are getting too close.*

I glanced up at Damon throgh my eyelashes. He glared at me. Anger flashed through his eyes. I turned away, suddenly scared to be in his embrace. I took a couple deep breaths to center myself. When I looked back up at him again, his eyes were filled with affection.

Did I just imagine the anger? I wondered to myself.

Damon stopped dancing and whispered in my ear, "The play's about to start." He brushed my hair back and tenderly kissed my earlobe. Fire and ice burned through my body—desire and fear fighting one another. A moan of ecstasy escaped my lips, and I tilted my head back. His lips crushed against mine. My hands clutched his hair, pulling him closer to me.

He was the first to pull away. A smile engulfed his face. "Yeah, I like this Dacia." His fingers traced my jawline and along my neck. He lowered me onto the blanket with him. Lounging on his side and propped up on his elbow, he drew me against him. His hand rested on my shoulder. Every so often his finger brushed against my neck, sending shivers of excitement through my body.

At first, I had trouble concentrating on *Faust*, but soon I found myself captivated by the performance. When it was over, Damon sat up and looked into my eyes. "So, what did you think of it?"

"It was really good." I fiddled with the necklace Mavros had given me. "I never knew Faust ended up in Heaven."

"Just because you do one thing you shouldn't, doesn't mean God will forsake you." He traced a fingertip along my cheek. "It just means you followed a different path than expected."

I knew this conversation should mean something to me, but before I figured it out, Damon leaned over me. His lips brushed against my forehead, my eyes, and my nose before finding my mouth. All thought of our conversation was gone.

Chapter 32

Just Friends

Sunday morning, I woke up conflicted. Damon was everything a girl could ask for—loving, romantic, exciting, gorgeous. I felt a connection to him even though I knew I shouldn't. My heart still belonged to Cody, but after my date with Damon, I had doubts for the first time. Shaking my head, I wondered if he still had some control over my thoughts.

I pulled Cody's pillow closer to me. His scent barely lingered on it. The thought of losing him caused my breath to catch in my throat and emptiness to spread through my body.

I sat up and put my head in my hands. *Can I fix this?* I wondered. I dragged my fingers through my hair, getting ready to face the day.

"Morning," Dan said.

I half-smiled at him. "Do you think Cody will see me to-day?"

"I don't know, but I know it took all he had to stay away from you yesterday."

"So, how did things go last night?" Samantha asked from her bed.

I looked down at my bare feet. *I need to trim my toenails,* I thought. "It was …" I stopped and cleared my throat. "It was easy, a perfect date. He was wonderful and charming. And, he was controlling me." I looked up at them, my eyes begging them to understand. "I didn't invite him in, and I don't remember making any promises. But, I feel horrible this morning, and Cody's pillow …" A sob shook my shoulders as it escaped my lips. "It doesn't smell like him anymore." My voice trailed off.

Samantha climbed out of her loft, sat on the couch beside me, and rubbed my back. "You can't hold yourself responsible for anything you did while he was controlling you."

I didn't look at her. I shook my head and said, "Is that how you'd feel? If Dan was with another girl, would it matter? Even if you knew she was controlling him? That he was doing it for the good of mankind?"

She looked at Dan for a while before answering. "No, I'd be jealous, angry." She turned back to me, and her chin dropped to her chest. "Hurt."

"If you knew the way Mavros and Damon make me feel, if you knew what they make me think, you probably wouldn't blame Cody for running off." Tears rolled out of my eyes, pooling in my hands.

"Cody didn't run off," Dan said, his voice was soft and sympathetic. "He did what he thought would help keep Mavros away, and it's killing him not to be with you."

"Then tell him to come; tell him I need him." My eyes pleaded with him to make it happen. "I know now that I can't get through this without him."

I got up, grabbed my bathroom bag, and headed out into the hall. Once there, I stared at Aurelia's door. I needed to know what happened after the play. I needed to know if I made Damon any promises because I couldn't remember getting in his car, the ride home, anything.

Aurelia's door opened. "Well, are you coming in?" Her lips curled up in a friendly smile.

"I'm not sure." I kicked my foot against the floor. "Do I want to know what happened last night?"

She motioned me in, closing the door behind me.

I held my hands over my face, covering my eyes. "I need to know if I'm going to cause the end of the world. I don't remember anything after the play."

"You promised—" My gasp stopped her sentence short. She raised one eyebrow at me and finished. "To see him again today. He will be here to pick you up at 3:00."

"Oh …" I sank to the floor. "That's all? I can live with that."

"Only if you are careful." She stared down at me with her hands on her hips and her lips pursed. "I cannot interfere, lest I cause the end of the world. You will have to keep your head today, Dacia."

"Then I have to see Cody." I looked up at her through my fingers. "Somebody will have to convince him of that."

"If Dan does not succeed, I will talk to him."

When I got back from my shower, Cody was seated in Cookie Monster. I stood in the doorway, staring at the back of his head. My heart stopped in my chest, and uncertainty filled my body. The one person I wanted to see more than anybody in the world was here, and I had no idea what to say to him or how to act. Did he want to see me? Was he here only because Dan or Aurelia made him come?

"Hi," I said as I stepped into the room. My eyes went to Samantha for help, but she didn't offer any.

Dan stood and reached his hand out for Samantha's. "Why don't we let them have some time alone?"

"No!" Cody's voice filled the room. The muscles tightened in his neck and jaw. His eyes narrowed, daring anybody to challenge his order.

"I think it would be best," Samantha said.

"No. Sit down. We're all *friends* here, nothing more."

The blood drained from my face. Somewhere in the back of my mind, I registered the pain I felt when my body crashed to the floor. Somewhere the sun shone and birds sang, but not for me. My world was consumed by shadows and darkness. "You … you can't mean that. You just can't."

"I explained, Dacia." Cody knelt in front of me. "Won't work if we're together."

I looked into his eyes and saw the pain he was trying to hide. My hand brushed against his, and he jerked away from me. "Can't do this." His voice was husky. He raked his fingers through his hair, leaving patches standing on end. "Can't touch you. Look at you. Then leave you. Need all or nothing, and can't have it all right now."

"If you're not with me, Mavros'll win. I didn't see you for one day, and when I was with Damon, I couldn't remember what you looked like." Tears pooled in my eyes. "If you stay away longer, he might steal all my memories of you."

Cody sat back, making sure not to touch me. "If he knows we're together, what's to keep him from killing you? He killed Elizabeth."

"Aurelia told you that you'd have to stay by her side," Samantha reminded him.

"I will. As her friend, with you. Can't be her boyfriend. Mavros can't see us like that. Can't hold hands. Can't hug or kiss you. Can't hold you." For a moment, Cody's guard slipped. He looked as if he'd seen his favorite dog run over right before his eyes. "Don't want this, but gotta be this way."

"Fine." I stood and walked away from Cody. I couldn't stand being so close to him without touching him. "Then stay over here and hang out today like friends. I'll sit in Big Bird, and you can sit in Cookie Monster. We can play games or watch a movie or whatever, but I need you with me for as long as you can handle it. Damon is coming over at 3:00, and I can't face him without being with you first."

"Aaaah, why?" His head fell forward, and he pulled at his hair.

How much of this can Cody take? How long can I fight Mavros' hold without Cody by my side? I grabbed a bottle of water and sat in Big Bird. "I don't remember anything after the play last night. I could've given him the world, but Aurelia said all I did was promise to see him again."

Cody looked up at me, his blue eyes stormy. "I'll stay. No promises."

I projected my thoughts only to him, *I'm so sorry. I know this isn't easy. I know it's killing you. I also know I love you and only you.*

He looked at me and smiled, a sad, heartbroken imitation of a smile.

The four of us played Yahtzee and tried to pretend like all was right in the world, but it wasn't. Cody and I should've been snuggled up with each other. At the very least, we should've been able to look at each other, but every time our eyes met, Cody turned his head away.

When our game was over, Cody got up, went to the desk, grabbed a notebook and pen, and sat back down. I watched him write. The first part came out quickly. Then he tapped the pen against his lips while he stared at the paper. He scribbled a few more things down, ripped the page out of the notebook, folded it in half, and handed it to me.

"Got stuff to do," he said without looking at me. "See you later."

I raised my hand in a half-hearted wave but couldn't find my voice to say anything. I sat staring at the paper he'd given to me. I wanted to know what it said, but I was terrified to open it.

"Well," Samantha said.

Dan scribbled a note and held it up for us to read. *Mavros could be watching.*

"No matter how you feel about Damon," he said, "Cody will always be your friend. He was your friend before you started dating. I don't think anything will change that."

I looked up at Dan and smiled. "Thanks." I prepared myself for the worst, unfolded the paper, and began reading.

Dacia,

This is the hardest thing I've ever done, pretending like I don't care, like I don't love you. I want to wrap my arms around you and pull you close, but I know if Mavros sees us together, he'll know you're not serious about Damon. I can't let him hurt you. But in trying to protect you, I'm the one hurting you. For that, I'll be eternally sorry.

I want you to know that whatever this looks like to you, I still love you. I still want forever. I made a promise, and I have no intention of taking it back. We're just going to have to be careful 'til this is over.

Watch your back, be careful, and don't do anything stupid.

All my love,
Cody

I pressed the letter against my chest as tears ran down my cheeks.

"Is everything okay?" Samantha asked.

I nodded and held the letter out to her. While she and Dan read it, I said, "Cody's stepping back so I can be with Damon."

"Speaking of which"—Samantha looked toward the door—"he'll be here soon. You should get ready."

"Yeah," I agreed but didn't get up.

I dressed in blue jeans and a hoodie—with Cody's note folded up in the pocket. I didn't remember if Damon told me what he had in mind, but unless I had to, I wasn't going to admit that to him. If he knew he had that effect on me, it could be disastrous.

I sat outside on a park bench waiting for him to show up. I didn't want to make up an excuse for not inviting him in, and with being so close to the mountains, I could tell him I waited here because it wouldn't be too long before the first snowfall of the year.

I felt Damon walking up but pretended not to notice. He didn't need to know I could sense his presence. He slid onto the bench and put his arm around my shoulders. I leaned in like a normal girlfriend would do with her boyfriend, but it sickened me. "What are you doing out here, Princess?"

"Waiting for you." I smiled up at him. "It's a nice day, and there won't be too many more of them before winter hits."

"What would you like to do this afternoon?"

"Well, we should stick around here. I have some home-work to finish up on tonight."

We sat in silence. My hand was on Cody's note. I was hoping that by having it with me I could keep control of my thoughts.

"You seem distracted." Damon rubbed his thumb along my neck. "Is something bothering you?"

I tried to smile at him, but it felt forced. "I'm okay."

"Is Cody being a jerk?"

Rage filled my chest, threatening to explode from my mouth as soon as I opened it. I took several deep breaths and answered, "No, he wants me to be happy, and he wants to be friends."

Damon's expression darkened before he could stop it. "I doubt that's all he wants."

"So do I, but at least he's not being a sore loser." I snug-gled up closer to him, in an attempt to keep him from seeing my face. "Let's not talk about Cody. If I want to talk about him, I can sit with Samantha and Dan."

"Okay, let's talk about us then. How long will you have to date me before you take off his ring," he asked, pulling on my promise ring.

"I'm not wearing it on my left hand anymore. It doesn't have the same meaning now." I looked down at my hand. I'd tried to take it off. I'd put it back in its box, but I couldn't bear to leave it behind. I wanted some sort of reminder of what was real, what was important. I pulled my lip into my mouth and looked at Damon. "If you want, I'll give it back to Cody."

"When you're ready." He pressed my fingers to his mouth. "He was a big part of your life. When you're ready to let go of him, you will."

"Thanks."

"Anything for you." He pulled me to my feet. Taking my hand in his, he started walking.

"Where are we going?"

"Nowhere. I just thought you should get your mind off whatever's troubling you, and it's not going to happen sitting there." He let go of my hand and wrapped his arm around my shoulders. At first, I dropped my hand to my side. Then I remembered we were dating now, so I slipped it around his waist.

"Did you have a good time last night?" I asked, looking up at him.

His lips formed into a crooked smile. "Yes. One of the best nights of my life. You were very passionate."

Heat crept up my cheeks. He stopped walking and tipped my chin up. "I didn't mean to embarrass you."

"It's okay."

"You're normally so reserved. It was a nice change." He bent down, resting his forehead on mine.

My heart thudded, trying to break free from my chest, and my breathing hitched in anticipation. When he pressed his velvet lips against mine, a spark ignited inside me until it grew into a raging inferno. Damon started to pull back, but with my hands tangled in his hair, I held his head down.

"Don't stop, please." My voice sounded low and throaty.

"I think we better," he whispered against my lips. "We have an audience."

Several students looked at us. I lowered my head and put my hands in my pouch. As soon as my fingers brushed against Cody's note, I regained control. My head dropped even lower, weighed down by overwhelming guilt and regret.

"I need to go." I turned away from him and sprinted back to my dorm. I stopped outside the door, not sure if I was ready to face my friends. *Does it matter? They'll find out eventually.* My steps were slow and measured as I walked down the hall. I was looking for an excuse to turn around, but I knew if I did, there was a chance I'd see Damon again.

"Hey," Samantha said when I got back, "how are you doing?"

I shrugged my shoulders and shook my head, staring at the carpet. "Believe everything you hear about me, no matter how repulsive it sounds."

"Why? What happened?" Dan asked.

"It seems Damon was controlling me, and we gave several students a show. It'll crush Cody when he hears about it."

"Maybe he won't find out," Samantha said.

"Yeah, right." I barked out a laugh. "He will."

Chapter 33

It's My Life

Mavros and I stand on a rocky outcrop, looking at the scenery below us. Tiny specks move along winding roads. From here, life down there seems insignificant. I step away from the edge. "I'm tired. Can we go back now?"

Mavros turns to face me. He looks exhausted; dark rings circle his normally vibrant eyes. "Join me, Dacia." He kicks at the ground. "I don't want to go back to the Abyss."

"I can't be with you." I shake my head. "There is no happy ending for the two of us, just an ending. I'm sorry."

His hands rise palms up in front of him, then fall to his sides. "You don't want the life that has been set before you. Change your path. If you don't, you'll endure hardship after hardship. Bind yourself to me. I promise your life will be better if you do."

I fold my hands behind my head and glance up. Fluffy white clouds dot the deep blue sky. "I know my life isn't going to be easy, but it's the life I was given." I lower my head, looking him in the eyes. "God chose me for whatever reason. I can't back down from that."

"Is that what you think?" He shakes his head and laughs. A cynical smile plays on his lips. "God didn't choose you for this life. It was a roll of the dice, the luck of the draw. There is no divine intervention."

"I don't believe that. This is my fate, my destiny." Anger flares inside of me, and I narrow my eyes at him. "It was given to me by God. For some reason, He chose me. For some reason, He believed in me … believed I could handle this."

"Sure, if that's what you want to think." He shrugs and steps toward me. "If you truly believe that, then there is more you should know. You haven't been told the whole truth. There's more to the prophecy. You will never find happiness or relief. Yours will be a tortured life."

"Maybe so—" I chew on my lip "—but there is good in it."

Mavros' eyes flash with anger. "So be it." He spins on his heel and vanishes, leaving behind a puff of black smoke.

Shaking off the last dregs of slumber, I tried to hold onto my dream. Could it be true? Was Mavros right? Was there more to the prophecy than I was told? If so, why was it being hidden from me? I got up off the couch, grabbed my bathroom bag, and headed out into the hall. Instead of going to the bathroom, though, I found myself knocking on Aurelia's door.

She opened the door. Her blouse and slacks were wrinkle-free, not a hair out of place, and her skin looked perfect. "Hello, Dacia. Is everything okay?"

I felt like a disheveled mess. "Yeah, well … not really." I rocked from one foot to the other. "Can we talk? Do you have a minute?"

"Sure, come in." She moved aside and ushered me through the door. Her room was filled with plants. Tall ones skimmed the ceiling. Vines spread across the floor. Leaves spilled over the edges of hanging baskets. Some flowered. Some didn't. But, all of them were thriving.

As soon as she shut the door, I turned toward her. "In my dream last night, Mavros told me there was more to the prophecy. Do you know anything about it?" Before I finished asking, I knew the answer. I saw it in her eyes. Whatever I hadn't been told was bad. "Just tell me, please. I need to know."

"I am truly sorry, Dacia" She tilted her head. "The elders will not allow me to tell you. With time, everything will become clear. Until then, you have to be patient."

I threw myself on her couch and tugged my hand down my face. "Why can't somebody tell me? Why does my life have to be a secret … *from me?*"

She sat beside me, rubbing my back. "Prophecies are not meant to be divulged until the time is at hand. If you know the remainder of it, you might try to change things. In the end, it could destroy you."

I pulled away from her. "Not knowing could do the same." I stood and headed for the door.

"Do not dwell on this."

"Yeah … sure … whatever. Just one more thing for me not to worry about if I somehow manage to make it through this week."

Chapter 34

Two Sides To The Same Coin

Classes were difficult the days following my date with Damon. Instead of walking to them with Cody, Damon walked with me. His arm was either wrapped around my shoulders, around my waist, or we were holding hands. In class, he scooted his chair as close to me as he could. If he couldn't hold my hand, he made sure his leg or foot touched mine. All of this was hard on me, but it had to have been hell on Cody.

Cody didn't acknowledge my presence, didn't so much as look at me. I knew it was better this way, but I wanted to talk to him to make sure he was okay.

I carried Cody's letter with me everywhere I went. Since the day after our date, Damon hadn't controlled my mind, but

I had no way of knowing if it was because he hadn't tried or because I had steeled my mind against him.

Damon threw my bag over his shoulder before placing his hand on the small of my back and leading me through the doors. The crisp air was a slap in the face, snapping me out of my stupor and relieving some of my stress. I closed my eyes and sucked in a deep breath.

"You seem tense today."

I looked up at Damon and nodded. "A little."

He led me to one of the benches and knelt in front of me. Holding my hands in his, he looked me in the eyes. "You know who I am; don't you?"

My heart slammed to a stop, and my mouth fell open. I snapped it closed. Where did this question come from? Why now? I wanted to lie to him, but with him staring into my eyes, I couldn't. I looked down and nodded. "Yeah." I dragged my hand down my face. "Mavros."

"And you've known from the beginning?" He rubbed his thumbs over the back of my hands.

I looked at him from behind my eyelashes. "Yep."

He stood up, turning his back on me. "Did the *Dragon* tell you?"

"No"—I shook my head—"*Aurelia* didn't tell me. She didn't know. I figured it out that first day in class."

His eyebrows rose in disbelief.

Students walked by. I hoped Cody was far away from here so he wouldn't see me with Damon. "Don't you remember me asking if you knew Mavros? Your eyes gave you away." I remembered that day and chuckled. "Well, that and the fact that you barely even glanced at Aurelia. All of the guys and a lot of the girls here drool over her."

"Why this form?" He paced in front of me. "Why do you prefer Damon?"

I shoved my hands in my pouch and slumped against the back of the bench. "I feel safer with you."

"Why?" He shook his head. "They're both me."

"Because I don't like being controlled, and when I met you as Damon, you didn't try to control me."

He looked away for a moment. I could almost see the gears turning in his head. "So, you hung out with me so I wouldn't come to you as Mavros and control you?"

"At first, but then I found that …" I gazed over his shoulder, not wanting to meet his eyes. "Well … I like you. You can be quite charming when you want to be."

Before my eyes, he became Mavros. His features were as stunning as the first time I'd seen him. I sucked in a breath, waiting for him to control me, but he didn't. "I know what you're thinking. You're thinking, 'He's a demon. There's no good in him.' But, Dacia, there is good and there is bad in everything. They are two sides to the same coin. Each and every one of us has both of those sides. Each of us has the capability to do great things, and each of us has the power to do the unspeakable. The side that is encouraged is the side that becomes dominant." He took my hands in his again. "If you help nurture the good in me,

I can do great things. Without you …" He shook his head and looked up, his eyes pleading with me to understand. "I can't do them on my own. If I go back to the Abyss, the only thing for me there is hatred and corruption. Which side do you think will win then?"

A chipmunk scurried across the sidewalk and disappeared into the trees. "If that's true, why should there be any hope for you now? You've only been back from the Abyss for a short time. How can there be any good left in you?"

"There wasn't, not until I met you. Before I met you"—passion burned in his eyes, and I wanted to trust him—"I never had a reason to nurture the good, to let it grow."

I rubbed my hand down my face. "How can I be sure you're not just saying this?"

"Can't you trust me?"

"I want to."

He reached up and brushed the hair back from my eyes. His fingers traced down my face and neck. I shivered from the contact. "I know it's not me you want to be with. I see how you watch Cody. I want you to be happy, but if you choose him, happiness will elude you."

"What if you're wrong?" I whispered.

"Ah, Dacia." Mavros shook his head, and his shoulders sagged. "It breaks my heart that you didn't even try to deny your affection for the boy."

My head fell forward. I couldn't believe I let him trick me so easily. "I'm trying." I looked up into his eyes. "I've spent this past week with you. I haven't spoken to Cody." I lifted my hand. "I quit wearing his ring. I'm trying to be open-minded. I'm trying to make the best decision, to do what's right."

"And, I appreciate that, but you're going to have to decide. If you choose me, Cody can still be part of your life." His features rearranged until I found myself looking at Damon. "If you choose Cody, you'll never see me again. You say you're my friend. Am I that easy to let go of?"

I closed my eyes, lowering my head. "Something tells me that no matter what choice I make, I'll lose."

"You could be happy with me." He squeezed my knee.

I knew he was right. He made me happy, made me feel alive. It might've all been in my head, but that thought never even occurred to me until I wasn't with him anymore. "Yeah, I *could* be, but *will* I be?"

"The choice is yours." He cupped my cheek. When he pulled his hand away, the touch was tender, like a whisper on my skin. "Don't wait 'til it's too late."

I sensed Damon walk away. When I opened my eyes, I was on the bench alone, a single tear dripping down my cheek. I walked back to my dorm room with my head hung low. I knew Cody would be my choice, but Mavros was right. I'd miss my friendship with Damon. How could I live with myself, sending a friend to the Abyss?

There was one bright spot in an otherwise dreary day. Mavros hadn't threatened the lives of my friends.

Muffled voices sounded from behind my door. As soon as I opened it, they quieted. Cody, Samantha, and Dan looked up at me, their faces riddled with guilt. "If I interrupted something, I can leave." I turned back to the door.

"No," Cody said. "Your room. I'll leave."

My shoulders slumped forward, and fresh tears dampened my eyelashes. "I wish you wouldn't. Mavros knows how I feel about you."

"How do you know?" Cody's voice was steely. "How do you know we aren't fooling him?"

"Because he knows everything." I spun around to face them. Cody's eyes were hollow. He looked haggard, broken. "He knows that I know Damon is him. He knows I love you. He told me. He knows everything. We were only fooling ourselves. Please, Cody. Please, don't go."

He took a couple of steps toward me and then hesitated. "Don't know what to do, Dacia. Wanna stay, but don't want you to get hurt because of me."

"If he knows," Samantha said, "what difference does it make? Stay. You two deserve happiness. Dacia'll think of a way to end this without anybody being hurt."

"Why don't we go get something to eat?" Dan grabbed Samantha by the hand. "Excuse me," he said when he got to the door.

I moved to the side, and Cody and I were left in awkward silence. I slumped back against the door, my chin falling to my chest. "I can't do this without you. I know you want to protect me, but I need you. I feel like I've already lost you, and I don't think I can handle it any longer."

Cody stepped closer, but I didn't look up. Silence filled the room making my heart race and my breathing ragged. I felt like all the air was being sucked out of the room. Then Cody spoke, filling the room with warmth and light. His voice was hopeful. "Been thinking, can you or Aurelia create an illusion?"

I looked up at him, my eyebrows crinkled in confusion. "Like what?"

"Could make it look like you were sleeping here, but actually, uh …" Heat crept up his face from his neck. "Actually stay with me in my room."

"Oh." A smile spread across my face. "I don't know. You realize Sarah would kill us."

"Only if she knows."

"I can't, but let's see if Aurelia can." I reached my hand out. When he took it in his, my spirits lifted.

We walked across the hall, and Aurelia opened the door before we knocked. She looked at our hands and raised her eyebrow in an unasked question.

"Cody and I have something we want to ask you," I said.

We sat down on her loveseat, and Cody told her what he wanted. "Can you help?"

Aurelia tapped her finger against her chin, reminding me of Sarah. "Dacia would not be able to do this herself. As soon as she fell asleep, the spell would break."

I let out a heavy sigh. "Oh."

"I can do it for you, though." She stood amongst her plants, trailing her fingers over the leaves.

"But don't you need to sleep?" I asked.

"Not every night. Dragons are not like people. Our sleep patterns vary. There are times when I do not sleep for weeks on end."

"Hmph. Weird." I tilted my head and thought about it for a minute. "I never knew."

"I will make it look like you are sleeping on the couch. You will either have to teleport to Cody's room or make yourself invisible and walk over there. Stay hidden. Who knows what Mavros will do if he finds out things are not what they seem."

"Thank you." Cody's eyes were alight with happiness.

I jumped up and hugged Aurelia. "Thanks. I need this. Time with Cody, I mean. I feel like I'm losing myself."

"It is my pleasure." She smiled. *You need to find yourself before it is too late.*

"Can you make sure Cody gets back to his room safely?" I asked. "If he goes back over with me, Mavros will know something is up."

"Yes."

I turned to face Cody, wrapping my arms around his neck. "I'll be there tonight, but I need to wait until Samantha and Dan get back. They have to know it's an illusion."

"Sure." His fingers lingered on my arm. "Don't take too long."

I went back to my room and wrote a note explaining our plan. As soon as Samantha and Dan returned, I handed it to them. "Read this."

"Oh." Samantha looked up from the note, smiling.

I put my finger over my lips to keep her silenced. Dan grinned and handed the paper back to me. A small fire burning in the palm of my hand destroyed the evidence. "I'm going to hit the showers." I winked. "I'll be back soon."

On my way to the bathroom, I checked in with Aurelia. *I'm taking a shower. From there, I'll teleport to Cody's room. Is that okay?*

Yes, be careful, she warned.

As planned, I teleported into Cody's room. His back was turned to me. He sat on the couch, staring blankly at the TV. "Hi," I said.

He jumped up. "Scared me."

"Sorry." I walked over and stood in front of him, not sure how to act or what to do.

Cody slowly lifted his hands toward my neck. He tilted my head back and looked hungrily into my eyes. His lips pressed against mine with an urgency that let me know how much he'd missed me. His hands traced a path from my neck to my shoulders and down my arms. When they found my hips, he pulled me closer to him, moaning with desire. I wrapped my legs around his waist and twined my fingers in his hair, never wanting to let go.

When he pulled away from me, I shivered in anticipation of another touch. I leaned my head back and looked up at his face. His blue eyes shone with happiness.

"Missed you." His voice was filled with desire.

I planted kisses along his neck. "I've missed you too." I slid my hands under his shirt, kneading his back. "That was too long to go without you."

We spent the evening lying on the couch in each other's arms. The TV was on, but neither of us looked away from each other long enough to know what was playing.

When I could barely keep my eyes open, Cody got up, reached his hand down, and led me to his bed. I rested my head against Cody's chest, his arms wrapped around me, and I felt a sense of serenity fill my body and mind. *This is where I belong*, I thought. *There are no other options for me.*

Chapter 35

The Way Life Should Be

$\mathcal{I}$ woke up in Cody's arms, the morning sun streaming in through the window and Aurelia's voice echoing in my head. *Dacia, you need to get back here before too many people are awake. You cannot risk being seen teleporting into the bathroom.*

Okay. Give me a few minutes. Nuzzled against Cody, I watched him sleep. This was what I wanted. It wouldn't last for eternity, but a lifetime spent with him would be one of happiness.

I gently shook his arm. "Cody, wake up."

"Everything okay?" He bolted upright, a look of fear chased away the peaceful expression from moments before.

I brushed my finger along his forehead, trying to erase his dismay. "Yeah, but I have to go."

"Be back tonight?" He propped himself on his arm.

I ran my hand along his bare chest, wanting to stay with him but knowing I couldn't. "As long as Aurelia is okay with it."

I started to roll out of bed, but Cody caught my wrist and pulled me to him. He brushed back my hair and sighed. His lips touched mine in a gentle promise. "I love you. Be careful."

"I love you, too, and I will." Before I teleported, I turned invisible.

Cody sat on the edge of the bed and pulled his hands through his hair. He stood. His eyes looked haunted. I didn't know if I should wrap my arms around him or not let him know I'd seen his torment.

Still unsure of what to do, I stepped forward. The floor creaked.

Cody looked right at me without seeing me. "Dacia?" His face reverted to its expressionless mask. He stretched his arm out. Before he could touch me, I teleported.

Standing in the corner of the bathroom, I dropped my chin to my chest and tugged my hand through my hair, wondering if I'd made the right decision. I lifted my head. *Aurelia, can you send my doppelganger out of the room?*

She is on her way.

Okay. Guilt weighed on me. I hated what I was doing to Cody and that he felt the need to hide it from me.

Dan and Samantha were still sleeping when I crept into my room. I sat down on the couch and picked up my book.

I was deep into reading when I heard my name. Looking up, I tried to figure out who said it. Samantha and Dan were still sleeping. I walked to the window. Damon stood on the lawn, gazing at my window. When I looked out, a grin spread across his face. He motioned for me to come down to him.

"Might as well," I said to myself. "I'm sure I'll have to spend time with him today." I stuck a bookmark in my book and jotted down a quick note to Samantha before walking out into the hallway.

Aurelia waited for me, arms folded across her chest. "I sensed him calling you. Be careful."

I nodded my head and sighed. "I'll be glad when this is over, only five days to go."

"I fear these will be the worst five." Worry furrowed her brow.

"I know." I looked down the hall toward the door. "I better go before he comes looking for me." As I walked outside, I tried to get in the right frame of mind. I needed to leave my guilt behind and gather my wits.

Damon leaned against his Mustang, arms folded over his chest. As I approached, he opened up the passenger door for me.

Before getting in, I asked, "Where are we going?"

"For a ride." He helped me into his car and shut the door.

Aurelia, I'm leaving. I don't know where he's taking me.

I will keep an eye on you.

Thanks.

Damon climbed in behind the steering wheel and peeled out of the parking lot. He turned onto a gravel road I'd never been on before. I looked out the window, enjoying the mountain view. A thrill of excitement ran through me when Damon took my hand in his.

"I thought it would be nice to get off campus for the day." His voice radiated menace. "There are too many distractions there."

My mind was filled with images of Cody and me. Somehow Damon projected them into my thoughts. Some were real, memories of mine seen from Damon's perspective. Others were horrible, images of Cody suffering. Cody chained to a dungeon wall, deep wounds covering his bloody body.

"Stop!" I ripped my hand out of his. "Stop. I told you I'm trying."

Damon's lips turned up in a cruel smile. "Yeah, that's what you said."

"I'm here with you now." I brushed my fingers along the back of his hand.

His fingers intertwined with mine. "For now, but what about tonight? Will you stay with me tonight?"

My breath caught, and I felt trapped. I couldn't say yes. It would break Cody. I couldn't say no because Mavros would know. "Oh … I, uh, I don't know. Where do you even stay? Do you have a dorm room?"

"No, I don't sleep." He laughed. "However, I would enjoy the feel of you in my arms while you slept."

My stomach constricted, and I discreetly swallowed the lump in my throat. "I don't know if I'm ready for that."

He squeezed my hand. My fingers pressed together, grinding the bones against each other. "Then how can I believe you're trying?"

"That's a really big step." Images of Cody and I sleeping on the couch flashed through my head like a slide show.

"But with him, you're ready?"

"He's been part of my life forever. You've been part of my life for a few weeks." I tugged my hand through my hair. I needed to find the right argument without upsetting him. "Where would we even stay?"

"Your room."

"Oh."

"Think about it." His voice softened, and he turned toward me.

Looking into his eyes, I felt my trepidation fade away. A warm tingly sensation spread through my body, and I thought about what it would be like lying with him, feeling his muscular arms holding me while I slept.

No! The thought struck me like lightning on a clear day. *You cannot give into him, Dacia.*

Damon slammed on his brakes. I lunged forward, stopped by a jerk of the seatbelt. He turned in his seat and hissed through gritted teeth, "Tell your dragon to stay out of this."

"You heard her?"

"Not exactly." He snarled at me. His canines elongated. "I know she's in your head, but I can't hear what she is telling you."

Aurelia, he can tell when you contact me. Please don't make him angry.

I waited for a response, and when I didn't get one, I assumed my message went through loud and clear. I looked over at Damon and smiled. "I told her to stay out of this." I reached up and traced my fingers along his jaw. "What I do when I'm with you has nothing to do with her."

"Precisely." He cupped my face in his hands and drew me closer to him. I expected him to press his lips against mine. Instead, he said, "And that's why dragons shouldn't be allowed to live. If she tries to interfere again, I'll end her. Understand?"

The pressure increased on my jaws, making it hard to think or move. "Yes," I squeaked through immobile lips.

"You might want to let her know." He relaxed his grip. "I'm playing for keeps this time." He slid his hands down to my shoulders. His features softened, warming his eyes. "I can't lose you. You mean too much to me."

The dark depths of his irises drew me in. "I'll let her know next time I see her."

He faced forward, put the car in gear, and drove off. I stared out the window.

Damon's wrath terrified me. I had no idea where he was taking me and if Aurelia was still watching over me. He sped down the gravel road, fishtailing around the curves. Veins bulged in his neck.

"Wh—" My voice cracked. I cleared my throat and started again. "Where are we going?"

"You'll see."

My imagination was getting the best of me. My heart raced, and my hands shook. He'd always told me where he was taking me. He'd never been this evasive before. Nefarious' cave and Draconian's dungeons popped into my mind. Would he try to keep me somewhere until I gave into him? Would he return me to the Abyss?

I stuck my hand in my pocket and clutched Cody's note. Then I focused on my breathing. I needed to control my fear. I needed to play my part and keep myself and my friends safe. "I've never been this way before. It's pretty."

"Not many people come back here. It's secluded, the perfect place for a picnic." He smiled at me, a smile that made warning bells ring in my head.

I shifted in my seat. "That sounds nice."

Damon pulled off the road near a creek. He stepped out, then walked around to my side opening the door for me. He held his hand out, and I took it, allowing him to help me out of the car.

Water rushed over rocks, smoothing and rounding them as it called me closer. "I love this sound." I closed my eyes and let the rhythm of nature calm me. "That and the smell of pines. They bring me to life."

Damon grabbed the picnic basket out of his car before taking hold of my hand and leading me over boulders and across the stream. "On the other side of these trees"—he lifted my hand with his and pointed in front of us—"is a lake. That's our destination."

Leading me through the forest, Damon never let go of my hand. Normally, I wouldn't have been able to fight his hold on me, but I clutched Cody's letter and pictured his blue eyes.

We stepped out of the trees, and mountains rose behind the lake, casting their reflections over the calm water. "This is beautiful. I can't believe we're the only ones here."

"Most people only venture where their maps tell them to, but for you, I needed to find someplace magnificent." He lifted my hand, brushing his lips against the back of it. Then he pulled away. He took a blanket out of the basket and spread it over the grass. I sat down and focused my attention on the scenery. Damon's fingertips brushed against my cheek. "You can't give the mountains all your attention. Save some for me."

"This is the perfect spot, but I could never ignore you." I smiled at him, hoping I was a good enough actress for him to think I was under his control.

Damon pulled me closer. Our eyes met, and he held me transfixed with his gaze. It felt like he was peering into my soul, searching for answers I wouldn't give him. While held by his stare, I tried to read his mind, but I was met by a brick wall.

Damon's expression hardened, and he turned away from me. "Would you like to go for a walk, or are you hungry?"

"Let's walk."

We strolled to the lake. My left hand was held in Damon's, and my right one was shoved in my hoodie pocket, clutching Cody's letter. At the water's edge, Damon spun me around, yanking my hand out of my pocket and sending the letter flying through the air. He clasped my hand in his and danced to a song I couldn't hear. A chill shuddered through my chest as I watched the paper sink below the surface.

"I hope that wasn't anything important," Damon whispered.

His words caressed my ear, and my control slipped. "Just a list of things to do."

"If you choose me—" he trailed kisses along my neck and up my ear "—servants will be responsible for all the mundane tasks. Your only job will be to enjoy life."

My legs weakened, and I slumped against him. "That's hard to imagine."

"But, once you have it, it's hard to imagine life without."

By the time we got back to campus, the sun sat low in the sky. Damon took my hand in his. "Did you decide?" His eyes filled with hope.

I knew this was coming, but I wasn't ready for it. I shook my head. "How can I say yes with Aurelia right across the hall? I can't let the two of you hurt each other."

His grip tightened on my hand, igniting a spark of anger in his eyes. "That *dragon* has caused me nothing but trouble."

"I'll see you tomorrow, though; won't I?"

"Yes, tomorrow." He raised my hand to his lips, then got out and opened my door for me, reaching down to help me out of the car. "Today was a good day. They could all be this way." He kissed my ear, my neck, and my cheek, finally bringing his lips against mine. Warmth tingled through my body as all thoughts of Cody were replaced with Damon. "Invite me in. Let me stay with you tonight."

I led him toward the dormitory, urging him to walk faster. *What are you doing?* I heard Arion's voice in my head. *You can't do this!*

I stopped near Wisteria Hall's entrance and shook my head, dropping Damon's hand. "I … I'm sorry. I can't." I turned and ran inside, not stopping until I was in my room. I leaned against the closed door, resisting the urge to bang my head on it.

Are you okay? Aurelia's voice rang through my head.

Yeah. Damon was controlling me. I almost let him in here.

Lying in Cody's bed with his arms wrapped around me, I couldn't keep my mind from wandering, from wondering how it would feel to lie in Damon's embrace. I let out a long, dramatic sigh.

"What's wrong?" Cody lifted his arm out from under me so he could prop himself up with it. With his other hand, he ran his fingers through my hair, brushing it back from my face.

I looked over his shoulder, knowing there was no way I could look in his eyes and answer him. "I can't stop thinking about Damon."

His arm slipped, but he didn't say anything.

"I've been keeping your letter with me." I looked into his haunted eyes. "I think it was keeping him from controlling me. But, Damon must've known. He made me lose it today. It's at the bottom of a lake somewhere up in the mountains, and I can't help but think that if I'd had it with me all day, I wouldn't be feeling this way now."

"So you think he was controlling you?" His voice was flat and emotionless.

"I know he was, but what I don't know is why I can't stop thinking about him now."

Cody rolled onto his back and stared at the ceiling.

"I feel like I'm losing myself." My voice cracked at the end.

"If he's what you want—"

"He's not!" I sat up and looked into his eyes. "You're the one I want."

"Then why?"

"I don't know. That's what I'm trying to explain." I let out a huff and flopped down on the pillows. "Maybe I'm not saying it right."

The look he gave me was filled with unbridled pain. He turned away. "Help me understand."

Clutching the hair on top of my head, I stared at the ceiling. *How can I explain so he'll understand?* "I guess I wonder if there's some residual effect. Like somehow he's controlling some of my thoughts but not all of them, kinda like when he used to call me to him."

"Think that's it?" His voice rose. "Maybe he's calling, but since you're farther away, it's making you think of him, not go to him?"

"I don't know." I rolled onto my side and put my hand on Cody's chest. "What I do know is that this is not me. He is not what I want. That's why I'm so frustrated. I don't want to think about Damon, especially when I'm with you."

He put his hand over mine. "We came up with one way." His eyes lit up mischievously, and he pulled me on top of him.

"How could I have forgotten?" I laughed before bringing my lips down on his.

Chapter 36

*M*avros stands with one foot on Cody's bloody chest. "You're not fooling me, Dacia." His mouth turns up in a sneer. "You're only fooling people like Cassandra, people who aren't intelligent enough to see beyond what's on the surface."

I try to keep my focus on Mavros. Every time I glance at Cody, Mavros inflicts more pain on him. "You can't expect me to give up nineteen years of my life just because you showed up on my doorstep like a little, lost kitten." The wind whips my hair around my face.

His face twists in anger. "Yes, I can. I am a god." He presses his foot down, and Cody moans. "He's a mere mortal."

Thunder crashes in response to Mavros' actions, and rain hammers the ground.

"No," I say softly, shaking my head. "No, you're not a god. You're a demon. There's a big difference, one I thought even you could see."

Mavros pounces, transforming into the panther. His claws dig into my shoulders as he knocks me to the rocky ground. His fangs press into my throat, not breaking the skin but threatening to. I close my eyes, waiting for his jaws to clench, to pierce my jugular vein.

Instead, his weight shifts, lightening. Mavros' ebony eyes stare down into mine. "If you choose *the boy*, you will watch him die. If you choose me, he can enjoy a long, happy life." He smooths the wet hair off my face. "Nobody can make this decision for you, and nobody but you can save your friends. The choice should be simple, but every drop of rain tells me you're going to make the wrong decision."

"*Choice? What choice?*" A humorless laugh flees from my shaking head.

"I told you I was playing for keeps." He sits up, straddling my waist, and holds my hands down. "You and Cody are about to wake up. Are you going to tell him that he's going to live or that you're sacrificing him?"

I woke with a start. My breath caught in my throat as I flung myself into a sitting position. The sheet slid down my body. Goosebumps rose on my arms. My tank top did little to stop the chill.

"You okay?" Cody's voice was groggy from being startled awake. "Bad dream?" He rubbed my arms in a calming gesture.

I jerked my head from side to side, searching the shadows for Mavros. I knew the room was blessed, but I felt his presence, his anger, and hatred. "I'm not sure it was a dream." I leaned into Cody's embrace, needing his strength and love. "I think Mavros was in my head."

He blew out a heavy sigh. "What's he want?"

"For me to choose him." I folded my arms over his, tightening his hold on me, hoping it would chase away my fears. "What else?"

"You can't." His voice had a desperate edge to it.

"Do I have a choice?" I tilted my head and looked up at him.

His eyes opened wide, and his muscles tensed. "Yeah … me." A tortured expression crossed his face. "Choose me."

I turned so I was facing him. "If I choose you, he'll kill you. That doesn't seem like much of a choice to me."

"Choose me." His thumb brushed against my cheek. "Then save me."

I drew my fingers over my eyes, trying to pull myself together. "If only it were that easy."

Damon and I strolled across campus. His arm was thrown over my shoulder, not lovingly but possessively. My body tensed when Cassandra and Bryce came into view … until I realized they were holding hands.

"Dacia," Bryce said. I looked at him, not sure what to expect. His smile was warm, and happiness sparkled in his pale eyes. "Thanks for the push you gave Cassi."

"Yeah, uh sure." I stumbled over the words.

Bryce nudged Cassandra playfully. She cleared her throat and shifted her weight from foot to foot. "Thanks," she mumbled. "You were right."

"No problem."

Damon started to pull me away but not before Cassandra said, "You should really be with Cody, though. It's obvious the two of you belong together."

"She's with me." Damon snarled. His fingers dug into my shoulder. Panther claws tore through my skin.

"Let's go," I said through clenched teeth. We rounded a corner, and I pulled Damon behind a couple of spruce trees. I grabbed the neckline of my hoodie and pulled it down over my shoulder exposing five bloody claw marks. My eyes narrowed, and I curled my hands into fists. "Since I don't heal from demon wounds on my own, I need to go see Aurelia." I spun on my heel, but I only made it one step before Damon's hand clamped down on my other shoulder.

"I'm sorry, Dacia." He stood in front of me, looking like he might shatter into a thousand pieces if I walked off. "I never meant to hurt you. Please believe me."

I pulled away from him. On the outside, I looked calm, but on the inside, a storm raged, threatening to break free and destroy everything in its path. "For someone who doesn't mean to hurt me, you sure do it a lot."

"You have to believe me when I say it was not intentional." He put his hand on my injured shoulder and closed his eyes. I sucked in a quick breath as the pain moved from my wounds toward his fingertips. When Damon opened his eyes, the only evidence that I'd been hurt was the blood on my shirt. If I'd have gone to Aurelia, it would've taken days to heal it.

Fury wrapped around my muscles, tightening them. My fists clenched, and my jaw clamped down. When I spoke, the words were soft, but there were sharp edges on them. "Why didn't you do that when you attacked me before school started? You could've saved me three days of my life and a whole lot of pain."

His eyes widened in surprise. "I couldn't." Pain clouded his face. "You wouldn't let me. I begged you to invite me in so I could help you." He reached toward me but let his hand drop. "There was no way for me to heal you. I couldn't even see you."

I stared at him, trying to figure out if he was telling me the truth or just trying to placate me.

"When you told me you were still injured, I healed you. Didn't you realize it?" He took a step closer to me. His shoulders slumped, and he looked broken. "The first time I met you, I healed you." He stretched his hand toward me. "You never knew?"

I shook my head, backing away from him. I thought about that day at the park, about how I'd been surprised when I got in my truck and my shoulder no longer ached. Had it really been him?

"I drew the venom out. I never meant to hurt you. I didn't know you weren't healing. If you'd have told me, I would've helped you sooner." He took a step back and lowered his head. "Please forgive me."

The storm raging inside me died down until I was in control. I nodded at him. "This time, but never again."

Samantha looked up from her homework. "Sarah called while you were out. She'd like to see you today if you have time."

I dropped my chin to my chest and shook my head. "I shouldn't have kept her in the dark this whole time."

"I'm surprised she didn't call sooner." She tapped her pen against her notebook.

Pulling my bloody sweatshirt over my head, I grabbed a new one, picked up the phone, and waited for Sarah to answer. "Hello."

"Hey." I ran my hand through my hair. "Samantha said you called."

"I did. Can you come to my office? I'd like to talk to you."

"Sure. Is anyone there? Can I just show up?"

"The coast is clear."

"Okay, see ya in a few." I hung up the phone. "I guess I'll be back." I teleported to Sarah's office. Guilt washed over me when I looked around the room where I'd spent so much of my first semester.

"I wish I could travel like that." Sarah sat on one of the couches, pouring lemonade into a glass. "Would you like some?" She held up the pitcher.

"Sure." I sat down across from her, grabbing my glass. "I'm sorry I haven't been here more. I have no excuse for it." I took a drink, not realizing how thirsty I was.

She waved her hand. "Don't worry about that. It's probably best."

"Really?" My eyebrows puckered together.

"Yes. Aurelia keeps me filled in. It keeps me off the demon's radar and makes it so there's one less person for you to watch over."

"I hadn't thought of it that way." I set my empty glass on the coffee table.

"How are you holding up?"

I looked down at my lap. "Not too good. I only have four days to figure out how to defeat Mavros, and I have no idea. I can't say yes to him, but I also can't say no to him. I can't let him kill my friends, but I can't let him have the world either. And, if he's what he seems like most of the time I'm around him, I can't imagine sending him back to the Abyss." I looked into Sarah's hazel eyes, hoping she would understand.

She nodded. "I've heard nothing but good things about him from all the teachers. It's amazing how a demon can seem like such a good person, but you have to understand that he's not."

My hands clenched. "How can you be sure?"

"Demons are evil, crafty, manipulative creatures bent on destruction." She leaned forward with her elbows on her knees.

A muscle in my jaw ticked. "And angels are the exact opposite."

"Right." Her eyebrows pinched together, and she sounded unsure.

"Then how do you explain Lucifer?" A tight fist of rage clenched inside me. None of them knew what Damon could be like. None of them had seen the despair in his eyes when he worried about going back to the Abyss. "And, if he can be evil, how can we be so sure no demons are good?"

"How many times has Mavros in any of his forms attacked you?" She shifted on the couch, looking uncomfortable. "How many times has he controlled you? If he's good, he wouldn't do that. If he's good, he wouldn't threaten to kill your friends if you don't choose him. I know you want to believe he can change, but he can't."

I refilled my glass and took a drink while I thought about what she'd said. "Most of the time, I would agree with you, but there are times when he looks so honest and sincere that it breaks my heart to think about sending him back. Then there are times like today."

"What happened today?" Her body went rigid.

"Bryce and Cassandra thanked me for hooking them up." I laughed. "Can you believe that? Anyway, Cassandra told me I should be with Cody, not Damon, and Damon's claws extended into my shoulder. He healed me; he didn't have to. Why would he unless there is some good in him?"

"Because he wants you to believe he's changing. He wants you to believe you have the ability to make him better."

I tugged my hand through my hair. "What if I can?"

"You can't." She sat on the coffee table and patted my leg. "This is a game to him, and if he wins, it's one hell of a prize."

I leaned back, resting my head against the couch. "I have no intention of letting him stay, but I don't know how to send him back either."

"You'll figure something out." Her tone was sympathetic.

I couldn't help but laugh. "You sound just like Cody."

Her face turned solemn. "How's he doing?"

"This is killing him, but he's doing his best to hide it." I remembered his expression yesterday when he thought I was gone, and my heart broke a little more.

"I noticed you're not wearing the ring he gave you." She pointed at my finger.

I looked down at my hand and sighed. "Damon commented on it, so I thought it'd be best not to wear it all the time."

"As hard as it must be for you and Cody, I think that's a good idea." She patted my knee one more time before standing up. "You have to do your best not to let Mavros or Damon or whoever know how you feel about Cody."

"He knows."

She spun around and looked at me. Her eyebrows rose until they were covered by her hair. Surprise and fear mingled together on her face. She cleared her throat and regained her usual composure. "Are you sure?"

"Yes, but I told him I'm trying." I twisted the strings on my hoodie together and stared at the edge of the coffee table. "It seems like he's buying it."

"I hope so."

I pressed my hands down on the couch on either side of me. "If it's okay with you, I'm supposed to meet everyone for supper." My stomach churned. I pinched my eyes shut and stood.

"What is it?" Sarah's voice was soft, concerned.

"Nothing." I tugged a shaking hand through my hair. "Just a feeling."

She clasped my shoulder. "If you need to talk, I'm here."

"Thanks." I closed my eyes, and when I opened them again, I stood in my room with Samantha, Dan, and Cody looking at me. I looked into Cody's blue eyes and fought the urge to throw myself into his arms. Instead, I asked, "Anybody hungry?"

"Starved," Cody answered.

We walked to the cafeteria. Cody and I were separated by Dan and Samantha. I tried not to glance at him, not to seem interested in him at all, but I'm sure I failed miserably. I got a chicken Caesar salad and a glass of water and sat down beside Samantha, leaving two chairs between myself and Cody. When he talked, I looked at my food or around the room, even though I was hanging on his every word.

I was almost done eating when the chair beside me scraped against the floor. I looked up into Damon's eyes. "May I?"

I glanced around the table and shrugged. "Uh, sure."

Damon scooted the chair right next to mine, sat down, and threw his arm over my shoulders, never looking away from Cody. Cody's expression darkened. His jaw clenched, and his eyes narrowed to slits.

Still watching Cody, Damon traced his fingers from my ear to my chin. I clutched my fork in my fist. *You're supposed to be his girlfriend,* I reminded myself.

I looked up at him through my eyelashes and curved my lips into what I hoped was a convincing smile. "Damon, let me finish eating. Then we can go for a walk or something."

"That's okay. I just wanted this." He cupped my face in his hands and leaned forward. I felt his breath on my ear. I wanted to pull away, but I fought the urge. "Will you kiss me in front of him, or have you made your decision?" he whispered so only I could hear him.

My heart plummeted as I closed the gap. I wrapped my arms around his neck and pressed my lips against his. He pulled me onto his lap. His fingertips brushed the skin on my back and sent shivers of desire through my body.

With a crash, something fell. I jumped up and turned to see what had happened. Cody's chair was lying on the floor, and he was darting toward the door. The noise in the cafeteria quieted until the humming of the air conditioner was all that could be heard. One hundred and fifty eyes turned to stare at me.

Damon chuckled softly. "My work here is done. I'll see you in class tomorrow."

I reached out and grabbed his hand, yanking him back. "What was that for?"

He smiled at me, not just any smile. This was a smile that melted the hard edges of my anger, softening me, almost making me forget what I wanted to say.

I shook my head, trying to regain my concentration. "Please leave him alone."

"Oh, I have no intention of harming him tonight. I've had my fun for today." He wrapped his arm around my waist and pulled me closer until our bodies were pressed together. Desire burned in his eyes. "Can I come to your room tonight?"

"After that stunt you just pulled," a red-faced Samantha yelled at him, "you're not welcome." Dan's hands wrapped around her waist, restraining her.

"Like you could stop me, little girl." Damon's voice was so cold that I trembled.

I pulled myself together. "She just did. I can't invite you in now."

He took a step back. "Your time is running out. I'd advise you to think about what's best for you and your friends." He turned and sauntered through the room.

"You have to go after Cody." Samantha clutched the back of her chair. Her eyes darted toward the door. "You have to make sure he's safe."

A black hole opened up inside of my chest, sucking all of my joy, all of my happiness, and all of my hope into it. My arms hung limply at my sides, and my eyes burned. "He won't want to see me."

"Go." Dan pointed. "We'll give you a minute."

"No." I tugged my hand through my hair, looking from them to the door. "You better come along. Samantha just pissed Damon off. I need to make sure you guys stay safe, too."

As we walked through the cafeteria, students—too anxious to wait until we were out of earshot—began whispering. "What do they see in her?" "She could have a piece of me." "What a slut!" "Cody's better off without her." "I could cheer him up." "But Damon's so hot. Can you blame her?" "What was that about?"

I kept my head up, not letting them know I heard what they were saying about me, but by the time I got outside, my eyes were full of unshed tears. I wrapped my arms around my waist, trying to hold myself together.

The sun was below the mountains, turning the sky dark blue. A few stars dotted the heavens, but it was still bright enough out to see. Unlike me, Cody had made it more than a few steps outside the door.

"Where do you think he went?" Samantha rested her hand on my shoulder.

"I … I don't know." My lip trembled. "I hope he didn't confront Damon."

Dan stood in front of me, holding my gaze with his. "See if Aurelia knows where he is."

Aurelia, do you know where Cody is?

I thought he was with you. She sounded confused. I imagined her perfectly trimmed eyebrows pinching together.

I shook my head at Dan and Samantha to let them know she didn't know where Cody was. *He was.*

What happened?

Damon. I projected images of what had happened to her.

Arion and I will help you find him.

Thanks. I pulled my bottom lip into my mouth and fought the urge to cry. "She doesn't know where he is, but they'll help us find him."

"I'm sure he's fine." Samantha squeezed my shoulder before walking away. "Damon said he wouldn't hurt him tonight."

Dan snorted. "And you trust him?"

"Da-aan." Samantha shot him a look that let him know she didn't think he was helping.

You can sense him. Aurelia's voice sounded in my head.

Only when he's close.

Start close to you. Then push your thoughts out until you find him.

I'll try. I stood still and searched for Cody's aura, scared that when I found him, he wouldn't want to see me.

It will not work if you do not want it to.

What do you mean? Anger flared through me again. *Of course, I want it to!*

Calm down, Dacia. You have to want it more than you fear it.

Oh. I pictured Cody leaving the cafeteria. I saw how betrayed and hurt he felt. *I don't know if I can.*

Then you will fail, and Cody may not remain safe.

I closed my eyes and took several deep breaths. Then I pressed my consciousness out, searching for Cody's combination of strength and love. My head hurt from the strain, but I didn't find him.

We walked toward the dorms. I stopped every few feet, searching for Cody, hoping to find him safe, praying Mavros would keep his word and leave Cody alone.

I found him, Arion said. *He is in the gymnasium. I will keep an eye on him until you get there.*

Thank you, Arion. I made sure I sent sincere gratitude along with my thoughts. *I owe you.*

No, I have yet to repay my debt. Must I remind you? You saved my life.

I sprinted to Lupine Fieldhouse with Dan and Samantha lagging behind. My only concern was making sure Cody was safe. As I reached for the door, something glistened in the corner of my eye. Turning, I watched Arion step out of the bushes. He shimmered like a diamond in the sunlight.

Patting his neck, I asked, "Can you get Dan and Samantha back to our room and keep them safe?"

He bowed slightly. "Consider it done."

Samantha squeezed my arm. "Good luck."

"Take your time." Dan patted my shoulder.

When they left, I went in. Several students were in the first room lifting weights and riding stationary bikes, but Cody wasn't among them. I glanced at the pool as I walked by, not seeing him there either.

I scanned each room as I passed it. I found Cody where I expected he'd be, shooting hoops. A few other students were playing a game on the far side of the court.

I grabbed a ball and dribbled toward the basket. When I was by the free-throw line, I tossed the ball up. My shot missed, not coming anywhere near the hoop. My arms were trembling and weak. I went after the ball and held it against my hip.

"Why are you here?" Cody asked without taking his eyes off his shots and rebounds.

The sharp edge of his voice pierced my chest. "I needed to make sure you were safe."

"I am." He dribbled to a different hoop. "Leave."

"I, uh." I stopped and cleared my throat. "I also need to explain."

"Explain what? I saw." His breathing accelerated. He shot again and ran after his rebound. "Don't want you here. Don't want to hear it." He grabbed the ball and shot it immediately. The net swished, and he chased after it. "Leave me alone."

His words were filled with malice and hit me like physical blows. Their impact sucked the breath from my lungs and left me reeling. "I didn't have a choice." The words left my mouth of their own accord.

"You didn't have to be so passionate! You didn't have to want it." He turned toward me, and in his face, I saw all the grief and heartache he felt.

My ball dropped to the ground and rolled across the court. "Is that what you think—that I wanted it?" I walked toward him, using my powers to force him to face me without moving away. I pressed my mouth against his, parting his lips with my tongue. His hands wrapped around me, and a moan escaped his throat. I wanted to keep kissing him, to have him hold me and love me, but I wanted it to be real, to be his choice. I stepped back and released him. "Do you still think I had a choice? Do you think I could control myself?"

He looked down at the floor, kicking at nothing.

"I chose to lean in and kiss him because he told me if I didn't, he would know my mind was made up. I didn't choose to keep kissing him. I didn't choose to be passionate." I turned and walked away. "I know it doesn't seem like it, but I'm doing the best I can. And, I love you."

Cody didn't stop me from leaving, didn't make a sound, and with each step I took, I felt a piece of my heart tear away. Each shard caused more pain than any demon or dragon could ever inflict on me.

I closed the door behind me and collapsed. Sobs tore through my chest. Tremors threatened to tear my limbs from my body, but I didn't care. I'd just lost the most important thing in my life, and I couldn't blame him for giving up on me.

Strong arms lifted me from the ground like I was a small child. I looked into Cody's face. His blue eyes were as hard as ice. "Not safe for you on your own." His voice was distant. His muscles were taut. Instead of feeling comforted by his embrace, I felt like I was being held by a stranger, or worse yet, by an enemy.

"I … can …" A sob choked my words. I wiped the tears from my face but couldn't stop new ones from falling. "I can walk."

He set me down beside him, making sure my footing was steady before striding away. He took me to my room, never looking at me or saying anything to me. When I stepped inside, he turned and trudged down the hallway.

"Oh, Dacia, I'm sorry," Samantha said, sending a fresh wave of tears flowing from my eyes.

Dan walked over and rested his hand on my shoulder. "Give him some time." He turned to Samantha and said, "I'm going to make sure he doesn't do anything stupid."

"Thanks." I tried to smile at him, but my lips formed into a look of pain instead.

Samantha brushed her lips over Dan's. "Be safe."

"I will."

When he left, Samantha led me over to the couch. "He'll forgive you."

"Why would he?" I remembered the pain in his expression, the heartache.

She stood in front of me with her arms folded over her chest. Her foot tapped against the lavender carpet. "Because he loves you, and it's not like you wanted this."

"Are you sure?" I clutched the panther pendant. Heat flowed through my hand and up my arm. I jerked on it, trying once again to pull it off, but it didn't budge.

She crossed her arms over her chest and glared at me. "Yes, I'm sure."

"I think Sarah is right." I tucked the necklace under my hoodie. "Damon wouldn't have done that to Cody if he was good."

Samantha sat beside me "She's not the only one who feels that way about him. We all do."

"Everyone but me." I held my head in my hands.

She pulled me into a one-armed hug. "But, you're the only one he was trying to convince otherwise, and now that you know, hopefully, you can stop him."

"Let's hope." I leaned my head against hers.

The phone rang, piercing the silence. "Please answer that," I said with a desperate edge to my voice.

She picked it up. "Hello ... Oh, okay. See you in the morning ... Love you, too." She hung up and walked back to the couch. "Cody's fine. They're in their room. They're staying there tonight. I'm sorry."

I wasn't surprised that Cody didn't want me with him, but I felt more pieces of my heart tear apart nevertheless. I got up, grabbed my bathroom bag and pajamas, turned to Samantha, and said, "I'll be back."

"Hang on. I'll go with you."

I knew she was coming to make sure I didn't do anything stupid, so I turned to face her. "I'm not going to run off. I'm not going to challenge Mavros or get myself killed. I'm just going to get ready for bed."

She put her hand on her hip and glared at me. "If it's all the same, I'm coming anyway. I need to get ready for bed, too."

Chapter 37

Apology Not Accepted

The pull was overwhelming. I tried to fight his call, but without Cody, I didn't have the strength. One moment, I was pacing in front of the couch. The next, I was standing in the trees behind the dorm face to face with Mavros. Dressed all in black, he blended into the shadows.

"Why tonight?" Anger tightened my chest. "Haven't you caused enough trouble for one day?"

"I wanted to apologize." He looked into my eyes but didn't try to control me.

"Oh, okay." I nodded my head and a humorless laugh escaped my lips. "Sure you did."

He lowered his head to his chest. "It wasn't my intention to hurt you. I'm truly sorry."

"Apology not accepted." Fire ignited in my hand. I looked at the flames in surprise. I hadn't lost control for a long time. Closing my fist, I extinguished them. "Cody and I were there as friends, nothing more, and you pulled that stunt. I was afraid he'd wait for you and give you no choice but to kill him."

Mavros closed the distance between us. "Maybe to everybody else, it looked like you and Cody were there as friends, but I know you've been lying in his arms at night." His hand brushed my neck, sliding under my t-shirt. He lifted the panther necklace between his fingers, then leaned in, his eyes hard. "I know where you are at all times. I could've stopped you. I could've made you come to me instead, but even though it was breaking my heart, I let you go to him. I went to you tonight to see if you would hurt him the way you've been hurting me these last few nights. I needed to know if there was still a chance for us. Can't you see what you mean to me?"

"No, I can't." I glared at him, too angry to hide my true feelings. "I see that you can be kind and gentle with me when you want to but cruel and heartless to my friends. They couldn't see any good in you even when I could."

He brushed a curl behind my ear. His fingers were soft but not manipulative. "Your friends don't know me like you do. You've seen the true me. You bring out the good in me. For you, I can change."

I stepped back. "Stay away from me tomorrow. I need some time to think." Without waiting for an answer, I turned and walked back to my room. Branches and rocks stabbed at my feet. The pain kept my anger from turning to sorrow.

"Is everything okay?" Samantha asked as soon as I opened the door.

I rolled my eyes without meaning to. "No. Nothing's okay." I tugged my fingers through my hair and slumped down onto the couch, holding my head between my hands. "Mavros apologized. He knows I've been staying with Cody. He knows everything. How could I have been so stupid? How could I think he wouldn't know? How could I think for even one minute that we were fooling him?"

"It's not your fault."

"Whatever." I clutched Cody's pillow and lay down. "I told him to stay away from me tomorrow."

Chapter 38

Cody didn't show up to Scientific Computing Monday. Dan, escorted by an invisible Arion, met us at Kalmia Hall. He shook his head, not meeting my eyes. "He's not ready to see you."

I nodded, not trusting my voice to hold up without cracking. *Will you or Aurelia keep an eye on him today?* I asked Arion.

Of course.

We went into the classroom. I scanned the seats and didn't see Damon there either. I sat through class without hearing anything Professor Granite said. When it was over, I followed Samantha and Dan out into the hallway in a zombie-like state.

Tuesday morning, Dan showed up for Mythology without Cody. He wrapped his arms around Samantha in a quick hug. Then he squeezed my shoulder. "He's still not ready."

"Oh." My heart dropped like an elevator with no cables holding it up. "Is he okay? Should I check on him?"

"No. Give him his space." Sympathy softened his masculine features. "He's trying to cope. If he doesn't talk to you by supper tonight, I'll bring him to you myself."

I bowed my head and swallowed the lump in my throat.

We went into the classroom, taking our customary spots. I doodled on my notepad, waiting for class to start. Right after Dr. Cedar walked in, Samantha leaned over and whispered, "Damon isn't here."

I shook my head. "No, he didn't show up this morning either."

"Well, at least that's a blessing."

"Actually, it's making me a nervous wreck." I couldn't help but wonder what he was up to. I'd never expected him to stay away for one day, let alone two. With only a few days left to win me over or return to the Abyss, I thought he'd be pressuring me constantly. I'd even wondered if he'd kidnap me to keep me from hiding in my room all day on the last day he could be on Earth. "I can't help but feel like he's sitting somewhere plotting his revenge."

Dan glanced at me around Samantha. "That seems likely."

Dr. Cedar discussed Greek Gods, but I didn't hear a word of his lecture. I couldn't focus on anything but my own mistakes.

After class, we stood outside Primrose Hall. Aurelia and I waited apart from Dan and Samantha, giving them the semblance of privacy.

Seeing them with their arms around each other sent a piercing pain through my chest. Cody would be better off if he stayed away from me, but I was lost without him.

I squeezed my eyes shut, willing my tears not to fall. "Go with him, Samantha. Aurelia's with me. I'll be fine. I won't do anything stupid."

"Are you sure?"

I nodded and cleared my throat. "Bring him back to me. Okay?"

She hugged me, and I hung on longer than I should have.

Aurelia, I'll teleport back to my room. Will you see them safely to Dan's?

Yes, I will take them there. Stay safe.

You too.

I walked between Primrose Hall and Quartz Building. Hiding in the shadows, I teleported to my room. I stood by the door alone. Silence filled the space, and the emptiness beat down on me. I needed Cody's strength. Setting my bag down, I found a note on my floor. I snatched it up, hoping Cody was ready to see me, but when I opened it, it wasn't Cody's handwriting I was looking at. It was Damon's.

My Dearest Dacia,

I stayed true to my word and left you alone yesterday. Now, I would like you to return the favor and meet me outside on our bench at 4:00. If you are not there, I will understand that you still need more time.

With all my love,
Damon

My first impulse was to crumple the letter up and set it on fire, but I restrained myself. Deep down I knew I had to see him. I only had until Thursday to keep up the charade.

By the time I read his note and looked at the clock, it was already 3:51. I grabbed a bottle of water and my book and darted out the door. I dodged people in the hallway and raced down the stairs. Once outside, I sprinted toward the bench.

I had no idea what Damon would do if he showed up and I wasn't there. My legs burned with each step, and I made a promise to myself to spend more time in the gym.

Rounding a corner, I spotted the bench. It was empty. I pulled my phone out of my pocket and looked at the clock. 3:56. I set my book and water down, then stretched my legs.

Damon, in either of his forms, still hadn't arrived. I sat on the bench and gulped my water. Then I read a few chapters before looking up, wondering where he was. "One more chapter," I said out loud, "then I'm going back to my room."

I started reading the next chapter when I heard Aurelia's voice. *Mavros took them.*

A hand latched onto my arm, spinning me around. I sucked in a breath as my heart leaped to my throat. Then I was yanked into Mavros' Abyss.

"Sorry, I'm late. It took me longer to find your friends than I had planned, but don't worry. They are safely hidden." I heard Damon's voice but couldn't see him. "But, if you choose wrong tomorrow—"

Panic rose inside me, making my voice high-pitched. "What do you mean tomorrow? I have two more days."

"No. *I*. Have. Until. Tomorrow. Then you will send me back to the Abyss, but not before I take care of your friends. Or, you will choose me and save us all."

"No," I gasped. "Let them go. Don't hurt them."

"I told you from the beginning this would happen if you didn't choose me."

"Please … please let them go." Icy fingers of dread pulled on my legs, dragging me to my hands and knees. "I waited for you."

"Yes, but that doesn't mean you plan to choose me." His voice sounded closer now. "I didn't want to give you the chance to squirrel your friends away." His fingers brushed my cheek, and I jerked away from his touch. "If you want to see them alive again, you'll have to face me. Tomorrow, Dacia. If I don't have the answer I want by tomorrow, you will watch your friends die. When I'm done with them, I'll end your miserable life."

"Why can't you just let them go?" I asked through my tears.

"I tried to be the good guy. I tried to be reasonable, but you wouldn't join me. Now, I've run out of time for games, so I'm playing hardball. If you want them to live, you'll have to join me."

I wrapped my arms around my legs, hugging them to my chest. "Isn't there another way for you to stay on Earth?"

"If there was, don't you think I would've found it by now?" His voice rose in anger. "Your dragons made it so the only way is for me to be bound to a mortal." Damon stood in front of me. I blinked back the light, waiting for my eyes to adjust. We were back by the bench. I wondered if we'd ever really left here. The back of his hand brushed against my cheek. When he spoke again, his voice was soft and loving. "I chose you, Dacia. You were supposed to be my saving grace."

After what he'd just told me, I wasn't in the mood to play games. However, I should've thought about what I was going to say before I opened my mouth. "Just a word of wisdom for next time, maybe you should choose somebody who hasn't already given their heart away."

His face hardened, and he pulled his hand away from me. His fingers curled into a fist. "If you've already made your decision, maybe I should just get rid of your friends now."

"No … no, you can't." I reached for his hand. "I have until tomorrow."

"Make the right choice." He disappeared in a wisp of smoke.

Not knowing what to do, I returned to my room. I sat on the couch with my knees folded into my chest, staring into space, unable to see through my clouded eyes.

Aurelia teleported into my room. "I am sorry, Dacia. When Mavros came, I was powerless to stop him. I cannot interfere. Arion could have, but not me."

"No, he couldn't." It took all my energy just to lift my head up to look at Aurelia. "Mavros would've killed him." I swiped at my eyes. "It's my fault. If Cody wasn't mad at me for kissing Damon and enjoying it, he would've been with me. Samantha and Dan would've been with us. Now they're gone, and I don't know how to get them back."

Aurelia rubbed my back. "Dacia, none of this is your fault."

"I don't want to do this right now." I grabbed a tissue and blew my nose. "Can you leave me alone for a while? I need to figure out what to do, and I can't concentrate at all."

She nodded. "I will be here if you need me."

I wondered if she teleported to her room or just turned invisible.

I sat in the dark, staring at the promise ring on my finger, wondering how Cody could want this life. He'd never be safe as long as he was with me. I understood now why Peter Parker tried to push Mary Jane away. As much as I loved Cody, it wasn't fair to put him through this.

Wherever Mavros took them, I was sure it wasn't pleasant, and although I wouldn't stop until I got them back, this night would stick with them for the rest of their lives. I hoped against hope they weren't in the black nothingness where he'd stuck me.

I'd never be able to guarantee their safety. Aurelia had all but told me that evil would find me no matter where I went or what I did. My powers were too intense to hide, and everybody would want me for their own.

I twirled the ring around my finger. The selfless thing to do would be to give it back to Cody … to tell him to move on. It wasn't a promise to a demon. It was breakable, but could I do it? Was I that selfless?

My head bobbed, so I got up to get another pop. Without Cody here to keep my dreams at bay, I was terrified to sleep. I plopped down in Cookie Monster, drinking my fourth one—hoping the caffeine would keep me up—staring at the TV.

A knock on the door startled me. "It's three in the morning. Who'd be bothering me this late?" I asked no one. I got up and stumbled to the door, peering through the peephole before opening it.

"How are you holding up?" Aurelia asked. I should've known it was her. I should've sensed her.

"All right, as long as I don't think about it," I answered as she strolled into my room. "I figured out my mistake. The panther attacked me the day before Mavros showed up at the park. I forgot to count that day." I plopped down, and my head landed in my hands. "I could've kept them safe if I would've realized it sooner."

She sat down beside me on the couch and put her arm around my shoulders. "None of us made that connection. Do not blame yourself."

I lifted my head. Anger chased away my self-pity. "Really, I'm the only one who should've made the connection. Nobody else was there when it happened."

"But we all knew."

"Whatever." I shrugged, and her arm slipped down my back. "I don't know how I'm going to stop Mavros or how I'll get them free. I guess if worse comes to worst, I'll have to join him."

"Dacia, no." Aurelia gasped. "That will not help anybody. He will still kill them, and the world will suffer greatly."

"I can't watch them die." I looked down at my bare feet. "I'm not strong enough for that."

"I know." She rubbed my arm. "However, no matter what, Mavros must return to the Abyss."

I stood up and looked into her golden eyes. "Are you sure he would destroy the planet? Are you sure he just doesn't want to stay on Earth?"

"Yes." She nodded. "I am."

"But … how do you know? What makes you so sure?" I started pacing behind the couch.

She tilted her head, and there was a long pause while she had a conversation with someone unseen. "I can sense evil. It is a gift given to all gold dragons, and Dacia, he is evil incarnate."

"Why didn't you tell me before?" I felt like she'd been holding back important information from me, keeping me in the dark.

"I have to tread carefully." She rolled her neck. "I am not sure I should tell you this, but after tomorrow—well, later to-day—it will no longer matter."

"So … what is it?" My teeth gritted together with impatience.

"When I was gathering information about Mavros, I had to go to the council of elders."

"What?"

"Elder gold dragons." She looked over her shoulder at me. "They told me the truth behind the curse put on Mavros. At one time, he was free to roam Earth. When the elders found out about his plot for destruction, they cursed him. However, in doing so, they gave up the rights for all gold dragons to stop him in the future."

I sat beside her. "So, that was why Mavros told you that you couldn't interfere." I remembered the day Aurelia had taken me out to see him.

"Correct. I cannot interfere in any way."

"So, I'll be on my own." My hands twisted in my lap. "Good to know. I might've counted on your help."

"It is not much, but I want you to have this." I looked up in time to see a dagger appear in her hands. She held it out, but I didn't take it.

Staring at the gold blade, I asked, "What am I supposed to do with that?"

She slid it into its scabbard and pressed it forward until I took it from her. "The purity of the gold will be harmful to him. It might help you until you can figure out something better."

"Hopefully, I think of something soon." I dragged my hand through my hair. "I'm … no, *they* are running out of time."

"Get some sleep, Dacia." She squeezed my shoulder. "You are going to need your wits about you tomorrow."

"I can't." I heard the hysterical edge in my voice. "Cody isn't here to keep the nightmares away, and I can't face the dreams that are waiting for me tonight."

"Very well." She patted my shoulder, then stood to leave. "See you in the morning."

Chapter 39

It's All Fun And Games

Waiting for Mavros, I can't remember ever feeling so alone. My heart aches for my friends. Cody's absence is like a punch in the gut. It's been years since I've gone this long without seeing him. I need his strength and love to help center me.

I pace back and forth trying to discover a way to defeat Mavros. Nothing has come to mind yet, and time's running out.

High above me, I hear the familiar sound of dragon wings. I look up expecting to see Aurelia, but it isn't her. Instead, it's an enormous three-headed beast. Close to the same size as Aurelia, it's as black as night with wings that remind me of Nefarious.

As it nears, I see the creature in more detail. Each of its three heads looks similar. They're angular with a bony frill at the base of the neck. Instead of being scaly, the creature has smooth, greasy-looking skin. Its long, muscular body cuts through the air. Its tail ends in an arrow-shaped tip. Hanging from its talons are Cody, Samantha, and Dan. They aren't moving, but I sense their auras.

Are you ready to give yourself to me in exchange for your friends' lives? Mavros' voice echoes in my head.

Where are you?

Flying above you, he answers. *How can you not see me?*

I saw that beast. I let him sense my disgust. *I figured it was your pet.*

This is me. The real me. He laughs, and it's an evil laugh.

The hairs on the back of my neck lift in response. How am I supposed to stand against this monster? I glance at the jeweled hilt of Aurelia's dagger stuck in my belt and laugh without humor.

What will it be, Dacia? Mavros' smooth voice coming from the beast flying above me is an affront to nature. *Will you watch me tear your friends apart, or will you be mine? My time on Earth is coming to an end. If you don't make your decision soon, your time will also be at an end.*

I rub the back of my neck. *How much time?*

My time ends soon enough. When it does, you'll either be standing by my side or lying lifelessly at my feet. Choose wisely.

Put them down. I step toward him. *Put them down and come to me as Damon—the man who won my friendship.*

I never cared about your love or friendship. His voice is filled with disdain. *All you ever were to me was a gateway ... a gate that I needed to open in order to avoid defeat.*

I'd known he was a demon all along, but I'd thought I'd meant something to him. I thought our friendship had been real. A lump wedges in the back of my throat, but I won't let him see me cry over him. "I'll make you a promise, Mavros. As long as you're in this form, I'll never be yours!"

He drops Samantha and Dan from where he soars. I lift my hands as if to catch them. It's an instinctual reaction, but it cushions their fall.

Mavros lands with Cody on a ledge high above me. The beast dissolves into a black mist and floats down. When it re-forms, Mavros stands in front of me. "I'm here, not quite as you requested." His expression is tender and loving.

"Did you mean it?" My eyes burn.

He tilts his head. "Mean what?"

"That you never wanted my friendship or love ... that I was only a gate."

"I don't know if you realize this, so I'll speak slowly for you." His eyes darken with hatred. "I ... am ... a ... *demon*! I don't care about you. I don't care about any lowly human— never have, never will."

"Then why did you act like you did?" Tears pool in my eyes, and that makes me even angrier. "Why didn't you just kidnap me or them from the beginning and force me to choose? Why didn't you drop me in the Abyss and leave me there until I caved? Why did you lie and manipulate me?"

His eyes twinkle with amusement. "Ah, can't you see how much more fun it was my way? I spent 999 years waiting to get back to this rock. Why shouldn't I have some pleasure? The end result is the same." He trails his finger down the side of my face. Gone is the magic, the electricity of his touch. Now my skin crawls with revulsion. "But seeing you—someone with such high morals—befriend a demon, *that* makes life worth living. Now you can choose me, or you can choose death." He steps away from me, lifting his shoulder in a halfhearted shrug. "It doesn't matter either way."

Still staring into his eyes, I slide the dagger out of my belt. I plunge it deep into his chest. He screams in pain.

I teleport to Cody, grab him and teleport to Samantha and Dan. As I reach for Samantha's hand, Mavros grabs my shoulders and jerks me backward.

"Nice try." He snarls, throwing me to the ground.

I land with a thud. The breath escapes from my lungs. A wave of dizziness crashes over me. I lie gasping for air and watch Mavros slash his claws across Cody's neck. Blood gurgles up from his mouth, and his aura flickers out. Mavros moves on to Samantha, killing her in the same fashion. Then Dan. There's nothing I can do to help them. I can't move. I can't think. I still can't even breathe.

I close my eyes, and when I open them, the panther stands over me. *You made the wrong decision, Dacia. We could've been great together. Now, you will rot in the ground like all your kind.*

His teeth tear into my throat. With my last breath, all I can think about is how I failed my friends.

"Dacia." I heard Aurelia say. Had she been there? Did she stop Mavros?

"Dacia," she said again. "Dacia, wake up."

I opened my eyes to find her standing above me. "I fell asleep?" My voice was hoarse.

"Yes. You are injured. Hold still while I heal you." She held her hands to my neck, and a cool sensation ran through my body.

I went to the sink and cleaned the blood off me. "If that was a premonition, today isn't going to go very well."

"Then, we should hope it was not one."

"Are you going with me?" I changed shirts, throwing the blood-soaked one in the trash.

"I plan to."

"Well, then it wasn't a premonition. You and Arion were nowhere to be seen in my dream."

"I may not be able to help you defeat him, but I will be there to support you and to heal you if I can," she said. "If it is within my power, I will also try to get our friends to safety."

Chapter 40

No Greater Love

$\mathcal{F}$ar from Phlox University, I awaited Mavros. Mountains rose all around me. Boulders the size of cars littered the ground, stacked haphazardly on top of each other. Tucked against the rocks, clumps of wildflowers thrived. Marmots sunned themselves on stones. Pikas scurried about, collecting grasses.

I stood in the shadows, praying Mavros would show up with my friends and I'd somehow be able to save us all. If I had to promise myself to him to save them, I would.

Even though I couldn't see or sense them, Aurelia and Arion came with me. Aurelia hoped that by remaining unseen Mavros wouldn't be able to tell they were with me.

While waiting for Mavros to show up, my imagination wandered down dark paths. Images of my friends being tortured and dying flashed through my mind. I saw their bodies broken and bleeding. A hundred different scenarios. A hundred different deaths. With each vision that pulsed in front of my eyes, my resolve weakened.

As I paced the clearing for the nth time, I heard the sound of enormous wings above me, and I realized I was about to relive my nightmare. My hands trembled, and my skin was cold and clammy. I fought to steel myself, but the fear only worsened.

I reached out for Cody's aura, finding his strength and love. There was something new mixed in with it. It took me a moment to realize what it was … sorrow. My heart dropped. It was my fault that emotion was tied to him now.

The regret lessened my fear. I looked to the sky, searching for any means to defeat Mavros.

Watching the beast, it occurred to me how gracefully he soared through the air. His body moved in sync with the breeze as he made his way toward me, and I wondered if air was Mavros' element or if it was fire.

He landed fifty yards from me. Before my eyes, the creature morphed into Mavros. Samantha and Dan fell to the ground in front of him, but he held Cody by the neck. Relief washed over me. This was not going to be an instant replay of my nightmare. Mavros had already changed it.

"What is your decision, Dacia?" he asked in his silken voice. "If you choose to be mine, I will let your friends live.

If not … I'll tear them apart limb from limb, piece by bloody piece. You won't be able to save them."

"Let them go." I clenched my fists and stepped toward him. "Once they are safe, I'll give you my decision."

Laughter was his only response.

His reaction infuriated me. "I don't trust you."

"You have my word, Dacia. I cannot go back on it." He eased his grip on Cody's neck. "My word is binding."

"Why me?" I asked.

"Power." He smiled, and it was wicked.

"So many girls would've bound themselves to you already." I strode closer to him. "Why not choose one of them?"

"To you, 999 years is ten lifetimes or more. To me, it's the blink of an eye. I'm a demon. I'd rather twist somebody who is righteous and moral than somebody who's already repulsive and vile. If you send me back to the Abyss, it was worth it to see you befriend a demon." His features morphed until he looked like Damon. Then he changed back into Mavros again.

"So, it was just a game to you?" My stomach dropped. "None of it was real?"

"None of it. I. Am. A. *Demon*!" His roar echoed through the clearing. The sounds of the forest hushed. His lips turned up in a sarcastic smile. "And, you were right about demons. We're all evil. If you live through this, you'll do well to remember that."

It shouldn't have bothered me, but I was crushed. How could all the time we spent together mean nothing to him? I knew he was a demon. I knew there was a chance he was evil, but some of the time I'd spent with Mavros and with Damon had been enjoyable. I'd thought he liked me. I'd thought there was good in him.

"But …" I pulled on my bottom lip. *Why did it matter what he thought of me? Why did I care?* "I saw all those emotions in your eyes. You couldn't have been faking that."

"A gift of mine." He laughed. "Apparently, one that works well on you."

A mixture of emotions had my stomach twisting and turning. I felt betrayed, stupid, scared, and angry. How could I have trusted a demon? How'd I think this would end? Did I really think he'd just walk away without a fight?

"Your decision, Dacia." The words were filled with revulsion. "Cody will die first if you choose incorrectly or wait too long." Cody squirmed as Mavros' grip tightened around his neck.

I held my hand up. "Wait."

He cocked his head and loosened his grip on Cody.

"What will happen if I say yes?" There was no way out of this. No way that my friends would walk away unharmed. No way for Cody and I to remain together.

Surprise flickered across his features. "Your power will sustain us for eternity. You will want for nothing."

"How much longer?" I dropped my head and rubbed my face. A world without Cody wouldn't be worth living in. Could I choose Mavros to keep him alive?

"Sunset."

I don't know where it came from, but I found the answer I'd been waiting for. I knew how to defeat Mavros. I just wasn't sure if I had the strength to do it. It was one thing to face death head-on, but it was another thing to take a life.

Looking at Cody hanging limply in Mavros' clutches, I knew Mavros wouldn't wait long to hear my decision before he killed him. Seeing that, I made up my mind. I had no other choice. I'd take a life, and I'd deal with the consequences later if I could.

I had to time it just right. If I acted too early, nobody would be saved. If I waited too long, Mavros would kill Cody. My plan depended upon surprise. If Mavros suspected my actions, I'd fail. My life and the lives of my friends would be forfeit.

As the light faded from the sky, I sensed Mavros' urgency. "Mavros!" I shouted. "Don't hurt him."

"Will you be mine, Dacia?" His voice was silken once again, and his eyes filled with hope.

"What would you do to stay?" A field of boulders separated us. I needed him closer.

He lowered Cody slightly. A look of confusion crossed his face. "Anything."

"Then come to me now."

He dropped Cody and strolled toward me, scrambling over the rocks. "Your wish, my command."

When he was closer to me than to Cody, I held up the golden dagger Aurelia had given me. It felt strange in my hand. It didn't belong there, but what choice did I have?

"What are you going to do with that little toy?" Mavros' laughter echoed through the valley.

I didn't respond to Mavros. Instead, I projected my thoughts to Aurelia. *Aurelia, I need you and Arion to get them out of here, and I need you to promise to keep them safe.*

What are you doing, Dacia?

Mavros' features distorted. He was no longer the beautiful man. He looked like the demon he was. "The *dragon* cannot interfere!"

"Not with you and me." I shook my head, then thought to Aurelia, *The only thing I can. I'm sending Mavros back to the Abyss, saving the world, and saving my friends.* I couldn't let her talk me out of it. I couldn't feel her sympathy for me. I had no other choice. It was the only way.

Dacia, no! her voice echoed in my head.

There's no other way. Please, please keep them safe. Tears ran down my cheeks, and I knew it was time.

"Mavros, you messed with the wrong person this time." I lifted the dagger in front of me with both hands to let him know I was serious.

"No, Dacia," he yelled as he sprinted toward me.

I saw defeat in Mavros' eyes, and that gave me the strength to do what I needed to. "Please let this be the right choice," I whispered to God.

The sunset turned the sky a brilliant pink as I plunged the knife into my heart. My friends screamed. Mavros roared. Arion's wings beat against the night sky. I imagined him carrying Samantha and Dan to safety.

Mavros knelt beside me. "Finally, a worthy opponent." He brushed the hair back from my face. His hands were tender.

Each beat of my heart pulled the tip of the knife farther into it, cutting and tearing the tissue. Piercing pain erupted in my chest. Blood gushed from my mouth.

Darkness wrapped its cold arms around me.

৪৩৭০ଓ

Chapter 41

A golden light shone above me.

This is different.

The other times I'd died, I'd stood on the shore of Falcon Lake awaiting a boat to carry me off to who knows where. It'd been peaceful and relaxing. After experiencing it, I was no longer afraid of death. As long as it was for a good cause, I welcomed it.

But, what was with this light? Is this what other people described? Should I head toward it? How, though? I couldn't feel my body. I wasn't even sure if I had one anymore.

The light didn't go away. It hovered right above me. "Dacia," a distant voice said. "Dacia."

I didn't have the strength to answer. I didn't even know if I'd be able to. It kept repeating my name, but it grew softer and softer until I drifted off into nothingness once again.

"Dacia." The voice was warm but unfamiliar.

I opened my eyes. I was sprawled out on the beach. Waves caressed the shore like a long-lost lover. The sound relaxed me. The air smelled cool and refreshing. I took a deep breath, closing my eyes and relishing the feel of oxygen in my lungs. When I opened them again, Death stood above me. Even from below, I couldn't see his face underneath the cowl. "Oh, uh, hello." I sat up, brushing the sand off my arms. "So is this it?"

"You sacrificed yourself to save your friends." His voice was soft and compassionate.

"Yes." I stared out over the water. "I didn't know how else to defeat Mavros."

He knelt beside me. "Few would have found the courage. Now you must choose."

"Choose?" My eyebrows pinched together, and I bit my lip. "Choose what?"

His hand rested on my shoulder, surprisingly warm and soothing. "You walk a fine line between the worlds. You may choose to go back to your life, or you may begin your journey with me."

Looking at the boat, I remembered the serenity I'd felt when it came for me before. The faces of my friends and family reflecting in Falcon Lake's water caught my attention. I was torn between peace and love. Turning to Death, I said, "As much as I'd enjoy the tranquility you're offering me, I should go back. Aurelia says the world needs me."

He bowed his head. "A wise decision." He stood and lowered his hand to help me to my feet. "Fare thee well, Dacia Wolf. We will meet again someday."

Chapter 42

Life After Death

*M*y body shuddered as fresh, pine-scented air returned to my lungs. I opened my eyes to see a billion stars twinkling above me. Sitting up, my muscles ached like the day after a vigorous workout. My shirt was soaked in blood. As I stood, I noticed the moonlight glint off the blade of the knife Aurelia had given me. I picked it up and replaced it in the scabbard hanging on my belt. After one more look at the night sky, I projected my thoughts to Aurelia. *I'm alive.*

Her thoughts came back to me, and I felt all her emotions in them—excitement, relief, respect, and affection. *Thank God. Is Mavros gone?*

I think so. He said he only had until sunset.

Stay there. We will return to you.

Moments later, my friends surrounded me. Looking into their tear-streaked faces, my stomach churned. "I'm sorry." I looked down at my hands. "It was the only way."

Cody closed the distance between us. "Never do that again." He lifted me into his arms.

My feet dangled above the ground as Cody pressed his lips against mine. Flames shot through me, warming my cold body. I pushed back, looking him in the eyes. "I'm so sorry, Cody."

He pressed his forehead to mine. "You couldn't help it. He controlled you."

"But—"

"No buts. I was a jerk. If I'd've dealt, we would've been together. He wouldn't've kidnapped us." He set me on the ground, keeping his arm around my waist, and looked at Dan and Samantha. "Forgive my stupidity?"

Samantha's lips curved upward. "Of course."

"Sure, Bro." Dan punched Cody's shoulder.

Samantha wrapped her arms around me. Since Cody wouldn't let go, it was a little awkward. "We thought you were gone."

"I was." The blood on my clothes was evidence enough. I pressed my hand to my chest but felt no pain. "You were wrong about me."

"What do you mean?" Samantha frowned.

"I pulled the trigger."

Samantha shook her head. "That doesn't count. You knew you'd live."

"Nope." I made a popping sound with the p. "I hoped I would, but I didn't know. Aurelia's never been able to tell me for sure."

"Why'd you do it then?" Dan wrapped his arms around Samantha and rested his head on top of hers.

"It was the only thing I thought might save you." I shrugged like it was no big deal. "Saving the world and saving you three seemed more important than saving me."

Cody pulled me tighter against his side, wrapping both arms around me. "Not sure 'bout that."

I slipped my arms around his waist and nodded at Aurelia and Arion. "Thank you for getting them to safety."

"You are welcome," Arion said.

"It was the least I could do—" Aurelia hung her head "—after endangering their lives to begin with."

"Wasn't your fault." Cody's voice was low and steady. "Mavros was taking us no matter what."

My eyelids drooped, and I stumbled backward, nearly pulling Cody over.

"You okay?" He steadied me.

I opened my mouth in a wide yawn. "I'm dead tired."

"Not funny." Cody lifted me into his arms.

I laid my head against his chest. "A little funny."

Chapter 43

Sunlight streamed in through the window. I snuggled against Cody, relishing the feel of him beside me. "Morning."

He looked at me—his eyes shining—and chuckled. "Morning's come and gone."

"Oh." Images from last night flashed through my mind. "It's over; isn't it?" I closed my eyes and let out a deep breath. I couldn't remember much of what had happened after coming back to life. I didn't remember showering or climbing into Cody's bed. "It wasn't a dream. It's really over."

"Yeah, it is."

"We made it." I couldn't believe it. It didn't sound real. Mavros was gone, and I was in Cody's arms. "So, you've just been lying here with me all morning?"

Cody traced my collar bone with a delicate touch of his fingertips. "No place I'd rather be."

Stretching my arms over my head, I exposed a strip of flesh along my stomach. Cody's hand slid along my bare skin. My heart fluttered, and I leaned into his touch. "Can we stay here all day?"

"I'd like to, but they're waiting." He started to get out of bed.

I flattened my palm against his chest. My gaze never left his eyes as I brought my lips to his. He rolled onto his back, pulling me with him. The kiss started slow and gentle but quickly became searing. His hands ran up my spine and along my shoulder blades, pressing me tightly against him. A moan escaped from deep within my throat. Cody pulled his mouth away from mine, kissing my chin, my neck, and my ear.

"None of this would have happened if we'd been together." My voice was ragged.

"Yeah." He trailed his fingers along my hairline and then followed my jaw.

I closed my eyes and softly moaned.

"Won't happen 'til you're ready."

I rolled back onto the bed, propping up my head on my hand. "I know. I'm just saying it's weird that one little thing … one left turn in Albuquerque … could've changed everything."

"Okay, Bugs." Cody laughed. It was a wonderful sound, one that I'd missed over the past month. With Mavros out of the picture, I hoped it would come easier to him now. "So … want to get married before something else happens?"

"No." I looked away, not wanting him to see the sadness in my eyes. "I want to marry you, but I don't expect you to. I'd understand if you never want to."

He jerked back as if I'd slapped him. "Why?"

"My life isn't exactly the kind of thing I would wish on anybody … especially not someone I love as much as you." I folded my arms around myself, waiting for the pain that would break me when he agreed. He deserved better, and he had to know that.

"Accepted that." He turned my face toward his. "Don't want anybody else."

I bit my lip, not wanting to ask but needing to. "Even with all that I'll put you through?"

"Another girl'd be boring." He smiled, brushing his hand over my cheek. "Love you. Forever. You wanna get married today, we can."

My heart swelled. Somehow, after everything I'd put him through, Cody still wanted me in his life. "We can wait, but when that day comes, it'll be the best day of my life."

"Mine too." He brushed his lips over mine. "Shall we go?"

"Yeah." I sighed. "I'm sure they're wondering where we are."

We climbed out of bed, and I stood in front of his mirror, combing my fingers through my hair while he threw a t-shirt on. "Okay." I grabbed his hand and teleported into my room. Samantha and Dan were curled up on the couch together. *Aurelia, we're here if you would like to come over.*

An instant later, Aurelia and Sarah stood beside us. "Did you sleep well?" Aurelia asked.

"Like I died."

Cody groaned, Dan chuckled, Sarah tilted her head, and Samantha said, "Too soon."

Sarah held up a sack filled with sandwiches and chips. "I thought you might be hungry."

"Always," Cody said.

I walked over to the refrigerator and grabbed drinks for everyone. Then I piled on the couch with Cody, Dan, and Samantha, leaving the chairs for Aurelia and Sarah. I picked up a sandwich and took a bite. "Well, where do I start?" I asked no one in particular.

I popped the top on my soda and took a drink. "I wasn't surprised when Mavros showed up as a three-headed dragon."

Aurelia's head snapped toward me, and she growled. "That was not a dragon."

"Sorry." I held my hands up. "I didn't know what to call it."

"A demon." Her voice was feral.

"Well, I wasn't surprised. I think he was going for shock and awe, but I saw it in my dream. Anyway, I had no idea what to do. In fact, Tuesday night, I told Aurelia that I might have to promise to be with him." I looked down at my hands not wanting to see their reactions. "I didn't know how to stop him or how to save all of you."

"He'd've killed us." Cody placed his hand over mine.

I shook my head. "You don't know that."

"We do." Dan pulled Samantha closer to him as if shielding her from the memory.

"Yeah, he told us that no matter what it was our last night." Samantha's face was ashen. "I'm glad to be sitting here."

"Wow." I closed my eyes and dropped my head to my chest. "I'm sorry I ever thought he could be good."

Cody caressed my hand. "Don't have to be. You saved us."

"Maybe not, but I am." I tugged my other hand through my hair, wondering how I could be such a fool. "Where'd he take you?"

Samantha visibly shuddered, and Dan rubbed his hands over her arms.

"I'm so sorry. He only threw me in his version of the Abyss for a few minutes at a time, and it about did me in. I can't imagine what you went through."

"We had each other." The color had drained from Dan's face. "You were by yourself."

"Can we just forget about it?" Samantha's voice shook.

Cody's muscles were tense, his eyes wide. "Love to. Don't think it'll happen."

Understanding that they needed the subject changed, I said, "Anyway, Aurelia gave me that knife. I knew I wouldn't be able to use it against Mavros. I tried in my dream, and you all died. I couldn't see a way out. I was still contemplating saying yes."

"So, you killed yourself." Cody shook his head. "Lucky it didn't work."

I snorted. "What makes you think it didn't work?"

"You're sitting here." Samantha waved her arm, gesturing toward me.

By some miracle or the grace of God, I was sitting with them, but it wasn't because I hadn't died. I glanced at all of their faces and felt my heart swell. The people sitting here with me were some of the most important ones in my life. I'd be eternally grateful for their love and support. I focused on Aurelia. "How long between me stabbing myself and telling you I was alive."

"Almost two hours."

My mouth fell open. "Oh, wow."

"We were …" Cody cleared his throat and started again. "We were going back at midnight."

"Aurelia thought we should wait to make sure Mavros was gone." Samantha's shoulders slumped.

"I was dead." My voice wobbled. "For almost two hours." The reality sank in, leaving me feeling numb. I wondered what the light I'd seen meant. Had Mavros tried to save me, hoping I'd change my mind and choose him after all?

"Dacia?" Cody's voice was soft, hesitant.

My lips hinted at a smile. "Death gave me a choice. I chose to come back. I was scared you'd still hate me"—I took Cody's hand in mine—"but you didn't."

"Never hated you." His forehead creased, and pain filled his eyes. "I was a jerk. Couldn't handle it. I'm sorry."

I squeezed Cody's hand. "He told me we'd meet again."

"Who did?" Sarah leaned forward, resting her elbows on her knees. "Mavros?"

"No." I shook my head. "Death."

A slight smile tugged at Aurelia's lips. "You made the right decision."

"Yeah, I did." I fidgeted with the panther necklace, wondering if it would come off now and not sure if I was ready for it to. "Like I told Mavros, my life might be difficult, but God gave it to me for a reason."

Chapter 44

Hard To Say Goodbye

Monday, I resumed classes. I needed to get back to normal, but it wasn't as easy as it had been after Nefarious or Draconian.

I sat in Scientific Computing, watching the door and trying not to stare at Damon's empty desk. Mavros needed to be returned to the Abyss, but Damon had been my friend. For several days, I'd spent most of my free time with him. I had come to appreciate his humor, his attentiveness, his charm, and even his cockiness. I knew Mavros was a demon who wanted to destroy the world, but as Damon, he never acted that way.

I felt like a friend of mine had died, but nobody shared my grief. No one understood what I was going through.

Cody slipped his hand under my desk and patted my knee, smiling sadly at me. I turned away from him and wiped my eyes.

When class ended, Cody didn't get up. He held onto my hand, keeping me there with him. "Go on," he said to the others. "We'll catch up."

As soon as they were gone, he leaned closer to me. "I get it."

I traced the grain pattern on the desk with my fingertip. "How can you?"

"He was a friend." He shrugged. "He's gone. You're sad, angry, guilty, and—" his jaw tightened, and his voice sounded strangled "—you probably miss him."

I stared at him, trying to figure out how he could be so understanding. It had been hard enough for him to see me with Damon, and now he had to see me pining for him. "I'm sorry."

He helped me to my feet. "Me, too."

That night I lay in Cody's arms. His breathing was slow and even. I pulled away from him and slowly sat up. I walked over to the window and looked out at the school grounds. For the past month, I probably would've seen Mavros, Damon, or the panther out there, gazing up at me. It was time for me to realize I would never see him again. I needed to let go of him for me and for Cody.

I reached up and grasped the clasp of the necklace, preparing to be burned or shocked. I pulled back the latch, and the necklace came off. It dangled from my fingers. The panther seemed to suck all of the light into it.

I set it down on Cody's desk and whispered, "Goodbye."

Fire dances along my fingers and up my arms. The blue flames are mine, but I have no control over them. They spin and twirl leaping across my skin, covering my body.

Their beauty is mesmerizing, lulling me into a hypnotic state. I stare unblinking, as the flames flicker from dark to light blue.

The fire shoots higher, burning all the oxygen from the air. I gasp for breath. My heart gallops, racing faster and faster.

I try to freeze the flames, to douse them, but nothing I do works.

My head pounds. My eyes widen. I try to teleport, but instead, I fall to my hands and knees, fighting for breath.

Darkness creeps in at the edges of my vision. I clutch my throat.

Something moves toward me. My head slumps to the ground, and I stare at a pointy-toed pair of boots.

Shadows engulf me.

"Dacia, breathe." Cody pumped my chest.

I sucked in a breath and choked on it, bolting into a sitting position.

"Are you hurt?" His eyes were bright, and his pulse pounded in his neck. "Dacia?" His hands shook as he reached for me.

"I—" I coughed "—I'm okay." My voice was a hoarse whisper through my burning throat.

He wrapped his arms around me. "Starting again?"

"I think so." I rested my head on his shoulder. "Whatever it was, it used my powers against me."

He ran his hand through my hair. I think it was as much to calm him as me.

The End

The best thing that you can do to support an author,
especially an indie author, is to leave a review.

Not only do your reviews help new readers find us,
they help the algorithms guide more people to our books.
In turn, that makes it possible for us to keep writing.

Positive reviews bring a bright spot to our day,
and reviews with constructive criticism help
us figure out how to make our books better.

Acknowledgments

It's really hard for me to write the acknowledgments. There are so many people who have helped me along the way, and I think I thanked them all in the first two books.

Cheryl Gage and Jeff Oyster helped me edit this book and gave me suggestions for what to change, so I'd like to thank them. Cheryl was very excited about this book, and since she never read Young Adult or Fantasy before reading my books, I'd like to give her a double thank you for giving my books a chance.

Jeff, Jami, and Jesse are amazing. Their love and support mean everything to me. I can't imagine a world without them in it.

I would like to add a special thank you to the readers who are excited about my books and can't wait for the next ones. It's a wonderful feeling knowing that people enjoy reading what I write.

Once again, I'd like to thank God for leading me to this path and giving me the shove I needed to walk down it.

A special thank you to J.K. Rowling for inspiring me to start writing again.

And for reading this to the end:

If you liked this story, you can join my mailing list.
Drop by my website <u>MandiOyster.com</u>
or if you have any comments,
shoot me a note at mandi@mandioyster.com.
I am always happy to hear from people who've read my work.
I try to answer every email I receive.

If you liked the story, please write a short review for me.
I greatly appreciate any kind words, even one or two
sentences go a long way. The number of reviews a
book receives improves how well a book does.

Facebook: <u>https://www.facebook.com/MandiOysterAuthor</u>
Instagram: <u>https://www.instagram.com/mandioyster/</u>
My web page: MandiOyster.com

About the Author

Mandi Oyster lives in Southwest Iowa in the middle of an enchanted forest where unicorns, fairies, and dragons abound. At least, that's what she assumes when she looks out into the trees. Her husband, two kids (when they're not away at college), four cats, and two chinchillas share the house with her. 

Besides being an author, she also runs her own editing business and works full-time as a digital prepress technician for a local printshop.

You can find her online at:
https://www.MandiOyster.com
https://www.facebook.com/MandiOysterAuthor
https://instagram.com/MandiOyster/

The Story Continues in …
Dacia Wolf
AND THE
DEMON MARK
Book 4

www.ingramcontent.com/pod-product-compliance
Lightning Source LLC
Chambersburg PA
CBHW060949190726
48286CB00005B/1487